I0603925

ISBN 978-1-0689591-1-0
Sing It Back

One

Thirty-one slashes of Sunset Pink lipstick marked the walls of the old house. Thirty-one days since Libby had last seen a sunset, or any sun at all except for the thin rays slanting through the ancient shutters over the windows of her room, illuminating nothing but the dust motes in the air. When she was a kid someone told her dust was from Mars, and she'd always wondered why it would bother coming here when it had all of outer space to explore. This room was proof that Mars-dust was a lie. That window hadn't been opened in at least fifty years but it was plenty dusty.

Libby poked at the remains of her last meal—another burger, cold just like the rest—picking up the crumbs and tossing them toward the gap in the baseboard. The mouse—she'd named it Pip—eased its whiskers out first and then followed, grabbing the largest crumb. It watched her with tiny black eyes while it ate.

It was nice to be treated with respect by at least one creature in this house. The mouse was a better conversationalist than her captors, as well.

She couldn't hear any voices now, or the TV or the music they sometimes played. She hadn't heard any of it since last night. No sign of people at all, just the usual coyotes in the evening and her. Not even a plane had gone over to rattle the old house. Had the apocalypse come and she'd missed it? Her own personal apocalypse had started thirty-one days ago at approximately 12:42 pm in the form of a panel van offering cheap cell service.

Over the next few hours the temperature outside dropped, and hunger made her even colder. Another lap around the room didn't warm her up as she'd hoped, even when she included the tiny bathroom, and the torn wool blanket didn't make a terribly comfortable shawl. Her only choice right now was to either start doing jumping jacks or hope her lipstick had nutritional value. It was fats and oils, right? Maybe some bug juice for colour and protein?

Sleep sounded good.

The bed slumped when she sat on it, the deep divot in the middle tried to pull her in but she resisted. She could see, just under the bed, the bit of rope they'd cut from her wrists before she woke up. It frayed at one end where she'd toyed with it. It wouldn't hold weight now, wouldn't rescue anyone. It would only snap and send her tumbling.

The grumble of an engine cut into the quiet, but it was the wrong pitch. Three vehicles, that's what she knew, and this was none of them, or maybe all at once. The engine was replaced by footsteps, a single masculine voice, one she didn't recognize. Anyway, the usual men never spoke outside anyway. No one answered him. Maybe the boss was finally here, to kill her, to sell her off to someone else. Maybe the apocalypse really had come and this was a ragtag band of survivors wanting to hole up in a remote farmhouse. She hoped they'd let her join them for good.

Libby's mother had told her once that flipping a coin isn't about letting the coin make the decision for you. It's about what happens while the coin is in the air, when you find yourself hoping which side it'll land on.

Hours earlier, when she realized she'd been abandoned, Libby searched her feelings and found herself not caring whether she lived or died. Now, though, the coin was in the air and she dared to hope for rescue.

Her world focused on the sounds, the key in the front door lock, the creaking of the floor boards in the kitchen. A text alert.

What?

Then the same voice, a pleasant baritone. "That's odd." A bit louder, "Hello?" More footsteps. "Anyone here?"

Libby ached to call out to him, but what if he really was here to kill her? Her brain fuzzed out, unable to compare the risks and possibilities.

A moment of silence, then, "Looks like squatters have been in here. Recently, too."

Squatters. She latched on to that word, hoping it meant he was the owner of this trash heap. She tried to call out, but her faint squawk didn't reach him over his phone conversation. Sitting up, she let the bed screech, even though it hurt her ears, then knocked on the wall.

"There's someone here," she heard. "Or some thing." A scuffle of shoe against floor, then the doorknob rattled. She sobbed, slapping her hand over her mouth in what had become habit over the last month.

"The parlour door's locked," he said. "I've got to hang up and find the key. I'll be fine," he added after a second. "Yeah, ten minutes. Bye."

Libby made herself move, slumping against the door to get as close to him as she could. "I'm in here," she said, then tried again louder. "Here. In the locked room."

He came closer, his voice penetrating the wood close to her head, like he was leaning too. "Uh, hi. Do you have the key?"

"No. I think they keep it somewhere to your left of the door. On a hook maybe? Sometimes I hear it up high."

"What's your name?" he asked, moving away as he did.

"Libby. I was kidnapped."

"Shit."

She chuckled, an awful, croaking sound. "Yeah."

"I shouldn't touch this key until the police come."

She shut her eyes, suddenly exhausted again. "Please."

Another long moment, and then, "All right. I'll just have to be careful."

She backed away, pulling the blanket tighter around herself and kept listening to the tiny noises that meant he'd found the key and was trying the lock.

"There," he said, and the latch popped. "Open it from your side, so I'm not touching the knob, too."

She reached out, almost expecting the knob to dissolve under her hand and leave her trapped, but no, it was solid metal and turned with only slight resistance. She peered around the door, and the guy, early-forties maybe?, short brown hair, kind eyes, smiled just a little.

"My name is Michael Ballard." He held out his hand and she took it, let him help her out of the room because all of a sudden the world was blurry and all she could focus on was the warmth of his skin. "Let's go outside and call the police, okay?"

She nodded, her throat too thick for use, and let him lead her into the sun.

On January first, at 12:42 pm, three men had grabbed Libby Wyatt and put her in a van. They drugged her with sleeping pills and drove off, leaving her messenger bag on the street where she dropped it. Only one person noticed; everyone else was sleeping off their New Year's Eve hangovers.

They tossed her wallet out the window on the parkway. It landed in a parking lot to be discovered a few days later. They kept her phone.

They'd brought her to some place called Gore's Landing.

The bastards had kidnapped her from Toronto and brought her to a lake of all places, and not even properly on the lake, but to just south of it. The only reason Michael had been around was because he was checking up on the property. She laughed. She'd been doing that a lot in the hours since her rescue. "I've never even heard of this place," she said, still giddy over having a real live person to talk to. "I don't think I've even flown over it."

"This isn't the best introduction, I'll admit." Michael pulled the cheap, orange, plastic chair closer to her hospital bed and sat down.

"If I'm going to have PTSD flashbacks about a town it might as well be one I have no reason to visit."

"I'd be more worried about farms. Going to back to Picton might be hard."

Right. Of course he'd think that. "I have no reason to go back. My Mom disowned me. Disinherited me."

He looked uncomfortable, but of course he looked uncomfortable.

"Let me guess, other than answering the normal questions she didn't get involved at all. Have they called yet to tell her that her secret shame survived her thirty-one day captivity?"

"Libby," he began. His voice was soft—calm, even but not monotonous—a warm baritone with a bit of rasp to it. Whatever he had to tell her would sound good in that voice. "Thirty-seven days."

"What?" How had she lost a week? She hadn't miscounted; she'd come up with a consistent tally every day.

"That's how long you were gone." He leaned forward, elbows on his knees, and looked her straight in the eye. "You do have some family, don't you? Someone you can stay with until you adjust?"

"Nope. This made-for-TV movie sucks."

"It's not over yet. We haven't even reached the first commercial break."

She laughed again, and really, it was getting ridiculous. "I like you."

His eyes crinkled up at the corners. "Good. You seem like you need someone on your side while you're in a strange city."

Libby had to pee, which was awesome because the doctor told her she could leave when she was properly hydrated again and she did not want to spend any more time in a hospital than she had to. Unfortunately, the only clean clothing she had was the gown she was wearing, so leaving might be an adventure. She could wear her shoes and her jacket, but everything else was rank. Once again she thanked a non-existent god that she'd gotten a birth control shot that suppressed her periods. "Hey, do you think you could find me some clothes?"

"A victim's advocate is on her way with some fresh clothing. I'm also trying to get your ID out of evidence, but Toronto Police Service says it will take a court order."

Libby hauled herself out of the bed, trying not to flash him as she did. "I see some bullshit bureaucracy in my future."

There was something odd about the way he'd phrased that, she realized. "Are you a cop?"

He shrugged, then leaned over and rested his elbows on his knees. "I was."

Something about his voice told her not to ask. "Okay."

"Anyway, Detective Strickland is on her way. She'll hook you up with people to help you navigate it when you get back."

He was on his phone when she got out of the bathroom, texting or playing a game or something, so she watched the traffic out the window until he was done. "Anything interesting?" he asked, tucking his phone back in his pocket.

"I don't know, are stretch Hummers typical for Cobourg?"

"Not that I've noticed. But I'm not from around here either." He joined her at the window, and the heat radiating from him contrasted pleasantly with the cold at her front. She took a moment to be grateful that her kidnappers had left her alone; she'd hate to be afraid of other people.

"Where are you from? And what do you do, if you're not a cop anymore?"

"I work for a not-for-profit in Ottawa."

"Neat."

"Hello?" Someone knocked at the open door and Libby turned in time to see a woman a little older than her poke her head in. "I'm Riley, from Victim's Assistance. Can I come in?"

She didn't wait for Libby to say yes, just strolled in and set a plastic bag on the chair. "You are Elizabeth, correct? And is this your father?"

Wow, her information was wrong. "It's Libby, and he's very much not my father."

"Oh." She started pulling stuff out of the bag: some navy sweats, socks, basic underthings, a pouch of what was probably toiletries. "Well, we had to guess your size based on your photo, but it'll do until you can get home."

Libby grabbed the underwear and slipped them on under her gown, smiling when Michael turned away. She followed them with the sweatpants and socks, glad to be warmer. "Is there any cash in that bag? I'm kind of destitute at the moment."

Riley's pleasant half-smile slipped. "I wasn't aware of that. But we were told that you're from out of town, and one of our benefactors has a hotel room waiting for you, just for the night."

That would have to do.

"I can take you to the bank tomorrow," Michael said, turning his head only slightly. "We'll talk to the manager, see if you can access your account without ID. I can certainly vouch for your identity."

"That's going above and beyond, man, but I'll gladly take advantage of you. You can turn around now." Then she noticed a shadow at the door. "Actually, you can deal with whoever that is while I finish changing."

She grabbed the rest of the clothes and slipped into the bathroom. She'd washed as best she could earlier, but still felt incredibly grimy. She still stank, too, but the sweatshirt hid it better than the gown did. She wished she'd picked up the little kit.

She'd just have to be the hostess with the grossest for a while longer.

Someone knocked at the bathroom door, so Libby opened it before adjusting the drawstring on her pants. Riley came in and closed the door behind her and seriously, there was not enough room for even one person in there.

"I wanted to make sure you were okay," she said, her smile tight and practiced.

"As well as I can be."

"Do you need me to stay for a bit? If you want to talk we can kick those men out."

Men, plural? "I'm good. I'm sure sometime in the future I'll freak out, but right now I'm glad to be free." It might even be the truth. Libby's emotions always took a while to catch up to her circumstances. Her friends always thought it was funny, the way she could be the calm one in a crisis and then faint dead away as soon as the crisis was over.

"You know yourself best. I'll head out, but I'll leave my business card on the table, okay?"

"Sounds good."

Libby followed her out, intending to go get a nurse so she could check out, but stopped short. The man talking to the detective was stout, with sleek white hair and a bit of a slump, and it took a moment for it to click. He was her parents' lawyer. She hadn't seen him in years, since they'd formally written her out of their will. He was kind to her then, but it was still a shock to see him here, now.

"Mr. Welles?"

"Libby." He held out both hands to her, and she slipped her hands into them, just a little overwhelmed at his presence. "I'm so glad to see you."

"How did you even know?"

"My dear, you're all over the news. The moment I heard, I cancelled all my meetings and caught the earliest flight."

And that, the sheer kindness from someone she'd met only twice in her life, was what did her in. Her knees buckled, and his hands tightened on hers while Michael caught her elbows as they eased her to the floor. The room blurred and she couldn't stop the choking sobs that wracked her body, no matter how she tried. All she knew was the hard floor and the two solid bodies nearby, murmuring words she didn't comprehend. Someone stroked her hair and that brought her out of it a bit. "Don't, I'm gross."

"I don't care," the old man said, and he cradled her against his side.

She didn't know how long she sat there, but when she looked up again Michael was talking to a nurse while packing up what little she had.

"Better?" Mr. Welles asked.

She nodded.

"Good, because I'm too old to be sitting on the floor this long." He stood up, still holding her hand, and didn't let go until she was on two feet. "Now, let's get out of here. We'll go to the hotel and get cleaned up, then we'll take Mr. Ballard to dinner, how's that?"

"I don't have clothes for dinner."

"We'll go somewhere it doesn't matter."

After a long, hot shower during which she used all the shampoo—and she would never, ever take nail clippers for granted again—and dinner of cheap Mexican food Julian Welles pulled her aside in the hotel lobby.

"Honey, I hate to do this right now, like this" he said, "but I have to get back to Kingston ASAP."

It felt like she was breathing syrup, but she swallowed and asked, "Do what?"

"While you were gone your father got sick. He died a couple of weeks later of brain cancer."

She said nothing. There was nothing she could say to that, without offending this man who'd helped her out. "Okay."

"I'm deeply sorry," he said. "The ceremony was lovely and his remains are in the forest." He pulled out his wallet and handed her a prepaid credit card. "It's the best I can do. Buy yourself some clothes and a train ticket. Go see your Mom for a while."

"Thanks, but," she waved the credit card casually, "I think I'll use this to go back to Toronto instead. That okay?"

He nodded. "It's a gift. How you use it is up to you."

His taxi pulled up then, and in a few moments he was gone. She was alone again and it did not feel good. Her heartbeat sped up until it felt like it was trying to climb out of her throat. Her palms went sweaty. She must have made a noise because the woman at the reception desk asked if she needed anything.

Libby gestured at the two big armchairs in the corner. "Is it okay if I hang out here for a while?"

"Go right ahead. Let me know if you need anything."

"Thanks." She pulled the biggest novel she could find off the bookshelf. If she had to read herself into oblivion in order to go to bed, she would.

Libby did eventually sleep, but only by leaving her window cracked open despite the cold. Having fresh air made being locked in alone tolerable enough, but she still woke wanting desperately to get out among people. As soon as she was dressed—she was too shaky to take the time to shower—she bolted out of her room and down to the lobby, where she sat with another book until a decent hour.

Michael had other plans for dinner the night before, but he'd promised to pick her up and take her to breakfast and then to the station to meet Detective Strickland. He arrived in the lobby right on time, looking fresh and dapper, far more than he had the day before. Libby generally approved of men who wore shirts with actual buttons, but add a sport coat and a tie and she could even forgive the worn jeans. Not that she was much to look at herself, still in sweats, and he seemed to stop for a second as he looked at her.

"You still need clothes," he said, as if she hadn't noticed.

"Today would be great." She double-checked the location of the gift card—tucked into the side of her sock—and followed him to the car. "I don't suppose anything's open yet."

"I did some research last night. There's a discount clothing store near here that's open twenty-four hours. That should do, right?"

Fifteen minutes later they were sitting in a bagel place in a mall parking lot. Libby ordered peppermint tea and a croissant; she'd gotten used to one large meal a day, and even though the tacos she ordered at dinner had been mostly lettuce, she still felt a little oogy.

Michael, on the other hand, ordered a big, gooey egg and cheese sandwich that smelled like heaven. She was sure he could tell she was drinking in the scent, as unsatisfying as that was.

"You can have one, you know. I can afford it." He was smirking at her, but there was a shine of grease on his lower lip that betrayed him.

"If I do, I'll probably be sick. Maybe later."

While she shopped Michael sat in the car and did some insurance paperwork, but not before teasing her gently about both generating said paperwork and taking up the time he needed to finish it.

She managed to find a decent set of clothes for the week, fresh undies and a few other necessities, plus a small suitcase to put them in. "You look like you had a worse shift than I did," the cashier said as she scanned Libby's pile.

"This whole month has been hell." Libby gave her a tight smile. "But it can only get better."

"I hope so, for your sake."

Libby tore the credit card from its glue, then realized she had no idea how much it was worth. "Hey, can you let me know how much is on there?"

"It should be written on the envelope."

Libby opened the flap again to see the number 2000. She closed it again so she'd stop staring at it. "Huh. Right." Julian was even more generous than she'd expected. She should have realized he could afford it, given the half-memories she had of going out on his sailboat as a kid.

"Nice gift."

"I have to pay it back, but it is handy right now."

The clerk clipped the tags on a few of the clothes and Libby headed back into the change room to dress properly. She hated wearing sweatpants in public unless she was actually working out. Her father had drilled it into her head from childhood that sweats were for sweating, just like running shoes were for running, and both were terrible for the environment. So she'd never developed the habit, never become comfortable in them. She felt like she was wearing pyjamas if she tried.

She'd been wearing jeans when kidnapped. There were no jeans among her purchases now.

The police station wasn't far, in a completely charmless red brick building, clean and tidy, but not in any way new or interesting. Micheal led her to the check-in, then stepped to one side. "You okay from here?" he asked with a quick touch to her elbow.

"Yeah." She was feeling kind of light-headed, but didn't want to delay him more. "Thanks for everything."

"My pleasure. Call if you need anything more while you're here." He handed her a business card and then he was gone.

She vaguely recognized the man who came to get her, one of the first responders at the house yesterday. "I'll take you up to the detectives," he said, leading her through security to the back of the building.

For a minute she was overwhelmed by the noise, but then she realized almost everyone was clapping. For her. Which was a little off-putting considering she hadn't done anything. She smiled weakly and tried not to make eye-contact.

The officer waved them off–had they been clapping for him? He didn't do anything either– and continued to a small meeting room in the back corner. He pulled out a plastic chair for her and gestured back at the main area. "We don't get a lot of wins, not on kidnapping cases. Have a seat, I'll go get Detective Nash and Detective Strickland."

Detective Nash she remembered from yesterday, and Detective Toronto was super tall and was one of those people whose skin was so pale you could see all the veins underneath, and her smile when she saw Libby lit up the room. "Elizabeth Wyatt, you are a miracle."

She came around the table and shook Libby's hand until Libby thought it would fall off. "When Nash called and said they'd found you I honest to God checked the calendar to make sure it wasn't April first."

"I'm happy to be found, too." She sounded pathetic in the face of all that enthusiasm, but what else could she say? "Thanks for all your hard work."

Strickland took the chair across from her and dug around in her briefcase. "I got your wallet released from evidence." She handed it over and Libby had the strangest feeling that the green wool was now contaminated. She didn't want to touch the thing.

"Thanks." She made her self reach over. As quickly as she could she took out all her cards and the collection of random cookie fortunes, shoving them in her pockets. Then she left the wallet on the table, staring at her from the cracked cream Formica.

"When can I go home?" She blurted out, lost for anything else to say.

Nash answered. "We need to get a complete statement from you. After that you can go anywhere you want."

Home sounded good. Her apartment was paid in advance for a few more months, so she probably hadn't been evicted. Dealing with school bureaucracy over her missed classes might be interesting. Maybe Detective Strickland could write her a note. "Can we start now?"

"We can," Nash replied. "Just give me a minute to get set up." He left, then came back with a video camera and a few bottles of water.

The next hour was painful. All things considered, Libby had had an easy time of it; she wasn't abused in any way except having been locked up against her will. The painful part wasn't reciting the story, but in the parts she couldn't tell, the things she didn't remember or just didn't know. How had she missed counting an entire week of days? How was it that she'd never heard any of their names?

Her stomach roiled against the feeling of uselessness settling in. Both detectives were frowning, not at her, but at the table or their notepads. She knew they were hoping for details, for clues to who those bastards were, but Libby couldn't provide. "I'm sorry," she said, after failing to answer another question. Those seemed to be the only words she knew right now.

Nash patted her hand. "It's hardly your fault."

"Sounds like they were more careful once they got here," Strickland said. "If they hadn't dumped your wallet and fired up your computer we might still be looking in the city."

Libby finished her story with the last time she had contact with the men, the day before Michael showed up. "The short one brought me a burger and a milkshake. Then two of them left. The one who stayed behind, I heard him on the phone later, but I couldn't make out what he was saying. Then a car came by and he left. That's it." She didn't tell them about talking to the mouse. Her childhood fantasies of being Cinderella didn't seem relevant.

"How'd it go?" Michael asked when she got back to the car. "Not well, I take it."

"Got my stuff back," she replied. "I didn't have much to tell them; two white guys about my age. That narrows it down a lot."

Michael said nothing, probably knowing there was nothing anyone could say to help her. He dropped her off at the hotel, but she couldn't sit alone in her room and the current receptionist kept eyeing her suspiciously so she went down the street to sit in a doughnut shop and wonder what to do next. Yes, she wanted to go home, but how? Getting on a train seemed so mundane, yet completely out of her reach. Maybe she should just chill for another day until she remembered how to exist in the world.

But she really didn't want to stay here, just in case they were still around. The cops figured she'd been outright abandoned as a bad investment, but what if they still had use for her?

A shape appeared at her side and she jumped, spilling her tea over her hand.

"Sorry," the shape said, and Libby looked up into the smiling face of a strange woman. She reached for a napkin and wiped up the spill, not bothering to reply.

"I didn't mean to startle you." The woman sat down across from Libby and took a sip from her own cup.

"I'm easily startled."

"I can guess. I'm Adelaide Jones. I'm a reporter from Oshawa."

Libby must have looked surprised, because the other woman laughed.

"I get that reaction a lot. My parents figured, hey, if you're going to have a common last name, you might as well have an interesting first name." She took another sip of what smelled like coffee. "I know who you are."

"Good for you?" Despite how personable Adelaide Jones was, Libby wasn't in the mood to tell her story again. "I have nothing to say," she added with an apologetic shrug. "The detectives have been very kind and helpful."

Adelaide smiled and jotted a note down. "Where will you go next?"

"That's what I was just trying to decide." As a red herring she added, "I was thinking a beach and some sun would be nice."

"How did your captors treat you?"

"They fed me and left me alone. Look, you can get all this from Detective Nash. I know less than they do. I didn't even know what province I was in until the police showed up."

"It must have come as quite a shock to find out your father died."

Libby shrugged, finished the last of her tea, and stood up. "Look, I'm not a celebrity. I don't care how many celebrities my parents knew, I'm not part of their little club. So stop. Please."

She walked out and went back to her hotel, still uncertain about what to do next. She needed someone to talk it over with, so she called Michael and left a message.

He called her back late in the afternoon and she invited him to dinner in the hotel restaurant. She felt like she owed him, not just for the rescue but for everything else he'd done for her outside his formal duties.

On top of that, he was good company and she kind of wanted to pack him up and take him home with her so she wouldn't have to be alone.

She might even have the teeniest little crush on him — mostly his voice, and the way the corners of his eyes crinkled when he smiled. She'd always had a thing for older men; her type was summed up as short hair, neatly-dressed, smart, but not necessarily in that order. She liked a certain amount of sarcasm, too, and so she never had trouble finding someone to date once or twice, but in the Venn diagram of men, short hair and neatly dressed often overlapped with young in a segment labelled "pretentious assholes". Especially when it came to her musician classmates.

It was probably a good idea to leave soon, since coming on to Michael would probably just end in embarrassment for both of them.

Although he'd hinted he might be late, he was waiting in the lobby when she got there. "Busy afternoon?" she asked, eyeing the crisp white dress shirt and new jeans he definitely hadn't been wearing when he dropped her off at the station.

He chuckled and held the door to the restaurant for her. "Not so much busy as sweaty. I still have a lot of work to do on that property."

"Where you found me?"

"Yes. It belonged to my aunt and no one else in the family wanted to bother with it. So it's mine, now."

The restaurant was a bit more romantic than she might have wished: soft light, candles and flowers on the tables, white cloths and shining silver. Libby grinned up at Michael. "I have no intentions on your honour, I swear."

He returned her smile. "Good, because I'm in short supply."

That startled a laugh out of her, and she thought it might be the first genuine, non-hysterical laugh she'd had in over a month. His mouth softened, like he'd had the same realization, but whatever he might have said was interrupted by the hostess.

After they were seated, Libby realized she didn't have much to talk about besides her situation, which she really didn't want to talk about anymore. She took a long drink of her water before blurting out, "So tell me, Michael, is there a Mrs Michael? A bunch of little ones? 'Cause it occurs to me that you probably know what colour underwear I was wearing that fateful day and I only know your name."

"You also know my profession."

"Wow, two things!"

He set his menu aside and clasped his hands on the table in front of him. "I don't actually know that." Michael cleared his throat and she looked up to see him raise an eyebrow at her.

"I notice that you haven't answered my question," she said.

He continued not to answer for a moment, absorbed in flipping his cutlery over, fork, knife, spoon, then righting them again. "There used to be a Mrs Michael. No kids."

She could see that asking him to elaborate would be rude. "Seeing anyone?"

He smiled, then. "Yes, actually. For a few months now."

"Good."

He cocked his head to one side, asking without words.

Libby shrugged. "I like to see good people be happy."

The waiter came and took their order, so clearly it was time for a new topic. "You're a music major, right?" Michael asked.

"Voice with a sideline in conducting."

"Parli italiano?"

She couldn't help be impressed. "Si, un poco. Also Latin, German, and French. Un poco."

"My mother's Italian, from Florence. I'm fluent."

Turned out he also enjoyed all kinds of music, and was relatively familiar with the classics.

They continued to chat about music, branching out into other arts, until it was time for her to pay the bill.

"Let me drive you to the train station tomorrow," he said as they headed back to the lobby.

Libby felt her shoulders relax; she'd hadn't even known they were tense, but now that she thought about it, the idea of getting into a taxi, or worse, one of those shuttle vans, with a strange man made her shudder. "I would appreciate that." It didn't solve the problem of what she'd do on the other end, but she'd figure something out.

He shook her hand when he said goodbye the next morning. "Call me when you've got all your new contact information," and he lingered before letting go. "I appreciate knowing how you're doing." He took a sharp breath, as if to say something else, but let it out in a huff instead.

Libby was not in the best frame of mind, worried about the trip, but the strength and warmth of his hand settled her. She'd taken a mild sedative the doctor had given her, and combined with that she had just enough focus to get where she needed to go, so she didn't ask. "Of course. And thanks, for, you know. Everything."

"Good luck."

Two

Michael almost didn't notice her at first, in the crowd of commuters on the platform. A woman's voice soared clear and bright over the noise, so perfect he thought someone was playing a radio, but then the singing stopped and a few people started to clap. He'd heard that TTC buskers were professional but he hadn't considered what that meant. She started singing again, another folk song, as he neared. A few listeners broke away and he was finally able to see her face.

He would laugh, later, as he told her that he still didn't quite recognize her. Although he'd never forget her face peering around the door she'd looked nothing like this, wearing makeup, dark hair pulled back, smiling. Seven months had changed her. Then she dipped her head and it all snapped together. "Elizabeth," he breathed, taking a step closer. She was radiant while singing, like she lived each note. He tried to catch her eye but she gazed into some middle distance, not connecting with her audience visually. So he waited until the song ended and dropped a five in the little blanket-lined suitcase at her feet. "Libby," he said again, just loud enough to get her attention.

She focused on him, blinked, then gasped. "Michael!"

Then she flung herself at him, an armful of warm, soft girl. "Hi," he said, tentatively putting his arms around her. "Hey." Her perfume was a light floral and wood, but as he dropped his chin to her shoulder he caught a musty scent, like she hadn't washed her hair in a few days. "How are you?"

She pulled away, a flush colouring her cheeks. "I'm good."

"Really?" He kept eye contact until he was certain she was lying.

"What are you doing in Toronto?" she asked, bending down and turning her attention to the case full of tips.

"I live here now."

"Cool." She flicked a glance at him, wary. "I can't talk now or I'll lose money. Take care."

Michael backed away to study her as she began another song, then made a decision. He'd never broken the habit of keeping pen and notebook on him, so he scrawled a note and signed it, adding his contact info at the end, then dropped it in her case and headed to work.

From what he remembered she was an opera student in her third–possibly now fourth–year of a degree at Pickford. Why she was singing folk songs in a subway station during morning rush he didn't know, but he guessed everyone needed a hobby. She'd been in touch a few times after her rescue, letting him know that her room in residence was still free, that she was seeing a therapist, thanking him for the letter he wrote to the dean that let her jump back into her studies even after a month away.

He'd wanted to make sure she didn't suffer any more than she had to. When he examined later why he'd given her his contact info, he decided it was lingering guilt. It definitely had nothing to do with her bright smile or the feel of her in his arms.

A few hours later, under a tree in Allen Gardens, Libby stared at the note for a third time, hoping for some flash of insight, a sign from the universe telling her what to do. She could call him, tell him lies about school, about a job that wasn't embarrassing. She could pretend everything was perfect, that she'd moved on from her trauma, but if she was going to do that she might as well not bother calling him at all. The results would be the same.

But she remembered the look on Detective Faith Strickland's face, the pity and disappointment in her voice when she checked on someone she thought was an ordinary homeless person in the park and turned out to be one of her cases. The realization that Libby hadn't been worthy of rescue at all had hit them both, and Libby had run off without a word.

She blew a raspberry at the note and tucked it in her pocket with her phone, the cash she'd made, and her ID, everything that mattered to her. She spread out the blanket to cover the damp grass, set her back against the tree, and slept until her alarm went off. She'd learned not to spend too much time in any one park, so she gave herself an hour to nap, knowing she looked less like a typical homeless person and more like the student she used to be. Still, patterns would get you noticed, and not just by the cops. She'd learned a lot since getting kicked out of school.

When she woke dusk was nearing and she was due at work soon, so she packed up her blanket in the shoulder bag she carried and walked the few blocks up Jarvis. Sometimes she could be early and help the bartender wipe down the tables, but if she did that too often they might start questioning her about it, and she could not lose this job. So most nights she got there just early enough to shower and do her hair.

Hazel, the owner, had given her a locker to keep her performance dresses and shoes in, and that's where she stowed most of her important stuff; clothes, music, toiletries, snacks, she stuffed the locker as full as she could. She didn't dare leave cash in it, although she trusted the other employees, but she had a bank account still so that was good. Her former roommate, Rain, let her use her dorm apartment as a mailing address and storage unit, probably partly to keep an eye on her and partly out of regret and guilt.

Libby saw Rain maybe every other week. She'd gotten a major role in the fall term play, so not only was she busy with rehearsals and socializing with the cast, but it was better for her if Libby kept her emotional bullshit away. Rain was going places, and Libby was happy for her.

The only people who seemed happy for Libby were the people at work, and if you'd told her last year that she'd feel most comfortable in a BDSM club, however exclusive... well, she probably would have had to ask what BDSM was before laughing. But the dommes and doms and subs and whoever were happy that Libby loved her job singing in their bar, happy she hung out with them in their lounge between sets, happy to teach her about their jobs. They might not be quite so happy if they knew she didn't have a place to go at night, but she didn't dare tell them and lose their respect.

Michael had seemed glad to see her. In the days during and after her rescue she hadn't seen him smile much, but this morning at the station his whole face showed his delight, especially after she recognized him. She hadn't noticed, before, how handsome he was in that way some older men had: wide jawline and high forehead, a cheek so smooth she'd expected it to be cool against hers, short dark hair that might have a hint of grey at the temples.

And there was another good reason not to call him. There was no way he'd be interested in a lying child like her.

"You've always had a bit of a hero thing going on," Claudine told Michael later that night. "Jeanine's death only made it worse." She rescued his glass from the edge of the coffee table and refreshed their G&Ts from the generous supply in her sideboard.

Michael had worked over his motivations all day with no resolution. Finally he'd put away his data entry work and come—not home, this wasn't his home no matter how long he stayed here—to Claudine for advice.

She'd been his best friend for years and knew him better even than most of the people he'd dated, and when he'd taken the transfer she'd offered him a room in her house and a shoulder to lean on when she had time between her job in the city archives and her evening appointments.

"That's not even a bit true," he replied. He wasn't that heroic. "And it's not like there's a pot and kettle situation here, not at all, Captain Fellowes."

"Tell me then," she sat across from him this time, in the big grey armchair, her back to the wall of glass that overlooked her minuscule backyard, "when your captain back in Ottawa transferred you to head of community policing, what did you choose to do instead?"

He'd quit in protest and taken the job her husband David had pointed out to him as a local case analyst at his national not-for-profit. "Fine, I get it. I have a deep-seated need to rescue people."

They both looked up at the sound of the lock turning in the front door. "It's not like that's a bad thing," Claudine replied before getting up to greet her husband and kids. She turned at the hall and stared down at him. "Within reason."

Michael stayed where he was. The front hall of the narrow rowhouse got crowded enough with two adults and two kids plus the dogs. He'd been staying with them long enough to ignore all but the most basic politeness now. He was part of the family.

"Uncle Mikey!" Lucy ran into the living room, still dressed in her soccer gear. "We won!"

"That's great!" He admired the ribbon she held up as proof. "Hey, did your mom tell you to call me Uncle Mikey?"

She nodded, her multitude of braids flying. "That's okay, right?"

"It's perfect." She ran off and he glared up at Claudine. "Just for that I'm leaving wet towels all over the bathroom floor."

"Won't be much different from our last girlfriend, then," David said from behind her, a cheeky grin making his dimples stand out.

Michael listened to the sounds of the house, his friends talking about their days, their kids shouting upstairs, the dogs' nails clicking along the hardwood as they came to say hello. "I should go," he said, surprising himself. "I mean, I should start looking for my own place. I've imposed on you long enough."

David frowned at him. "If that's what you want. But you're welcome to stay."

"We like a full house," Claudine added as she sat on the arm of David's chair. "And you might as well be family."

"Don't misunderstand. I love it here. But things will change. You two will get a new girlfriend. I'll start dating again." He looked at Dave. "And I don't want it to get uncomfortable at work if anyone finds out."

Claudine waved his concern away. "We're really good at secrets in this house. Speaking of, one of my clients just texted me. I'm going to go make some money to keep you two in the style to which you've become accustomed." She swept out of the living room, calling out behind her, "Don't forget to eat."

"Anyway," Michael said to Dave, "I can't keep sponging off you forever."

Dave leaned forward, his elbows on his knees. "I get it. And despite what Claudine says, it might affect work. I am your boss. But let us help. Between the two of us we have a lot of contacts in this city."

It would be stupid of Michael not to agree to that.

Libby's shift went as usual and if she was maybe a little extra flirtatious with the guy at the front table as she sang it paid off with the twenty he left for her at the bar. In the bathroom she shed her stage persona and put on her homeless chic again. She really needed to hit the laundromat the next day. She didn't own a lot of underwear now, and finding a way to hand wash her really fucking expensive bras (which was all of them; they'd been the first clothes she packed when she was kicked out of residence) was getting harder. When winter set in it would be worse.

Not for the first time she wondered if she shouldn't just pack up and go someplace warmer. But that seemed like committing to the whole homeless life, choosing to go where it was easier. She could find a small town, a cheap place to live, but what would she do there? Her whole life, her whole experience, was singing. She could probably work on a farm if she had to, but that would seriously be giving up the dream.

No, Toronto had the opera scene she wanted to be part of. It had the club she worked in and people who would give her money just to entertain them for a few minutes while they waited for a train. It had the few people who were on her side. Funny, she'd always wondered why poor people stayed here. Now she knew.

The nights were getting colder, so she traded her lighter day jacket for warm wool when she left the club. With her blanket and some shelter from the wind she'd be fine. She'd been fine since May, after all. There was a park near the club, tucked between two buildings, that she hadn't been to in a while. When the shrubs were fully leafed out she could hide between them and the concrete wall and she wouldn't be obvious from the street.

She wasn't the only one who had that idea. She hopped the fence to find Dale, a panhandler who sometimes worked near Yonge and Dundas where Libby busked on the weekends. Dale was hardcore homeless, knew everything there was to know and guarded her secret hideouts from everyone, including Libby at her nicest. She looked about seventy, skin wrinkled and blonde hair dulled from poor nutrition, but was really in her fifties. She'd just been on the street for that long.

"Oh, hell," Dale said, seeing Libby. "Beth, right?"

"Yep. Sorry to intrude."

"Big enough for both of us, I guess." Dale pulled her bags closer around her, making a little fort. "It's getting cold you know. You should give up this experiment or assignment or whatever and go home. Winter's too rough for you."

Libby stashed her suitcase and backpack behind the fluffiest bush and spread out her blanket. "I'm not slumming it for kicks, Dale. This is the real deal for me."

"More's the pity. I can tell you don't want to be here. Not like me."

"We can't always get what we want."

"That's for damn sure. Your family all gone?"

Libby swallowed the sudden lump in her throat. "In every way that matters."

Dale was quiet until Libby put her head down. "Hey, you look tidy and clean; nobody bothers you in stores I bet. You think you could get me some face cream? Some kind that's good for winter?"

"I'll see what I can do." Dale probably thought she'd shoplift it, but so far Libby hadn't had to resort to that. Between her two jobs she had enough cash to buy little things. She tried not to because she was saving up to go back to school, or maybe just get voice lessons on her own so she could start auditioning again.

She wasn't going to be here forever.

"Hey Dale?"

"Yeah?"

"I don't sleep a whole lot, but when I do I might start yelling. Just so you know."

"I hear you."

Libby always slept better with company now, and that night was no different. Her alarm went off at dawn, actually waking her from a pleasant dream. Dale was already gone.

It didn't take Michael as long as he'd expected to find a new place to live. He knew what neighbourhoods to look in and what he generally wanted. His price was flexible and people were generally receptive to his story. And being a single man over forty in Toronto wasn't such a liability, but he still worked in mention of his widowed status when he could just to stack the deck.

After a month of daily trips to see apartments he finally found one that worked for him, a condo in Swansea, two bedrooms, east-facing, recently renovated. It wasn't perfectly his style but he liked it enough to put up with the red oak floors and dark granite counter-tops. Oliver would have loved it, but Oliver wasn't here.

But his new place, while comfortable, was missing something, and it took him a bit to realize it was noise. Company. Claudine's house was busy, with her and David and the kids, a kind of busy he found he missed. He'd spent too long alone and relished being in the same room as another person even without interacting. He brushed it off at first as stress from his new situation, but the more often he went home to an empty apartment the more he found himself trying not to.

He partially solved the loneliness problem one Saturday, about two weeks in, when his meanderings took him through a neighbourhood near his apartment. He stopped at a cat shelter storefront to watch kittens in the window then thought why the hell not? He had no good reason now not to get a pet. Those kittens needed real homes and he had one to give.

Inside, the shelter was busy. Not quite crowded, he had no problem moving around, but more people than he expected inspecting the kittens in cages around the room. He waited for a moment behind a family to get his turn at a trio of orange tabbies, but gave up when an employee came with a key to open the cage.

The next cage over had an older cat, a scruffy tortoiseshell much like the one he'd had as a kid, and he waggled his fingers at her. She ignored him, and since he wanted a little more interaction and a little less nostalgia he stepped to the next cage over.

Immediately a white paw slid out between the bars to bat at his coat. He petted the pink toe beans and the cat, an enormous grey tuxedo-patterned male, meowed at him. "Hello," Michael replied as he read the information sheet.

Jeeves is a cuddler who prefers to sit beside you rather than on you. He's a great jumper and loves to be up high. He has been with us for two months and is looking forward to finding his forever home. Recently neutered, he still displays some tomcat behaviours and is best suited to a single pet home.

He was a three year old short hair, possibly a Siamese or Ragdoll mix, no major health issues. Michael looked around for an employee and caught the eye of a young man who came over immediately.

"Are you interested in the big boy? Adult cats have a reduced adoption fee."

Jeeves had switched to rubbing his chin against Michael's fingers, and Michael chuckled. "I think he picked me rather than the other way around."

The employee grinned and opened the cage to rub the cat's head. "He does that. He's super friendly and very entertaining. He was abandoned and the owners didn't want him back."

Michael had always been a sucker for a hard luck case. "I'll take him."

After signing all the papers he made a quick trip to a pet store for supplies, dropped them off at home, and went back for Jeeves.

"I don't know if I can keep calling you that," he said as the cat sniffed his way around his new living room. "It might be too dignified for a cat. You've got great PR, sure, but I've known other cats and as a species you aren't as graceful as you're purported to be."

As if to prove his point the cat tried to jump to the top of the bookcase and misjudged, scrabbling for a hold before finally hauling himself up by sheer will. "I see I made the right choice in you."

The cat settled on the bookcase, then his mouth dropped open and his tongue slid forward. "Dork." The cat made a noise that sounded like agreement and proceeded to look as regal and aloof as you could with your tongue hanging out.

Michael spent the next few minutes sending Claudine cat pictures and texting her stupid things about having found the love of his life. It wasn't human companionship, but at least it kept him from talking to himself.

Claudine had been right when she said his work would consume him, but having the cat made him sure to go home at a reasonable hour. He hadn't yet had a day where he needed to go back to work after feeding Jeeves, but it would come; in the innocence business deadlines came swiftly. He liked having a routine again, someone who depended on him if only for a scratch behind the ears. When he needed to talk to people, people he didn't work with, he went to cafes, the park, or he called up Claudine.

He was good. He didn't need anything more. He rarely thought about Oliver at all these days.

Michael passed through the St George subway station twice a day now that he lived in Queens. Libby wasn't always working—there seemed to be a rotation among the buskers at the bottom of the stairs—but when she was he always tried to stop and listen. Sometimes she accompanied herself on a guitar, other times she just sang.

Today she had the guitar out, singing Johnny Cash's *Don't Go Near the Water*. Her playlist was heavy on environmental protest songs, he'd noticed, Joni Mitchell, Cat Stevens, and a bunch he didn't recognize, which made sense considering her upbringing. He'd done the bare minimum of research into her parents' religion when he met her, but from what he knew she was doing the equivalent of singing hymns here. Anyone else who left home the way she did— escaped from her mother's cult—would be trying to bury their past, not proclaim it to several thousand Torontonians.

This little connection, him listening to her sing, was the only contact they had. She hadn't called or emailed him, hadn't even come over to say hi between songs though she always acknowledged his presence with a smile.

Something was up. He usually knew when someone was hiding something; years as a cop and even more years hiding parts of his own identity had given him a sense for it. But he couldn't push, didn't have the right to push. As long as he could meet her here a few times a week and see that she was physically safe he had to let her be. Besides, she lived in a dorm and was surrounded by other students. Her kidnapping was a fluke. Odds of it happening again were low.

He waited for the smile and waved back, then moved on, expecting to hear the next song behind him, but instead she called out to him. He went back and waited while she handed the guitar off to a scruffy young guy and collected up her tips. "Hey," she said when she was done. "You busy right now?"

Work could wait a few minutes. "What do you need?"

"Just a break from singing." She tucked a strand of limp brown hair behind her ear. "Fridays and Saturdays I sing at a club in the evenings, so I try not to stress my voice too much. Stuart there," she indicated over her shoulder, "shares my time slot and lets me use his guitar."

"Care for a coffee?" The kiosk outside wasn't quite the zoo it usually was right now.

"I would love one." They joined the line and she asked, "So what are you doing here? In Toronto I mean."

He shrugged. "Transfer. I needed to get out of Ottawa and the only opening was here. Plus I know the boss, here."

"Neat." Her forehead creased. "You never told me what you do, except "not for profit"."

"We advocate for people who are unjustly imprisoned."

"By whose standards of justice?"

"That's another part of our work, trying to change the current standards."

"Wow, I mean, I already knew you were my hero, but I guess you're other people's too."

Embarrassment washed over him. "Don't say that. I get enough of that from my friend Claudine."

"Nuh-uh. You rescued me from starving to death. No takebacks." She gave him a playful smile.

Clearly there was nothing he could do but change the subject. "Which club do you sing at?"

He was not expecting her to turn away, frowning, before answering. "It's a private club," she said, staring intently at the specials board.

It was their turn to order so he didn't get a follow up question. He had a pretty good idea, though, considering Claudine's second job.

After receiving their drinks they found a free bench and sat for a bit. Michael groped for something to say, then noticed an ad for pizza. "You still taking Italian?"

"That was last year. French, too." She laughed. "You'll get this: I had a panic attack in the middle of French and nearly sent Madame Martineau into premature labour with a manuel scolaire. I had to give all my profs permission to throw things at me if they needed to get my attention."

"Ow."

"Yeah, it stopped being funny when my composition prof brought a squirt bottle."

Michael sipped his coffee. "How are the panic attacks now?"

There it was again, that tell, that glance at the ground. "About the same. Nightmares, too. I don't sleep much."

"I know how that is. You can call me, you know. Any time you need to talk about it. I've been there."

She snorted. "Did your therapist say you had no right to have PTSD because at least you weren't raped?"

He hissed air in through his teeth. "You couldn't get a new therapist?"

"There weren't any available in the time I needed one. You know, ten sessions in five weeks or you can't keep your spot in residence and by the way your insurance only covers ten sessions." She glanced up, then back down to her cup. "Did I tell you I socked my roommate my first day back? She surprised me from behind. You'd think people would know better these days."

"You'd think. People make all kinds of assumptions about trauma, though." He chuckled at a bitter memory. "How many times have you been told to just get over it?"

She groaned and slapped her forehead lightly. "Or the worst—no, wait, the rape thing was the worst—when they tell you to Think Positive! Hang in there, it'll get better!" She rolled her eyes. "I mean, I'm sure it will? But I'm also pretty sure ignoring it isn't the way to go."

"It isn't." Michael checked the clock on his phone. "Hey, I really do need to get to work. But I'm serious about calling me. If you need anything."

"Thanks. And you know where to find me if you," she emphasized the word, "need anything."

He saluted her with his empty cup and went down to his platform. She may have been joking, but it wasn't like he had a lot of friends in the city. He might take her up on it.

Libby had thought her days of manual labour at The Farm were oppressive, but her days now were rapidly taking top place. Job, other job, laundromat, eat, try to sleep, try not to get caught trying to sleep, scour audition notices and wonder if she was still qualified. Check in with the free counselling services to see if she was near the top of the waiting list yet. Feel guilty for taking a spot on the waiting list that someone else might need more. Eyes up, walk with purpose, don't draw attention.

The only place she got to relax, to be herself, was at the club. Not just when she was singing, but any evening she could go in and hang out. At first she went just to be comfortable for an hour or two, but she actually fit in with these women and men and non-binary people. She had things to say to them, and more especially to learn from them.

Her favourites were Erica, a slender, redheaded, masculine-presenting enby who liked to talk about gardening and country music, and Adria, a tall woman with a Master's in history and arm muscles Libby envied.

"You know," Adria said one slow evening, "we run classes if you're interested." She sat down with Libby and the domme she'd been talking to. "You could sit in on a couple."

Libby hesitated. "Classes on what? 'Cause Celeste was just talking about bloodplay and that's a hard no for me."

Adria shrugged one shoulder. "Whatever interests you. They're mostly beginner level on the common kinks — bondage, pain play, dominance, that kind of thing."

Celeste touched Libby's knee lightly. "And we all have things we won't do. Kink is a spectrum not a binary. Me, I prefer to work with a knife rather than fists." She shook her head, dyed blonde waves breaking against her jaw. "So barbaric."

Adria simply flipped her off and said to Libby. "Anyway, if you do come you should probably think about using a different name, like we do. You probably should be using one on stage anyway, to protect your identity."

She was already Beth on the street; she didn't need another name to have to remember. "I don't have much of an identity to protect," she replied.

Adria pointed a squared-off fingernail at her. "That is a completely different issue."

A quiet chime sounded from Libby's pocket. "That means I have a set to do." She stood up and smoothed down the skirt of her tight black and white dress. "Goodnight, everyone."

"Fix your lipstick, sweetie," Celeste called after her.

Because Libby would have forgotten. Damn, back in school she had it perfected: the makeup, the subtle jewellery, the dresses and skirts and tailored blouses, all chosen to make her classmates and teachers take her seriously, to hide the small mistakes she made as she assimilated to Outside culture. But now she'd lapsed, the hardship of her life making that sort of thing less important. Except it was only less important on the street, not here at work. And it wouldn't be at auditions and working in opera, either where only the principals had their own makeup artists.

She stopped in the dressing room to swipe another slick of red on her lips and to put herself into her jazz kitten persona. She'd always loved acting, and sometimes all she had to do was wink at herself in the mirror to rev up her ego.

This was one of those nights.

Three

Sunday morning Libby woke to the sight of an elderly man lying near her in the park. He was like her, trying to stay out of the biting wind that had picked up overnight. Normally she'd found it best to stay out of the way of the lifers like him and Dale, but she didn't like the uneven gasps of his breath, the way he didn't move when she called out to him, the blue tinge of his lips and eyelids.

So she did the only thing she could think of, she called 911. The dispatcher answered immediately and Libby told her story, modified. Old man collapsed, trouble breathing, not responsive. She didn't say he was homeless; she'd heard the stories of street people being ignored even by emergency services. Then she packed up her own gear and pretended to simply have been taking an early stroll, maybe going home after a fun night.

Until the paramedics showed up about five minutes later. "That was quick," she said as a guy dropped out of the passenger side before the ambulance was even parked. She immediately felt stupid, because of course his focus was on his patient.

He glanced up at her. "We were just around the corner. Slow morning. I'm Ray, this is my partner Kerry." He gestured with his thumb back at the woman who was now getting gear out of the truck.

"Beth."

"What can you tell me?" Ray asked, and without even thinking about lying, Libby answered.

"I woke up and he was right there, but his breathing sounded awful, wet and shaky, and he wouldn't wake up. So I called you."

"You know his name?"

"Never seen him before."

"This not your usual area?"

"I move around a lot."

"Okay." He went back to his patient, who Kerry was already working on, loosening clothing and attaching equipment.

She zoned out their technical jargon as they worked. Early Sundays were usually her favourite time of the week, with only the occasional jogger to interrupt the quiet. When she was still in school she'd often spend Sunday mornings outside on the lawn, reading, pretending she was back home at The Farm. Now the stone wall she sat on was cold through her cotton pants; she'd have to go to Rain's to replace her clothes with a warmer set. Her cheeks were still numb from the night but the air would warm up soon. She hadn't been this hyper-aware of fall weather changes since, well, ever. Even at home she'd never needed to worry, she could always run back to the bunkhouse if she needed something.

She felt horrible and shallow when she found her attention wandering to Ray's looks. He wasn't that much taller than she was, but he had to be strong, given the width of his shoulders and the size of his biceps. Kerry was no weakling either, but Libby couldn't stop staring at Ray. He was handsome, too, with short, dark blond hair and a full mouth, skin that was far too tan for a blond guy who worked indoors all day, current circumstances notwithstanding.

He stood up suddenly and she looked away, sure she'd been caught, but he simply went over to the ambulance and brought out the stretcher. They loaded the man up and as Kerry cleared up their gear Ray came over to Libby.

"Here." He handed her a ten dollar bill. She didn't bother refusing it. "Get yourself some breakfast over there." He indicated the diner just opening up. "I'll be off shift after this call. Stick around?"

She saw no reason not to. "Sure."

Was he doing the right thing? Ray had no idea, but when he recognized the woman calling herself Beth he couldn't just let it go. Giving her money might have been a bad idea, he realized on the way to the hospital, but it was the first way he thought of to keep her in a place he could find her again.

So he had no plan, no clue of what to say to her, or even if he should say more than "Hey, weren't you kidnapped?" But he was committed now. He'd asked her to stay so he should at least show up. And if she wanted to stay lost, that was her business.

He was honestly surprised to see her outside the diner when he got there. He'd been delayed with paperwork before he could leave and he was sure she'd be gone, but nope, there she was, sitting on a concrete planter, cup in hand, looking at something on her phone.

That should probably have been his first clue.

"I actually do have money, you know," she said to him before he could even say hi. "I work two jobs. Just because I can't afford a place to live in this city doesn't mean I need charity. And I don't need saving."

Sure, okay, she had enough cash to buy her own coffee, but why sit outside? He glanced over at the diner and winced; the clientele weren't exactly friendly looking, all slicked-back hair and swagger, tired mouths and dead eyes. He'd bet there was more than one concealed weapon in there. No wonder she'd gotten her coffee to go.

No wonder she was sitting on a planter looking at the street instead of on the bench facing the window.

She tried to hand him his ten back, but he stopped her. "It wasn't charity. It was a ploy to get you to stay so I could ask you a couple of questions."

"Uh huh." But she tucked the bill away again, so he counted it as a win. "So how is he? The man from earlier?" Her concern was sincere and completely charming. She definitely wasn't from around here.

"You know what the worst part of my job is?" he asked. He sat on the end of the planter, half on the corner so he could face her a bit. Now that he had the time to look at her he saw the dark circles under her eyes, the red patch on her lower lip where it split, how dry and tight the rest of her skin was.

"The vomit?"

Ray almost laughed. "That's pretty bad, yeah. But the worst part is that after I get them through the doors of the ER I never hear about them again."

"Never?"

He shrugged. "Some of them, the special cases, I get called out to over and over. Others, a few memorable ones, the ER nurses will talk about when it's slow. But most of them I have no idea." Sometimes he thought it was better not to know.

"So you're out there saving lives. Maybe."

The side they were on faced the park and he looked that way instead. It was a pretty nice park, probably had lots of flowers in the summer. As places to sleep outside went, it could be a lot worse. "Yup."

"Not in it for the glory, huh?"

He had his own question for her and didn't bother with subtlety. "Are you Elizabeth Wyatt?"

He hadn't even noticed she was tense until she slumped back in her seat with a weak laugh. "Is that all you want to know? Yeah, I'm Libby Wyatt."

"Ray Lee. So, Libby, why are you out here calling yourself Beth?"

She drank the last of whatever was in the cup and tossed it in the nearby recycling bin. "I'm undercover."

"Bullshit. Were the reports wrong? We got an update saying you'd been found."

"Oh, I was found. But it turns out it's not so easy to just jump back into your life after a thing like that." She took another look at her phone then stashed it in her pocket. "Maybe I should go back to the farm." From anyone else saying that he'd have expected them to sound wistful, but she sounded resigned. Tired.

"If Toronto's so bad to you, why stick around?"

"Because I have a dream, and where better to realize your dreams than here?" She gestured widely at the street, the park, the growing number of people out early on a Sunday morning. Her arms fell back to her sides and her shoulders slumped. "Dreams suck, sometimes."

"I've heard it's not the dreams so much as what you have to do to make them come true."

She hummed. "Do you have any dreams, or is being a paramedic everything you wanted?"

It was a fair question. "It was when I started out." He shrugged it off and added, "I have some personal dreams, too, that won't be so easy."

"Personal dreams, that sounds dirty."

A startled chuckle burst out of him. "Some of them really are."

"And the rest?" she asked, eyes wide, maybe intrigued just a little bit.

What was he doing, talking so intimately to someone he'd only just met? Maybe that was it, it was easier to tell the private stuff to strangers than to your friends.

He'd been quiet too long. "Let me guess," she said, turning towards him. "White picket fence, a dog. Spouse."

"I'm more of a city loft kind of guy than a yard kind. Dogs are good. I like most animals, at least the ones I've met. Can't speak for toucans. They could be assholes."

"And note that he doesn't mention gender of spouse," she said in a conspiratorial tone.

He took a good look at her, liking what he saw, for the most part, but especially the sparkle in her eye that wasn't there an hour ago. "I'm mostly gay."

"Mostly."

"Every once in a while a woman comes along who grabs my attention." He let her see him looking, see him enjoying the long dark hair, proud nose, impish tilt to her mouth. Hints of a curvy body under her coat.

"Should I be flattered?"

He studied her again. "Feel free."

Head cocked to one side, she studied him as well, then seemed to come to a decision. "So, Ray Lee, do you have any plans tonight?"

Ray was not expecting that. "Not so much, no. Why?"

"'Cause I'm going to a friend's place this afternoon, which means I get to do things like shower and do my hair and find warmer clothes. All this in preparation for a concert me and my busking buddies are giving tonight in Riverdale Park. Want to come?"

It wasn't far from his house, and suddenly he really did want to go. "What do you do as a busker?"

"I train toucans."

"Well, I'm in."

She narrowed her eyes at him. "Really?"

"Sure, I need to find out if they're assholes or not."

And that's how Ray got a date with a homeless woman. He would not be telling his friends at the department about that part.

Ray got to the park late, not that they'd set a strict time or anything, but she'd mentioned she'd be performing around seven and he didn't get there until about ten after. Of course she didn't notice because she was singing. Ray wasn't sure what he'd expected her to be doing— probably not handling birds—but the singing kind of came as a surprise. She was pretty good, too, for all that he knew of opera and despite the fact that the acoustics in a park were shit. Her song was classical, maybe opera? Even if she'd told him she sang he still wouldn't have expected that.

She finished singing and waited out the applause, then started another, a lighter sounding song, prettier, German, kind of familiar, and Ray was struck by how little vocabulary he had to describe vocal music. He chuckled to himself and the guy next to him looked over sharply.

Ray stared back. "Problem?" He hadn't spoiled for a fight in a long time, not since high school, but something about the way this guy was watching him, like a cougar deciding if it wants to eat you right away or play with you a little first, put him on edge.

But the guy—and now that Ray looked at him he saw he was attractive in a clean-cut, older guy kind of way—just shook his head. "Wondering what was funny."

Ray pointed up at Libby. "She invited me here and I don't have a fucking clue what I'm listening to."

"Well, I don't speak German, but I keep hearing the word 'fish' in there. And I think my washing machine plays this when it's done."

Oh. "I'm an idiot." The guy raised a questioning eyebrow at him. "It's Schubert's Trout Quintet. Or a piece of it, at least." Ray should have recognized it earlier. His dad would crucify him for not recognizing Schubert.

"Usually she sings folk," the guy said, watching Libby again. "I hear her at St George station a few days a week when I'm going into work."

"She's good."

"She's studying opera at Pickford."

"That explains it, then." Dreams, she'd said. Dreams you could only chase in a big city. You could make lots of dreams happen in small towns but some could only happen in the biggest of cities. Opera was one of them. And tuition would make a hell of a dent in your housing budget.

Libby finished her song and left the makeshift stage. The guy drifted away, maybe to put some cash in the donation box, maybe to catch a train. Another performer came on and introduced herself before pulling out an honest to god nose flute. Ray searched for Libby in a sea of heads, but couldn't find her. Probably she was getting a glass of water after all that. He waited around a bit longer, actually gaining an appreciation for nose flute music. It didn't hurt that she was playing classic rock on the thing.

"Hey." A hand clasped around his arm and he turned, startled, but it was Libby, finally, smiling and full of energy.

"Hey, nice job up there."

"Thanks. You like classical?" She tugged his arm and he followed her out of the crowd around the performers and on to one of the paths leading towards Sumach Street.

"Some. My dad was a conductor, but I don't know a lot of vocal stuff." They stopped near a big tree and Libby stood with her back against it.

"But I know you have a good voice. Excellent pitch."

"I work hard."

"It shows." Ray joined her against the tree and watched the evening dogwalkers as they went by. "You've got some fans of your own," he said eventually. "I talked to a guy who seems to look forward to hearing you in the mornings."

"Yeah, I've got a few." She smiled at some memory. "Some come talk to me when it's slow, but there aren't many."

"You like it? Busking?"

Her smile brightened. "I do. I mean, I wouldn't want to try to live off it, but it's good for now."

"So what's your second job? You said you had two."

She licked her lips and let her eyes drift past his shoulder. "I sing jazz at a private club."

"Jazz, folk, and opera?" His dad would probably tell her to specialize.

"Wow, you really have been talking to my regulars But those pieces I sang weren't opera, they were lieder. Art songs." The sound of a trumpet coming from the performance area interrupted her and she stood on her toes to look. "Tim isn't supposed to be on yet. Something must have happened to make him switch. Anyway, folk music is like breathing. I grew up on those songs, especially the environmentalist stuff. It's easy and it's different from what everyone else is doing."

"Sparing your voice for opera."

"Exactly." The trumpet stopped in the middle of a phrase. "Look, I gotta go see what's up over there." She pulled out her phone and flicked the screen a few times. "Yeah, I missed a few texts."

Ray held out his hand for her phone. "Let me give you my number. We can get together again."

She didn't even hesitate to hand it over. "Great." He gave it back and she was gone, disappearing into the crowd again.

"Holy shit, Libby." Rain clutched Libby's arm and wouldn't let go. "Not what I was expecting."

Libby jerked her arm again—she needed to fix this cordless mic before Tim was done—and this time Rain let up. "What were you expecting?"

Rain didn't answer for a second, and when she did she sounded ashamed, which was new for Rain. "A guy who'd date a homeless person?" she said, barely loud enough to hear. "Either a complete sleaze or, I don't know, a nerd type. Someone who can't interact with normal people."

"I'm ignoring the implication that homeless equals abnormal." Libby wrapped electrical tape around the battery case and hoped it would hold the contacts in place. "And I told you he's a paramedic. That implies certain social skills, and, I might add, compassion."

"And I totally believe you now."

"Now?" She handed the mic back to Stuart, and turned, putting her hands on her hips just like the women who raised her.

"You have to admit you were sheltered until you came here." Rain had been the first person Libby could trust to help her assimilate instead of make fun of her or deliberately mislead her. "He could have been lying to you."

She wasn't wrong, and although Libby preferred to think she'd learned everything she needed to in her first year away from The Farm, she knew there were still huge gaps in her experience, even after three years. "Did I forget to mention the part where I called the ambulance he arrived in?"

"Uh, yeah? You did."

Oops. Libby glanced back at Ray, but he was gone. "Sorry. Yeah, there was an old man and I called 911 and that's how I met him." She settled back into one of the performer's chairs, tugging Rain down to sit beside her. "And we never said anything about dating."

"You said, and I quote: 'then we flirted a bit'. How does that not mean dating?"

"Whatever. Shut up and listen to the music."

"Fine way to treat someone who lets you use her expensive conditioner."

"I said thank you. I even brought you hot chocolate." Good hot chocolate, too. The kind that was too good to buy for herself.

"True."

"He gave me his phone number," Libby finally admitted after a few minutes of silence. "Just now, when we talked."

"Told you." Rain patted Libby's hand. "And anyway, what's the problem with that?"

"He's says he's not trying to rescue me, but he might be."

"You need rescuing."

It was an argument Libby was tired of, so she didn't bother responding. She and Rain, despite their vastly different backgrounds, had practically been sisters since the day they met. Even living together hadn't dampened their love for each other. Even Libby's troubles hadn't. This argument might.

"It's getting colder," Rain said, avoiding Libby's eye.

Gee, she hadn't noticed. "It's still pretty warm during the day."

"I've got some money stashed away." Rain started picking at her cuticles. "You know, if you decide one night it's too cold and you want a hotel room."

Libby slung her arm around Rain and pulled her tight. "I have enough money of my own. And I promise," she waited for Rain to look at her, "I will use it if it gets too bad. Okay?"

"If you freeze to death I'll only blame myself," Rain said with a sly glance up.

"Oh, that's low."

Ray waited for Libby through her last set and the clean-up. "Where'd your friend go?"

Libby jumped, one hand fluttering to her throat. He hadn't meant to startle her. Hadn't thought he could in a small crowd like this.

"Ray." She sighed his name, dropping her hand as she saw him properly. "She had to go home. Her mother has a weekly Skype appointment."

"So," he said, shoving his hands in his jeans pockets. "It occurred to me that this might be a date."

"If it is I've been a terrible partner." She finished gathering up her gear and slung her bag over her shoulder. "But I can be better."

"Good."

As they stepped out from the cover of trees she shivered at the sudden change in temperature and a gust of wind stole her voice for a second so he couldn't quite hear what she said. "Damn," she added.

"You gonna be okay out here?" She had a good hat and gloves, and a cozy-looking scarf in a dark stripe. Her coat could be better, but at least she was wearing wool and synthetics.

"Yeah." Her smile was uncertain, but he chose to believe her.

The cold had put pink in her cheeks and lips and a sparkle in her eye. She was stunning in a way that wasn't precisely beautiful, with her wide-set eyes and strong jaw. "Want to come back to my place?"

"Are you asking because you think I need a warm place to sleep? Or because you want my company?"

"The second." He let his gaze drift over her figure, hidden under her coat. "Definitely the second."

Something hot flashed in her eyes and her mouth melted into a wicked smile. "Then let's go."

Libby hadn't been intending to sleep with Ray that night, but there was something about the way he stood, relaxed, confident, tight jeans and tighter jacket showing off all his best features, that made her libido stand up and say whoa. She wasn't usually the type to fuck a guy the day she met him but she hadn't actually had much of a sex drive—she'd tried more than once—since, well, since. No way was she going to ignore it now.

It was a short trip on the streetcar to his place. His house—an actual house not too far from Queen's Park—was surprisingly nice. Someone with actual, if outdated and overblown, decorating sense had done it at some point, but someone with different taste had taken over and made it his. Ray, obviously, was the second person, and she figured the first was whoever had the place before him. It was an odd combination of damask wallpaper, brocades, and punk rock. "I grew up here," he said when she mentioned it. "Took over from my folks when they moved to the country. You want something to drink?" He motioned to the kitchen and took a step back.

"Nope." She tugged off her sweater and tossed it over a chair.

He grinned. "Something to eat?"

"Nope." She'd already left her boots at the door so she took the pins out of her hair and let it drop.

Ray got the hint and closed the few steps between them, sliding his hand around her waist to tug her the remaining inches to him. "A nap?"

"Not yet." She pulled herself up his body to reach his mouth, already open and waiting for her. His lips were soft, soft enough to make Libby embarrassed about how chapped hers were, but she ceased to care when his tongue, slick and strong, glided against hers, causing a tingle that swept to her toes.

She stifled a moan, delighted at the power of her arousal. Then his lips slid to the sweet spot under her ear and she couldn't have held back the high-pitched keen even if she tried.

She needed to touch him as much as she needed to be touched and it was just so easy to slip her hand down the back of his jeans and squeeze. He thrust, the hard ridge of his cock pressing against her stomach; on tiptoes she could just angle herself enough to rub where she needed it most. "Couch," she said, tugging at his hair.

"Yeah, okay." He walked her backward until she could pull him down on top of her, sweet and heavy, making her pulse pound in her ears. She spread her legs and let him settle between them. The noise he made was somewhere between a moan and a laugh.

"What?"

He buried his face in the crook of her neck. "I just realized I actually haven't been with a woman in about a decade."

"I don't think it's something you can forget how to do." His hand glided up her rib cage to cup her breast. "There, see?"

He tweaked her nipple in retaliation. She swatted his ass, making him thrust again so perfectly that she started to come. "Shit," she gasped, and held his hips down, grinding against him.

He got the idea, rutting into her, talking the whole time, "Yeah, come on, let me hear you, Libby," dissolving into babble as her brain whited out.

When she stopped shaking she blinked up at his stupid smile. "Well. That was unexpected."

"But not unwelcome."

"Definitely not." She tapped his shoulder a couple of times. "Get up."

He didn't question, didn't hesitate, although a cute frown creased his forehead until she guided him back down and straddled his thighs. "Your turn." She released the button on his jeans and peeled down the zipper before digging her fingers into both sides and easing them, and his briefs, down just enough to free his cock. His sigh of relief turned into a gasp when she trailed her fingertips lightly over the head. It was hot and smooth in her hand and she toyed with it, enjoying the silken skin.

"Please," he panted.

She tightened her grip in response, watching his face, feeling the pulse in her palm, hearing his breaths grow shorter and sharper until finally he spilled on to his stomach. She held him gently through the aftershocks, releasing him only when he pulled her down to kiss, careful of the mess. She slid to the side, wedging herself between him and the back of the couch. "Now I'll have that nap."

Ray laughed and rolled away, off the couch. "You'd be more comfortable in my bed," he said, heading into what she supposed was the bathroom.

And there it was. She couldn't stay. She couldn't let herself spend the night in his bed, and then maybe the next, couldn't start a relationship until she was sure a breakup wouldn't leave her homeless again. She made herself get up, taking a moment to enjoy how relaxed her muscles were, then tidied her clothing.

The bathroom door opened as she was tying her boot, and Ray stopped dead when he saw. "Going somewhere?"

Libby pulled the bow tight and stood up. "Yeah, I gotta...," she fumbled for a convincing lie but settled on, "I can't stay."

He tried to hide the disappointment, but Libby saw right through him. "Oh. You want to get together again sometime?"

Hat, scarf, coat, Libby busied herself so she didn't have to look at him while she turned him down. "I don't think that's a good idea." He was ridiculously hot and sweet and she might be able to fall for him if she let herself, but she'd sworn off relationships until her life was more stable. "I have enough to worry about. I can't add a relationship to the mess that is my life right now."

Ray opened his mouth, but shut it again without saying anything.

"I'm sorry, really," Libby said, one hand already on the doorknob. "I do like you and all, but this is the way it has to be. For me. Right now."

"Sure. Of course." He found his shirt and pulled it on again. "Take care."

With nothing more to say, Libby left.

Four

The small amount of sleep Libby got ended with her contorted in a strange position that left her with a headache that no amount of self-massage would get rid of.

"Great," she said to her pocket mirror. She didn't want to resort to pain medication, but she'd booked today's workshop—and paid for it—back in April, before everything went to hell. "You're no less talented now than you were back then. You're just a little twitchier. And you talk to yourself." That probably wasn't a liability. She'd heard worse about opera singers.

Rosie Klein had been artist in residence at Pickford the previous year—Libby had taken a masterclass with her in November while prepping for the holiday gala—and now she was holding a workshop at her studio, one that had required an audition and two references to get into. This was Libby's last chance to work with one of her idols, no way was she going to blow it.

Ms. Klein's studio was up in St Clair West, a trip split between streetcar and bus, giving Libby enough time to gather herself together. Only a few minutes early, Libby went in and found a seat with the others, getting oriented and trying to decide what she'd sing when invited up. She'd been working on *Una voce poco fa* when she was kicked out at the end of term but by that point Ms. Klein had been away on tour in Europe, and what Ms. Klein didn't know Libby was bad at she couldn't make Libby sing.

Usually Libby volunteered to be the first one to do anything rather than wait nervously, but this time she let others go first and second. So when Ms. Klein called her name she was prepared, doubly so when she asked, "You did *Figaro* last year, right?" They'd been talking about register changes, which Libby did easily.

But then she got up and couldn't control her nerves. On the little stage she started to shake; her voice cracked and wheezed and then refused to produce anything. Then she was on the floor, weeping silently. Someone wearing a light perfume had an arm around her, but otherwise the world was empty.

"This is so stupid," she said to herself. "Why is this happening?"

Whoever was next to her nudged her enough to get her off the floor and then guided her out the main door.

Libby opened her eyes and recognized the dress Ms Klein was wearing. Great. She had to humiliate herself in front of someone she one day wanted to be.

"Nerves?" Ms. Klein asked gently.

Libby's chuckle was more of a gurgle through the phlegm in her throat. "I wish."

"I heard your Cherubino last year. You've nothing to worry about."

Libby didn't want to explain, but she wasn't sure she could sit through well-meaning advice based on incredibly wrong assumptions. "This is going to sound melodramatic, but bear with me, please."

Ms Klein waited.

"On New Year's Day I was kidnapped," Libby began. "I was held for thirty-seven days in a room with only myself and a mouse for company." She laughed, feeling the crackle in her throat. "Sounds like Cinderella. Anyway, I had to entertain myself or I knew I'd end up just imagining worse and worse things, you know? So I recited poetry to myself. I played movies in my head. But I didn't sing. I had to save one thing from being associated with that time."

"Well," Ms. Klein said eventually, and Libby had never appreciated an upper class English accent more. "You've good enough reason to cry."

"I sing now. I sing folk, I sing jazz. But every time I try opera, my one true love... I can't." She was hot and scummy with sweat and mucus and just wanted to go home, wherever that was. "I can't access it anymore. I spent so long protecting myself that I just can't find myself anymore."

"You will." She tapped Libby under her chin and smiled brightly. "I must get back so the others don't think I'm playing favourites to the poor, kidnapped girl."

Libby watched the door close after her before taking the deep breath she hadn't managed on stage and going back inside. Her time was up, wasted, and Ms. Klein had to move on to the other students. And although Libby might not be able to sing right now but she could listen and take notes.

Several times over the next month Libby thought about texting Ray to explain, or apologize, or something. She hated that she might have hurt him, but when she really sat down and considered the situation she kept coming to the same conclusion: Don't.

Because she'd have to ask why he was hurt. She hadn't done anything thousands of men hadn't done and she certainly hadn't made any promises. So was he hurt because she refused his charity? That was his problem, not hers.

So she didn't text him and he didn't contact her and life goes on, right?

She did hear from Michael, this time by phone. He must have been in touch with Detective Strickland, because Faith (they were totally on a first name basis now) had called her and asked if she could give Michael Libby's contact info. She'd said yes, because what harm could it do?

Still, she was pretty surprised to actually get a call from him; she stood staring at her phone for so long she almost didn't answer in time. "What's up?" The lounge at work was too populated to have the kind of conversation it might turn out to be, so she took herself up to one of the conference rooms.

"I need a favour."

What could he possibly need from her? "Okay."

"I have to go out of town day after tomorrow, and I need someone to look after my cat." When she didn't reply, he continued, "The only other person I know in the city is allergic, and also really busy. Could you manage?"

"For how long?"

"Two weeks."

"You're lucky I like cats."

"Is that a yes?" His voice was all teasing amusement. She'd love to have him read a book to her or something.

"You don't live in, like, Barrie, do you?"

"Swansea, not far from Runnymede."

That was doable. And then he played what he didn't know was a high card. "You could even stay at my place, if you wanted. Actually, that would be best. I haven't had him very long and he's really needy. If he gets too lonely I might come home to all my furniture destroyed."

"Okay, yeah. Sounds good."

He was busy in the morning, so they made plans for her to go to his place the next afternoon for the tour. She hung up with an enormous feeling of relief and went back down to the club with an unaccustomed smile on her face.

She usually had fun during her sets, but the one she did next was particularly good. She got a lot of tips, too, and by the time she was ready to leave she thought she might actually be able to pull her life together again. She was just putting on her jacket and checking the pockets when Adria stopped her.

As much as Libby liked Adria, she tensed up. She was sure Adria knew Libby's situation, but she never said anything, just looked the other way when Libby used the shower or fell asleep in the employee lounge.

"You got a minute?" Adria asked.

"Sure, what's up?"

"I'm teaching a session on Japanese rope bondage tomorrow morning, and my sub had to cancel. Do you think you could step in? It's just a beginner class, so nothing too exotic or painful."

Libby froze. It wasn't that she wasn't a little kinky, but she'd never been restrained, certainly not since her kidnapping. What if she had a panic attack? But she trusted Adria to know when Libby had to stop, trusted her to listen to a safeword. It was her job, after all.

Adria must have seen it all on her face because she smiled weakly and said, "Never mind, I can easily find someone else."

Libby reached out, stopping short of grabbing her arm. "No, wait. I was just trying to decide if it would trigger me. I don't think it will."

"This is a public session. Anyone could be there."

"Will I have to be naked?"

The answer was no, and they discussed for a few minutes what she could wear. "Are you sure you can do this?" Adria asked again.

"I want to."

The class was at ten, so Libby made sure to get there at nine so she could have time to shower and dry her hair. With the money Adria was paying her maybe she could afford to get it cut, short and easy to wash. Except that she'd have to keep getting it cut or risk looking like a slob, so the trade-off was paying for cuts or paying for the occasional hotel room so she could at least relax, if not sleep.

She dressed in the tight, plain dark t-shirt and boy shorts they'd discussed, no underwire, hair braided, nothing that would impede her circulation under the ropes or hide what Adria was doing.

The class wasn't on the client level, but in the parlour they used for staff meetings. It was warm, the heat already on to combat the November chill, but nerves made her nipples look huge poking out the fabric of her purple shirt and she wanted to cross her arms to hide them, but students were drifting in so she pretended it was exam day in soprano class and tried to project calm and confidence. Unlike with her examiners, though, she didn't dare look anyone in the eye; she didn't want to invite conversation. She sat on the low velvet bench in the middle of the room and stared at her hands in her lap.

It was easier than she thought, being quiet and still. She was better at it than she used to be. She shied away from the thought that she had practised being quiet and still, a whole month of it. She actually liked the idea of not having to be on, projecting at an audience, to not always have to think about every move she made, the meaning and import, to have to remember lines or lyrics or where her mark was. All she had to do now was follow instructions, no decision-making, nothing to remember.

Adria started talking to the class, ignoring Libby. At least, that's what Libby thought until she heard her name.

"...already consented, or she wouldn't be here, but who knows what's changed in the last twenty minutes?"

A few people laughed, and Libby was surprised to see Adria frown at them. "Everyone has special circumstances; emotional and physical states can change in an instant. Don't ever presume consent." She turned to Libby. "Libby, will you let me tie you up?"

She nodded. "I'd like to try."

"And will you tell me if anything feels wrong?"

Adria had already told Libby about the stoplight system, so Libby nodded again. "Yellow means proceed with caution. Red means stop immediately."

Adria addressed her class again. "And for the top, 'proceed with caution' means 'check in frequently and watch for signs of physical and emotional distress.'"

She pulled out a series of lime green ropes of various sizes. She'd had Libby look at them, feel them, beforehand, so she didn't have any surprises. They were soft, and just holding them, wrapping them lightly around her wrists, hadn't made her uncomfortable in the slightest.

You'd think someone who worked with floggers, straps and buckles, rope, would have rough hands, but Adria's hands were smooth, the backs a satiny dark brown that glowed with health.

Libby relaxed, deeper than in what felt like years, and more than once, while Adria was demonstrating a complicated pattern that didn't require Libby to move, she started to fall asleep, right there, sitting up. Except it wasn't quite sleep; she could still hear Adria and the audience questions, could answer when Adria checked in with her, could feel the ropes constricting her, holding her, supporting her, but it was all so far away, like being under water in a warm bath. She was free of thought, of fear. If she had a concept of heaven, it might be this.

Adria said her name once, twice, and Libby fought to answer yet still stay in that calm place.

"You okay?"

"Yeah," she sighed.

"Nothing's too tight? Circulation's normal?" She tickled the tip of Libby's finger.

Libby wiggled it back at her. "All green."

"You sound drunk." A smattering of laughter greeted her, and Libby joined in.

"I feel awesome."

"You look pretty damn good, too. Take a look."

Libby opened her eyes to sight down her body. The ropes, some white now, different sizes for different purposes, criss-crossed her torso, binding her arms to her body and her legs together. Even her fingers were wrapped and she remembered that—it had been hard to ignore someone playing with her hand—each top knuckle bound to the next. She wiggled them again, feeling only slight give. "I've got webbed fingers."

More laughter, low and intimate.

"Sit up straight, show it all off." Adria pressed her hand to Libby's lower back and posed her like a doll. With her legs bound together hip to toe she felt oddly demure despite her state of undress. Bolder, she looked at the assembled students for the first time, five of them, it turned out, and nearly swallowed her tongue when she saw Michael. She raised her eyebrows at him and he ducked his head, a slight smile turning his mouth up. If she'd seen him earlier she might have been uncomfortable with his presence, but now he just added to the warm hum inside her.

He watched Libby's face relax as Claudine, who was Adria here, worked the ropes, the creases between her eyebrows smoothing out, and he realized that he was seeing her for the first time, the woman in the photos from before her kidnapping. He hadn't known this about her, was sure she wouldn't want him to know the one thing about herself she'd managed to keep secret through the media attention.

Then she was sitting up, looking at him, and he winked in acknowledgement. Her smile was loose, woozy, and she seemed just as content as a few minutes earlier. She was beautiful in a way he'd never noticed before, even though she was slightly too thin compared to her photos. He tried not to let his gaze linger on her curves, even though he had the perfect excuse of studying the pattern of ropes.

But then Claudine called the students up to look at the knots before they'd try their own on practice dolls – actual blow-up dolls ("They'll tell you if the rope's too tight," Claudine had said. "Don't leave any wrinkles.")

When Michael made it to the front of the line he didn't speak to Libby, nor did she to him. It was all strictly professional among Claudine and the strangers. He honestly did want to learn this, not get distracted by someone he barely knew. He ignored the way she inhaled sharply when he leaned in to get a closer look at a particularly intricate knot on her thigh. During practice he only went back to her when he needed to, and when he looked up from his doll later she was gone and he hadn't noticed. They still had an appointment this afternoon, although it was hard to reconcile this Libby with the one he'd talked to yesterday.

Claudine dismissed them and he gathered his jacket and his notes, going over what he'd learned, trying to fix it in his memory before distraction erased it.

Distraction came sooner than he expected, because as he stepped on to the sidewalk he heard his name called in a voice that was rapidly becoming familiar. He turned and there she was, leaning against the wrought iron rail. She had the same travelling case she had before, and a warm-looking hat and scarf with her coat this time. "Hi."

Libby wasn't sure why she waited for him. After all, they had plans to meet at his place later, and would that be weird now? It was mostly curiosity that prompted her to call his name when he came out of the building. Curiosity and the memory of that wink he'd tossed her earlier, which felt like a shared secret. The warm way he smiled at her, the way he didn't hesitate to come to her, that was gratifying. Feeling immensely silly, she reached out one finger and poked him in the shoulder. His jacket, a dark grey wool, was soft.

His face crinkled, puzzled. "What?"

"I'm just having a hard time believing you're here," she said. "I mean, you were my knight in shining flannel, virtuous above all, and here you are learning to tie people up for fun."

He laughed, leaning against the railing next to her. "Well, I certainly didn't expect to see you."

"Just earning a little extra money." Libby took a deep breath and decided to come clean. "I work here on the weekends. Singing, in the bar."

"You used to work in a museum, right?"

She nodded. "They didn't have a position for me when I got back." Got back. What a stupid way to put it, but honestly, she was tired of the word 'kidnapped'. And it wasn't like he didn't know already.

"And the busking fills in the rest?"

"You'd be surprised what buskers can pull in. Some people make an actual living at it."

"Good thing you have your scholarship, hey?"

Libby couldn't bring herself to lie to him, so she settled for a non-committal hum. "Do you want to go get some lunch with me? I know a place with great soup." If she was lucky he'd offer to pay.

"Sounds delightful." He honest-to-god offered her his arm then and didn't let go the whole three blocks to the café.

Libby loved this little shop. It always smelled wonderful, like fried onions and curry. You had the option of getting a big chunk of bread and butter with your soup or one of their pasta salads. Best, they always had something vegetarian, and on a good day it was chili.

The walls were a friendly medium blue and the white plasticky tables were usually spotless.

She never had to worry about blending in, because this wasn't a popular place for anyone but the locals, the construction workers, the nurses from the nearby hospital. And sometimes, when she went in after work, Anna behind the counter would give her a free cup of mint tea to go.

Over lunch she told Michael stories about her former classmates and professors, of roles she'd played in student productions. When she tired of talking about herself—which happened pretty quickly—she asked why he left Ottawa. "You seemed like you had a good thing going, there."

"I did." And suddenly he wouldn't look at her, preferring to slowly spread butter on every millimetre of his bread. "There's something I didn't tell you back then."

It was going around. "Oh?"

He glanced up for a second and then laboriously dipped a chunk of bread into his soup and ate it. "You asked me if I was seeing anyone."

"You said you were."

"Yeah. Oliver." He said it almost too quietly, directing it at his food and not her.

"So you're bi?" She was watching his face, the startled look that came over it, and amended her question. "Or what? Because you said you used to be married to a woman."

He started looking at her again as he spoke. "Yes. Anyway, he got tenure. Decided to buy a house and asked me not to move with him."

"Shitty."

"Yeah." He was still angry, months later, she could see it in the way his lips thinned. "It got harder to stay there, and I'd already been offered a position here, so I took it."

Libby remembered that. "Your friend's husband."

"Right."

Libby thought there was a story there, but she didn't ask. "So tell me something else – how'd you find out about Adria's class? Does she advertise?"

Something small changed in his face, like he thought her question was amusing. "She does, actually. But I have a friend who pestered me into learning more about what she does."

Jesus. She had not expected that. "Your friend's a domme?"

He nodded. "Pro."

"Neat. So now what? Did you like it?"

He ate his soup, slowly and carefully, before answering. "Maybe? You obviously did."

"Shocking, I know. But yeah, it was nice. Comforting." Then she thought about it a second and laughed. "That's probably not the word most people would use."

"No, probably not." He cocked his head, thinking. "I like the artistic aspects, I guess."

Libby'd had these fantastic red patterns on her skin after. They'd faded too quickly, leaving her a little sad. "I never thought of it that way."

Michael leaned over the table and started talking with his hands, almost drawing a picture in front of her. "My friend has these coffee table books, big glossy things with the most beautiful photos of the art." He stopped suddenly like he couldn't put words to what he felt. "I'm not sure I've ever made anything beautiful before. I think I want that."

Libby nodded along with him. "One of the best things about singing with other people is that moment when you all hit your notes perfectly and the chord just hovers in the air like it took life on its own."

"It sounds amazing."

"I like to think it's a direct connection to the universe. Like we're tapping into some deep vibration and making it audible to the world." Suddenly feeling stupid—who was she to talk about the universe to someone so much more experienced?—she licked the butter off her thumb so she wouldn't have to look at him.

"Far out."

Okay, so flipping him the bird wasn't the most mature response, but he laughed and she had pretty much been raised by hippies, so he wasn't wrong.

After lunch they went directly to his apartment in Swansea. Everything she needed was in the two bags she had with her, but she pretended like she was making lists of what she'd need to pack for two weeks away from home. "Nice place," was all she said at first, taking a few slow steps into the living area. The walls were creamy and mostly bare, but the red oak floor had a soft, modern rug under the seating area and his couch looked new and comfy. Mostly, though, she cared that the place was warm and had good light.

"Thanks." He hung up her coat and led her deeper into the apartment. Around the corner she could see past the living area into a nice-sized galley kitchen with a breakfast bar. Three doors led off the hall beside it.

A warm body thumped against her calf. "Oh! Kitty, hi!" The cat busied himself headbutting her knees until she picked him up.

"This is Jeeves, also known as Lord of Destruction. Don't leave anything you love on the floor or he'll kick it to shreds. Otherwise he's very sweet."

"Got it. I grew up with cats on The Farm." She gave the cat a scratch on the ear. "You boys are all alike, aren't you?" He wriggled out of her arms and wandered off. "At least he's not clingy."

"Oh he is; he's just going to sit by his bowl in hopes I'll feed him. Can I get you anything? Water?"

Libby took a better look around while he got her drink. She drifted over to his music collection first, a weird mix of vinyl, CDs, and an MP3 player. The music itself was just as eclectic; jazz, a lot of stuff she didn't recognize, a smattering of classical and opera. Billie Holiday beside Leonard Cohen, John Lee Hooker beside Joni Mitchell. She wondered what he had in digital.

She heard his footsteps approaching, which she assumed was on purpose. "You can put something on if you'd like."

She took the glass from him with one hand and slipped a record out of the stack. "How about this? I've never heard of this band."

Michael chuckled as he let the vinyl drop from the sleeve. "Cocteau Twins? Of that entire subgenre in my collection you managed to pick one you might actually like." He cued it up and she listened while he gave her a tour of the apartment.

His bedroom was much like the outer rooms, but with pictures on the walls, photos she made a vow to examine later. "You can use my bed, if you want. I don't have a guest bed yet."

"Sure." If she could sleep. She'd managed to make her sleep problem a benefit these past few months, but given a bed and absolute privacy, had anything changed?

"You okay? Having second thoughts?"

She jerked her head up, unaware that she'd been staring at the wood grain on the floor. "No, I'm fine. Just tired."

"You working again tonight?"

She nodded. "I should probably go get a nap so I can focus later."

He escorted her out. "I'll make a list of things you should know, about the apartment and the cat. Can you be here tomorrow at seven am?"

"Yeah, absolutely." She got out of there as graciously as she could, stopping to give Jeeves a goodbye pat.

On the subway back downtown she stared out the window at the blackness, overwhelmed by the idea that she might not be better, that all this might actually have gotten worse, that she was irretrievably lost.

Five

Libby spent the night in the park near Michael's building so she wouldn't be late, hoping desperately that he wasn't the sort of person who jogged early in the morning. If he was she didn't see him, so she called herself lucky (ha!) and did her best to look normal before going over there.

When she knocked on the door she could smell coffee, and she really did call herself lucky, then. Even better, Michael answered the door wearing an apron over his jeans and dress shirt and she smelled eggs and cheese and toasted bread. "Breakfast?" he offered, leading the way into the kitchen.

"Yes, please." She dropped her bags on the way and sat at the breakfast bar separating the little kitchen from the living room. There was a plate set out for her, which he dropped half a cheese omelette on. "Classy," she said, picking up the fork and digging in.

"Yeah well, I'm sticking you with the dishes," he replied. "Anything in your coffee?"

She shook her head no; her mouth was too full to talk. The mug he set in front of her smelled amazing. Coffee had been forbidden at The Farm, the carbon footprint and workers' rights issues making it evil, and she'd deliberately cultivated a taste for it when she got out. That and chocolate.

He sat down opposite her and ate, going over the things she needed to know while he did. He'd actually written out a list, with everything from the building manager's email to the address of the vet's office. There were also detailed instructions on feeding the cat, watering the plants, and who to call if anything disastrous happened (someone named Claudine in Cabbagetown).

When he got up to leave she stood too, following him to the door to see him out. "Have a safe trip," she said as he grabbed his suitcase.

"Thanks. Be safe." He turned around and absently kissed her on the temple, then he was gone, out the door to the airport, and she was alone in his house with his cat.

"Weird," she told Jeeves when he hopped up next to her on the counter. Weird, but kind of sweet. It made her think fondly of her last relationship, which really wasn't something she should be thinking fondly of. It hadn't ended badly, but it needed to stay ended.

She took her pack into the bedroom and dug out some relatively fresh clothes. She'd been able to do laundry a few days before and had a shirt that she'd only worn once since. It smelled okay, so she grabbed it and her toiletries kit and searched for the bathroom. She'd thought the bathroom at work was heaven, but this was something else. White on white on white, yes, but sparkling clean. An open shelf was stuffed with fluffy bath sheets in a dark, welcoming teal, and the shower curtain had a coral trellis pattern. Most importantly, the place felt like someone lived there. There were toiletries scattered about the counter, and the shower contained a modest array of bottles plus an antique-looking safety razor, shaving soap, and mirror. The air still smelled faintly herbal. She didn't waste any time setting out her own stuff and turning on the hot water.

Heaven was a hot shower and no time limit.

Eventually she had to get out. She was really curious about what kind of internet and TV service Michael had. It had been a while since she'd had privacy and unlimited bandwidth. She had some reading to catch up on. But first she needed to check out auditions. She was barely qualified for even the smaller companies, but she had to try, right? Especially now that she wouldn't have a degree to point to.

When she left school she'd talked to her instructors about mentoring, about where to go without education, and they'd given her some good advice. Her voice coach had given her a membership to a website that listed auditions and industry news. So far she hadn't been qualified for most of the roles that came up, even without her opera-block, but smaller companies were starting up and she was looking at a broader range of musical theatre now, not just opera. She didn't want to, but she was out of choices. If she couldn't get past her brain's refusal to sing opera she'd need other options.

Her luck today was holding. There was an audition for a small company, an emergency listing, for the day after tomorrow. She didn't have much time to practice, but she hadn't forgotten any of her pieces. She just needed to brush up. And maybe switch things up a bit.

Libby hadn't seriously auditioned for anything until she got kicked out. In school, auditions were merely a formality; profs knew everyone's skills, and only freshmen had to worry about proving themselves. Of course, upperclassmen didn't bother even trying for roles outside their particular talents.

A year ago, Libby would never have auditioned for a contralto part, but at this point she'd take whatever she could get. She had managed to extend her lower register— something she'd never even tried at school— mostly in an effort to produce the sexier voice required by her night job, so she might even not make an ass of herself. She tried not to think about how she'd probably lost a lot of the colour in her higher register after six months without real practice.

She emailed the address on the ad to arrange an audition time, then settled in for a day of quiet relaxation.

Libby's definition of 'too quiet' had changed a lot since she left The Farm. It had changed even more since her kidnapping. Now, even with the windows open and constant traffic, this area of the city was too quiet for her. She tried to sleep during the day, hoping that the higher noise level would help, but her schedule was just too fragmented for that to work. And on the days she could spend the whole time at Michael's sleep just wouldn't come. Peaceful sleep, at least.

The building had a limited gym in the basement, just a few treadmills and some free weights, but Libby made full use of them each night, trying to wear herself out enough to pass out completely. It didn't work, but at least she felt good for a little while after; hard, physical labour was just another part of her life until she'd moved away and she found she missed it just a little.

The best part, the part she could get used to, was having a fridge. Her first day at the grocery store she ended up with a basket full of produce, far too much for a single person, even over two weeks. She pared it down to things she didn't get often, the treats that didn't come with cheap food: kiwis, fresh soybeans, leafy greens. It was amazing how hard it was to get leaf lettuce or spinach without either paying twelve dollars for a salad or having to pick meat out of it.

And at the end of each day she got to snuggle with a big, warm, furry beast, and sometimes, if he climbed up on her chest and tucked his head under her chin, she could sleep.

Her first audition of five was in a rundown office-building in Etobicoke, not exactly the high-class operation she'd always hoped she'd work for, but it was a start. The hour travel time wasn't great, but hey, there was an enormous park she could spend nights in if her schedule didn't allow time to get back to downtown.

There wasn't anyone in the front office when she entered, but a big sign pointed her down the hall to a meeting room. After one look she turned right back around, nearly slamming her knee into the corner in her need to get the fuck out of that hall.

Shit. Why had she not considered that her former classmates might be here? And why did there have to be so many of them? Okay, it was only two, and Nicole and Diana might as well be a single entity anyway, but still, of all of them, those two were the worst. Nicole was the class clown, except her humour was rooted in caricature and humiliation, cloaked in a way that made her targets—who were also her adoring audience—unaware they were the ones being mocked. Diana did everything Nicole did, but in anticipation, like a canary in a coal mine or a trial balloon. Nicole then either swept in and covered the path Diana had laid in her own glory or left her to twist in the wind. The truly pathetic part was that Diana had no clue she was being used. She was just happy to be a snide, self-important part of Nicole's story.

And here they were, auditioning for the same show. Libby almost walked out.

She couldn't, though, not and call herself an opera singer. This was the dream she'd been working so hard for, she couldn't give it up just because the Society of Twits was here too. She tidied her clothes and pulled out her phone, then started typing texts to her own number as she walked to join the two-person line.

"Oh look, it's Lily. Hi Lily."

Libby ignored her—her name wasn't Lily, after all; Diana might have been talking to someone else—and read the text that just came through. This app was the best buck she'd ever spent.

A hand waved between her face and her phone. "Lily. I nearly didn't recognize you. You used to be so fat."

Libby pretended surprise as she looked up from her phone, in time to see Diana glance back at Nicole for approval of her little jab. "Hi," she gave them her best stage smile. "It's Libby, not

Lily. But you always did have a poor memory, didn't you?"

Oh, that was not a happy look. "We haven't seen you in class for a while."

As if the whole school didn't know she'd had to leave. "Oh, you know how it is. You get a great singing job and school seems so unnecessary."

Nicole stopped pretending not to listen to them. "You got a gig? Then what are you doing here?"

"There's always time for more when you don't have to bother with classes. I'm surprised to see you two here. I always thought you were more suited to musicals."

"How dare you? Say what you want about me but don't you dare slander Nicole!"

"I can defend myself, Diana."

"But you never do, because you're just too good a person."

"Or maybe it's because she has you to be her guard dog." Libby suspected that Nicole would be decent enough—contemptuous sense of humour aside—if she didn't always have Diana jumping in to defend her or to tell everyone what Nicole really meant. But no one would ever know, because Diana was always around. "Or do I mean purse dog?"

Libby could have sworn she saw Nicole smile a little at that. Whatever Diana was about to say was cut off when a woman in her mid-thirties came out of the meeting room.

Libby had a moment of horror that she'd heard everything, but if she did she wasn't acknowledging it. "I'm Helen, the director. Who's next?"

Nicole introduced herself and followed Helen inside. In turn she was followed by Diana, already making excuses for how necessary her presence was.

Fifteen minutes later, they both walked out. Helen thanked Nicole for her time and told her she'd get back to her, a brush off as clear as anything Libby had ever heard.

As soon as the door closed behind them, Diana started practically shouting. "Sexist assholes!" She stopped in front of Libby. "They have a scene where everybody's going to be naked!"

"Is it only women in the scene?"

"No. But no way am I auditioning for sexist pigs like them!"

"If men are just as naked as the women, I don't understand how that's sexist."

"Well, you're obviously just not feminist enough."

Libby blinked at her in disbelief. "Okay then."

Nicole dragged her away before the conversation, if you could call it that, went any farther. A moment later Helen came back out. "You're the last one?"

"Looks like it."

The room is a standard meeting room, without even a piano, but that wasn't a big deal for Libby. "So what's the role? Your ad didn't mention which opera."

"Handel's *Serse*. It's a new translation."

"Interesting." Libby put her coat and bag on one of the chairs, trying to get comfortable. "I don't know it at all. I've only heard the name."

Helen's face was a mixture of excitement and fatigue. "You should know that we've already cast the contralto. We only have one role left, the soprano Atalanta."

"Well, I'm a soprano. What kind of a mood would you like?"

"How about something with some spirit?"

Libby had a couple of songs that hit that mark. "How many times have you heard *Agitata* today?"

Helen groaned. "As long as you're not murdering *Queen of the Night*. Go ahead."

Libby started strong, sure she was in the right key, and she might have been, but it didn't matter because her heart was pounding, her breath short, and therefore her sixteenth notes were muddy, sliding around and getting in each other's way. She tried to stand up taller and support more, but between her anxiety and her lack of practice it was hopeless. She could read the disappointment on Helen's face, too.

She finished as strongly as she could, acting the hell out of the rest of the piece to try to make up for her faults. At least she'd hit the big intervals correctly, and hadn't fumbled memorization. "Not too bad, I hope?"

"No, not too bad." Helen's smile was as gentle as her words. "Unfortunately, you need training that I don't have the time and resources to give you. We need to get this production up and perfect as quickly as possible."

Libby tried to swallow the lump in her throat, but it just grew worse. She needed to get out of there before she did something stupid like cry. "Thanks anyway."

"Keep an eye on our auditions and come back when you've got your degree."

"Sure."

She found a quiet spot in the park across the street and cried until her throat hurt.

Michael was glad to be home, which was a strange feeling considering he hadn't really considered Toronto home before. It had taken a while, but there it was, assimilation. He'd dropped his bags off at the apartment, taken a quick shower—no sign of Libby except a note telling him she was at work, which at this time on a Saturday meant busking—and was meeting Claudine at Allen Gardens. It was too late in the year for the park to look anything but scraggly and brown, but she led him into the Edwardian-era conservatory. He paused in the entry to take off his hat and gloves, to open his coat.

"It's quiet." It was like being in a glass bottle, surrounded by the city, but protected from the worst of it.

"I like the peace," Claudine replied, bending over an orchid to examine the petals more closely.

They walked for a while, changing climates every few minutes in a whirlwind tour of vegetation. "I did some thinking while I was in Ottawa," he said finally. "I've decided to start dating again."

"Okay. And you need to talk about this why?"

"Because life is hard and this is a big city."

He'd given her his most pathetic face, so she laughed and replied, "Fair enough."

"How do you meet people here?"

He'd caught her off guard, she genuinely looked confused. "I met David in university. We tend to meet our girlfriends at fetish events. What do I know about it?"

"Surely you've learned something. By osmosis, maybe." He gently touched the spine on a barrel cactus, letting it go before it broke the skin of his finger. "And considering your other job, you must have heard a lot of stories."

"So, would you rather hear about the academics who met at work or the artists who met at work? Or maybe the sex workers who met at work."

"I'm sensing a theme."

"We work a lot." She shot him a playful glance. "And no, you can't have my husband. He's straight."

They reached the exit and stood outside for a while, watching a couple of sparrows flit around the remains of a formal garden. "This is nice," Michael said eventually. The day was if anything a little colder now, but he was reluctant to leave just yet. "You grew up here, didn't you?" They'd spent a lot of time talking while on duty, but the combined forces of vigilance and it being twenty years past meant he was hazy on the details.

"In Mississauga. But my grandmother lived just over there." She pointed at a brown apartment building, one that looked just like all the rest of them. "We'd come here every Sunday after church."

"Then you should have known how cold it would be before you brought me here."

"You're from Ottawa. You can handle it." A poke in the ribs left him almost wishing he'd never moved out of her house. He missed having a friend he saw every day. David was a great guy, but you couldn't really horse around with the boss.

"I left my heated mittens in my other parka."

Claudine turned and started down the west path, towards the street. "You know, you should come to the club some night. The bar I mean; only clients get to see the rest. You might meet someone."

"Someone kinky."

She shrugged one shoulder. "Sure. Or not. Members are allowed to bring friends into the bar area. And don't pretend you weren't at my ropes class."

"It was more curiosity than anything." Curiosity he'd had since he'd first learned about it a few years earlier. He'd never been into anything but light bondage, but the book on shibari that Claudine had at home had struck him deeply. He'd never thought he had artistic inclinations, but there you go.

"You were pretty good. You should come to the next one." They passed a brightly decorated store front and she stopped in front of it. "Hey, what are you doing for Christmas?"

Despite the reminders all around him, Michael had avoided thinking about it. "There's a work party."

"And the day itself?" Claudine leaned back against the wall, facing the street. Neither of them had lost the itch that came of having your back exposed.

"Probably sit at home and be glad I'm not travelling."

She was watching something, but he didn't bother to look. "You should come to our house. My mashed potatoes are fantastic."

"All right."

"Bring your boyfriend."

What? "I don't have a boyfriend."

"You might by Christmas." She nodded in the direction of the café across from them. "That stocky guy over there's been eyeing you for a few minutes."

He looked, just in time to see the guy look away quickly. "How do you know he's not looking at you?"

"No one looks at me when I'm not either Madame Adria or someone's mom. I make sure of it." Her phone rang and she pulled it out of her pocket. "You should go over and talk to him."

He was pretty attractive, in a prize-fighter kind of way. And Michael did need to warm up before heading home.

Claudine's call was from David, something about Lucy's recital that night. She had to go home, but Michael was still considering introducing himself. He finally got up and crossed the street, amused at how the guy suddenly wasn't looking anywhere at but at his cup.

The café was warm and they had hot cider liberally dosed with caramel syrup, which sounded fantastic. He ordered, then while he waited he tried to catch Blondie's eye. From here he could see the broad shoulders and crooked nose, the obvious strength in his frame, and he wondered for a minute if he really was a boxer. His build was less gym rat, more 'I haul heavy things for a living'. Far more attractive, in Michael's opinion.

The barista called his name and the guy looked up, giving Michael a shy smile when he caught him. That was clearly his cue.

Michael took his cup over. "May I join you?"

"Sure." His eyes were light brown, his hair natural or a good fake. "Hey, you got the cider. Did you get extra cinnamon? This place never uses enough."

He took a sip and had to agree. "I wasn't aware. It's my first time in this neighbourhood."

"You new to the city, or just visiting?"

"New. I'm from Ottawa."

"Oh." The guy's wary smile brightened. "Cool. I'm Dragos." He said it with a short -sh on the end. Something must have shown on Michael's face, because he laughed. "I know, right? Nobody calls me that."

"Michael. What should I call you?"

"I mostly go by Ray. We've met before, you know."

He did look a bit familiar. "When?"

"Riverdale Park. There was a concert of buskers. We talked for a bit about one of the performers."

Right. He'd laughed and Michael had thought he was laughing at Libby. "I remember. I was speculating, before I came in here, on if you're a fighter."

Ray snorted. "Only if you count death as an opponent. Paramedic."

That explained the build. "Tough job."

"It is at that. Let me guess, you're an accountant."

That wasn't an unusual guess. For some reason, no matter how long he'd spent in the Army and as a police officer, Michael exuded harmlessness. It was helpful, at times. "Not even close."

"Banker?"

"Nope."

"Venture capitalist."

He was clearly having fun with this, but Michael decided to let him off the hook. "Case analyst for Innocence Canada."

"So you're a lawyer."

Michael laughed. "Former cop."

"Gotta admit I would not have guessed that." Ray got the connection instantly. "Left in a bad way?"

"They objected to my boyfriend."

"Ouch. Your friend live around here?" Ray asked, gesturing towards the window to where Claudine no longer stood.

"No, she just likes it here." He took a chance and added, "She and her husband inherited a house in Cabbagetown."

"Nice. So we might see each other again sometime, you and me?" Ray glanced down and away, uncertain. "Or we could see each other again sooner, and not accidentally."

"Bold." Michael smiled when Ray looked up again. "I like that."

This time when Ray looked away it was more bashful than nervous. "Yeah, well. I'm old enough to not care if I make an ass of myself now and then."

"Good. I much prefer that to people who are so careful they never take a chance."

"So you would like to go out with me sometime."

"Absolutely."

"How about tonight? I'm on shift at eleven, but I could make some dinner, see how the evening goes."

"I almost literally just got back from two weeks away. Could we make it Saturday?"

"A little cliché, but all right."

Michael had to agree through his laughter.

Ray had recognized Michael instantly; that's why he'd been staring at him. He felt stupid to have been caught, but he'd gone a little blank, stunned. That could not be the same guy who gave him a death glare. No way was that soft smile part of the same face as those cold eyes. But then he remembered the fondness with which he'd watched Libby, the same stillness in his posture, and yeah, it was him. It only made sense when he learned Michael was a cop, then it all came together.

But getting caught staring hadn't worked out too bad, he'd gotten a date out of it after all. He probably shouldn't have offered to make the guy dinner, but hey, Ray had skills. He was a creative genius in the kitchen. Among other places.

He just had to hope this date went better than his last one.

He hadn't heard from Libby again, hadn't even let himself cruise by her busking spot to check up on her. He didn't want to be that guy even a little bit, didn't want her thinking he was out to rescue her or change her or make her feel beholden to him in any way, so he tried to stop remembering the curve of her cheek when she smiled.

Michael was a much better choice.

Six

It felt weird for Libby to be using her key in the apartment door, knowing Michael was probably home. She was the hired help, and yet not. She hadn't forgotten the distracted kiss Michael had given her when he left, but she kind of hoped he had.

"Hey, kitty-cat," she said when Jeeves appeared. "Is your Daddy home yet?"

A rustle from the bedroom gave him away and his head popped out of the door. "I'm not that cat's father."

Libby grinned up at him from where she knelt on the floor with Jeeves. "Poor guy. No wonder he was such a suck with me, if you keep denying him."

"He's a grown cat. He'll have to learn to live with the pain."

Libby got up off the floor. She wanted to hug him, but wasn't sure how he'd react. "Good trip?"

Michael shrugged. "Good in that we got something accomplished, yes. The subject matter? Not pleasant."

"I'll get out of your hair soon, then." She moved past him to the bathroom and cringed when she saw all the dry-erase notes she'd left the bathroom mirror. A quick wipe with some toilet paper got rid of them. She had the list of auditions in her phone and everything else was moot now that she was moving back out.

She was already packed, her bag against the living room wall, all traces of her gone except for a few things in the bathroom. "I wanted to make sure you were actually coming home today," she explained, stuffing her toiletries kit into her backpack. "The weather's supposed to turn nasty soon."

"How'd the auditions go?"

Closing her eyes, she sighed. "I'm too out of practice. I thought for sure that after—" she cut herself off. It never helped to share too much.

Michael slid his hand around her upper arm and squeezed gently. "I know it doesn't mean much, but I think you're great."

Her smile was weak, but it was definitely a smile. "Thanks. And it means more than you realize." She picked up her coat and slipped it on. "Now, I have to get going."

She was out the door before she noticed she had his warmest scarf draped around her neck. She'd been wearing it all week because her old one was, well, old, and his was better. She could give it back later.

Out in the cold again, but this time with a small picnic blanket she'd picked up at Goodwill. At this rate she'd need a bigger bag soon. How many years did it take to reach the shopping cart level of homelessness? She hoped she never got there. She'd always prefer to be able to run.

The night was bad. She spent it shivering, trying to sleep upright on a park bench, and even if she'd been able to sleep like a normal person, the shivering would have kept her awake all night anyway. "I wonder what it would take to get arrested? At least it's warm in jail." Great, she was talking out loud to herself.

She wanted a hot shower but no way was she getting one. It would feel great up until her hair froze. She decided to walk, visit a part of the city that was out of her usual territory. Walking would keep her warm and who knew what she'd discover? She also worried about being recognized, about becoming, unintentionally, a threat to other street people or a burden to shopkeepers and the residents who had things like homes and rights. If she ever got out of this situation she'd seriously consider becoming an advocate for unhoused people.

It was almost harder, this time, to go from relative comfort to the street. The first time she had no idea what was in store for her or how long she'd be out there. In her head she'd just be a couple of weeks until she made enough money to find a place to live. But she'd failed every roommate interview, all of them baulking at either the homeless thing or her getting kicked out, and even so, she still couldn't manage first and last month's rent plus a security deposit. Not if she also wanted to eat and buy a TTC pass so she could get to her two jobs.

This time she knew how she'd live and it made it harder to leave. If anything, it made her even more of a failure, even though she'd always known her break from school would be temporary. She'd always thought homelessness would be temporary too.

Don't blame yourself, Rain kept telling her. It's your parents' fault for being unrealistic. It's the kidnappers' fault. It's a problem with the system that kicked out a talented young woman because of a mental health problem.

Well, Libby did have a way of directing her hurt and anger at one of the perpetrators, and she was ready to take advantage of it.

Shortly after she returned to Toronto Libby had been harassed by reporters. They hovered outside her classes, her residence, one or two at a time, asking questions Libby mostly couldn't answer to their satisfaction. There'd been a few small articles, but with no juicy details or suspects to vilify, they had little to write about.

Later a different crop of journalists emailed and phoned her with requests for interviews, some about the kidnapping, some about her father's death, others about her childhood at The Farm. Those she paid special attention to. Her childhood and eventual exile weren't something she talked about much. She hated the pity people treated her with when they knew, hated the word cult–she had this weirdly protective thing going on about her parents. They weren't bad people, as such. Just misguided. She'd always felt bad for the other kids, the ones still going through what she'd experienced, but she couldn't do anything to really help.

She'd never wanted the extra attention a full scale article would bring; having been held for a month had been bad enough and at the time she just wanted to get back to her real life. But her current real life wasn't worth the trouble of keeping her mouth shut anymore, and the slight chance that something good could come of it made her decision easy. She was in a special position and she knew it; earlier stories had been published, but with anonymous sources in small venues. But she had name recognition, and maybe it was time. Not maybe. It was time. But which paper? Somewhere in cloud storage she had a list of journalists who'd called her, and their papers. It was both awesome and frightening to think she could make the Star or the New York Times. Again, only this time deliberately.

The next morning she found a warm, busy lobby with free wifi and spent an hour poking through her phone (it took her less than a minute to find the list; the rest of the time she spent distracted, cleaning up old, irrelevant shit and reorganizing her bookmarks). She also accessed the database of church members; her mom never changed her password. Surprise surprise, two of the five journalists were in the database, one at a high rank. She deleted their names as violently as one could on a touch screen.

Of the remaining three, she read what she could of their work, the human interest stuff at least, to make sure she was trusting her life story to the right person. She chose Adelaide Bukhari, an independent writer who'd made a lot of promises that Libby liked. She called and left a message, reminding Adelaide of the conversation they'd had in Cobourg. Then, out of curiosity more than anything, she looked up if there was such a thing as an interview contract.

After that, she just had to figure out what she was going to say.

The morning of the interview, Libby had it all worked out. She had the questions in advance and knew exactly how the afternoon would go. She even got to the cafe early to have some lunch before Adelaide arrived. But as the hour drew near, her throat closed up and she started to shake. She pulled her coat back on and went for a quick walk, hoping to work out some of the tension.

Libby had rarely in her life been nervous, and most of those times had been in the past ten months. Her life had been easy; she was rich and white and pretty enough. Her parents were charismatic and goodwill towards them encompassed her as well. She was a natural performer and nerves were just things that sent signals through your body.

But this was possibly the most important thing she'd ever done; nothing else, not the As or the Ds she'd earned in school, none of it mattered in the world.

A part of her whispered that this didn't matter either, that the church would go on as it always had, ignoring negative attention because if you had enough money, you didn't have to care. You just bought another ad campaign, opened another facility in a new town. And of course you owned the best private lawyers and half the court system.

The whispering did make her wonder – was it bad enough? She knew that because of her parents' rank she'd been sheltered. Her punishments hadn't been as severe as the other kids. She'd never been taken away from her friends to live in one of the other communes. If she'd continued on as an adult she'd eventually have taken her mother's rank with all its pay and perquisites.

Then the part of her brain which wasn't still ten years old and indoctrinated kicked that other part and said: But that's how they lure people in, with the promise of a better life for your kids. The longer you stayed in, the higher your rank, the higher your pay, and your kids would benefit when they grew up. That is the problem. And if it wasn't so bad why did so many people want to write about it?

She was going to have the meeting anyway, that was a given. She'd tell the truth and let others sort it out.

The interview wasn't as awkward as Libby had been expecting. Adelaide had done some research, and had a good set of questions that didn't leave Libby feeling like a teen with an irrational hatred of Mommy. She led Libby through aspects of her life that mattered to the article and left others alone, never being intrusive, always making sure Libby was comfortable. They spent a couple of hours talking until Libby had to leave for her other job. It was nice. She'd never really had a chance to talk to someone rational about her past; the first few times she'd mentioned it to her friends at school they'd been appalled and had asked all kinds of intrusive questions, wanting salacious details rather than letting her talk. Yeah, Libby had left, but she was conflicted, even now, about all of it.

But Adelaide merely wanted confirmation of rumour from someone who'd known the church leaders, who'd heard the decision-making processes from a young age. It was good, almost cathartic, to finally talk about it to someone who was fair and kind.

And if parts of her story made Adelaide frown and begin writing more frantically, well, Libby knew she was just telling the truth.

She got to work early, feeling good enough to hang out with the dommes in the lounge before her first set. Socializing wasn't something she'd set out to do in a really long time, Alex and Rain aside, but these women (and the two men and one enby) in this space were safe. They were curious about her, but no one asked for details. They all had things they couldn't or wouldn't talk about, and even though Libby wasn't one of them, they included her well enough. But she still kept out of their way, only speaking when spoken to, using the wifi, trying not to sound like a snob when she had to admit that she didn't own a TV and so had no opinions on the latest season of whatever they were talking about.

When she was done her first set, Adria met her at the door with a bottle of water. Libby drank about half of it down without stopping; she'd spent most of her day singing or talking in some way, and she was starting to sound raspy in a way that wasn't entirely sexy.

"How'd you like to be my sub for another class?" Adria asked, letting Libby past her to sit down.

"Ropes again?" If Libby's heart hadn't already been pounding from her performance, she was sure it would be at the suggestion. As it was, excitement fluttered in her throat. She drank again, trying not to let it show too much.

"Refresher and a slightly more advanced lesson."

She didn't even have to think about it. "Sure." Libby fought down the embarrassment that threatened. She'd own it, just like all the rest of the people who came here. "I liked it."

"I could tell. I thought you might like a chance to explore that side of you little more."

"I would, yes. Please." Her break was over and she had to get back on stage. "Text me the details?"

"Come find me after your last set. I have a client who might want an audience, if you're up for it."

That was a little more than Libby's fragile brain could handle, so she just nodded and went back out. She'd already made the decision before her first song was over, because of course she'd take a good excuse to stay past her shift in a place that had long felt like home. Maybe she'd even get paid a bit for it. It didn't occur to her to wonder what kind of scene Adria was doing, with what kind of client. It didn't matter, she'd do it anyway.

She asked, of course, because she'd listened to the others in the lounge. Not that they bad-mouthed their clients, because they didn't, but they talked about craft the way voice students did. She'd learned a lot, and not just about BDSM.

"He generally likes being hit, but sometimes he'll request humiliation." She looked expectant, like Libby should answer.

Libby remembered what Adria had told her before the class, and responded honestly. "I don't think I can watch humiliation. Personal reasons."

"Okay. I'll talk to him when he comes in and get you if he wants the usual. I'll introduce you and you can decide from there if you want to watch. Both of you have the option to tap out at any time, you understand?"

"Yes."

Libby waited in the lounge, taking the opportunity to grab a piece of the birthday cake that was still sitting around. If she was lucky it would still be there when she was ready to leave and she could take another piece, calories to get her through a cold night.

Adria came to get her as she was finishing, and as they walked she filled Libby in on a few other matters of etiquette. It was a busy night at the club, but Libby didn't look around much. Not that there was much to see—the actual scenes took place in private rooms—but when she was on stage the patrons' faces blurred together. Running into them in the hallway, occasionally in fetish gear? Not easy to ignore, especially when they were faces she knew, when they were celebrities and politicians, and once she thought she saw the mother of one of her former classmates.

The client, who Adria called Kevin, seemed nice, eager to meet her without being creepy. He wasn't much older than Libby, neatly dressed and groomed, and attractive. Libby might have dated him under other circumstances. There was a chair for Libby, set right in Kevin's eyeline from his position tied to a rack thing and goddamn if Libby was going to be more involved in this she had to learn some terminology.

Not that she wanted to be more involved. She was involved just enough for the moment.

Maybe.

She watched Kevin's face as Adria punched him in the back and wondered if that's what she'd looked like while tied up. Peaceful. Happy. Relaxed.

Winter arrived suddenly and viciously. The temperature dropped twenty degrees overnight and when Libby checked her reflection in the diner bathroom the next morning her cheeks were red and chapped. She'd spent the worst of the night huddled in a niche in the facade of a church, dozing. Terrified, she'd startled awake with every unfamiliar noise, dreading the moment someone would find her and send her away. Or worse, call the police. Worst case, she'd fall asleep and freeze to death.

Libby was a good student; as soon as she resigned herself to her fate she'd done all the research, and knew the places the hardcore homeless spent cold nights. The packed places were train and bus stations, abandoned buildings, and smaller parks, but she was afraid that as soon as she set foot in one of those enclaves she'd be identified as a poseur and robbed. So she'd made the decision to get as much sleep as she could during the day in public, doing her best to look like a student. Now, though, she wasn't sure she could manage, even without snow on the ground.

In the diner bathroom she fussed with her hair to buy time before she went back out into the cold. The sky was the flat grey that usually meant snow, and she needed to get her winter coat and boots from Rain before that happened. It was too early to call, but she'd be warm enough in the subway station while she sang. She could get in touch with Rain later.

If she couldn't get her warm clothes today she'd have to scrounge up the cash for a bed in a hostel, because no way was she risking a homeless shelter, even if that wouldn't be ethically despicable. Other people needed them more. She could get by. This was temporary.

She warmed up, both physically and musically, on the subway to her station. It was still early even for commuters, and the car wasn't so full that she'd be disturbing anyone. Even so, she had a moment of fear when an older woman, dressed like Libby's grandma used to back when she was still allowed at The Farm, approached her out of nowhere.

"Are you that girl who sings at St George?"

Libby was so startled by the question all she could do was nod.

"You have a beautiful voice, and it's nice to hear folk songs." She fumbled in her purse for a few seconds before coming up with a toonie. "Here. I'm not going to be able to hear you today, and I always drop a little something in your box."

"Oh. Thank you, you're so kind." Libby took the coin and stashed it away. "Hey, the next time you do pass by, let me know if you have any requests. I might be able to work something in."

The woman smiled brightly, and she was maybe not as old as her clothes and purse suggested. "I'll do that." And then she went back to her seat, leaving Libby in something of a daze.

After that exchange her shift could only go well. She made a point, however, of noticing the people who approached her, especially those who stood and actually listened for more than a few seconds. It turned out she recognized a lot of them, probably having noticed them subconsciously. She had way more regulars than she'd thought, and it cheered her even more Someone even dropped a five into her case, which was new. Michael showed up, too, although he didn't do more than wave as he nearly ran past.

It was starting to be a great day.

When she was done she called Rain, who was home and eager to see her. "Sara's moving out next week," she said as she ushered Libby inside. "Heather and I are getting a new roommate after Christmas. The room will be empty until then."

It was a big risk for them to take. "Heather's okay with it?" Libby hadn't really met Heather, just for a few minutes here and there. If Libby was in her position she wasn't sure she'd agree.

"I told her everything and she wants to help." Rain started digging in the closet for Libby's stuff, tossing whatever she found out behind her. "With the caveat that you disappear if anyone starts to get suspicious."

"I don't want to make trouble for you." Her coat was musty smelling after so long in the back of the closet, unwashed, but Libby hoped it would air out. She didn't have the cash to get it dry-cleaned.

"We won't let you." Rain pulled herself out of the closet, holding one boot. "But I'd never forgive myself if you froze to death one night." She handed Libby the boot and went back in.

"This isn't mine."

Rain's head reappeared. "It isn't? Whose is it?"

"I've never seen it before."

"It's too big to be Heather's, and Sara would never wear those. So I guess if I find the mate you can have them."

Libby didn't argue. They looked far warmer than the boots she had, and big enough that she could put thick wool socks in them. They were ugly, but she had a feeling that by the time January came around she wouldn't care. Rain tossed her the other boot and came out with Libby's own pair, shutting the closet behind her.

"Sara's going to be back soon. Let me take you out for lunch."

And how could Libby refuse? She had to find a way to make it all up to Rain, and Heather as well, as soon as she could. Unfortunately, her skills and general resources didn't really lend themselves to gifts. 'As soon as she could' might end up being the better part of a year.

She still had to find a place to sleep for the rest of the week, and after lunch she wandered near the school. She didn't have student ID anymore so she couldn't even get into the building, but inspiration struck anyway, because that guy leaving was a particularly clingy ex who'd love to have her stay the night, assuming he was single.

If only her mom could see her now, prostituting herself for a bed to sleep in. Not that Libby wouldn't get anything out of it; Alex was a generous partner and that night with Ray had just maybe kickstarted her libido. Yeah, Libby had no problems with the idea.

Turned out, neither did Alex. She didn't tell him the whole truth, just that she needed a place for the night ("Roommates, you know?") and maybe some time with his bathtub. He even offered to pay for the pizza. After her bath he went down on her for a couple of minutes before she gave up and just straddled him, pretending to get off as he did. The time with Ray had clearly been a fluke. Maybe she'd been better rested, or more relaxed or whatever, but she was back to feeling like a goddamn victim again. Not even a tingle. The bastards had stolen this from her, too. Luckily Alex hadn't noticed her problem, which meant she didn't have to deal with him feeling bad for not making her come. She didn't think she could handle delicate masculine emotions right now.

She slept. Checking the time on her phone the next morning, she realized she slept for a full, uninterrupted eight hours. How long had it been since she'd done that? Nearly a year, since the kidnapping? She felt good. Blissful. Like she'd turned a corner. Like she could actually accomplish something. She wished she'd figured this trick out back in March, before her grades dropped too low to recover. She repressed the helpless feeling that punched into her chest. She wasn't getting back into school anytime soon, had lost her chance at a degree. But really, all she'd wanted to do was sing, and she was doing that. It didn't matter what or on which stage.

It didn't matter that as she went longer without formal training and practice she'd lose her operatic voice. Really, it didn't. Everything she'd worked so hard for? Insignificant. She could have stayed in Picton and sung to the school kids.

Fuck.

Alex moved beside her, waking. "Hey."

She rolled over and gave him her best smile. "Hi. We should do this again sometime."

"Or we could get back together, do it all the time." The hope on his face was heartbreaking.

Libby sat up, putting her back against the wall. "That's not going to happen."

"But—,"

"Dude, we made a deal last night. You remember why we broke up?"

He closed his eyes, as if it took effort to call up the details. "The sex was the only good thing about us." He said it like it was learned by rote, something he'd had to tell himself over and over.

"Yes. So why can't we leave it there? I come over, we fuck, we sleep, I say goodbye in the morning, like a standing gym date or something. Then eventually you find someone who'll go to church with you, who won't leave her clothes all over the floor, who'll be less snarky than I am."

"Right." Was she imagining that he looked relieved? What was going on in that guy's head? "So, next week?"

"Can we make it Thursday?" She had an audition Friday; maybe a decent night's rest beforehand would make the difference between yes and no.

"I'll make a note of it."

A thought struck Libby and she laughed. "Put it on your Google calendar and share it with me."

"Right. 'Make Libby's brains fall out with pleasure.' I'll share it publicly."

"You do that. Be sure to let me know what your Dad says." She got out of bed and started collecting her clothes. "I've got to go. I have to work."

In a subway station a bit later she got a message from his calendar: Meeting with Libby re: stress relief project. She snorted and added it to hers.

Now she just had to find someone for all the other nights.

Bad Mother: How the Church of the Eternal Mother Betrays Her Children

Libby Wyatt looks cold. She walks into my office (or the local cafe, same thing) wearing barely adequate winter gear. Her cheeks are pink, the kind of pink that you know will start to hurt when the skin warms up. For someone from Ontario, this is surprising behaviour.

"Yeah, well, on The Farm there's no complaining. Mother Earth gives us cold and snow, it's our duty to live with it instead of trying to get rid of it," Libby says when asked about it. "Old habits are hard to break." She gestures at her worn coat and mittens with holes in them. "Buying new when you can reuse is a sin."

Punishable by?

"Depends on your fitness level. For healthy, able people it's generally some kind of forced labour without food or breaks. For those less able," she pauses here, uncomfortable. "Corporal punishment, sometimes. Fasting, that kind of thing."

What we know about the Church of the Eternal Mother is piecemeal, rumour and urban legend piled on top of propaganda and genuine good deeds. We know that there are two Churches, the public one you see in every city—like other religions, you go there once or twice a week and then back to your normal life–the one with celebrity spokespersons, and the one in the compounds, where you live only and exactly the Church's doctrine.

Anyone can walk into a Church in the city and learn what it's about. Only members get to go to services, but becoming a member isn't difficult. In fact, it's the easiest paying job you'll ever get. Leaving is; it comes with signed NDAs and enormous breach of contract fees.

More and more, lately, former members are coming forward to speak, anonymously until now, about what they endured at The Farm and other compounds.

But Libby Wyatt is different. Libby Wyatt is not only a former member, she's the excommunicated only child of the Church's founder, Paula Percy. And she's ready to talk.

"You have to understand that it's hard for me to...." She pauses for a bit, careful in her word choice. "To know what's normal, out here in the world. I mean, so much of what happens every day outside the Church seems so horrible in comparison. My parents loved me. The couple who raised me for them protected me against injustice. Bullies were punished. Depression was treated, not stigmatized. That's more than a lot of non-Church kids get."

She goes on with a story.

"When I was ten and still in school—"

I interrupt her here. "Still in school? How old are most kids when they leave school?" I know the answer.

"Ten. Birthdays are January first, you leave school that year for planting and don't go back. You're apprenticed to someone, then you work from dawn to dark all year round. But that's just at The Farm. The other communities have their own rules depending on their needs."

I invite her to continue.

"So, one day we were playing soccer and one of the boys tried to stop the ball with his chest. The ball was going pretty fast and it stopped his heart. The medic couldn't revive him. Every kid there got mandatory time with the therapist after, to make sure we could handle what happened."

She laughs softly to herself. "When I got back after being kidnapped I had some issues with PTSD. Still do, actually. Anyway, I saw a therapist at school. It was one of the most frustrating experiences of my life. And the free public services are impossible to access without months of waiting. Mental health care out here is a joke."

I ask her about physical health care.

"There are things I didn't know about until I was excommunicated. I always thought we had great health care. We had a big hospital, after all, and no pharmaceutical companies telling us what to do or forcing us to use their drugs. If you got a cold—which barely anyone did because we had very little interaction with outsiders—you stayed in quarantine and one of the medics would care for you. If something else was wrong you went to the hospital. I visited the hospital a few times a year because it was also the administration building and that's where my mother worked. It's a big old house, bright and friendly and all the patients I saw looked pretty good for sick people."

But?

"But there are things you can't treat without pharmaceuticals. We had chemists who made drugs out of plants, but it turns out you can't cure cancer with garlic and acupuncture. Some people went to the hospital and never came back. Mom told me my Aunt Hailey fell in love with a potter and went to live with her, and that's why she didn't come home."

I ask her about homosexuality, sexuality in general.

"You do what you like, there." She chuckles and glances to one side conspiratorially. "We had better sex education, better education about anatomy in general than most people. You're given your first sex toy on your fifteenth birthday. I didn't even know what to do with it, but there it was, ready for me to figure it out."

And between people?

"You're encouraged to experiment with people near your own age. [Here Libby goes on to tell of her own exploration, completely unashamed. The magazine chooses not to print her words because they involve children under the legal age of consent.] Adults, there's no stigma about age between adults. Or number of partners or the sex of partners, as long as everyone's aware. As long as everyone either engendered or raised at least one child no one cared what else you did."

What about unplanned pregnancies?

"We had ways around them. We had ways to fix them. But most everyone done growing was happy to have a child if they were allowed."

Allowed?

"Certain couples could have sex, but not get pregnant. Rules about inbreeding are strict."

Ah.

When I first spoke to Libby, shortly after her rescue, she cracked a joke about the food her captors served. I ask her about it now.

"Cheeseburgers. One cheeseburger and a pop every day. If I wanted water I had to save a fast food cup and fill it from the sink in the bathroom. Which, by the way, they never cleaned. It was nasty after the first week."

Cheeseburgers are pretty great.

"I guess? I mean, if I ate meat, like, at all then sure. But we're vegetarian as a rule, so I was pretty sick for a while, eating mostly meat. But I got used to it eventually. Or my body did, anyway. I still can't stand the smell of them." She makes an 'ick' face. "And I'm not going to start eating meat voluntarily, ever."

A previous interview with a former Church member touched on physical standards within the community. I ask Libby to elaborate. Her expression flattens and I realize I've hit a personal issue.

"At The Farm you have to be fit. You have to be able to work hard and you have to show that you do."

With Libby's permission, I'll describe her as unnaturally skinny. Not in a skeletal, waif-like way—most people wouldn't look twice at her—but skinny in a way that's not right for her build. She's meant to look strong.

"I was always a bit too plump, no matter how hard I worked, no matter what I ate. I was told I looked lazy, unhealthy, like an outsider. I got punished a lot for it. When I was sixteen one of the elders called for a tribunal. They thought I was sneaking out of The Farm for what they called garbage food."

Pizza, ice cream, cheeseburgers?

"Exactly. I was sneaking out, but not for food."

What for?

"Music."

Until recently Libby was pursuing a degree in opera at The Pickford Performing Arts Academy, with a strong interest in composing.

"I liked to sit in a particular tree and look over the wall. One day I noticed a horse in the field next door. I'd never seen a horse that wasn't a draft, I'd only seen pictures, so I went out...." She stops and looks at me. "I'm not saying how. If I do they'll find a way to block it. I know they're paying attention to what I do out here, even if they're busy pretending I never existed. Anyway, I went over to look at the horse. It was a nice day and I sang as I walked. A girl, younger than me, called out to me. She said I had a nice voice. We became friends and I'd go over to listen to her parents CDs. Before that the only music I knew was what you'd call folk, with a bit of classical. Pre-twentieth century only. Rock, jazz, modern instrumental seemed miraculous to me."

I ask her how hard it was, after she left the Church, to assimilate to outside society.

"So hard. Just figuring out the medical stuff, like how often should I go to the dentist? That was hard. I'd never taken public transit. I'd never used money. And I didn't have a lot of cultural referents so most conversations went right over my head. I learned to smile and nod and hope no one noticed I was clueless. My roommate, Rain, helped a lot. She showed me a lot of the TV and movies I'd missed, the important ones. I got to watch my mom's TV show for the first time, too. She was a cute kid."

Paula Percy was the child star of Two-Ring Circus, which ran on NBC for most of the '70s. She became an environmental activist, founded The Church of the Eternal Mother, and eventually married Harrison Wyatt, then CEO of EarthSafe Technologies. Libby was born shortly after. We talk about her parents a bit.

"They were busy. Dad had his company in New York and eventually his Ambassadorship. Mom didn't stop travelling, advocating for the Earth, educating people. I was raised first by my mom's sister, then after she went away, after she died, the elders. I saw my parents a couple of times a year, but I never doubted they loved me. The Church is all about love and they were the greatest example."

She continues. "And that's the thing I miss about it. My folks, yes, absolutely, but it was more than just me and them. We had an enormous family made up of all different kinds of people. There was always something to do, someone to talk to. If you needed help, there was always someone who knew what you needed. There was always someone who cared, even if you had to ask a dozen people first. You had to force yourself to be alone, and even up in that tree I never felt lonely."

Love. It keeps coming up in Libby's interview. Love the Earth, love each other, love your children. But don't stop hitting them when they misbehave. Don't hesitate to starve them if they weigh even a pound over your ideal. Don't teach them science so they can make their own decisions about doctors and vaccines and genetically modified food. Love them, until they decide they want to pursue an education outside your rigidly-defined community.

"I saw my dad once, on Yonge Street," Libby says. "I crossed the street to stand in front of him as he walked toward me. He ignored me. Not like he saw me and chose not to admit it. He just didn't see me. I wasn't even dead to him. I had just never existed at all."

Harrison Wyatt collapsed in his office, comatose, while Libby was missing. He died in hospital twenty days later. A short week after that, a local man found Libby in the abandoned farmhouse on his family property near Rice Lake.

I ask her if she wants to talk about her father's death. She shrugs. "There's not much to say about it. I wasn't there. Even if I hadn't been kidnapped he still wouldn't have wanted me there."

Do you have anything to say to your mother?

"The fact that I'm doing this interview at all says everything I need to."

Eight

Saturday had Michael sitting at home, obsessing about how long it had been since he'd actually been on a date, so he figured he'd get out and do something. He caught a subway to Yonge Street, thinking maybe he could find some dessert to take tonight, since alcohol was out – Ray was still working nights.

In the PATH tunnel outside Dundas Station he got sidetracked, because Libby was singing.

She hadn't noticed him yet, so he indulged himself in listening to her voice, which had picked up a smoky tinge since the last time he'd heard her. Or maybe it was the song: slow, soulful, mournful. She sounded like she really believed what she was singing. He started noticing how tired she looked. The drooping eyelids might be an affectation for the song, but she hadn't even tried to hide the dark circles under them. She looked thin and brittle, so different from how he saw her in his memory. But she was an adult and it was none of his business.

That didn't mean he couldn't give her a little attention.

There was a bakery nearby that had excellent cookies, so he dashed out and came back with six: four snickerdoodles for after dinner, and two of an oatmeal caramel concoction for Libby. The place had been busy, and he hoped she hadn't packed up by the time he got back. She hadn't, although she wasn't singing anymore. She sat on the floor against a wall, sipping from a reusable water bottle and counting her donation box.

"Hey," he said, kneeling down beside her.

She almost bowled him over completely. He tried not to drop the cookies as she flung herself into his arms again. "I have had the shittiest day, you have no idea. It's awesome to see you," she said, somewhere in the vicinity of his neck.

"Okay." He stroked her back a little. She even felt thinner, and when had he even bothered to notice her under his hands?

She pulled away, shaking her head at her own reaction. "Sorry. I'm all over the place these days. Stress is a killer."

"I brought you something." He took out the cookies in their little paper bag and handed them to her. The rich, sweet aroma wafted up, almost overpowering the winter smells of wet wool and fake pumpkin pie spice.

She grinned and put it to her nose, taking a deep sniff. "Caramel. How did you know?"

"You mentioned it when we went to breakfast that first day. You wanted the caramel bagel, but thought it might be too rich. You got the plain one instead."

She blinked at him. "How do you remember that?"

"Partly training. Partly because you're the most interesting thing I've ever found in my house. It's hard to forget." He shrugged. "You're hard to forget."

Her smile turned sweet and she unwrapped a cookie and took a bite. "Oh my god," she said through a mouthful. "It's still warm."

"Good."

"Fucking fantastic." She finished the treat in three more bites, ate the second just as quickly, then crumpled the paper and tossed into a nearby trashcan. "Hey, you've got to see this." She reached into her donation box and pulled out something that sparkled.

He took it, and realized it was a cut glass music note on a plastic thread. "A Christmas ornament?"

"I guess so? I don't have a lot of experience with Christmas." She held it up and it spun slowly, catching the light. "But I can't believe someone just gave it to me!"

"Maybe they gave one to every panhandler."

She slapped his coat sleeve. "Don't. Don't hurt me like that."

"You have fans. Doesn't surprise me at all."

The warm smile she gave him was repayment enough for the cookies. "Anyway, I'm done here. You busy?"

"Not until later."

"Want to take a walk?"

"Absolutely."

Most of the time Libby thought she was doomed to a life of hyperactive emotions and physical hardship. But every once in a while something awesome would happen that made her think everything would be okay. A gift from a fan, surprise cookies, a walk downtown with a friend, just like a normal person.

It was hard to believe this was the same street she'd come through this morning. It was snowing now, perfectly white, marred only by occasional tracks. Libby sighed. She missed playing in the snow, of being able to roll around and have a snowball fight and then go inside where it was warm and change clothes, maybe have some hot peppermint tea.

She shivered at the thought of being wet in the cold; her whole snow experience was changed, now.

"You cold?"

"A little."

"Come here." He held his arm out at shoulder level, and how could she not snuggle into the curve of his body? Libby was well-aware of how touch-starved she was, which was weird because she'd never thought she touched people much before, and she took comfort in winding her arm around his waist in turn.

It was harder to walk that way, especially once she decided to rest her cheek against his shoulder. He smelled amazing, she'd noticed it earlier—spicy and warm, a trace of citrus cologne on his scarf—and she wanted desperately to bury her nose into his neck again.

"Better?"

"Mmm."

She felt more than heard him chuckle. "I have a date tonight and here I am canoodling with a woman."

"Canoodling."

"It's a good word."

"It's a great word, one of my favourites at the moment." She turned to the more interesting topic. "A date, huh? Is he cute? Or is it she?"

"He. And he's more ruggedly handsome than cute. At least, from my point of view, not being a twenty-something woman."

"What's his name?"

"Dragos." It sounded like he swallowed his tongue at the end.

"Slavic?"

"I assume so. I didn't ask."

Libby was far too curious for her own good, her guardians had always told her. This was just too good to pass by though. "When did you meet him?"

"A week ago."

"Seriously?" She lifted her head so quickly her hat slid off and she had to resettle it before her ears froze.

"Ridiculous, I know." He flicked the pompom on her hat. "I only made the decision to start dating again while I was away, and then there he was, asking me out."

She snorted. "Seize the moment."

"I usually do."

"Usually at this point in the conversation I'd make sure my friend was going somewhere safe-ish and had an exit plan. You want my phone number for if you need to escape?"

"I'm going to his place, and while he probably outweighs me by fifty pounds of muscle, I'm a sneaky fighter." He paused as if weighing his thoughts. "Besides, I already have your number."

"A cop on speed dial. My life just keeps spinning farther and farther from where my parents wanted it to be."

"Former cop. And is that bad?"

"Fuck, no. It's perfect."

He laughed for real, then, and she hid a smile in his arm. She hadn't been this comfortable with a guy since, well, ever. Since she started dating. The realization that she would actually let him tie her up in private stopped her forward momentum. She stumbled when he kept walking, pulling her off balance.

"You okay?"

"Yeah. Just noticed something."

He nodded and didn't ask further, but she kind of wanted to talk about it. "Are you always this cuddly with near-strangers?"

He seemed to have think about it, if the frown he gave the street ahead of them was any indication. "No, I don't think so. There are some people I instantly connect with, like Claudine and David, but this isn't usual even with them."

Faint nausea rose in her throat. "So what is this, some kind of overprotective bullshit?"

Michael stopped and turned to her, putting his hands on her shoulders. "I can't say there isn't some protectiveness in there. It's not unusual for people in our situation to bond in lesser ways."

"That's a lot of qualifying negatives in there."

He shrugged and dropped his hands to his pockets. "Our situation is unique. But I do genuinely like you, what I've gotten to know."

Better, but Libby still had some reservations. "So why did you talk to me that morning?"

"I was lonely. You were a familiar face."

She very nearly laughed at the contradiction between the embarrassment in his voice and how his face betrayed none of it. "Okay. I'll buy that. Listen, I should go. I've got to get some sleep before work tonight," she said. If Rain or Heather were home she'd be able to sleep on the couch, just as long as she could convince them to stay in the room. If not, well, she'd read somewhere that just pretending to sleep could be pretty restful. Might as well give that a shot.

Michael carefully looped his fingers around her wrist, over the new bones she had showing. She hadn't realized he'd noticed. "You were my biggest success. Take care of yourself."

She had to turn away before he saw the tears collecting in her eyes. "I try."

"I brought cookies," was Michael's opening line when Ray greeted him at the door. It worked just as well the second time, because Ray invited him in right away, reaching for the sack Michael was holding out.

"Hey thanks, I didn't have anything planned for dessert." He backed away to the side, holding the door. "Come on in."

The first thing that hit Michael was the scent in the air, thyme and mushrooms. and something roasted in olive oil. "Smells amazing," he said, taking off his boots.

Ray came back from the kitchen and helped him with his coat. "Thanks. I realized I didn't know what you eat, so I went with a classic." He cocked his head to one side. "Well, one of my classics. But always a crowd pleaser, even among the carnivores."

Michael followed him into the living room. "You're vegetarian?"

"Is that going to be a problem?" Ray looked back at him with a slight frown.

"Not at all." Michael might have issues cooking for him, but he could adapt. "I'm pretty omnivorous, though."

Ray nodded and went into the kitchen to dig through the fridge. "Does that include beer? I'm not on shift until eleven, which means I can have one as long as it's now."

Michael accepted the cold bottle with thanks and an offer to help with the cooking, but Ray brushed him off. "It's mostly done. Just the mushroom gravy to put together."

Leaning on the counter to one side of him, Michael watched Ray work, his short, thick fingers holding delicate glass bowls of liquid, steady enough not to spill, the way his tongue peeked out as he tasted the mixture. The way the muscles in his bare arms flexed as he stirred.

Ray's eyes flicked towards him once, twice, then finally, with a small smile, he leaned over and brushed his lips across Michael's, his tongue flicking out for a taste. He pulled back a bit. "You think I can't see you watching?"

Michael grinned at him. "I was hoping you would." He slid his hand up Ray's arm and tugged him closer. "Turn off the burner," he said, pleased when Ray immediately complied.

Michael had always liked being with men who could overpower him, so when Ray crowded him into the counter he didn't resist. Ray was a little shorter than he was, so Michael had to lean down to kiss him. He didn't hold back, delving in as soon as he could, relishing the feel once again of a mouth under his, warm weight pressing into him. Michael's hand fit perfectly into the small of Ray's back, then slid under his t-shirt to caress soft skin. Ray's mouth left his and Michael bared his neck to him as Ray nibbled down his jaw to the shivery spot under his ear.

He parted his thighs, letting Ray in closer, and Ray murmured a soft word as he pressed their cocks together.

"Yeah," Michael said as he got a good feel of what Ray was packing in his tight jeans.

Ray snickered in his ear, the gust of breath making him shudder. "Dinner's getting cold."

Two could play that game. Michael shimmied out from his position between Ray and the counter, walked over to a cabinet and asked, "Where are the plates?"

Ray's glare was poisonous, but he pointed out the dish cupboard and started pulling food out of the oven.

The meal turned out to be a dish which Ray vacillated between calling meatloaf and veggie loaf, both of which were wrong. "And 'tofu loaf' is just awkward," he added with a grin.

"I don't care what you call it, it's delicious." Michael wasn't even lying; it was fantastic, as were the roasted potatoes and vinegary green beans.

The lingering arousal from earlier wasn't helped by Ray's calf against his under the table, but he could ignore it in order to eat. They wouldn't have time tonight for anything complicated, and Michael liked letting sexual tension build. Jeanine had called him a tease more than once, but he liked a slow burn, it added an extra dimension to sex, a ferocity he enjoyed.

So they talked, mostly, about everything they could think of, and when they retired to the couch with coffee they kept talking. It was easy, comfortable. And, when it came time to leave, his reluctance to go made perfect sense.

Nine

Michael and Ray had three more dates in quick succession ("It was the cookies," Ray would tell people later, "They were just that good.") before Christmas, with a mutual decision to not attend each other's office parties.

"I'm out at work, that's not a problem," Ray said when he brought it up. "I just think it's too soon for me to be seen dating a cop."

"Ex-cop."

"That might be worse, actually."

"Well, I'm not out at work, and I'm not sure bringing a man to the holiday party is the way to manage it smoothly."

"I can attest to that. Unless you want to be put under a microscope the whole evening."

"You didn't."

Ray shook his head in dismay at his younger self. "I wanted to make a scene. I just hadn't thought the scene would involve questions about who was on top."

Michael wanted to ask, but didn't.

Ray waited, an invitational eyebrow raised, but then continued talking. "I figured I'd take my sister to the party anyway; she wants to meet one the guys. Apparently he helped a friend of hers last year and she'd like to thank him. She's coming down for two weeks."

"Do I get to see you at all, if your family's in town?"

"I think I can manage an evening away from them. Maybe even two."

Michael didn't have much time off at Christmas, being the new guy, but it wasn't like he had family duties he was ignoring in favour of work. Christmas morning he spent watching old movies with Jeeves on his lap and a mug of hot chocolate in his hand, admiring the coloured lights he'd put up around the living room. He hadn't bothered with a tree, but he'd still managed a faintly festive air.

At noon precisely he got a text message from Libby.

Merry Christmas. Did I do that right? :P

Delighted, he typed out a reply: *Happy Ordinary Day in December.*

Dork.

You have no idea. What are you up to today?

A moment passed before her reply came: *Movie marathon. Been a while since I had the time.*

Same here. The movies, not the time. He'd had a lot of time, recently, but every time he pulled up Netflix he got mired in option block.

Today's theme: BEM.

He frowned at his phone. *Bem?*

Bug eyed monsters.

Have fun.

I regret nothing!

Inspired, he called Ray, who was in the middle of cooking dinner. "You should come over tomorrow," he said during a lull.

"I should?" There was an amused lilt in Ray's voice.

"You should."

"And if I don't?"

"Then you might miss something."

"And what would that something be?" Michael heard a woman's voice in the background. "Yes," Ray said to the other person. "I am talking to a boy. Now fuck off."

"Time away from your sister, apparently."

"And?"

"I have a very comfortable couch."

"Oh really?"

"You should try it out."

The pause on the other end is almost enough to make Michael backtrack, but he can hear the smile in Ray's voice when he speaks. "Yeah, okay. I can do that."

Michael spent the rest of the afternoon cleaning the bathroom and washing his better set of sheets before heading out to Claudine's for Christmas dinner. In the end, it didn't matter, because he got called in to work around midnight and had to cancel. New information plus an imminent appeal meant all hands on deck for his office, for as long as it took to verify. If they could keep the man from going back to prison after his appeal Michael would consider his job well done, even though this wasn't his client.

Around seven his eyes finally blurred too much to read, so he took a quick nap in an office set aside for that purpose. When he woke up he almost went right back to sleep because he was clearly hallucinating the voice he heard at reception. Ray's voice. He'd convinced himself it was a coincidence up until he walked out there and saw that it actually was Ray, with a tray of coffee and a bakery box.

Ray caught sight of him and wandered over, after handing off all but one of the coffees to the person he'd been talking to. "I brought breakfast," he said, opening the box and showing off a selection of egg and bagel sandwiches. "Got 'em downstairs. They're still mostly hot."

"Bless you," Michael said as he reached for one.

"Take two. You probably didn't have dinner."

Michael had shared some of the curry David had ordered in, but he'd gladly eat as many of the amazing smelling sandwiches as he could. He took a second, and then called out to let the others know they were available.

"How did you even get in here?" he asked as he led Ray to his desk. His screen had long gone dark and he left it that way. Ray didn't need to see the photos.

"Flashed my credentials. That usually works."

"Worked for me."

"And here I thought you wanted me for my wit."

"Nope. It's the arms." He unwrapped the sandwich and wondered how something so ordinary could smell so heavenly before eating the thing in three bites. The second went down almost as quickly. "Have I said thank you yet? Because thank you."

Ray chuckled gently. "I think you need more sleep."

"Probably. I'm going to make a call and then I can head home."

"I'll see you another day, then."

Michael had a moment of indecision – should he kiss Ray goodbye? Would he have kissed Jeanine? Probably not. The moment passed when he could have, and Ray was turning away. He was overthinking this coming out thing. It would have to wait.

If you forced Michael to admit that he still had a Google alert set up for Libby's name, relic of their initial meeting, he'd say it was because he's lazy, because he never thinks about cleaning up his tech. Which is partially true, but not in the important ways. The idea of erasing Libby's name had felt like erasing her, like making her short presence in his life never have happened. She was his success, the kind he rarely got, and if you erased your successes what were you left with?

If he'd thought about it, he was also hoping to see her successes, to know that the woman he'd helped when it mattered most was making the most of her life. He really hadn't expected a couple of dozen links in one day, each referencing an article titled *Bad Mother: How the Church of the Eternal Mother Betrays Her Children.*

Curious, he clicked through to the article. Libby hadn't said much about her parents beyond telling him about her father's death. He was positive she hadn't mentioned their religious preferences, but here Libby was talking about one of the most loathed institutions from the position of a high-ranking insider.

Libby Wyatt looks cold. She walks into my office (or my local café, same thing) wearing barely adequate winter gear. Her cheeks are pink, the kind of pink that you know will start to hurt when the skin warms up. For someone from Ontario, this is surprising behaviour.

"Yeah, well, on The Farm there's no complaining. Mother Earth gives us cold and snow, it's our duty to live with it instead of trying to get rid of it," Libby says when asked about it. "Old habits are hard to break." She gestures at her worn coat and mittens with holes in them. "Buying new when you can reuse is a sin."

Punishable by?

Michael stopped reading. He felt sleazy, learning about Libby this way. There are things you should learn about your friends in person, in a quiet room over a cup of tea or a glass of something alcoholic, not from a secondhand source on a glowing screen. He closed his browser window, unwilling to even glance at the rest, then he deleted the alert.

Why did it feel so wrong? What was he doing, caring so much for this young woman? He shouldn't be in contact at all, wouldn't be except for the serendipity of his new job, of the near-impossibility of their meeting again as they did. Twice, in totally different parts of the city, different even from the ones they lived and worked in. Or went to school in, in her case. If he'd been a man who believed in fate, in kismet, he'd be taking it as a sign. But coincidences happened, and even a big city could be terribly small sometimes.

He was drawn to her, though. She'd come out of a terrible situation with her sense of humour intact and a determined smile on her face. He admired that resolution to not let your tragedies rule your life; it was a lesson he'd worked hard to learn after Jeanine's death. And now, having got to know her a bit, he saw she was warm and caring beyond the sarcasm and jokes. She was adventurous, too. Claudine had said that ropes class was her first time with any kind of submission, but she'd dived in without fear. He liked that a lot, not just because he was curious if she'd submit to him. He saw potential in her as a friend, someone who'd jump off a cliff with you if you asked, then mock you later for your form. He thought she and Ray might get along well too. The chances they'd gang up on him were high, but he was willing to take the risk.

Ten

Libby thought the week of staying at Rain's would be great, just what she needed to start feeling like her usual self. A couple of nights of sleep in a warm, dry, comfortable bed, time and space to take care of some personal hygiene, meals that involved a variety of foods. Just what she needed. And for the most part yes. But she'd forgotten one major issue – she still couldn't sleep alone. Cat naps on the subway and in the lounge at work were still the most rest she ever got.

She'd once heard some kids talk about sleeping on the subway, how if you rode the Yonge-University line from one end to the other no one would get suspicious until you'd had a good two hours. If you switched cars you might get another couple in. That sounded like a really fucking good idea right about now, when she was back out on the street with nowhere to go, but the TTC shut down at two AM so she'd still have to find a place to spend the coldest part of the night.

With no real plan other than to keep moving and stay warm and conscious, she continued walking north. This block was mostly offices and store front businesses that closed up at six pm, so the only light came from the street lamps and the occasional car. She should have gone one block over, then at least there'd be apartments, she'd see lights, candles, flickering blue TVs. Signs of life. Signs that she wasn't alone in an enormous city. Because right now, if she blocked out the noise, she could almost believe that she was the only person left in the world. It wasn't a comfortable feeling.

She tried to stay on east-west streets as much as possible; the wind coming south down the concrete canyons was brutal. Her face was numb, her hands shoved into her pockets were only slightly less so. She tried not to think about her feet. As long as they still worked, she couldn't care. There'd been a thaw over the last day, and every intersection was a lake of slowly refreezing slush. Just a few hours ago she'd been with Rain, warm and comfortable on the couch, watching a movie and drinking homemade spiced chai. Now her teeth chattered so hard she thought the enamel might chip.

A noise crackled behind her, caught her attention, distracted her from the mouth of the alley to her side, and at first she thought she slipped as she turned, because the world tilted sideways, but that was a person behind her, grabbing her, twisting. She yelped in surprise, but that was the only sound she managed to get out of her suddenly closed throat. Her hands were still in her pockets; she struggled to get them out and get her feet under her, get into a position where she could fight back. She slid around, trying to dodge, and this time she really did slip, whacking her head on the brick.

Pain disoriented her for a moment, letting her attacker, attackers now, get their hands on her. She kicked wildly and heard a grunt, but didn't even have time for satisfaction before she a cloth covered her face. Lavender. The bag smelled like lavender. Hysterical giggles didn't make it out of her mouth, they rose up to force themselves out as tears.

In the distance a woman shouted, and Libby could only hope she was in a better situation.

"Get her feet," one of the men said, and a set of hands gripped her ankles over her boots. "Toss her in the car and let's go."

Running footsteps, coming closer.

She kicked out again without hitting anything. "Stop it, Elizabeth," the one at her head shouted. "Shit, they said this would be easy."

"Hey! Get away from her." The woman's voice was nearer now, her shout angry, not scared.

The arms supporting Libby dropped away and she crumpled to the ground. She heard running, more than one person, then the same crackling noise, and finally the faint whine of an electric engine.

The bag slid off her head, taking her hat with it.

"You okay, honey?"

Her rescuer wasn't nearly as bundled up as she should be, Libby thought. "Where'd you come from?"

The woman helped Libby stand before answering. "I was in my office and saw you through the window." She pointed at an open door across the street. "Let's go inside and call the police. My name's Rivkah. You're Elizabeth?"

Libby nodded, then corrected her. "Libby."

In the office Libby held her off; there was no point in calling 911 now, not when she was safe. Instead she thumbed through her contacts, looking for Detective Strickland. The phone started to ring but Libby's pulse rushed so loudly in her ears that she could barely hear it. Her hands grew numb and somewhere in the distance she heard a voice, but before she could respond the world went black.

She woke in a hospital. "Shit," she said, letting her head fall back to the pillow. She wasn't hooked up to an IV, so bonus, but her muscles were pretty weak still and her head was thumping a tympani solo.

"Oh good, you're awake."

Startled, Libby sat up, only realizing halfway that it was such an incredibly bad idea. She kept going, though, hoping that upright might feel better.

"Fuck." She touched the side of her head that hurt worst. At least it wasn't bandaged.

"Sorry." Detective Strickland stood at Libby's right, phone in her hand. "You're not severely injured. A few scrapes, a bump on your head. Panic attack."

"Yeah, I know what those feel like by now." She realized she was wearing her street clothes, not a gown. "How long have I been here?"

"About twenty minutes. The paramedics gave you a mild sedative, that's why you were asleep."

She remembered bits now, of people getting her off the floor, the ride in the ambulance, freaking out when the EMT touched her wrist. "Okay. Can I go?"

"I think the doctor wants to talk to you, but after that they'll let you come to the station with me."

"Sure. Whatever you need me to do."

The doctor gave her a quick assessment and let her go. Detective Strickland put her in a car and drove her to the station, letting Libby tell her the bare bones story. Libby had a weird moment when she realized she'd never been to this station before, the place where her first kidnapping had been investigated.

They took over a small conference room for privacy. Libby sat down and thought about what she would say as the detective went out for a moment and came back with a bottle of water.

"This seems familiar," Libby quipped, taking the bottle and cracking it open.

Faith took a seat on the other side of the table and leaned her elbows on the brown fake wood surface. "Too familiar."

After a long drink, Libby decided to just say it. "I know this seems really crazy and paranoid, but it was the same guys."

She'd expected some surprise from Faith, perhaps a denial, but she Faith simply glanced down at her notes. "Rivkah Stanley said they called you by name."

Right. Libby'd forgotten that. "Yes. Also, the bag they put over my head smelled like lavender."

Faith stared at her for a second. "Lavender?"

"The first time, last year, it smelled like that too."

"You didn't mention that at the time."

She took another sip of water. "I didn't remember until it happened again." The pad of her thumb fit perfectly into a divot on the edge of the table. "I don't remember much at all of that first time. But I'm certain they were the same people."

It was Detective Strickland who called Michael. "I know you're not in the PD anymore, but I'd like your input on the new information we have, and Libby's fine with it."

He agreed and headed over to her precinct. As he walked from the subway station he realized he was passing near where the first kidnapping took place, so he quickly detoured to see it. Like most other crime scenes, there was nothing marking the location as special, no physical sign that someone's life was irreparably altered. The city moved on. The architecture forgot.

He continued to the station. Strickland met him at the front desk and led him back through the bullpen to her desk. It was tidier than his had ever been. He hoped that meant she was on top of her work and not that she'd given up and was tossing everything in a drawer to forget.

"What I can't figure out," he told Strickland after she briefed him, "is why they waited so long to try again. They must be working a long timeline."

"She has been difficult to track down."

"As a student she keeps a regular schedule. She even lives in the same place."

Strickland frowned. "She didn't tell you? She lost her scholarship and her housing. She's been sleeping rough since last spring. I came across her during the summer and she told me everything. Been keeping an eye on her ever since. She moves around a lot."

His thoughts were running in all directions, none tracking the conversation. She'd lied to him. Or had she? Had he made assumptions, had she just not corrected him? The part of him that had been a cop for twelve years said lies of omission were still lies, but the part that remembered being twenty-six understood about pride and losing face with someone you respected. The part of him who'd lost his wife understood not wanting pity. "But she's working."

"Two jobs as far as I know. She's doing her best, even if she'd be better off in almost any other city."

Michael understood that, having gone through it when his wife died. "This is where her friends are."

Strickland gave him a pointed look. "And she doesn't want or need you rescuing her again."

He let himself sigh and lean against the desk. "You think she's happy on the streets?"

"I think she's content." She rummaged through her files and came out with Libby's. "I think she's got a plan to rescue herself."

He followed her as she led him through the halls. "You know as well as I do that it rarely works out that way."

"Maybe this time it will."

"You're awfully optimistic for a cop."

She paused with her hand on the knob of a conference room. "Optimism is why I became a cop. You?"

"Desperation, mostly. Maybe a little bit of optimism."

She led him into the room to Libby, who looked like actual hell. He chose the seat beside her and when she dropped her hand to his he squeezed it as hard as he could without hurting her.

When Strickland was done with them it was nearly morning. Michael bought himself and Libby a couple of slices of pizza which they ate while she walked him back to his train station.

Michael couldn't stop thinking about what Strickland had told him and tried to figure out how to phrase his question without pissing Libby off. It was clear she didn't want him to know about her living conditions, but it was also clear that she was in danger, if not from the kidnappers then from the cold or random violence. It didn't help that he was still recovering from finding out that she lied to him, that she didn't trust him enough to tell him what was going on. "Why didn't you tell me?" he burst out, finally.

She spun around to face him, walking backward a few steps. "Tell you what?" She sounded genuinely confused, her eyes still a little glazed.

"That you aren't in school anymore? That you're unhoused?"

By her glare he could tell he hadn't managed to control his prejudices. "Because it's none of your business?"

Fair enough. He trotted a few steps to catch up. "I thought we were becoming friends."

The glare faded, and she turned her eyes down. "We are. I hope." She glanced at him again, something like sorrow caressing her mouth. "But I don't want help. I don't want pity. I got into this on my own, I can get out. I've almost got enough money."

"Enough for what?"

She didn't answer.

"Detective Strickland told me you lost your scholarship."

She shrugged. "Turns out when you miss a month of school, can't sleep, and have near daily panic attacks your grades go down. Who knew?"

"They couldn't give you any kind of consideration?"

She chuckled low in her throat, a desperate, fake laugh. "Nope. Too many other people needed the money. People with, you know, jobs and caring parents."

"That's unfair."

She stopped walking and raised a disbelieving eyebrow at him. "That's what's unfair?"

"Did you tell them exactly what happened to you?"

"I did. So did Detective Nash. And Detective Strickland. And all the news media." She snorted. "I'm not an idiot, you know." She started walking again and he was forced to play catch up.

"I know. But even after over a decade on the police force I still can't get over how thoughtless people can be."

"Voice lessons." His confusion must have shown because she explained. "I have almost enough money for voice lessons. I fucked up an audition; I fucked up five auditions. I don't have the skills anymore because I have no way of really practising. I have to get them back so I can start auditioning again."

"You're still focused on opera?"

"It's what I love."

"But you have to admit you're pretty good with the folk tunes."

She didn't look at him, choosing to focus on the slush puddle to her right. "It's not the same."

He had nothing to say to that. They continued walking for another block without speaking. Then he surprised even himself with what he said next. "Move in with me." Now that he'd said it, he liked the idea. She disappeared from his side and he turned back to see she'd stopped dead.

"What?" Her voice was barely audible, whether from surprise or the truck going by he didn't know, but he took the few steps back to her.

"I have an extra room. I work long evenings sometimes. The cat will appreciate the company." He tried to think of it from her point of view. "And so will I."

She was thinking about it, he could tell. He could only imagine the way she'd been living the past few months, especially since the snow started, but she had to be considering it after the day's stress.

Then her jaw tensed, she stuffed her hands in her pockets, and he knew then what her answer would be.

"No." She glanced at him sideways, waiting for his reaction.

What could he do? He was in no position to force her, and it seemed Strickland was right. "Okay," he said, after too long a pause for comfort. "But the offer stands. You know where I live, come over any time."

They walked a few more blocks in silence, until finally she lifted her head to him. "Thanks." It was barely audible, and he acknowledged it with a nod. Now was not the time for anything more.

Eleven

This audition began with a lecture. "We're creating an avant-garde production of *Figaro*," the man on the stage said. He hadn't introduced himself, and Libby wondered if she was supposed to recognize him. The ad hadn't given names, not even of the company, so her ability to research before going in was limited. She peered at him from her position halfway back in the theatre, hoping to be able to pin an identity on him, but nope.

Someone to her left was fidgeting, giving her hope that she wasn't the only inexperienced candidate there. It was hard to tell ages in the half-dark of the audience, and age didn't always translate to experience anyway.

She'd tuned out some of what the guy was saying; not like it mattered to her what kind of interpretation they went for. She didn't have room to pick and choose her roles, and although avant-garde anything wasn't her favourite, she need a foot in the door, a line on her resume, even if the line just read '

chorus'.

"...so keep your seats and have your music ready." He walked off the stage like he had someplace better to be, and that place wasn't in the audience.

The first name was called and as the singer took the stage Libby sighed.

"It can't be that bad." The guy next to her leaned towards her slightly, his arm warming hers on the rest between them. He was about her age, nice looking, dressed well in suit pants and a waistcoat.

Libby shook her head. "Look at her. She's got so much presence that she nearly fills the stage all by herself." Libby could hardly look away from her, and when she started to sing the effect was even more prominent.

"She's always been magnetic, even when we were kids."

"You know her?" She looked from her back to him, noticing the identical skin tone and eye shape, the similar jaw lines and cheekbones. "Siblings?"

He grinned. "Yup."

Holy shit. "And you audition for the same shows? What if you got cast as lovers?"

"Never happen. She's an alto and I'm a bass."

"Thank fuck for stereotyping, I guess." She listened to her for a moment more. "Hey, *Figaro* doesn't have an alto part."

"Maybe that's the avant-garde deal?" He shrugged. "The ad asked for all voices."

"Weird."

He introduced himself as Benny, and the two of them traded comments on the other singers until it was Libby's turn.

She'd decided on something less common this time, and was glad she did given the number of repeats they'd had to listen to. This time she was singing a soubrette piece, hoping the restricted range and simplicity of the role would suit her current voice. She thought she did well, better than her previous auditions, certainly, and when she sat back down Benny gave her a thumbs up. She didn't have to stay, but she'd already missed the best hours of busking just travelling out here, and even if she left now by the time she got back it wouldn't be worth the effort to set up and sing.

She woke when Benny jostled her arm. "Oh," she said, noting the activity on the stage. She'd obviously been asleep for a while, because the man from earlier was climbing the stairs again. "I didn't snore, did I?" she asked Benny, horrified.

"Not so anyone but me could hear you."

Wiping the sleep grit from her eyes, she tried to concentrate on what the man in front was saying, but the room was warm and she'd slept deeply enough that she was still in a state of lassitude. "Did he just...?"

"What the fuck?" Benny replied, and when she glanced at him his face was clouded. "This was all a trick?"

The man continued to speak over the rising noise of the crowd. "So we periodically hold mock auditions to scope out the new talent. We've got your names and contact information, as well as your results. Some of you may be hearing from us in the future."

"I gave up a shift for this," Libby said, feeling a bubble of anger well in her chest. The bubble was threatening to turn to tears, so she grabbed her things to leave.

"I need to get so drunk," Benny said, gathering his own coat and bag. "I don't even care what time it is, this bullshit requires medicating."

"Amen," said a woman in the row above them.

Benny grinned at her. "You're welcome to join me, Mel."

Libby looked closer at the woman, but seeing as she was white she probably wasn't another sister. "You guys know each other?"

"We grew up in the same neighbourhood," Mel replied, shoving her hat down over her ears.

The crowd was clearing out and Benny's sister, Dinah, joined them. "We going out?"

"Fuck yes," Benny said. "You coming, Libby?"

She could use some company, and she had a few dollars to spare for a cup of coffee, if not booze. "Sure, sounds good."

"I don't have any money," Mel said as they filed out of the hall. "How about we go to my place and drink up what's left from the party?"

"To be honest," Libby said, shouldering the door open, "that sounds even better than going out."

They picked up food on the way, draining the last of Libby's cash for the week. There'd be a cheque waiting for her at the club the next day, but she was out of luck until she could deposit it.

Mel's place was tiny, and shared with three others, but nice enough. The four of them filled the little living room-slash-Mel's bedroom, sprawled in beanbag chairs that lived in a stack in the corner when not in use. Libby ended up with a tall glass of cheap gin and cheaper grapefruit juice that made a nice palate cleanser for the cheap Italian they were eating. She hadn't had anything so delicious in ages.

Her tolerance was shot, though; she hadn't had alcohol in nearly a year. It didn't take much for her to begin the high-pitched giggling Rain had teased her so much about. She slumped farther into her beanbag and wiggled the toe poking out of her sock as Dinah told them a complicated story about one of her restaurant customers.

She was starting to doze off when Benny got her attention. "Where do you work, Libby?"

"Huh? Oh." She was still a little loopy, so she didn't even consider prevaricating. "I busk during the week and sing at a private club on weekends."

The response wasn't what she'd expected. "Wow," Mel said, real admiration in her voice. "You're the only one of us making money actually singing."

Libby contemplated her toe. The nail was a bit long; personal grooming wasn't a priority right now. "I hadn't thought of it that way, but yeah, I guess. I mean, It's not opera, but at least I'm singing, right?"

They questioned her about both jobs, what she sang generally, how much money she made. She had to lie at that point, because she couldn't admit her living situation; she'd been frozen out once before when she'd owned up to it, and she liked these people. She didn't want to risk their friendship. "I make enough," she told them, "just barely. I'm saving up for a coach so I can stop fucking up these auditions."

Having turned the conversation back to auditioning, Libby relaxed again, listening. It had been so long since she'd socialized in a group that she was having a hard time adapting. She was either listening too much or interrupting too much – her instincts had gone all kablooey.

There was only so much she could blame on being drunk when it was clear she'd had the same drink for an hour. It was nice, though. She was having a good time.

She zoned out for a bit, possibly fell asleep, until Benny collapsed on her beanbag, displacing her to one side. He was warm and comfortable, so she didn't much care. She looked around, blinking when she saw Mel and Dinah making out on the floor. "Huh."

"Yeah, they do that every so often," Benny said, passing over a bowl of popcorn. "They're both straight, but they like kissing. It's a comfort thing. Stress reduction without having to deal with relationships."

That sounded amazing to Libby. Not so much the lack of romance, but having someone you could touch whenever you wanted to? She could barely remember what that felt like. As close as she and Rain were, they didn't have the kind of friendship that included cuddling. A pit opened in her stomach and she tried to think of something else so the tears wouldn't fall.

Benny leaned closer, towering over her slightly. "You want to know how I deal with anxiety?"

Not really? She raised her eyebrows at him, not wanting to commit to a 'yes', but curious anyway.

He lifted the hem of his sweater, revealing a waist cincher. "Strangely enough, the compression really helps with my social anxiety. I read about it on a blog, and it totally works."

But.... "How do you sing in it?"

"It's not tight enough to affect my breathing, and my posture is amazing. The support actually helps a lot."

Libby had noticed. "Holy crap I thought that was just excellent training."

"Well, that too."

"I need to get one of those. The corset and the training."

Benny pulled out his phone. "What's your number? I'll text you the shop name."

"And the name of your coach."

They chatted until Libby dozed off again, and she woke up happy, even with the crick in her neck and a full bladder. Everyone else was asleep too, sprawled all over the floor and beanbags. Someone had covered Libby with a quilt that looked handmade. She stroked the fabric, contemplating going back to sleep, but then Mel opened her eyes.

"Morning," Libby said quietly. "Sorry about just crashing."

Mel squinted against the winter sun streaming through the uncovered window. "No problem. Everyone does it." She struggled out of her position nestled against Dinah, stretching as she stood.

Libby got to her feet as well, and folded the quilt before tossing it on her chair. "That doesn't mean it's okay for a stranger."

Mel shrugged it off and went over to the little kitchenette. "Coffee? It's only instant, but there's whipped cream."

Libby nodded, then took a minute to use the bathroom before joining her, careful not to wake the siblings. The hiss of the can of coconut cream seemed horribly loud in the quiet apartment, and Libby had to find her phone to check the time. It was nine and she wasn't busking today; she was working at the club that night, an evening class with Adria then her usual gig.

Mel asked her about busking, so Libby gave her the lowdown, telling some of her better stories about her regulars, until Mel interrupted her.

"What does your boyfriend think about you hanging out in subway stations all the time?"

Libby blinked away an image of Michael laughing; she must still be half asleep to have come up with that. "Don't have one. I need to take care of me right now, you know?" It was bullshit, but it was the kind of bullshit most women went along with.

"I get it." Mel was nodding along. "Auditioning comes first. Then, once you've hit the COC, you can think about relationships." She shrugged one slim shoulder. "Or not."

"Yeah." Except any prestigious company seemed an impossible goal now. Once, when she was still in school and getting high marks from her teachers, sure. But now? She'd be lucky to get a place in a small town light opera. "I've got to go, say bye to the others for me? Benny's got my contact info." She got out of there as quickly as was polite, and before the crushing depression hit.

Twelve

Michael hadn't seen Libby face to face in over a month, not until now. They'd texted once in a while, but he was determined to let her live the way she'd chosen as long as she was healthy. But now that he was looking he could see she wasn't healthy, not really. Physically she looked fine, well-fed and hydrated, even like she'd gotten some sleep recently. But there was something off about her affect – she wasn't making eye contact with anyone, not even Claudine, and she'd barely looked at him. Usually she had a warm smile for him, and okay, it seemed a bit patronizing to assume something was wrong because she didn't smile at him. But she really did seem subdued. Even when he'd first found her there'd been an energy about her, a way of drawing attention that her ordeal hadn't tarnished. Now, though, it was gone. She moved as little as possible, lethargic. Apathetic.

Michael recognized the signs.

This class was much smaller, only three students, and Claudine had promised them some hands on time practicing ties on a real person. He went last, watching as the others perfected knots, as Claudine talked them through certain patterns, but mostly watching

Libby. He'd hoped she'd react the same way she did last time, zoned out and happy, but she didn't. She stayed fully engaged the whole time. At one point she'd looked like she was about to cry, so much so that Claudine stopped the student and took her aside to talk.

When it was Michael's turn he swallowed his nerves and put on his impartial cop face. Libby rewarded his effort with a grimace that was probably supposed to be a smile. "Hey," she said, barely above a whisper.

"Long time no see." He busied himself organizing the ties he wanted to use, absolving her of any need to respond. He thought he heard a quiet huff of a laugh, and a quick glance proved him right.

When he turned back she showed no sign of humour, or anything other than blankness. He lifted her hand, giving it a squeeze before binding her wrists together. "Sit up, please."

She obeyed, raising her torso but leaving her legs flat on the settee. He left her arms where they were, tied in front, and began a simple weave of diamonds down the centre of her chest. He got turned around at one point and Claudine had to help him out, which at least made Libby look at him for a few seconds. She mostly watched his hands as if hypnotized by the motion. By the time he was halfway down, her upper arms held tightly to her sides, she'd relaxed, closed her eyes. Her breathing deepened as well, and he could almost believe she was sleeping if she hadn't still been holding herself upright. She'd gone someplace peaceful, and he couldn't begrudge her that.

After class he went to the bar to see her act. He'd only ever heard her in the subway, competing with the noise of the crowd and the rush of trains. Here, in the low light, just her up there with no competition, it felt private. Intimate. For a moment it was too much, and he looked down at the table, tracing a scratch in the surface with his thumb before he could turn to her again.

Her voice and movements were precise, trained and cultivated to produce the desired effect, but what startled him was her face. She looked as she had while tied up – content, relaxed. She truly loved what she did and it showed in every micro-expression. The crease that had rested between her eyebrows as she set up was gone. The delicate lift in the corners of her mouth might have been an effect of singing, but the way it lingered between songs wasn't. This was her passion, and it was so powerful that Michael, dazed, wondered if he'd ever experienced anything like it. It was her job and her one true love and her escape.

And it was a fucking shame that she couldn't enjoy the rest of her life to the same extent.

Libby finished her set, the only one tonight, with You're Getting to Be a Habit with Me just for Michael. She'd faltered when she saw him out there, watching her. He was at a table off to her left, about halfway back, one she didn't look to often, so she hadn't seen him until her second song. She'd tried to ignore him after that, to regain some of what she'd had earlier when wrapped snugly in soft rope, his hands deft and mostly accurate. They were good hands, strong and broad, with thick fingers. As she sang she'd imagined the tight bands around her, the tug of movement as he looped rope around rope and secured knots. It helped, it helped so much, and she wondered if it would be tacky to ask Adria to fashion her something to wear on stage. Nothing fancy, just a rope corset, maybe. Something protective.

After the last song she went down to him, something she usually didn't do. She liked to keep a distance between herself and the regulars, maintain some semblance of professionalism, of privacy, but this was different. Michael was different.

"Great job," he said, standing up to greet her. "I had no idea. You're so completely different up there, not like your day job at all."

"Yeah, well, here I don't have to worry about anyone making off with my tips."

The bartender, Trish this time, turned on the stereo, puncturing the quiet. Michael watched Libby with such affection, such tenderness, that she started tearing up right there. She blinked rapidly, fighting it off, and was moderately successful.

She just couldn't look him in the face anymore.

"Is there some place we can talk?" he said, touching the inside of her wrist with two of those sturdy fingers.

Trying to decide if she could afford the emotional fallout was more effort than it was worth. "Give me a minute to finish up here and I'll meet you at the door."

She watched him walk out and an unexpected loneliness crashed into her. "Suck it up, Libby, you had your chance," she muttered to herself as she crossed over to the bar.

She got her tips from Trish and then changed quickly, not bothering to wash her face and change her hair from socialite to student; her hat and scarf would cover everything. The weather forecast had promised deep cold that night, and she was as prepared as she could be. None of her usual crash pads were available; Rain was away, Jenna, her former boss, was having a dinner party, and Alex had a new girlfriend. There were one or two other guys she could call up to trade sex for a warm place to sleep, but she couldn't be bothered to make the effort they'd require.

If the wrap she threw on over her jacket was really a blanket, no one mentioned it as she left.

Michael noticed it immediately, of course. She watched him take in the red and yellow plaid monstrosity, a frown forming as he did. "You got a place to sleep tonight?"

And just like that Libby was so goddamn tired. She sighed, cursing herself when she started crying again. She attempted flippancy, but failed miserably. "Why, you offering?"

He wrapped one arm around her, pulling her into his side. "Come on."

She didn't bother to resent the relief that flooded through her as he took her home.

They didn't talk at all on the train, they just sat together, touching shoulders, Libby's duffle across their laps. Libby didn't know what to say besides thank you, and there was only so often you could say it before people got annoyed and stopped giving you things. The lights on the train were too bright, so she closed her eyes and just let the time pass, deliberately not thinking about any of the things that were marked with land mines in her brain right now.

She wondered if Michael had a bed in the guest room yet. If Jeeves would remember how he'd sit with her while she watched TV, his front half propped up on her thigh, back half on the couch. If that box of microwave popcorn she liked was still in the pantry.

If he had ropes at home.

The thought made her shiver, and his arm slid up and around her shoulders, holding her close again, and it was a natural thing to rest her head against his chest and fall asleep.

"Libby."

Something moved her, in a way that was different from the train, and she woke. "Sorry."

The affection in his face was almost overwhelming. "Not a problem. But our stop is coming up."

Right. "But I was comfy," she whined, only partly joking.

He laughed softly. "But wouldn't you rather be wrapped in a fuzzy blanket and sipping hot chocolate?"

"Dear god, yes."

The apartment looked the same, and Libby wasn't sure why she thought it might have changed. Other people, real people with real lives, didn't change the place they slept every night.

"You can put your stuff in this room," he said, leading her across the living room to the room he was using as storage. "Sorry there's no bed."

"This is so much better than where I've been sleeping, you have no idea. And I can sleep on the couch, it's not a problem." She tossed her duffle in the corner. "There. All unpacked."

"Have you eaten?" He stopped and rephrased. "Sorry. Are you interested in dinner? I've got some leftovers from earlier."

"Sure. Let me know if there's anything I can do."

"Make yourself at home. Take a shower if you want."

She pulled a lock of hair to her face, wrinkling her nose as she sniffed it. "Yeah, that's probably a good idea."

Dinner smelled incredible, all tomato and spices. Music was playing, upbeat rock, but nothing she recognized. She watched Michael from the door for a moment; she'd never expected him to be the dancing-alone-while-you-work type, but there he was, shaking that thing like the singer told him to. He had a surprisingly nice ass for a guy his age.

"Oh hey."

She snapped her eyes up to his face as quickly as she could.

"Feel better?"

"Immensely." She sat on a stool at the breakfast bar and started braiding her hair. She was too tired to hold up a hair dryer right now. There was a mug of hot chocolate already in place.

He brought her a dish of rice swimming in oily eggplant sauce, which just solidified her belief that she was in heaven, then sat down across from her.

She was just loading up her fork when he spoke. "Move in with me."

No way was she wasting this food, so she settled for glaring at him while she savoured the bite. "I already said no," she answered eventually, sounding weak even to herself.

"I get that you want to take care of yourself, that you've been doing it for a really long time." He took a sip from a cup that smelled like chocolate. "Long enough that you maybe don't know how to depend on others."

He wasn't wrong. Parenting at The Farm pretty much ended when a kid hit puberty and was therefore old enough to work. She didn't answer.

"And you were doing well, I could see that. You were taking care of yourself enough to work and go on auditions. But something changed in the last month even beyond the attempted kidnapping."

"More like a lot of little things all at once," she replied, staring at her food instead of the absolute kindness and understanding in his eyes.

"And now it's harder. You're tired and hungry, both literally and metaphorically, and it's beating you down rather than the other way around."

All Libby could do was nod and eat.

"So maybe it's time to try another strategy."

She looked up at that, startled and pleased at having it phrased that way. "Plan B."

"Exactly."

She made herself think it through before accepting. "How much?"

"Pardon?"

"How much is the rent?" It made her perversely glad that she startled him with that question.

"What can you afford? Including your voice lessons," he added.

Yow, tough question. "I could cook and clean?"

"Can you? Cook?"

"Sort of? I could learn. It's not that hard, right?"

"Depends if you can follow instructions."

"I'm great at that."

"So you'll do it?"

She put her hand over his. "Will you promise me that you'll kick me out if you need to? I hate this enough, I don't want to be a burden, too."

He turned his hand over and grasped hers, his palm soft against her dried out skin. "I promise. Can I ask how much money you do have?"

She wanted him to know, wanted him to get that she was taking care of herself just fine. "Just over five thousand."

"For a year working two jobs."

"One job, two nights a week, plus tips from the busking. Minus food, TTC pass, phone service, dresses and makeup for work, and the occasional hotel."

"Well, that answers my next question."

"Which one?"

He watched her for a moment while she ate. "If you're able to finish your degree."

Libby dropped her fork, then fished it carefully out of the rice. That was not the question she was expecting. "Not likely." She licked the sauce off her fingers.

A crease appeared between his brows. "Does it bother you?"

Libby did him the courtesy of actually thinking about it. "You know, I'm not sure it does. The auditions I've been to, they care more about technique than credentials. That's why I need lessons again. I've lost my polish."

"Torch songs will do that to you."

"Yeah, and belting out *Big Yellow Taxi* across a crowded subway station." She took another bite. "This is really delicious. You've got to teach me to make it."

"It's really easy, too. I'm glad you like it."

She didn't tell him she wasn't getting a lot of good food these days. She figured he knew that part already. "So. Last time I saw you that wasn't at the police station you were about to have a date. How'd that go?"

He was an engaging speaker, she knew that already, but he made her laugh a few times with his story of his utterly mundane date and the few follow-ups they'd had. She thought she might like Dragos, if she ever got to meet him. "...and then I got caught up with work and haven't talked to him in nearly a week."

"Oh, no, quelle horreur! A week!" She got up to refill her water from the fridge and saw there was milk. Suddenly she was craving it and realized she'd hadn't had a glass of milk in god knows how long. Since the last time she was here, maybe. "How have you not wasted away from pining?"

"You're hilarious," he said, totally deadpan, his face so bland and unimpressed that she nearly burst out laughing again. "I'm so glad I invited you to live with me."

"Fine." She sighed and sat back down with her brimming glass of milk. "Big tough cop can't take a little teasing."

"That's it. You're out of here. Pack your things and go."

For a second Libby thought he was serious, that's how good an actor he was, but she called his bluff by tearing up, throwing in a lower lip tremor for effect. "But... but...."

He smiled and pointed an accusing finger at her. "Okay, don't ever do that again. That's just sad and totally uncalled for."

"Whatever, you can't resist."

"I actually can. I just pity you enough not to."

"Ooh." That one hurt, just a tiny bit. She finished her drink and decided to take her end of their bargain seriously. "Want me to clean up?"

"I'll get it. You look like you need to sleep."

She did, but she also didn't want to be a bad guest. "Mind if I pick out a book?"

"Anything you want."

The bookcase was decently large, if filled with non-fiction of the legal system kind. She slid out a big white cookbook that promised her it held the basics and flopped down on the couch. Halfway through the chapter on salads, lulled by the sound of Michael puttering around the kitchen, she fell asleep.

She woke in the pitch black room and listened. Nothing. Asshat and Douchepotato must not have come back. They rarely did, choosing to spend their nights in comfort, she assumed.

She felt disoriented, like she'd lost time. Like the way you feel when your brain is awake but your body is still in sleep paralysis. There were the lipstick drawings she'd made on the walls, yellow-flowered wallpaper behind them.

The mouse she shared her cage with was making noise, an awful, raspy noise, interspersed with keening. "Shut up," she yelled, but it came out like nothing, a hoarse whisper. She tried again. Nothing.

There was a siren in the distance now, oh god, were they coming to rescue her? Something tickled at her memory, a voice. A man.

"Libby."

Hands grabbed her and she struggled, she fought as hard as she could. They were going to move her, she knew, they'd move her and the sirens would never find her again. An arm came around her and she threw her head back, hoping to crack his skull with hers. She'd rather die than spend another night here.

"I don't think you really mean that."

Somewhere a cat meowed and suddenly her hand was full of warm fur. She opened her eyes and, in the light from the bedroom door, recognized Michael in the distance and his cat head-butting her dangling hand. "Shit."

The cat jumped to her lap, giving her soulful eyes and mewing like he was worried about her. She petted him and waited for her heart rate to go down, for the lump to leave her throat.

"Nightmare?" Another, dim light came on and Michael knelt beside the couch.

"Sorry."

"Don't be. I have enough of my own, I'm used to it." He joined her in scritching the cat, getting behind his ears and making him purr louder.

"Then you don't need me waking you as well."

"I'll just sleep later, then. I have a fairly flexible schedule. Care to tell me about it?"

"Not really. Just the usual reliving of the trauma."

"Right." He turned on the table lamp behind her. "I actually like those better than the ones where you're stuck in some confusing yet frightening situation you can't get out of."

"Huh. Yeah, those are weird." Her mouth tasted awful. She must have fallen asleep without brushing her teeth and he didn't bother waking her. She had a blanket over her that she didn't remember from earlier. "Give me a minute?"

He nodded, and she went to brush her teeth and pee. She didn't want to go back to sleep, but it was after eleven. She should probably try, as futile as it seemed right now.

"I didn't mean to make you hide in your room," she told Michael when she went back out. He'd rearranged the throw pillows and straightened the blanket, which the cat was now curled up on.

"You didn't. I stayed out here working for a while, and only just a few minutes ago turned off the lights."

That explained the nightmare, if the room suddenly went dark and quiet. "Well, I'm probably not going back to sleep for a bit, so if you want to come back out...." She shrugged. She had to finish reading the cookbook anyway.

"Mind if I steal some of the couch and turn on the TV?"

"Go for it."

Michael wasn't really interested in watching TV, but Libby looked terrible so he put on a comedy show and waited for her to stop shaking. She wrapped herself up in the blanket and opened her book, but she wasn't really reading. Her eyes weren't moving and she didn't turn pages often enough for a book with so many pictures. Her body curled around itself like she was cold, despite her wool cocoon. She was stuck in the nightmare, still, either the one she just woke from or the one she'd lived for so long.

The only parts of her not tucked away neatly were her hands and the one foot resting against his thigh. It flexed and he patted it without thinking, then left his hand there when she relaxed a little. He could feel the chill of her skin through her threadbare sock. "Hey, it's a bit cold in here," he said, squeezing her foot. "You think I could share that blanket?"

"What?" She really hadn't been engaged with her surroundings. "Oh, yeah."

A bit too quickly she sat up beside him, throwing the blanket over them both and tucking herself into his side. All he could see of her was her head, and not even that when she laid it on his shoulder and slipped her left hand between his right arm and his side. She stopped shaking, her breathing evened out, and gradually her skin warmed to the temperature of his. She even laughed a few times at the TV, and he resigned himself to sleeping upright on the couch if that's what it took.

When she fell asleep again, though, it was against the arm of the couch in her original position. She'd stolen the blanket and left Michael cold, so he went to bed, dimming the lights but not dousing them completely.

His own dreams were rough; he didn't remember details the next morning, but each time he woke it was with a tremendous sense of guilt and shame, and he could only imagine he must have been dreaming about Jeanine. He'd wondered, over the years, what her last days were like. Her mother was with her until the day of her death and she'd told him Jeanine was happier, more positive. He never told her about the letter.

He woke again around dawn to hear Libby puttering around in the kitchen. He smelled coffee and toast, and it was comforting in a way that put him back to sleep until his alarm.

"We're out of jam," Libby told him from her position on the couch under a cat. "Sorry, but that bread is amazing. We might be out of that, too."

"S'fine." The whole scene was so ridiculously domestic that he stopped to just look at her for a minute, smiling. "Make a list of anything you want or need and I'll get groceries when I get back from work."

She sat up, dislodging the cat. "How about you make a list, and I'll do it. Since I have so much free time right now."

Jeeves head-butted Michael's shins a few times, earning a scratch on the ear. "That would be great. Have you fed the beast?"

"I have indeed fed the beast. And the cat, too." She laughed up at him, and for a moment he went giddy, months of worry shedding off him like water, worry he hadn't really known he had until suddenly it was gone.

"I'm gonna try this cooking thing," she added, "so let me know what you hate, or are allergic to or anything."

"There's very little I won't eat." To that end, he kept going into the kitchen to get his own breakfast. He sat at the peninsula and made the grocery list while he ate, drawing a little map to the bakery that made the bread and the shop where he bought jam. He also included the small list of foods he can't stand: chard, rapini, tempeh, sun-dried tomatoes. Nothing terribly common, unless you happened to have been raised vegetarian, like Libby. He wasn't taking any chances with tempeh.

He left the note with a half a dozen twenties, more than enough cash for the small list and whatever she needed for dinner and herself. He'd give her a couple of weeks to recover, both in mood and body, before they talked about her paying for her own personal items. For the moment, he could and would cover her if she wanted. He suspected she wouldn't.

"I did a thing," he said when Ray called him later.

"What kind of a thing?" He could hear the amusement in Ray's voice.

"A serious thing." Michael sighed and just told him. "There's this young woman. I helped her out of a jam a while ago and she needs a place

to stay. So I invited her to use my guest room."
When he realized he needed to tell Ray what
happened he'd decided to be completely open
about it. "Indefinitely."

"So you've got a roommate?" Thank God Ray
didn't sound anything other than mildly curious
now.

"Yes."

"Okay. Well, I've got my own news. Nothing
so interesting as a random new roomie, but
important. My grandmother is having eye
surgery next week."

"Oh no."

"Yeah, she'll be fine but she wants me to go up
and take care of her. I've got enough time off
saved up, so I'm leaving tomorrow."

Michael desperately tried to remember where
Ray's grandma lived. "London?"

"That's the place."

"For how long?"

"I've got ten days. I'm hoping I can convince
her to call in one of the nursing services for when
I leave."

Ten days. He could stand to be apart from
Ray for ten days. "Let me know when you get in."

"If it's not the middle of the night or
something."

After Michael went to work Libby stared at the cookbook—a different one than last night's—not really seeing it. Jeeves hadn't come back to her lap and even wrapping herself in the blanket didn't help her feel grounded. She checked the clock; it was already nearly noon and she was still in her sleep clothes. She hadn't even looked at the list.

A shower, that would make her feel better. A hot shower and some basic grooming usually went a long way to lifting her mood, and it did for a bit. She lost time again while blow drying her hair, nearly burning her ear with the hot plastic, so she gave that up.

Food. She'd promised Michael dinner and he'd left her more than enough cash. Really the man was stupidly generous, in a way she'd never expected him to be. Maybe it was just her? Idiot. She mentally smacked herself in the face. He knew he could trust her because she'd already proven herself trustworthy taking care of Jeeves while Michael was away.

So it was just her. Huh.

She grabbed the cash, the list, and a few fabric shopping bags and set out to explore the neighbourhood again.

She was fine up until she entered the grocery store. The bakery was great; the grey-haired woman behind the counter was helpful and quick with samples when Libby hesitated deciding between two savoury loaves. Her only trouble in the store with the jam was again one of decision, but she figured the stuff wouldn't spoil, so what the hell, get both the marmalade and the strawberry. Citrus fruit felt illicit, still, but strawberry jam in winter was normal.

It wasn't like Libby hadn't shopped in grocery stores before. She had, back when she lived with Rain, although that was more like a quick in and out for snacks and microwave meals. This time, though, she stood at the end of an aisle and couldn't figure out where to go next. She could read the signs, but they were meaningless. The sounds all blurred together, voices, carts squeaking, all of it was a mass of constant noise. All she could focus on was how thirsty she was, and how good that bottle of orange juice looked. But she didn't know the etiquette here. Could she drink the bottle while she shopped and then pay for it? Did she dare?

She grabbed the bottle and paid for it, drank it right there at the door and then tossed the bottle in her bag. The receipt she carefully stowed in her pocket in case anyone questioned why she had an empty bottle in her bag. If the store had recycling, she wouldn't have to be so paranoid. But she was better able to focus on shopping now, and she got through it with a minimum of drama.

Back home she put the perishables away, leaving the dinner ingredients out on the counter. Then she laid down, closed her eyes, and tried to concentrate on anything but how pathetic she was.

She was pulled out of her funk by her phone ringing. She didn't want to answer, didn't want to talk to anyone, but it was Michael and she was living in his house and she owed him basic courtesy. She slid her thumb over to answer and put a big, fake smile on her face. "Hey, what's up?"

"Your friend, the one you lived with," he paused long enough for her to supply him with a name.

"Rain."

"Rain. You said you still have possessions at her place."

Possessions instead of stuff. Is that how Faith had thought about her stuff while she was gone? "Some, yeah. Why?"

"I can borrow a car tonight if you want to pick it all up and move in properly."

Her brain went offline for like a nanosecond. Move in. As if this really was her home instead of her just pretending. "Let me call her and find out. I'm working tonight, too, but not 'til nine."

Rain answered her phone and was all too happy to set up some time. "You have no idea how relieved I am, Libby," and the warmth in her voice nearly knocked Libby over. "I've been so worried about you. Tell me all about it."

Huh. Libby hadn't thought that far ahead. On the surface, if you didn't know Michael, it looked pretty sleazy. She'd have to be careful. "Okay, you remember that guy who found me?"

Rain did, vaguely, and Libby laid out a history for them that wasn't far from the truth. She left out the bits at the classes; she hadn't even told Rain that she had a night job, let alone that it was at a BDSM club. She made up some stuff about his boyfriend, and added that Rain would get to meet him that night, but that they couldn't stay long.

She ended the conversation as quickly as she could, not wanting to either lie too much or get backed into a corner where she'd have to start telling truths. It was a precarious position, but she didn't want to ruin her relationship with Rain, the only person she knew who had an inkling of what it was like being raised by militant hippies. Her parents hadn't been members of the cult, but Rain had admitted to having researched it as a teenager. "It just seemed like a comfortable way to live, with only people who shared your values," she'd said, about a week into their friendship. "But then I kept looking, reading articles, and I went to one of the recruitment centres but the people there were creepy so I stopped."

That connection, those shared values, were one of the things that got them put together in residence in the first place. Rain had tried everything she could think of to keep Libby in school, even going so far as to ask her parents to pay for Libby's tuition. Of course they refused, and Rain had only told Libby herself about it much later, knowing that she would have objected at the time had she known.

Rain was her only real friend, besides Michael. She had been having some fun texting Benny and Mel, but a texting relationship of barely two days didn't count. Thinking of Benny led her to remember the link he'd sent her, and she wondered if having the corset, if wearing it casually would act like being bound. Maybe she could prevent what had happened at the grocery store from happening again.

The website he'd sent her to had a variety of options, both in styles and prices, but she really wished she could try them out before buying. Even the cheapest was still more than she was comfortable paying for something she couldn't test out. They didn't have a physical store, but there had to be something else like it. She was in Toronto, if she couldn't buy a cheap corset there they didn't exist.

Monday. She'd do it Monday, after her session at the station. That would give her something to look forward to. For now, she had dinner to make, which meant tearing apart the kitchen to make sure she had all the tools she needed.

Thirteen

The windows were open and the air in the apartment smelled like burned garlic. Not a pleasant scent, but not unexpected given Libby's inexperience cooking. Michael had burned a lot of garlic and onions when he started out.

Libby met him halfway to the kitchen and brandished a spoon at him. "Do not say it smells great in here. There is no lying to me, not even to make me feel better, got it?"

"Got it." He loosened his tie and followed her back to the stove. The garlic in the pan looked perfect swimming in a sauce of herbs and cannellinis. "Everything's under control?"

"If I need another set of hands I'll let you know."

He glanced at the recipe as he left, noting that it was one that was pretty easy yet looked and tasted impressive. Satisfied that she'd be fine, he settled in with his laptop to do some research. He'd had an idea earlier, but his timeline to implement it was short.

Dinner took longer than it should have, and the casserole was not exactly hot, but it tasted like it was supposed to, so both he and Libby counted it as a win.

"I know I promised to cook, but that took a really long time," she said, dragging a forkful of pasta through the sauce. "I'm not sure I should be doing this every night."

"Did you enjoy it?"

She stared at her plate for a second, then smiled up at him. "Yeah, I did." There was a touch of wonder in her voice.

"Then it'll go faster as you practice." He noticed her shoulders slump, just a touch. "But three times a week would be plenty, if that's what you're up to."

"Do I have to choose which days in advance?"

He studied her posture, the tired lines on her face. "No. Just let me know before I leave work, okay? Then I can plan to get groceries or take out or something."

She nodded and went back to her food. "Rain's going to be home all night. Do you want to go right after dinner?"

"Sounds good. I thought I'd drive you to work tonight and leave Claudine's car for her. I'll take transit home."

"Claudine?"

He had to think for a moment why she didn't know Claudine, and then he realized he'd stupidly outed her real name without checking with her first. "Ah, Adria."

"Wait, you know her well enough to borrow her car?"

Wincing, he replied to his broccoli, "Her husband's car, actually."

"You know her husband?" She blinked. "She has a husband?"

So he told her the whole story as they finished eating: Joining the Armed Forces, meeting a superior officer in Kuwait, getting to be friends with her, being reassigned, then a couple of years later being hand-picked for her unit supporting the UN transition in East Timor. Leaving the service for a career in law enforcement. Claudine leaving the service too, then picking up their friendship again. He left out a lot, but he knew Libby understood when she asked, "So you were pretty glad to get the job here, so you could see her more often."

"I was. Of course, it was her husband who hired me, but we get along well enough too."

"So does that mean she'll be over here sometimes?"

He couldn't figure out if she was nervous at the possibility, or interested. "I usually go over there. Her kids love me." He let the conversation drop, then, figuring if Libby wanted to see Claudine socially they could work it out themselves.

The Pickford Performing Arts Academy was at Front and Church, so getting there by car was as painless as it got driving in downtown. Libby directed him to a short-term parking garage under the residence hall. She'd gotten quieter as they drove, starting out telling him stories about her and Rain, then tapering off into a fidgety silence. Now she was hesitant, even stuttered a few times giving him directions. She led him upstairs without stopping to talk to anyone but the woman at the security desk, and even though he expressed interest in the practice rooms and lounges, she didn't give him a tour.

Alone in the elevator, he jostled her elbow with his. "What's up?"

She didn't look up from her shoes. "The top floor." A small curve in her lip betrayed her.

"Care to tell me what's got you so nervous?"

Shaking her head, she finally looked up at him. "I'll tell you later, when we're done here."

She took a deep breath before knocking on Rain's door, her old door, and pasted a big smile on her face that turned from obviously fake to natural when a tall South Asian woman answered.

"Libby!" She pulled Libby into a hug, ignoring Michael for the moment.

He followed them inside, feeling awkward with the flat boxes under his arm. He introduced himself, liking the suspicious look in Rain's eyes as she sized him up. She finally introduced herself with a firm handshake.

To the right of the front door was a closet taking up the rest of the wall, which Libby pretty much dove headfirst into. To the left was a hallway with four doors: three bedrooms and a bathroom, he guessed. The living area was barely big enough for the love seat, chair, and overloaded bookcase they had in there. A small counter housed a bar fridge, a toaster, and an electric kettle. A laptop on the couch had what looked like a paused TV show on the screen.

"I haven't had time to go through all the books," Rain told him, crossing to the overstuffed shelves in the living room. "I'll do that now."

Michael made himself useful putting together boxes and packing the books Rain handed to him. Libby moved on to another closet, coming out with two large garment bags and a couple of shoe boxes. "Performance clothes," she told him, setting the bags on the couch and dropping the shoes. "Ball gowns and high heels, the life of an opera singer."

"You'll get to wear them again," he said quietly, though perhaps not quietly enough given the puzzled smile Rain shot him.

The way Libby looked at him then made it all worth the effort. "Yeah, I will," she replied. She reached out and he enveloped her hand in his. "Thanks."

"My pleasure."

Rain was staring at them openly now. He raised his eyebrows innocently at her, and she went back to her task.

Down in the car, boxes and bags loaded, Michael broached the topic. "So. Rain's pretty worried about you."

Libby snorted, but didn't look away from the window. "She has been since I got kidnapped. God, she nearly cried when I came home, and then again when I got kicked out." She shrugged. "She's the only friend I had for a long time, and I hate lying to her."

Michael said nothing, waiting for her to explain.

"I haven't told her about the club. For someone who was raised by hippies she's surprisingly conventional. She also probably thinks you have less than honourable motives."

"Yeah, I got that impression. She doesn't have a great poker face."

"But she does. She must have wanted you to see what she's thinking."

That wasn't a comforting thought. "You know, we should go buy you a bed tomorrow. Get your room done up properly."

"That's," Libby paused and cleared her throat. "That's not necessary. I can sleep on the couch. Or the floor, even, if you don't want me camped out in the living room."

Over his dead body. "I was meaning to get a guest bed anyway. I have family who might want to visit."

"Well." She thumped her head against the window. "I can't argue with that."

"And a dresser, of course."

"Sure."

Michael carefully didn't smile. "A chair would be nice, maybe a small one. Oh, and a full length mirror, of course. For those ball gowns and high heels."

She peered at him sideways. "I thought you were talking about your relatives."

"Hey, you don't know my brother."

That got a laugh out of her. "You don't have a brother."

"Oh yeah, I told you that, didn't I?"

"And I remember a surprising amount, considering my state of mind at the time."

They'd never really talked about that first day, when she'd been in turns quiet and sarcastic, when he'd talked at her because she seemed more comfortable that way. "Strickland still hasn't got any leads?" he asked, keeping his attention on the road in front of them.

"Nope."

"Well, if she hasn't by next December you're staying inside on New Year's."

"I will happily lock myself in my room."

He'd been kidding, she was not. "Then we'd better make it comfortable."

She reached out and slapped him on the arm, laughing as she did. "Oh, let it go already. I'll choose furniture, fine. But it's your money, so you're the one deciding where we shop. Oh hey," she said, then stopped.

"What?"

"The guy you're dating, what's his name? Something with a D?"

"Ray."

She narrowed her eyes. "That's not the name you told me. Is this a new guy?"

"Nope, same one. His name really is Dragos. But everyone calls him Ray."

She nodded, understanding. "Right. Okay. So you were just fucking with me before."

"What can I say? Gotta have some fun. What about him?"

"Is he okay with this?"

He risked a glance at her. She was frowning, playing with her fingers as she did when she was agitated. "He's fine with it. I talked to him this afternoon."

"Good. I don't want to be in the way."

"I'll let you know if you are." He remembered something he wanted to ask her, too. "Tell me, why were you so nervous earlier?"

She tugged her hat down over her ears. "I wasn't sure how Rain would react to you. She thinks I can't take care of myself. There was a thing with a guy I had a date with."

"Invite her over sometime." He didn't know how to say he wanted her to feel at home. Everything he came up with sounded patronizing. "It's your home now too, invite whoever you want."

"Okay. Wild parties, coming up."

He chuckled at the thought. "Just remember to invite the neighbours so they won't complain."

Fourteen

Ugh. My roommate's getting all gooey about his boyfriend. Wanna hook up?

Ray stared at his phone, checked the name of the sender, then stared some more. He hadn't heard a damn thing from Libby since she walked out of his house, and now she wanted to get together?

Fuck it.

Seriously? You shut me down hard and now you're back for more? I feel used.

He waited a few seconds for a reply, and when it failed to appear he shoved his phone in his pocket and went back to sweeping the dog kibble off the floor.

Shit. Did I not apologize properly? Look, you have a home and I didn't and I have this amazing ability to see the future, one where you kept asking me every night to stay over and the relationship got weird really fast. Can you forgive me?

Well. That did make a lot of sense, and yeah, he could see where she'd get the idea seeing as the first thing he did was give her money.

Yeah, okay. But I'm seeing someone, so no booty calls.

Fair enough. Have a nice night.

Ray had a few more tasks to do before he could settle for the night. Grandma had already gone to bed with her audio book so he was just finishing up the cleaning. He could take a break for a minute to talk to Michael.

Home day after tomorrow, I think. Gran's doing better at navigating blind now. Plus my aunt's here, finally.

The response was almost immediate. *Good. Too soon to say I missed you?*

Nah. Missed you too. Being a Toronto native doesn't get me any cred at all here.

He could almost see the confused frown Michael would have when he got that.

You were expecting it to?

They don't know how to deal with me: European name= smart, blond = dumb. Paramedic = smart, muscled = dumb

You defy category.

I'm a mystery. Here's another: Gay = smart, apparently.

Gay people are smarter than straight people?

So I've been told. I shouldn't have admitted knowing who Debussy was.

Or stop going to bars near the university.

I'm talking about my cousins.

Okay, the Debussy thing wasn't his cousins, they knew his dad, had had almost all the same lectures Ray had. But there had been others at the party and then a bar trivia game and, well, comments had been made. After a moment he sent: *Grandma keeps trying to set me up with Nice Local Girl. Says NLG will have my babies. More important to have babies than to have love.*

Hope your parents don't think so.

My parents are awesome.

Not that they didn't want grandchildren, but his sister was a little more into that than he was.

Let me know when your flight gets in.

We'll go out. We haven't been out in public yet.

That's true.

Baby steps, that's what it would take to get Michael to come out again, and Ray was determined to coax the process along. He'd been content to let the issue alone for now, focussing instead on training for the firefighter exam next week. But once he'd passed that, and he would this time, he knew it, he'd have more time to think about it. To make plans.

"What is that on your face?" Libby asked as Michael entered the kitchen.

"What?" He started pulling pots and pans out of the drawer by the stove.

"That big stupid grin you've got going there."

"Oh, that. Ray's coming back."

"Ray." She frowned down at the papers she had set out on the peninsula. "Ray, boyfriend Ray?"

"That's the one."

"Dude, anything that makes you smile like that you'd better work at."

"I'm so glad we agree."

"Just let me know if you need me gone for a night. I can manage."

Michael figured that wouldn't be necessary; Ray had his own place if need be, and Michael predicted a lot of staying in. He started slicing onions and heard a snort from Libby.

"You're doing it again. Is he really that hot? 'Cause I know you've only had, like, three dates with him."

Michael turned his dopey grin on her. "He really, really is."

"Christ, I have got to get laid if you're going to be like this for the foreseeable future. You are ridiculous. Isn't he, Jeeves?"

The cat, well trained by now, replied with a brrt.

"Even the cat agrees with me."

"The cat always agrees with you."

"He's a smart cat."

"He once tried to jump into the nook in the shower." The shampoo bottle had exploded when it hit the floor, and Michael had his first and hopefully last experience rinsing a cat.

"He's smart where it counts."

There was no way Michael was going to win this one. She'd completely co-opted his cat in the space of a week. He was considering tossing her room to check for contraband treats.

Not that he didn't have a stash of catnip in the pantry. Michael embraced his hypocrisy.

"Anyway," he said, moving the onions to the pan, "that's my news. What are you up to there?"

She sighed down at the stack of what looked like forms in front of her. "Change of address, change of address, taxes—"

"You're doing your taxes already?"

"I'm checking to see what exactly applies to me. And if I'm in trouble because I completely blanked on the whole deal last year." She picked up a booklet from the bottom of the pile. "And scholarship information."

"You're thinking of going back?"

"If I can get funding? Sure. But once they look at my last set of transcripts, they'll probably reject me."

He had to give her credit for trying. "I make a good character reference, if it comes down to that."

"Sure, yeah, I'll just wave my forty-year-old, ex-cop roommate around. That's sure to work."

"Hey, the kind of people who sit on arts scholarship committees are the kind of people who think all cops are good and pure and just." He wouldn't be the first person to use that impression for his own purposes.

Her mouth twisted like she was suppressing something. "I am totally not going to make a joke about your boyfriend's ass."

"Thank you for your kindness."

Ray called Michael at work the next Thursday. "Dress up. We're celebrating."

He'd been mysterious ever since he got home, coy, clearly planning something, but there was another aspect to it, something Michael couldn't pin down. It seemed he was going to find out tonight. So how could he say no?

Ray hadn't told him where they were going that evening, just that he should meet him at the park outside Christie Station. Ray greeted him with a kiss, right there on the street, and Michael just gaped at him for a moment before exclaiming, "This is incredible."

Ray laughed, confused, before putting his arm around him and leading him east. "What? Christie Pits?"

"Being out, in public, with no worries."

"Well, not no worries, but I think between the two of us we can take 'em."

Remembering what Ray had said to him earlier, Michael asked, "So what are we celebrating?"

Ray grinned at him. "You are now dating a firefighter."

He couldn't resist. "Really? What's his name?"

"Asshole."

"That's a good name."

Ray took him to a Korean place, one that Michael had talked about wanting to go to, and he'd even ordered off-menu because he knew the owner. Course after course, the food delighted Michael, but equally entertaining was watching Ray with his.

After dessert, Ray grinned at him with delightful impishness and said, "Want to take a walk?"

Outside, Michael grabbed him by the scarf and tugged him in for short, hard kiss. "Thanks for remembering." He slid his hand into Ray's open coat and around his waist, pulling him closer. The cool air was refreshing after the warmth of the restaurant and he was happy to linger.

Ray curled his hands into Michael's lapels and kissed him again, longer and sweeter. "I thought we were walking."

"We can't walk to your place." He let his hand wander down the curve of Ray's ass.

"Is that a hint?"

Michael shook his head. "It's a promise." He kissed Ray again then released him to take his hand and lead him to the station.

Michael was still stunned at the realization that he didn't have to hide this side of himself here. His boss was arguably way kinkier than anything he and Ray could get up to—although Michael had managed not to learn details even while he lived with them—so he wasn't going to get fired for kissing his boyfriend in public. He spent the train ride to Bloor-Yonge Station with his hand on Ray's thigh, high enough to get the point across, not high enough to be indecent. The feeling of breaking the rules while not breaking the rules was almost vertigo-inducing.

Thirty minutes later Ray had him pinned to the inside of his front door and was fumbling at Michael's belt buckle. "Shit," Ray gasped, pulling his lips away from Michael's. He got the belt open and started working on button and zipper. His face was buried in Michael's neck, hot tongue swiping trails against his skin. "You smell amazing, did I tell you that?" The nip caught Michael off guard and he gasped. "Fucking amazing."

Michael's gasp turned into a deep chuckle. "My roommate sprayed me with her perfume this morning in retaliation for something I said."

"Well, it works for you." His chilled fingers warmed quickly as they slid down the front of Michael's briefs. "What did you say?"

Michael thrust helplessly up into Ray's hand. "I really don't want to talk about her while your hand is on my cock."

Ray laughed against the base of his ear, sending shivers down Michael's spine. "Jesus."

Michael removed his hands from their place down the back of Ray's jeans. "I know you have a bed in this place."

"You do, huh?" Ray started backing away, tugging Michael along by the front of his shirt, undoing the buttons as he went.

"If you don't that would be sad, because then how could I pin you down and rub all over you?"

Ray shivered and crashed them both into the wall, cradling Michael's head with his hand at the last second. "Or I could pin you right here."

Michael didn't tear off Ray's shirt; it was a nice shirt. He kissed him instead, distracting him while he undid the buttons, then spread the edges apart, gliding his hands over smooth skin and muscle. He broke the kiss to look: tanned expanse of chest, open jeans, no underwear, hard cock poking out. "God, you're gorgeous."

They'd already had the usual discussions and tests, so there was nothing holding them back. Ray's hands pushed down his own clothes and he eased forward, pressing them together. He clutched Ray to him and thrust up, rough hair tickling as he went. Ray gasped above him, his fingers digging wonderfully into Michael's shoulders. The space between them grew slick with sweat and spunk and it wasn't quite enough but neither wanted to stop.

All it took was a hand between them, cupping them together until Ray jerked and shuddered, and Michael felt the splash on his skin, warm and wet, and that was enough to send him over the edge with a groan.

"Next time I'm sucking you off," Ray said, his voice rough.

Michael's knees nearly gave out. "I have no problem with that."

"Good, 'cause next time is in about an hour." He pulled himself off Michael, a mess of wrinkled clothes and reddened skin, sweaty and tired and magnificent. "Water?" he offered as he shucked his clothes, leaving them piled in the hall where they fell.

"Please."

While Ray wandered bare-ass into the kitchen Michael took advantage of the bathroom, cleaning up as best he could without showering again. His pants were a wreck but his shirt remained unscathed, luckily, so he could borrow jeans and get home without embarrassing himself on the subway. He stripped down completely and joined Ray in the bedroom.

Ray couldn't help but keep a careful eye on Michael, even once he was in Ray's bed. The last person he'd slept with had bolted, and even though the circumstances were completely different he needed to make sure it wasn't him, that he wasn't the problem.

He was pretty sure he wasn't. This time. And if he walked out of the bathroom and found Michael dressed and ready to leave Ray promised himself he'd make him explain thoroughly before he let him go.

Not that he needed to worry, because Michael was looking up at him with all the energy and wariness of a sleepy panda cub and when Ray kissed him again he didn't show even the slightest interest in leaving.

It was after midnight when Michael got home, sleepy and sated and already looking forward to the next time he could see Ray. The neighbourhood was a quiet one and the street was empty of anything but the occasional car, typical for late night on a weekday.

So he almost didn't notice the bench outside his building; he'd walked past it hundreds of times without really noticing it, but this time something did catch his attention.

There was a body on it. Human, female. He took a few steps closer to assess if she was sleeping or drunk and recognized Libby's hat. Her face was covered with a scarf but he could see enough to know it was her and not just someone with a similar toque. "Libby," he said quietly, taking another step but keeping out of her reach. "Wake up."

She didn't move, and his heart jerked in his chest, but there, she was breathing. He ventured a step closer and called her name again. This time her eyelids fluttered and her hand twitched.

"Libby," he said louder this time. "Come on, wake up. It's time to go in."

She woke with a great, gasping breath, sitting upright almost faster than he could see. "Oh." She relaxed, just a bit. "It's you."

Now that she was aware of her surroundings, he came close enough to touch, kneeling before her so she wouldn't have to crane her neck. "You can come inside now. I'm going to bed." He held out his hand and she took it, standing as he did.

"Sure," she said, not letting go. He wasn't entirely sure she was completely awake yet, but the last thing he wanted was to come out here in the morning and find her frozen to the bench. The temperature had been dropping drastically, the mild few days turning back into winter. By morning there would likely be snow again.

She was oriented enough by the time they got inside that she could remove her own outer clothes. Michael was shocked to see that all she wore under her coat were flimsy flannel pyjamas. She might not have died, but her skin had been in danger. Now was not the time for a reminder; judging by her current state she hadn't been in her right mind when she went out there in the first place.

"More nightmares?" he asked.

She nodded as she pulled off a boot. "Little bit of panic attack thrown in."

"If you want to sleep on the couch, go ahead. I'll leave my door open if that'll help."

"It might, thanks." She levered herself up off the floor and dragged over to the couch, collapsing with the pillow in her arms

Michael grabbed the throw blanket and tucked it around her; it was chilly in the apartment, she must have opened a window.

"You smell good," she said, her eyes drifting closed.

"I smell like you."

"Me and sex."

He shoved the mental image that provided to the back of his head, never to be touched.

"You must have had a good time with Ray."

"I did."

She opened her eyes again, halfway. "What's he do? As a job, I mean. He works pretty strange hours."

"He's a firefighter." Michael couldn't hold back the grin.

"Wow. That explains it then."

"Which?"

"Both the schedule and the..." she searched for an appropriate word, "wonder with which you talk about him."

He ducked his head, a little dismayed at being so obvious.

"I want all the juicy details in the morning," she said, her voice tapering off into nearly nothing by the end.

Michael turned off most of the lights, leaving a dim one in the kitchen, and went to bed.

He woke again while it was still dark, and for a moment he couldn't figure out why he was awake. There was no unusual noise or light, and Jeeves was nestled into the small of his back, unmoving. Then he realized that the warmth of an extra body extended all the way up his back, not just in Jeeves's usual spot.

"Sorry," Libby said from behind him. "I'll find another option in the morning when I can think properly, okay?"

"All right. You got enough covers?"

"Yeah, thanks." She snuggled deeper into the bed, her back against his, and it was less than a minute before he heard her breathing settle into sleep.

His own sleep came less easily. Libby needed a real solution; she couldn't share his bed every night, it was ridiculous and inappropriate, but he couldn't just leave her to twist in the wind. She'd been depressed, even if she wouldn't admit it, but the more he talked about it to her the more he realized she wouldn't accept traditional help. All he could do was support her and hope she came around to the idea of spending money on medication. But this couldn't stand, he needed to have a life of his own, he needed to be able to spend the night away without worrying, he needed to be able to have Ray stay over without three in the bed.

Fifteen

Libby joined Benny in the lobby of the Artist's Factory. "You sure about this?" she asked, shedding her hat and gloves.

"I've heard you sing. You're good enough that she'll at least think about taking you on."

Benny had been hounding her for weeks, ever since she'd asked him who his teacher was. Finally she'd decided she had enough cash for a few months of remedial lessons, just to get her back on track.

Or so she told herself. She wasn't sure she wanted to know just how bad her voice had become. She could live with not knowing; rejection, well, outright rejection would mean the end of all hope.

She'd left everything she knew, everyone she loved, for the chance to sing opera. Not jazz, not pop or folk or madrigals, but opera. She'd been renounced by her own parents, robbed of love and community and any sense of belonging, just because she thought had something greater to give. If her voice failed her, if she failed the promise of her voice, what had she paid that price for?

And now she was stuck at the bottom of the stairs, unable to make her feet move.

"Do I have to hold your hand?" Benny watched her expectantly from a few steps up.

"Maybe?" She finally lifted her right foot and stepped up, telling herself that one person's opinion wasn't the opinion of everyone in the business. It was just one person, one teacher, and she had other, differing opinions to seek out. That's what she told herself all the way up the stairs and through the door.

The Factory was, in fact, a renovated factory, it looked exactly the way you'd expect: brick walls, exposed beams, enormous windows, everything Libby loved in a space. Andrea's office had dropped ceilings, though, not low like in a normal room, but low enough, and she guessed it was for the acoustics. A high ceiling like the original probably either echoed or absorbed all the sound. She'd missed that class because of kidnapping. Anatomical charts, mostly of the head, throat, and chest, decorated the walls along with photos of various productions.

Benny was introducing her, and Andrea, the teacher, looked genuinely happy to see them. "Benny's told me a lot about you," she said after he'd seen himself out. "He said you're a mezzo?"

Libby decided the best thing to do was fess up. "I'm trained as a lyric, that's where they put me at Pickford, but I've fucked my voice up by only singing a lot of folk and jazz, so I've been auditioning soubrette. My tessitura is lower than it used to be, but I think I've got more dramatic weight."

Andrea cocked her head to one side as she listened. "Let's test it."

Libby followed her over to the eight foot grand in the corner, standing to face her as she sat on bench. They ran through scales diatonic and chromatic scales, intervals and melisma, testing both her range and her comfort levels.

Finally Andrea dropped her hands into her lap and gazed at Libby, assessing. "Why are you singing so much jazz and folk?"

Libby told her the truth, about everything including being kicked out of school, which she hadn't even told Benny. When she was done, she shrugged and waited.

"Well," Andrea said eventually. "That's quite a story. So here's my professional opinion: you haven't damaged your voice, but you're on your way if you keep ignoring technique. I know most of the voice faculty at Pickford, so I know you've been taught certain methods, most of which I agree with. I'll let you know which ones I don't."

Libby had to work that out, but clearly Andrea was waiting for a response. "So you'll take me on?"

"I will. But you need to get back to your old habits. Eat properly, sleep properly, work your core, for God's sake. Support that voice, even when you're singing folk, especially when you're singing jazz. It can only help you. They may be more relaxed styles, but they can benefit from proper technique."

It was a good thing Libby was done singing, because she could barely breathe. "Right."

They worked out when her first lesson would be, and how much she would pay, which was way more than she'd hoped, and then she went down to meet Benny in the lobby.

"Told you," he said when he saw her face.

"Yeah, whatever." She tugged her hat over her head and swept past him. "Let's get out of here."

Libby was feeling so good that she invited Benny to lunch at a cafe she knew nearby, then corset shopping on Gerrard. She figured she shouldn't pay more than sixty dollars, not and be able to live with herself. It was a corset, for god's sake, not therapy or meds, and she didn't even know if it would work for her. After going to three stores she found one she liked, but they didn't carry the colour she wanted and she'd have to order it.

"I am having an awesome day," she told Benny as they left the store. "Want to come back to my place?" Michael had told her she could invite people over, but she hadn't yet tested that ability.

They'd ended up near the Eaton Centre, and she'd forgotten that the Church had a facility there, or maybe she'd never known, but there they were, walking down Yonge Street, and there it was, enormous shiny sign and all: Church of the Eternal Mother Discovery Centre.

Libby didn't even realize she'd stopped walking until someone bumped her from behind and she stumbled forward. Benny was a few steps ahead and she jogged to catch up, still staring at the building across the street. Her lunch made itself known again in the back of her throat, but she kept moving. She could do this. She wasn't cowardly enough that she couldn't walk past a building. Even this one.

She'd been by the Discovery Centre near Union Station when she first arrived in the city, mostly out of a morbid curiosity as to what they were telling people who weren't born into the life. It had been a modest storefront, which she now realized had been purposely designed to fit into the area, elegant and business-like. This one, however, took up the entire front of a building, smug and making promises aimed at harried workers and tourists looking for respite from an overwhelming city. There was a poster in the window advertising a seminar on community gardening, and another on personal sustainability, or, as the poster put it, How to Survive an Apocalypse.

"Fucking cult," Benny muttered beside her, gesturing at two women coming out of the building in their homemade wool clothing: natural dyed fabrics, felted boots, and all. "Did you read that article last month? The interview with the daughter of the founders?"

Flabbergasted was the only word that fit Libby's state of mind right then, because...Benny didn't know who she was. The article had used her name and it wasn't that common, her nickname at least, but he hadn't connected her with that poor ex-cultist.

"Benny," she said, and he noticed she'd stopped again. "Benny. I gave that interview." She was trying really hard not to use her 'wow, you're stupid' voice, but she probably slipped a little. She could be forgiven, considering how many people couldn't pass up the chance to show her they recognized her.

She pointed at the poster of the founders in front of their shiny, shiny greenhouse. "Those are my parents."

Benny laughed. "I'm shit at remembering names," he said, and began to say more but then two men their age came out of the Church and her heart seized up in her chest. Blackness crept in at the edges of her vision and she bumped into somebody as she ran, barely hearing the curses following her. She couldn't stop moving, if she did they'd catch her again, she had to get home she had to get away she had to run run run run hide. She heard, somewhere off in the distance, people shouting. Cars honked, flashed by in her periphery, but she didn't care, she had to keep going. There, she knew that place up ahead, that was good, that was great. Go there.

Sixteen

Michael was in a tedious meeting at police headquarters when his phone buzzed in his pocket. He took the excuse to leave, and he would forever be glad he did instead of ignoring it.

It was Libby. "Hey," he said, curious. "What's up?"

"Uh, hi." It was a male voice, young. "Do you know Libby?"

Shit. He tried to keep his voice steady and calm. "She lives with me."

"Oh. Uh, well, something's wrong with her, and she won't let me call an ambulance. You're her emergency number."

"Where are you?"

"Mackenzie House. The museum?"

He looked it up, grateful when it turned out to be almost directly south of him. "I can be there in ten minutes."

He ducked back into the meeting and made his excuses, citing a family emergency. His colleagues could take care of the rest. Then he took off on foot, dodging traffic when he had to. Even on a cold day the sidewalks were busy, there were too many people in the way, some sort of protest he didn't stop to identify. Then he caught a break, saw two people huddled under a tree. He got there as quickly as he could without drawing attention, slid past the little fence that roped off the yard, and found her, shaking, tears freezing on her red cheeks, a young Black man squatting beside her, holding the tips of her fingers in his.

Michael dropped to his knees in front of them, heedless of the snow, and took Libby's other hand in his. "Hey," he said softly, taking off her glove to feel her skin.

"Mike," she gasped, swallowing the rest of his name. "Do you have a gun?"

He didn't. "Why?"

She peeked around the trunk of the tree, looking west. "They're here. They saw me."

"Who?"

Libby didn't answer, just gasped for air and shook. The man patted her shoulder and Michael looked to him for a response.

He shrugged. "We were over on Yonge and we passed the Eternal Mother building, you know? Everything was fine, she was getting sarcastic at me because I didn't know she was that Libby Wyatt, and then she just started running. This is where I caught up to her and convinced her to stop. I'm Benny, by the way."

"Michael."

"So this is, what? PTSD flashback?"

"Something like that."

"And she lives with you." He sounded skeptical, and honestly, given the age difference, Michael couldn't blame him.

"Yes. Look, Benny, thanks for your help, but I should take her home now. Okay?"

"Sure. Have her call me when she's better."

Michael didn't say she might never be better, he just lifted Libby to her feet and then tried not to fall over when she threw herself at him and squeezed the life out of him. It was easy to get a cab in that part of town, but the ride was hampered a bit by the fact that she wouldn't let him go, not even when he had to fish around in his pocket for his wallet to pay the driver.

He got them both upstairs finally, and into the apartment. He detached her long enough to shed his winter gear, not expecting her to disappear around the corner.

"Little mouse, little mouse, won't you come out?" she was singing under her breath as she paced the length of the one protected wall of the living room. Her hands moved constantly, her right hand tugging at each left finger in turn, then the left doing the same to the right. He watched for a moment, just long enough to realize she wasn't going to calm on her own, not even here.

He stepped in when it looked like she was about to dislocate something, placing himself in front of her, risking being mistaken for an attacker, but he couldn't just stand there and do nothing.

She stopped, then tried to dodge around him, but he pulled her into his arms and held her tight. She relaxed almost immediately, still shaking, but no longer filled with the kind of tension that made you want to run or fight.

"God," she gasped into his shoulder. "Help me, I don't know what to do, I can't think, I can't breathe."

"Okay." He stroked her hair, desperate for a solution, then he remembered the look she had during the class, when he was binding her arms. He drew the scarf from around her neck and, catching her gaze, asked, "Can I tie you up for a minute?"

She nodded shakily, then replied, "Let's see."

He looped the scarf, an awkward, thick knit, around her wrist then wrapped it around her body, tightened it, then knotted it at her other wrist. It was poorly secured and wouldn't last long, but with her arms forced to her sides it mimicked a hug. He guided her to sit on the couch. "Let me get my real ropes."

When he got back with ropes and sharp scissors Jeeves had jumped up on her lap and was sniffing her face, kneading her chest as he did. "Good boy," Michael told him while setting him aside.

He unwrapped her with one hand, keeping a strong grip on her arm with the other. "Let's get your coat off, I want you to be comfortable."

She stripped out of her coat and sweater while he levered her boots off. "Lie down," he said, "and let me know if you want a pillow or something."

To his surprise she went to the floor instead of the couch, but that only made it easier for him to manoeuvre so he said nothing. He started with her wrists, copying what he'd done in class, but faster, with fewer decorative embellishments. "What happened?"

"It was them."

"Who?"

"The guys," she said, digging her heel into the floorboards, "They came out of the church building, just like they were normal people."

"Wait." He stopped what he was doing and leaned over to see her face properly.

"No, don't stop. I need this."

"Okay, but are you saying they were your kidnappers?"

"Yes."

Michael continued the repetition of wrap, knot, wrap, pleased as she relaxed incrementally with each iteration. "You're telling me your kidnappers are with your old church."

She nodded. "They came out. They were dressed like members."

"And this was the first indication you had?"

She closed her eyes and didn't answer.

He tried not to be angry with her, not until he got the whole story. "I'll finish here, then I'll call Strickland, but she might want to talk to you."

"Not today. I can't go out again today." She shook her head violently, as if unable to stop, and Michael set himself to work more calmly, trying to capture some of Claudine's steadiness and confidence. Confidence he didn't feel, working as he was with a real person for only the second time, one who was in distress he couldn't easily curtail. He reached her waist and must have hesitated, because she said, "Keep going," in a drowsy voice, so he kept going.

As she relaxed he was reluctant to ask her to move body parts for him, so he leaned over to look her in the eye again, stunned at how glazed she looked already. "Okay if I touch your legs? Your thighs?"

She nodded once, slightly, but that was enough. He continued down, a tight weave down her waist and hips, her thighs down to her knees, where he stopped. She appeared to be asleep and didn't object when he backed away.

He grabbed his phone quickly and came back to her, intent on calling Strickland and then Claudine.

To her surprise Libby didn't have a nightmare that night, for probably the first time since she started sleeping more than an hour at once.

She'd heard Michael talking, first in what she thought of as cop talk, then another call that was gentler, quieter. He'd roused her after that, making sure she was still good, that she could wiggle her fingers and toes, then left her to make dinner. He only released her, roused her, when it was time to eat. She ate wrapped in a blanket on the couch, watching PBS and talking about things that had nothing to do with how her day went.

She went to bed early, leaving the door open so the cat could come and go. She'd noticed the first time she was here that having the cat nearby, even just wandering around, let her sleep better. Having him on the bed was even better. Her nightmares had tailed off from terrifying replays of her kidnapping to anxiety dreams where she couldn't get to the top of a set of stairs.

The morning was good, although her face heated up when she saw the ropes and remembered the feel of Michael's hands on her, lifting her hips, grazing her thighs, never lingering, but enough to make her shy when she saw him at breakfast.

She tried to act normally, because the last thing she wanted was for him to think he'd injured her in any way. "So what did Faith have to say?" she asked eventually, needing to distract herself from the low level arousal humming at her.

"She wants to see you today, get a better description." He refilled her coffee, and she noticed he was still in his flannels and t-shirt instead of dressed for work. "I'll take you."

"Thanks." She didn't want to be alone, again, ever. "You know, you skip out on work a lot for me."

He laughed. "I have an agreement with the boss. And I'm just the guy who collects information. Yesterday I was in the meeting from hell. You did me a favour."

"Fuck you," she said, grinning. "Using my pain for your own pleasure." That hit a little too close to making her blush again, so she covered her face with her coffee mug.

To her great surprise she saw his face start to pink up, before he turned away to grab another bagel.

"Were you talking to Ray last night? After Faith?"

"No, it was Claudine. Adria." He busied himself splitting the bagel and slathering on cream cheese. "I needed some advice." He sat down opposite her. "I've never done this, you know. I only took the class in the first place because Claudine had some books around and the pictures were pretty." He shrugged. "And I like knots."

"Well." Libby cleared her throat to buy time. She really didn't know how to respond to such a confession. "I'm happy to act as your canvas, if you want."

He looked up. "Can I take pictures? No, wait, don't answer that, that was terrible."

But Libby had no problem with the idea. She'd done some research herself, and she'd seen both the uncomfortably sexual poses and the more evocative ones. "As long as it's tasteful porn."

The snort he let out then, his mouth full of bagel, was the least elegant thing she'd ever seen him do. But she'd made him laugh and that was pretty awesome.

Seventeen

Libby didn't take her time getting ready. She'd become an expert at making herself presentable in tight spaces and with little time, and she really just wanted to get this over with. She knew Michael did too, even though he didn't say so.

They took a cab to the police station, where Faith came to meet them almost immediately, ushering them to her desk.

Libby told her the whole story, from stopping in front of the church building to Michael meeting her in the park. She gave descriptions again, and looked at the sketches that had been done in Cobourg, making sure they matched. "So what now?" she asked when they'd gone over it all.

"Now you go home and we'll find them. We may not have names, but we know where they work."

A horrible realization swept over Libby. "It wasn't them, was it? I mean, it wasn't their idea to kidnap me." It had to have come from higher up. But why? Why would they do such a thing?

Some part of Libby, deep in the back of her brain, had always figured that she could go home, that if she did she'd be greeted with forgiveness and love. That she'd get back the family she lost when she left. But no. They hated her, they wanted to punish her. And they should, because she had betrayed everything they stood for. And so what if some of that stuff needed betraying because it was wrong or dangerous? She could have worked that out from inside, fixed it instead of throwing out all the good with the bad.

She'd come to a big city full of cars and other pollutants. She'd bought items with ridiculous carbon footprints just because they were cheap or new to her. Shoes, mangoes, nail polish, milk from factory-farmed cows, long showers, did she really need any of it? She flew in a plane to a competition once. Her planned career involved a lot more flying, more than the average Canadian.

She was the enemy, now.

But they could have just let her be, just one more deluded person who needed re-educating. Instead they'd done the worst to her. They'd drugged her. They'd left her alone. They'd made her eat meat.

She stood, nearly knocking her chair over. "I have to get to work soon."

Libby felt bad about being so abrupt as she hurried out, but she had to get out of there. She'd been trying to hold it together, but the idea was catching up to her, making her shake with rage and betrayal, because how dare they? This family who raised her, who she trusted for nearly twenty years, how could they do that to her? All she'd done was try to be her best self, and isn't that what they taught her? She'd come to understand over the years that the idea of 'best self' meant 'what we say is right' and she thought she'd gotten over how irrational it was, but it still hurt to think about.

She sat down on the sidewalk, back against the building. She'd left her coat inside, stupid in this weather, and the concrete and brick were icy, but she couldn't move, could barely think. Her eyes stung as her tears froze and she was hot, swollen, like she was going to break out of her skin. She wanted to rage, to destroy something, anything, even her hand against the brick, if only she could move.

Hands touched her shoulders, drew her close. She fought, struggled without seeing until she was wrapped in an embrace and the scent hit her – Michael's cologne. She struggled against him anyway, embracing the stress on her muscles, the way his arms tightened and made her fight harder but still didn't let her go. She finally was able to relax, lay her head against his chest, and everything became a warm, welcoming fog, like the last few seconds before falling asleep.

He said something to her that she didn't register.

"Muh?"

"Put your coat on."

"Can't. Inside."

"I brought it." He let go and she nearly fell forward, catching herself only as the cold hit her again. He held the coat for her as she slipped into the sleeves, then dug around in the pockets for her hat and mittens.

"Thanks." Bundled up again properly she was still cold; her wool pants and the back of her sweater were wet from sitting in the snow, but her fingers and ears were starting to get the feeling back. Her nose was going to start running any moment now and that was gonna suck because she didn't know where her hanky was.

"Where do you need to be?"

She had to think about it, her mind still fuzzy. "I lied. I don't have to work until later."

"Libby." He paused. "Is that the only thing you lied about?"

She let her head fall back against the wall. "I'm so tired, Michael."

"I know." He hadn't moved, his hands still on her shoulders.

"I think I knew they were church members?" Her throat ached with tears and stress. "I'm not sure. Some part of me must have, right?"

He leaned forward, pressing a warm kiss to her forehead. "We don't always know what we know."

"I'm sorry if I made things harder."

He slipped his hand around behind her and coaxed her away from the wall. "Come back inside."

"So I don't really think they waited a year because they couldn't find her. I think they waited because the new year is symbolic." Faith was being all Detective Strickland, explaining what had happened to someone who looked like a boss type. They all sat around a conference table, Faith at the head, Libby and Michael back by the door so she could leave again if she had to.

"I think you're right," Libby said, speaking for the first time since joining them again. "New Year's is a time of change," she told them, practically quoting the doctrine she'd been raised on. "They love change: growth, becoming something new, something more. Better than ordinary humans. It's the most important celebration of the year. It's also the day my mother got the idea for the church."

"So they kidnapped you for what? They wouldn't ransom you back to their own members, would they?"

Libby stared at Michael. "Did you even read the article?"

He shrugged. "It felt too personal. Too intimate."

"It was published in an international, highly-regarded news magazine with a readership of millions," she said. "It's not my lingerie drawer."

"No, it's just a painful period of your life."

"So tell me your most painful moment and then go read it."

"I'll think about it."

"Why try a second time?" Faith's boss interrupted, getting them back on topic. "Revenge for the article?"

"Maybe?" Libby hadn't planned on mentioning her punishment theory, but now that it was on the table she couldn't deny it. "Maybe they were trying to indoctrinate me again. Getting me back would negate the article. I could say it was all lies, I was cashing in on my fame."

Faith tapped the table with her pen thoughtfully. "And you're sure it was them?"

"Yes. There were a few things nagging at me after I talked to you. The first pair, they seemed familiar at first. Not like I'd met them ever, but like when you see the sibling of someone you know and you can't pinpoint why you think you know them. You know?"

"You're saying they're from the Picton congregation?"

"Okay, so not like a sibling. Maybe like how you can always tell a dancer by the way they stand." She checked out their puzzled faces. "Or maybe not."

"No, I get what you mean," Faith said. "Every group develops characteristics that identify them to others. But what are those characteristics in this case?"

"Arrogance? Self-assurance? They wore normal clothes, so I don't know. I was inside the group for too long and then not exposed to them at all. I can't tell."

"They never approached you here?"

"I was excommunicated. They weren't allowed to acknowledge my existence. And I did my best to avoid them when I knew where they were."

"I wonder if we could get membership information with photos."

She snorted. "Good luck. I might still have access, but there aren't photos. Which is surprising, really, because we had strict physical standards to maintain. Or reach, in most cases." Libby had always been a little too plump, a little too soft for their ideals. She'd never tasted caramel or fudge until college. Or hamburgers, but that was more about the animal-friendly diet than about her perceived fat. She shuddered at the memory of a month of fast food burgers. How could they do that and still call themselves loyal members? "So here's a question," she began, then laid out the burger conundrum to Faith and Michael.

"Maybe they're just bad vegetarians," Michael said.

"Or they had to feed you out of their own pockets and that was cheaper and easier than obeying the church law," Faith added. "The higher-ups didn't want a paper trail."

"Plus even they're cheap," Libby added. "I mean, if they wanted to give us a rule-change handout we had to pay for it. And that hemp paper is expensive."

Faith sighed. "We can't even assume the administration was in on it. What if it was personal? Maybe they wanted to make nice to her mother. Get promoted."

"They had long enough to do whatever it was they wanted," Michael said, "but they didn't."

"I did miss a week in my tally." Libby shrugged at their reactions. "I don't know, maybe they mastered mind control. Were there any banks robbed in the area that week?"

Michael laughed, at least. Faith kind of glared at her and Libby shrugged. "It just feels really stupid to me, okay? What could they possibly gain by getting me back except to punish me? They were the ones who kicked me out in the first place."

"That's what I'm going to find out," Faith replied. "That's why we're going to send someone out to take some pictures, then we'll call you in and see if you recognize them." She rapped her desk with her knuckles. "Then we'll ask them that question."

Michael went off to work, then, and Libby was shocked to realize it was only ten AM and she could still make her hours at St George Station. She needed to go home quickly, but she could make it with enough time to set up before the lunch rush.

If she kept busy enough, maybe she'd stop twitching every time she saw two blond guys together.

That night she went to bed as usual, leaving the door open so Jeeves could join her, but every time she drifted off she'd jerk awake again, heart pounding, convinced she was back there.

She got up and turned a night light on, a little one she'd bought with the kind of embarrassment that means you think people can read your mind. It didn't help.

Lying flat on her back with her pillow clutched to her chest helped, and she did sleep, but the nightmare she had was terrifying enough that her own scream woke her. She waited, panting, listening for anything that meant she'd woken Michael up, but all she heard was her own pulse pounding in her ears, her own breath rasping. Jeeves came in to check on her and she didn't protest when he settled himself on her sternum, tucking his head under her chin. But even the weight and living warmth and the buzz of his purr couldn't calm her, couldn't stop her from jumping at every noise, sure they were here to take her away again.

There was a noise outside her room, Michael getting up, and Jeeves abandoned her. She fell back into the jerky half-sleep she'd lived with for so long.

The next time she woke up was from the same damn nightmare, the one where she was trapped in a room the size of a closet, screaming voicelessly while sirens passed her by. "This is stupid," she said to her ceiling. "How is it possible that finding my abductors is fucking with me so much?"

She saw movement before the shadow at her door, followed by a soft knock. "Did you say something?" Michael asked.

Libby sat up, then folded her legs under her as she turned to face him. "Not to you. Just...," she waved her hand at the ceiling, "trying to work stuff out."

He leaned against the door frame. "Do you need anything?"

"Sleep?" She patted the bed beside her. "Come in if you want."

He did, and settled where she'd indicated. She was slightly behind him, so she couldn't see anything but the edge of his face, the corner of his eye, the curve of his chin. "I keep waking up thinking I'm back there, alone. Did I tell you that for a long time I couldn't fall asleep if I was alone?"

"No."

"I had to be in public. I slept in the library, in the lounges, on benches in the park. Under trees, pretending like I'd been studying and I'd fallen asleep like any student might. It was so quiet, in that farmhouse. I liked having background noise afterwards. Cars and people. Fountains. Dogs barking."

"Music?"

She shook her head. "Music and movies are in my head, they were the only thing that kept me sane that whole time. They don't help." She leaned her shoulder against his. "Then there's the smell. Dust and mould. Fast food. I can't walk past a McDonald's without feeling sick. But grass, car exhaust, asphalt, that's all good. Comforting."

Michael looked over at her window, firmly closed and locked. "And yet you don't open your window."

"You're paying the heating bill, not me. I didn't think it was my place."

He turned unexpectedly towards her, causing her weight to shift enough that she nearly fell into his lap. He caught her with a hand at her waist. "Do what you need to. I don't care. I'll turn down the heat and get out more blankets, if necessary."

Sighing, she took advantage of him and leaned back into his chest. "Why are you so nice to me? You've done so much, but I'm not your responsibility. Not since you handed me over to the EMTs."

His hold on her tightened, and his hand slid farther around her, coming to rest on her stomach just below her ribs. "I'm told I have a hero problem. I need to rescue people."

She pulled away a little to see his face in the weak light. "So it's not just me?" she teased.

"Sorry. You're not the first. It's why I joined the police force, and partly why I left, too." There was something sad in his expression, so she didn't push for details. She knew he had a wife who died, there wasn't much more she needed to know.

"Well, thanks. I'm not sure I've said that properly, yet." Her eyes were drifting shut now, and that familiar and scary relaxation was drifting over her.

"You're more than welcome," he said, as she fell asleep against his warmth.

Michael woke with the sun in his eyes. He closed them again and pulled the pillow he was clutching closer to his chest. His pillow sighed, which was weird, he must be dreaming. Come to think of it, the sun was weird, too, because his window didn't face east. And he usually closed his blinds.

His pillow shifted, settling back against him. He breathed in deeply, smelling perfume, something bright with a bit of smoke. He leaned into it and encountered long hair, which woke him up completely. He was in Libby's room, her bed, that's why it was so strange, and she was in his arms, asleep. He didn't know what time it was, but it was late enough that the winter sun was strong. They'd been asleep for hours without any nightmares.

Michael hadn't slept with a woman in his arms, in his bed, since Jeanine. It was comfortable. Too comfortable, perhaps, considering his current level of arousal. He felt like an idiot, a creep, for being turned on by Libby, who relied on him. But she was also a gorgeous woman who was determined not to rely on him, who would, one day, regain her life properly. She wasn't just physically attractive, but admirable.

He should move, but he didn't want to wake her. Based on what she'd told him at three AM she hadn't had a good night's sleep in ages, aside from the night he tied her up. He flushed at the memory of how she looked wrapped in his ropes, of the patterns left on her skin when he released her. He felt like an asshole, possessive of her, when all she wanted was his help.

She sighed again, and shifted until his erection was pressed against her rounded ass, and okay, now he really had to get up, no matter if she woke. He slid back, glad that he wasn't against the wall. His right arm was trapped between them, not under her, so all he had to do was remove the arm draped over her. He wiggled the fingers of his left hand, testing the grip she had on him, and realized he'd have to slide his hand down and out of her hand, along her sternum, hopefully not touching her any more inappropriately than he already was. He managed, eventually, creeping backward off the bed until his feet hit the floor.

She turned over before he got out the door, but he didn't think she woke.

It was already past eight, late for him, especially considering he'd taken a chunk of yesterday morning off. If he hurried he could still get to work by nine-thirty. If he stayed late he could get caught up. He'd been combing through databases and going through trial transcripts, so his work wasn't vital to anyone's safety, but he still wanted to get it done before the next case came up.

He was putting on coffee when Libby came out of her room, still sleepy-eyed and in pyjamas. "Hey," she said, before coming up and leaning on the counter beside him. "Did you sleep in my room last night?"

"Yeah, I fell asleep shortly after you did." He glanced at her, afraid of what she'd say. "It was inappropriate and I'm sorry."

"No, hey, it's fine. I slept great, actually." She scratched at her head. "When did you get up?"

"Just a few minutes ago."

She chuckled. "Oh, wow. I did sleep well if I didn't even notice."

"You were pretty out of it. I tried to get up after you fell asleep but you wouldn't let me, you just pulled me down with you, without even being conscious."

"I'm a cuddler," she said, amused.

Michael finished putting together the coffee and backed away from her. "I'm going to shower and then I have to get to work. What are you up to today?"

"Waiting for Detective Faith to call me and ask me to identify some assholes. Rain's coming over later to keep me from going batshit."

"Good luck with that." He caught the packet of filters she threw before it hit his face.

Eighteen

Libby hadn't told Michael because she didn't want to jinx it, but her next audition wasn't for an opera, it was for the scholarship committee at Pickford. She hadn't been planning on it, not at first, but then Dinah got a job, a real one, in the chorus at Opera Toronto and Libby got both insanely jealous and deeply depressed at her options.

She was nervous, but her lessons had brought her nearly back to where she'd been when she left school and she'd slept amazingly these past couple of weeks. Michael had been binding her in various ways in the evenings, trying to find out just how little would calm her enough to rest. They'd worked out a deal where he'd tie her up and she'd only sneak into his bed if she was desperate to sleep.

So she felt fucking fantastic and she looked nearly as good in her audition dress, which finally fit again. Even her hair was perfectly curled. She was going to rock this audition, get back into school, and get her life back.

She recognized almost everyone on the committee when she took the stage. They were all smiling politely; she had no idea if any recognized her, and if they did, whether that was bad or good. She smiled back at them, projecting strength and energy as well as she knew how, hoping she hadn't lost that inner vibrancy they'd praised so highly at her first audition.

"My name is Elizabeth Wyatt," she announced when the committee head gave her a nod. "I'm a soprano with a focus in opera." She went on to list everyone she'd studied under, a list which included some of her former and hopefully future professors. "I also have strong interests in jazz music and conducting."

The man at the end of the row looked up. "Jazz and opera, two very disparate styles. How will you handle that?"

Libby had decided it was best not to mention her job. She might not have it for long anyway. "My first love is always opera, but I've spent the last year expanding both my singing repertoire and my personal collection."

Another woman wrote something in pen on her notes, then asked, "Why do you want to attend the Pickford School?"

She'd planned for this, she'd written an emotional little speech and memorized it. Now she just hoped she didn't mess it up. "I have already been a student here, and I want to come back."

The man at the end nodded vigorously. "I thought I recognized your name."

Libby carefully didn't look any one of them in the eye as she spoke, but kept her gaze roving across the level of their eyebrows. "A little over a year ago I was kidnapped and held for over a month. I came back to my life at Pickford hoping that nothing had changed." Her mouth was suddenly dry, so she took a sip from her bottle of water before continuing. "But I had changed. Not only had I missed several weeks of classes but I was an emotional wreck. I tried my hardest to catch up, to keep up my standing, but I couldn't. I failed two classes and you made the only decision you could: to revoke my scholarship and give it to someone who would make better use of it. But as you can see I'm healthy again. I have excellent support and I'm as focused and driven as I was before the kidnapping. I won't fail again."

The other man spoke up. "I have your application here, but I'd like to hear it from you directly. Why do you need this scholarship?"

She took another deep breath and tried to look confident. "I have nothing. I was excommunicated from my religious commune for daring to want higher education. My parents disinherited me and refuse to acknowledge my existence. I work two jobs, which pay for my voice lessons and basic living expenses. I have no other recourse."

"And what will you be performing today?" the head asked, and Libby could have kissed her for changing the subject. She was smiling, too, a real smile, and that gave Libby a little boost.

She'd already given her sheet music to the pianist, so she nodded to her and stated, "*Venite, inginocchiatevi*, from *Le Nozze di Figaro*."

The piece was short, fairly simple, still within her soubrette range, and most importantly, fun. She'd picked it because she remembered talking to her classmates about their various audition pieces and they'd almost all picked the heavy, dramatic stuff. She wanted the judges to feel good when she sang.

And bonus, her Italian pronunciation was really good now. Michael had started shouting corrections every time she fumbled in his presence, so she knew what she was doing there.

She pulled it off. She sounded great, hit every note and every emotional state. She could practically see the other characters in the scene she was playing. She finished, curtseyed to the judges, thanked her pianist and retrieved her music, and walked out, just barely managing to make it to a bench before her throat closed up.

Her breath came noisily, echoing through the hall, growing worse as the vise tightened around her windpipe. Her vision greyed out so she did the only thing she could think of, she took a swallow of water. The pressure began to ease; her neck still throbbed but her breathing came more easily. "Wow, what an exciting new development!" she murmured to herself, and was shocked to find talking helped. She sat for a bit longer, recovering, and looked up what happened on her phone.

Laryngospasm, the internet told her, brought on by anxiety. At least it had hit after her audition, not before. PTSD sucked. But she already knew that.

She had a lesson soon, which was great because she had to talk to someone about her audition and Andrea was the only one she'd told. The fewer people she told now the fewer she'd have to have that awkward, 'Whoops, I failed!' conversation with.

Her phone rang and she didn't bother to look up at the caller, she just pressed green. "Hello."

"Libby, this is Detective Strickland."

Libby got up and found a quiet spot outside, where she wouldn't be overheard. "What can I do for you?"

"We've got two suspects here for you to identify."

Holy shit.

"Libby?"

"Uh, yeah. When do you need me there?" Her throat started to tighten again and she swallowed a few times to loosen it up.

"How's eight tomorrow morning?"

Libby blanked on her schedule, but she'd drop everything even if she remembered it. "Sure. Do I need to bring anything?"

"You might want to bring a friend. This could be difficult for you."

"I won't have to talk to them, will I?"

Faith gave her a long spiel about how safe she'd be and how they'd never know she was there, but Libby's brain was spinning too fast to catch most of it. "Okay, thanks," she said during a pause, hoping that was enough. "See you then."

She didn't tell Michael this, either. As she came home from her lesson he was just leaving to go to work; they'd gotten a case and from the look on his face it was a bad one. "They're all bad ones," he'd told her when she'd commented. "I'm going out of town tonight to talk to the family. I should be back tomorrow."

"I'll be fine on my own," she said, more out of hope than certainty.

She went through her usual evening routine, trying not to think about how empty the apartment was. She had Jeeves. She could turn on music, cook something that made the place smell good. She could just calm the fuck down.

So she turned on the music and cooked dinner and read a book with a cat on her lap, wrapped tightly in a blanket. She had a glass of wine, then another. When she went to bed she left the lights on, her bedroom door open, and all the windows cracked.

She slept, eventually, fitfully, but without nightmares – at least that she could remember. Morning brought a profound sense of relief with it. She felt like crap, but at least she had ways to keep herself occupied during the day, ways that included other people.

Except one of those ways included the absolute last people she wanted to see again. She texted Michael: Will putting those guys in jail make me feel better? Because he would know, right?

He replied: Maybe. Everyone reacts differently.

Not helpful at all, but she didn't bother telling him that. He probably figured that out.

Bring a friend, Faith had said, and Libby thought maybe of all her friends Rain deserved to be there. It was still early, she wouldn't be in classes yet.

Rain answered immediately. "Libby, what's up?"

She couldn't muster small talk right now. "The police want me to go identify some guys. Will you come with me?"

She didn't even have to finish her question. "What time and where?" Rain asked, with all the confidence and determination that had abandoned Libby.

Instead of meeting at the station Rain came to the apartment. She'd only been there once before but she knew her way around like it was her own, making Libby some chamomile tea to calm her and asking questions about her auditions to distract her.

"Thanks for calling me," she said eventually, as they sat together on the couch.

"It seemed like a good idea," Libby replied. "I wasn't sure if you'd want to be that involved, though."

"Honestly?" She sipped her own tea before continuing. "It's frightening. But it must be worse for you so of course I'd come."

Libby slumped over, leaning her face against the couch back. "You take such good care of me." Even at the beginning, when Libby was just learning how to cope outside in the real world, Rain had treated her with respect and helped her along, even quizzing her on slang and pop culture. "Sometimes I wish I could take care of you, too, but then I'm glad you don't have any reason for it."

Rain laughed. "All the times you sat and listened to my terrible monologues are enough."

Finally it was time to go down to the station. The trip was nearly an hour, but Rain kept Libby entertained the whole way by making her listen to random snippets of podcasts, which weren't a thing Libby was into except that Rain wanted her to be.

Faith met them at the front desk and took Libby back to an area she'd never seen. She tried not to look anyone in the eye as she passed; even though she'd lived here for a few years she still sometimes felt like the sheltered farm girl she'd once been. That they'd tried to make her into again.

At that moment her terror was swallowed up by anger. They'd tried to steal her away from the life she'd made, to take her back to the place where she was hated, ridiculed, where she—everything she was, everything she could be—was wasted. "I'm a good person," she said, mostly to herself. "I try to live a good life."

Faith glanced at her, curious. "Many of us do."

"And yet, it's not enough for them. Which is funny, because their way of life isn't enough for me. They called me selfish, you know that? My parents, the community. It's why they kicked me out in the first place. I made them do it. I wanted them to do it so I could be free. They're wrong, not me."

"From what I've heard, they're very wrong," Faith said. "Even aside from kidnapping and forcible confinement."

"So what I still don't understand is why they want me back." She flexed her rib cage, feeling the tight press of her new corset holding her together. The rush of her thoughts calmed a little, enough to let her recover.

"That's what I'm hoping to find out when I question them." They stopped so Faith could open a steel door and usher Libby in. She'd expected a one-way window with a bunch of men standing on the other side, a live identification, but a uniformed officer stood beside a table laid with photos, three rows of four, 4x6 colour headshots. Tension she hadn't know possessed her drained away. Libby scanned across the rows; they were all blondish men about her age, with roughly the same features. It must have taken work to find that many men to make up the extra ten.

But only one made her heart stop. "That one," she said, looking at the edge of the photo rather than at the face. "Bottom row, third one."

"Are you sure?"

"Absolutely."

"And the other one?"

She examined them again, avoiding the one guy. The eyes of one looked familiar, the mouth of another, but she'd couldn't say for sure. "I don't think he's here."

Faith cleared the photo and the officer laid out another set, these all dark haired. "How about here?"

Again, they all looked kind of familiar. "I don't know. If I could hear their voices, maybe, but it's hard to tell with pictures."

"It's all right. I doubt this guy will be hard to pressure. He'll tell us everything."

The officer led Libby out to the desk and that was it. She hugged Rain, hard, thankful that she was done. All she had to do now was wait for the police to do their jobs and find the rest of them.

Nineteen

Michael didn't get back to the city until early the next morning, exhausted from driving but unwilling to stay away even those few extra hours. He stumbled up the stairs, managing halfway before realizing he'd dropped a glove right at the bottom. He didn't care enough to go back for it; he'd get it later.

The door opened after only a little fumbling with his key, but it opened from the inside. "Hey," he said, leaning against the jamb. "How'd you know it was me?"

Libby grabbed his upper arm and pulled him in. "Your keys make a distinctive noise. Also you were talking to yourself."

"Huh. I really need to sleep." He dropped his stuff on the bench in the hall and took off his shoes, leaving them where they lay.

"You really do." She still had a hand on his arm, steadying him. "Did you help some people today?"

"I don't know, maybe." Michael managed to make it to the couch, where he collapsed at one end. He pulled the throw pillow from behind his back and settled in.

The cushion beside him sank down, and only then did he notice he'd let his eyes close. "Well, I identified one of my kidnappers today. Yesterday."

Michael opened his eyes to examine her expression. "You don't look relieved."

She shrugged. "It was only the one. There are still a few more, plus whoever hired them."

"But still, it's progress." The room went dark again.

"Faith says he should cave pretty quickly when she questions him."

"Good."

Warmth spread over his shoulder and squeezed. "Okay, well, you should go to bed."

"Mmm."

"Michael?"

He raised his right arm and she squirmed into his embrace. Her weight melted against him and he fell asleep.

Libby finished her book and dropped it on the floor, the only flat surface she could reach. She had her head on the pillow, which was now on Michael's lap, and could look up at him as he slept, his face soft and relaxed. Classic jawline combined with soft cheeks. Hairline slightly receding, but it looked okay because he kept it so short. His arm was around her waist, his head was dropped forward, as if he might kiss her, and....

Oh, fuck. She really wanted him to.

Was White Knight Syndrome really a thing? Was she only grateful to him, or was this real? And did it matter? He probably thought of her as a kid who needed his help, a way to make up for something in his past, maybe. His wife, something had gone bad with her.

And oh, wow, that was something else. He'd been married. He'd had real relationships, not just fuckbuddies and month-long sprees of dance clubs and sex. He was in a relationship, one that had potential. She needed to chill the fuck out.

She dug her phone out of her pocket to check the time – not even noon yet. She texted a quick question to Stuart and got a quick answer yes. Michael's arm was heavy and slack when she picked it up to roll off him, but he didn't wake. A shower, some food, and then a train ride to Stu's and she'd get over this stupid, childish crush on the person she could count on most.

Michael was still asleep when she got out of the shower, so she took pity on him and shook him gently. "Hey, get up and go to bed."

He blinked up at her, a small smile gracing his mouth. "Nope, can't."

"Then at least stretch out on the couch. I'm not going to massage your neck for you later. I have to work."

He did, putting his feet up and sliding down against the arm rest. "Hmm. Tell Claudine to call me back."

"Sure, if I see her." He was already asleep again.

She got back several hours later, a swing in her hips and a smile on her face.

"Is that what I look like after seeing Ray?" Michael asked as she flopped sideways into the big armchair.

"Is there a sappy look on my face?"

"Less sappy, more smug."

"Then I look only half like you look." She kicked one foot in the air and settled her head on the arm rest.

"It's true, you're only half as pretty as I am."

She snorted. "You wish."

"You've got kind of a big nose."

Her reply consisted entirely of raising her eyebrows and pointing at his hairline.

"Your+ lips are way too full."

She tilted her head so she could face him. "Seriously? That's the best you could do?"

He shrugged. "You're hideous, what can I say?" He raised his book up to hide his face, but she saw that smile anyway.

"How on earth did I end up with you as my best friend?" She dug under her hips for the soft toy fish she'd sat on.

"Clearly you're cursed."

She threw the fish at him, dropping it into his book. "So when do I get to meet Firefighter Ray?"

"When do I get to meet whoever put that smug look on your face?"

"Never. He's just a friend I busk with sometimes." She waggled her eyebrows at him.

His mouth dropped open slightly as he thought it through. "Stuart? Was that his name?"

"Yup." She kept her eyes on the upholstery.

The fish landed on her face. She brushed it off to the floor.

"He's pretty cute."

"I know, right?" She sat up and faced him. "He's adorable. Can't lie to save his life, but I like that. It's unusual." You had to learn how to lie at The Farm. It was the only way to survive. "And don't think I didn't notice you changing the subject away from Ray."

"Our schedules don't mesh that well, even without adding in yours." He slid to the floor and grabbed the fish back. At some point while she was gone he'd changed into a soft grey hooded sweatshirt and jeans. His feet were bare.

"Your toes are knobbly," she told him.

"I'm thinking of coming out at work."

"Non sequitur for the win." Then it hit her, what he said. "I'm sorry. I do actually remember what you said about the last time you were out at work."

He scrunched his face up in dismay. "Is it stupid to be worried? My boss would never hold it against me. I don't know that anyone else there is gay, but it's not like I socialize with most of them."

"What's the worst that could happen?" It was a genuine question. She actually didn't know the answer to that.

"That's the problem, I don't know. I'm not on the force anymore, and that's when it was worst. But even an uncomfortable work environment might not be worth it."

The answer seemed obvious to Libby. "So maybe you should socialize with them more. Get a feel for how they'd react."

He sighed and leaned back. "Maybe. They are predisposed to like Ray, since he brought breakfast back at Christmas."

"Wait, your co-workers have met Ray and I haven't? I am deeply insulted."

"He's too pretty." Michael was clearly joking, his tone gave him away. "I'm afraid you two will run away together."

"It's funny, but I've never had any luck with gay guys."

"I wonder why."

A completely awesome idea struck Libby. "Hey, you know what we should do?"

"I'm frightened already," Michael replied.

"We should have a dinner party. Adria, your boss, a couple of other people you work closely with. You can cook for them, and also feel them out about Ray."

He frowned, idly tapping the fish against his knee. "And how do we explain you?"

What? "What do you mean?"

"We're in a pretty strange situation here."

She really wasn't following him. "As roommates?"

"We're not exactly usual." He paused, then started ticking facts off on his fingers. "Our age difference, our different jobs, interests...how would we possibly have met?"

Libby squinted at him, as if it would make his intent clearer. "Why can't we tell the truth?"

"Well, first off, it's pretty strange. 'Yeah, I found her in this abandoned house so I brought her home to live with me.' Second, do you really want that story to be the first thing people know about you?"

She slid down to the floor opposite him. "It's the first thing people usually know about me. At least this way I can control the way it's told. We can make it sound like a wacky sitcom, if we want." She realized something and had to fight back the panic it caused. "Could this get you in trouble?" Her breathing escalated, her heart pounding without her permission. "Did you break some sort of code that could get you fired?"

"No, Libby," he took her hand as he spoke, "nothing like that. It just looks bad, that's all. The power differential...." It was like he was struggling to explain.

"What? Wait, you think they'll assume we're sleeping together? That's the only thing I can think of that would bring power into it. Unless you've been telling everyone you like to tie me up."

She could still bring that flush to his cheeks by talking about it. It was adorable. "No, of course not."

His hand still held hers, so she gave it a squeeze. "I don't care if they think that. Do you?"

"I'm afraid it will undermine my integrity."

"Ouch." She said it to joke, but it did hurt, just a bit, that people thought she couldn't make her own decisions. "Look, someone's going to make assumptions, and probably soon. Why not have some people over, they can meet me, we'll show them we have a healthy relationship of whatever kind. That way when less...charitable people find out you'll have them on your side. Right?"

He nodded. "I guess that goes for coming out too, doesn't it?"

"Well, they are more likely to slap you on the back and congratulate you for sleeping with me than with Ray."

"You haven't seen Ray."

"And we're back to this. Set it up, buddy, or I'll follow you on one of your dates."

"You wouldn't."

She took her hand back and placed it on her chest with a shocked gasp. "Michael? We had plans and now I find you here?" Her lower lip wobbled. "Who is he, Michael?"

"Oh, Jesus, no, please don't do that. No point in embarrassing yourself."

"Then set it up already."

"Fine. But I'm doing it on a day you have terrible hair."

"And you'll think about the dinner?"

"I'll think about the dinner."

Libby went to the club early that night; she had to talk to her accompanist, Taylor, about some new music, and now that she wasn't hiding something as huge as being homeless she felt free to come and go, to spend time chatting with the others.

It was a relief, having a job with people she liked, people she could trust to have her back. The museum had been fun, but she'd always been a bit out of place. The others were history students, most of whom had lived in the GTA their whole lives. An opera student from a farm in Prince Edward County, who'd only been exposed to pop culture for a few months when she got the job, didn't exactly fit in. These people, on the other hand, who'd chosen work they couldn't talk about in public, who'd chosen to follow their souls in spite of what their families and friends would say if they knew, they came from varied backgrounds. Libby was unique, sure, but not odd. She was an object of empathy, not pity or derision.

The locker room was empty when she got there, but the bench had a newspaper on it, open to page five. POLICE MAKE ARREST IN WYATT KIDNAPPING. Excellent. She'd have something to talk about tonight. She changed into her dress and fixed her hair; she'd be happy when the weather warmed up and she didn't have to wear hats anymore. Jewellery, shoes, water bottle, she was ready if she got sidetracked and ended up not being able to come back upstairs.

Taylor wasn't in the bar when Libby checked, so she went to the lounge to see if he was there. He wasn't, which was weird because he'd agreed to meeting Libby early to go over a few things. Adria was there, though, watching something on her phone.

"Michael says to call him back," Libby told her. She took off her heels and set them aside. They were gorgeous, but there was no point in wearing them if she didn't have to.

"What?" Adria barely looked up from her phone.

"Michael? Your old Army buddy? Has been trying to call you."

That got her attention. "Oh, right. I figured I'd wait until he'd had a chance to regroup." She thumbed a quick text message and then tucked her phone beside her. "I hear you had a big day yesterday."

"It wasn't as bad as I thought it would be."

"Yeah, well, wait until you have to testify."

Oh shit. She hadn't even thought of that. "I was kind of hoping they'd make some arrests, get some confessions, make some more arrests, get some more confessions, and then it would be all over."

"I obviously don't know the details, but it's unlikely."

"Great, more panic attacks. Hey, did he tell you he's been tying me up regularly?"

Adria laughed. "He's called me once or twice to ask questions." She leaned forward, serious. "You can call me too, you know. I'm not exclusively a top."

"I'm good for now." She did have something she'd wanted to ask someone. "Is it weird that I have no interest in anything else kinky? And that it's not sexual, like, at all?" She didn't let herself think the word 'yet'. She had no business thinking that.

"You are who you are. Some people might tell you there are rules about that kind of thing, but they're mostly pretentious assholes. The only rules are the ones about consent and caring."

"We definitely have those."

"Good." Adria glanced back down at her phone, but Libby had more questions.

"Hey, can I ask you something else adult?"

Her smile looked more tolerant than pleased. "Sure."

Libby bounced on her toes a bit, trying to work out sudden nervous energy. "Will people think it's weird that I'm staying with Michael and not paying rent or anything?"

"You're kind of hung up on weird, aren't you?"

"My entire life from birth to age twenty was the definition of weird. I have no baseline for the rest of society."

"It is unusual, but when you live in this city you get used to unusual living situations." Adria cocked her head. "Why?"

"I suggested he invite some of his co-workers over for dinner and he got squirrelly about how they might react to my presence."

"Hmm. Can't help you there."

Taylor poked his head in the door then. He apologized for being late, and then Libby had to get to work.

After Libby left, Michael felt safe calling Ray. The mood Libby was in—the mood both of them were in—she'd interrupt and they'd start bickering again instead of him actually getting to talk to Ray. Either that or she'd sit by quietly and take blackmail notes.

"Hey." Ray's voice was warm and soft, and Michael found himself smiling.

"Hi."

"You all recovered from your long day?"

"Not even close. Is it like this for you, that you can't let a case go?"

Ray chuckled. "You know every fire is different? You might think, looking at pictures, that they're all the same, but they're not. Not from the inside."

"Is that a yes?"

"Yeah, sometimes. I'm lucky, though, 'cause we don't have to wait long to find out if we passed or failed."

Suddenly energized, Michael got up, putting Ray on speaker, and headed to the kitchen. He'd had dinner, but he thought cookies sounded good. "What's different about the fires?"

"They way they move is predictable, right? But different buildings make different fires. This window is open, this door is closed. Dropped ceiling, half-wall, fully carpeted. Materials burn at different temperatures, make different colours and smells, different smoke."

Michael laid out ingredients while Ray talked: eggs, butter, sugar, flour, vanilla. He hunted for chocolate chips, but came up empty. Walnuts, then, and cinnamon. He set honey beside the sugar. "Sounds complicated. And beautiful."

"There's a reason people attribute mystical properties to it." He added, "My mother's a folklorist. Don't ever get her started on mystical fires. Hey, did you know the trees in Australia explode?"

Reflexively, Michael glanced at his phone on the counter. "You're kidding."

"Partly. The oil in them is flammable, so they go up really fast and spread the fire too quickly. Looks like an explosion."

"Wow." He beat the eggs, enjoying the ring of whisk against bowl.

"What are you doing over there?"

"Making cookies."

"I can be there in half an hour."

The oven was nearly preheated. "They'll be done by then."

"Great." He hung up.

Michael was just pulling the second pan from the oven when the intercom buzzed. He let Ray up, greeting him with a kiss and a cookie.

"Got a glass of milk to go with that?" Ray asked before he shoved the cookie in his mouth to deal with his boots.

"Maybe. Neither of us has been shopping in a few days." He checked, and there was just enough for two glasses. He set it all out, with the cooled cookies, on the peninsula.

Ray followed him into the kitchen, taking Libby's usual stool at the counter. "So where is this mysterious roommate?"

"Working." The cookies needed to come off the tray and the third batch go in the oven.

"Right. Singer at a nightclub." Ray scooped another off the plate while Michael worked. "So, is she one of those cases you can't let go?"

"No." He amended, "Well, she was at first. Now she's a friend."

"Always good to see a happy ending."

He closed the oven door and set the timer, then joined Ray at the counter. "We're not quite there yet. But they've got good leads on her kidnappers so it won't be long."

They shared a few moments of relaxed silence. "Why'd you become a cop?" Ray asked quietly.

Michael took a moment to break open a cookie, warm and spicy. "I was a month from the end of my last tour, ready to go get a degree, when my wife got sick. Huntington's." He couldn't look at Ray while he spoke; her death still hurt too much. "I didn't want to leave her to manage alone." He shrugged and finished his cookie. "I couldn't ask her to leave her family. Local PD seemed like the obvious choice."

"And after?"

He didn't have to ask after what. "I'd already spent a decade on the force. I was a detective, I had cases. Call it inertia, call it sunk cost fallacy, I don't know. Grief, maybe. The unwillingness to leave what we'd built together." Ray already knew how he'd ended up in Toronto. "How about you, you made any plans for if you have to give up active duty?"

Ray smiled like a thirty-year-old who'd never had a joint injury, then stretched his arms behind his head, giving Michael a good look at his biceps. "Marry rich, take up philanthropy. Or knitting."

"Good plan." Michael was ninety percent sure Ray had no clue about his personal wealth. He wasn't anywhere near the level Libby would be if she inherited, even after selling his aunt's farm, but it was enough that he didn't like to talk about it.

He rounded the counter and with a single finger traced the lines and curves of muscle showing on Ray's bare arm. "Bored boytoy would be a good look on you."

"You offering?"

"I don't know. This job certainly keeps you in good shape."

Ray cast a glance at the bedroom door, open enough to show the bed. "When's she due back, anyway? We wouldn't want to scandalize her."

Michael gave Ray his best disbelieving look. "Scandalize her? Impossible."

"You sure she's just a singer?"

"Just is not the word." He added, "She doesn't finish until midnight. We've got plenty of time."

Twenty

Michael was at work, mired in half-complete evidence databases and poorly-performed fingerprint analysis, so by the time Detective Strickland called he relished the break.

She got straight to the point. "We've got the rest of the kidnappers. Want to come to the arrest?" Like it was a party, or a concert. She didn't have to invite him, he was invested in the case same as she was.

"Yes, absolutely, tell me where to be."

He met her at her station to ride along with her. "We're going to the church itself. Our kidnappers are at a meeting. We'll get them all at once."

As she'd predicted the first guy, Jordan Wells, had told them everything, everything except the name of the person who'd ordered them to grab Libby. One of these guys would have the information Strickland needed, they had to count on that.

He'd been to the church building, stood outside it after the second attempt when Libby admitted who she thought was after her. He'd tried to take the character of the people who passed through the big double doors: members with their distinct dress and mannerisms (and how hard had Libby worked to rid herself of those physical tells?), curiosity-seekers, tourists, protesters. People just there for the seminars, not knowing they'd be in for hard sell proselytizing. And then, after her breakdown in the station that day, he'd gone back and read her interview, then followed it up with other articles, exposes and puff pieces both. The official website was a nightmare cloaked in good intentions. It was easy to see how otherwise intelligent people could get caught up in it.

"These guys aren't otherwise intelligent," Strickland told him when he brought it up. "Quite likely whoever's in charge chose the dumb ones to carry out their plans, gave them strict instructions for a while. When that communication ended for whatever reason they reverted to idiots."

They left the cars on Gould Street and walked. The building had too many doors, too many escape routes, and they couldn't give up any advantage by letting the members know the police had arrived. So stealth was the mode of the day, plain clothes, plain cars, surround and subdue before they even knew what was happening. Once the arrests had been made, then the uniforms and marked cars could arrive.

It went down perfectly, a textbook situation. No one had time to run, even if they had the inclination. Strickland was right, they were dumb, not even understanding they were in trouble until the cuffs went on.

While Strickland did a headcount, comparing them to the names Wells had given her, Michael thought about calling Libby, but it seemed rude to take that pleasure away from Strickland. After all, it had been her case long before Michael had even heard of Libby.

"You coming along while I book them?" Strickland asked as the trio were ushered into cars.

"Nah, I've got to get back to work."

"Did you call her?"

"Your case, your win, your call."

He didn't think it was possible for her smile to get any wider, but he got a good look at her teeth for a second. "Thanks, Ballard."

"No problem." He shook her hand and walked away, noticing for the first time just what a beautiful day it was.

Libby's day went like this:

First, she woke up when Michael left. Just as she was getting back to sleep Jeeves bounced up on her bed and decided he needed cuddles. She gave them to him for a few minutes, then, deciding she was awake, she got up and showered.

Breakfast, then practice. She was lucky, she had good enough pitch that she could get by with tapping out piano notes on a keyboard app on her phone. She'd have preferred an actual piano, but she didn't have the cash for even a little electronic one, and there were things she wasn't going to mention to Michael. He'd buy it for her, maybe even a little apartment size, and she didn't want to be indebted to him any more than she already was.

But she was slowly ceasing to care. Her life had been nothing but hard work, pain, deprivation. Desperation. She'd thought leaving The Farm was her best choice, but life here hadn't been much better. She'd only thought it was great being in school, getting to sing, to perform, but now that she thought about it, it had just been a different kind of hell. She'd been lonely. Her whole life up until then had been populated by a noisy, busy mob. Adults, children, they all worked together, they shared homes, beds, toys. Toronto was noisy and busy in a different way, anonymous and cold.

How weird was it that she missed a place of hardship and lies? By most legal standards she'd been abused by her parents and the other leaders. But something in her still yearned for the company of people who were all working together for a greater purpose. People who weren't competing except in the most jovial ways. Little backstabbing, less true hatred. And the part of her that yearned for that life again just may have found it with Michael.

They'd need at least a half-dozen more people to recreate the feeling, but they were pretty close as it was. Her voice cracked on an arpeggio. She blamed it on the octave rather than her train of thought. She tried it again, concentrating on her voice rather than her thoughts. Music had always been her escape. It was what made her special back on The Farm, but she'd lost it and it was still gone. She'd gotten some of it back, some of that escape, but not all of it.

But maybe she didn't need it anymore. Maybe it she could sing because she loved it, not because she was good at it, or because she needed it. And that's when she realized, in the middle of a staccato passage, that she loved singing jazz. Did she love opera?

Just the other night she'd been listening to The Magic Flute and she got chills during Queen of the Night. So yeah, she did still love it. Warmed up, she got out her sheet music and then her phone rang.

"Libby Wyatt." She'd picked up the habit of answering that way from Michael, she realized, but it came in handy.

"Miss Wyatt, good morning." The voice was familiar, but she couldn't pinpoint it. "This is Bridget Weymouth, from the Hayden Weymouth Scholarship Committee."

She'd gotten a letter last time, so it took her a moment to figure out what was going on. "Good morning."

"I'm calling to let you know that you've been approved for half-tuition for the autumn term."

Libby embarrassed herself with the startled squeal she let out before getting herself together. "Really? Thank you, Ms. Weymouth."

"Just don't let us down this time."

"I'll do my best."

They said their goodbyes, hung up, and then Libby collapsed cross-legged on the floor to just sit and breathe for a second. She thought she was having a panic attack, the shivers and light-headedness, except instead of fear she was elated. Excited. The first time this happened she had known she'd get the scholarship. She knew how good she was and that she deserved it. This felt like a gift rather than something she deserved. And now she had proof that she still loved opera and wanted to continue.

She could, and would, love both.

Energized, she went back to her music and worked her way through a few songs she knew well before tackling a new one. She was pounding out a difficult syncopation on the table when the phone rang again. Her heart stopped, sure that it was Bridget Weymouth again to tell her she'd made a mistake, but it wasn't, it was Faith Strickland and could Libby's day get any better? Because it was looking pretty perfect now.

She texted Michael. Did you hear?

I was there, he replied shortly. Watched the whole thing. And then a moment later, How are you feeling?

She thought about it for a minute. Good. Relieved.

Her phone rang and it was him. "It's not over yet, you know," he said without even a hello. "There's still a whole mess before we can get them to trial, plus the question of who set them on you in the first place."

A horrifying thought struck her. "Am I still in danger? Will they send others after me?"

His silence, short as it was, told her everything. "There's a chance. But the fact that they waited a whole year the last time might mean they'll wait. We have time."

"I have more news," she blurted out. There was no reason not to tell him, now. "I got my scholarship back."

Awkward silence followed. "Did I know you applied?" he asked weakly.

"No." She laughed when he sighed in relief. "I didn't want to say anything, just in case I failed."

"But you didn't! We should celebrate."

"Let's get dressed up and go out for drinks. Invite Ray."

"You want to hear someone else sing for once?"

It was like he read her mind, then she remembered that they'd had that conversation once. "Exactly."

This was, without a doubt, the strangest date Michael had ever been on. He thought he'd seen most of Libby's dresses as she went off to work at the club, but this was different. Her work dresses were usually jersey or satin, black or red, short sleeved, deep neckline, skirt just above the knee. Tight and conventionally sexy, but ordinary. Cheap.

This dress was remarkable. First off, it was orange. Bright, citrusy orange. From the waist up it was conservative: tailored, form-fitting chiffon top with long, belled sleeves that draped over her hands a bit, and a round neck. A short A-line skirt teased at what was beneath it, and he couldn't stop staring at the strip of creamy skin revealed between the hem and the thigh-high brown suede elf boots she wore with it. He'd seen her wearing far less, but somehow that flirty little peek of skin was what got to him.

She caught him staring. All she did was grin and say, "I know, right?"

He had to clear his throat before answering. "Very mod." He added, "I think my mother had a dress like that in the sixties."

"This might actually be from the sixties," she replied. She put on her coat, which was mercifully longer than the dress. "I found it in a two dollar box at a charity shop. It's amazing what you can get when you're willing to wear wild colours. I also got this fantastic lime green paisley skirt, but that's for summer."

"I look forward to seeing it."

"Don't let your boyfriend hear you say that."

Michael had opted for a piano bar, a little more upscale to justify dressing up, with good quality booze and even better music. Claudine had taken him there once, mostly to prove a point about gay bars, and he'd ended up liking it. It was art deco plush, a place you could pretend you were a more elegant person. He thought Libby would like it and he knew he was right the moment they walked in.

The whole room was round, three concentric circles of tables surrounding a centre hub of polished oak bar. Soft lighting shone down from crystal globes, sending shafts of colour to decorate the cream walls. The high-backed booths along the outside were upholstered in brown leather, and black velvet chairs adorned the rest of the tables. Music, clearly live, perhaps in another room, completed the ambience. Libby gazed around, eyes sparkling in the low light.

"You're the best," she said, and gave him a smack on the cheek that he hoped didn't leave lipstick behind. "Oh my god, there's an actual coat check girl."

They found Ray at a booth near the back. As they climbed the three stairs to that level he caught Ray checking them both out. He'd wondered if Ray had any bisexual tendencies, but he hadn't bothered to ask yet. Of course, checking out the woman in the orange mod dress didn't necessarily mean much. She was pretty eye-catching to anyone; she'd gotten more than a few compliments on the way over to the table.

Ray slid over from the middle, letting Michael sit with his back to the wall, although the booth was big enough they all could. He ended up between the two of them, which was appropriate enough.

His concern about the lipstick on his cheek was addressed as soon as he sat down, when Ray gave him a big smacking kiss in exactly the same spot then wiped it off with his thumb.

"Better?" Michael asked him, and Ray turned the gesture into a caress of his cheekbone.

"So much better with you here, you have no idea."

Michael had to kiss him properly for that.

"Wow," Libby interrupted. "And I thought Michael was sappy."

"Nice to meet you too, finally." Ray reached over the table to shake Libby's hand. She gave him a quizzical look, but took his hand anyway. "So, do you want to tell him, or should I?"

At first Libby had thought she was imagining it. The light at the table was soft, dim enough that it could have been a trick, making him look so much like Paramedic Ray. But then he spoke, and Libby never, ever forgot a voice.

"You go ahead," she said, still feeling slightly stunned.

Michael was watching them both, mild curiosity on his face and oh, boy, did she not want to do this. If Ray hadn't said anything she would have just pretended to be a stranger, she was okay with that. "What's going on?" Michael asked, eyes bouncing from Libby to Ray.

Ray placed both hands flat on the table before he spoke. "You remember the night we met, at the concert in the park?"

Michael nodded, but Libby had questions. "Wait, you two met then? When? How?"

The look Ray gave her was enough to shut her up. "We'll get to that later. Anyway," he said to Michael, "Libby and I met earlier that day and she invited me to the concert. She came home with me after."

She watched Michael's expression shift from expectant to confused. "You slept together?" He turned to Ray. "I thought you were gay."

"Mostly gay, it turns out," Libby said, and realized she really wasn't helping at all. "Anyway, it happened, and I was absolutely not interested in a relationship at the time because I thought he was trying to white knight me so I left kind of abruptly."

"And never got back to me."

She gave him a weak shrug. "Sorry. But hey! You're together now and everyone's good, right?"

Ray was watching Michael too, nervously, and Libby was suddenly really sorry if she'd managed to ruin what they had, but Michael didn't seem angry or anything. In fact, he looked amused, like when Jeeves did something stupid.

"A city of six and a half million people and this is what happens," he said.

Libby held up her hand, stopping him. "Don't you dare say anything about fate. I refuse to believe I got kidnapped to help your love life."

"Hey, yeah," Ray said to Libby. "I hear they caught the guys. Congratulations."

Michael watched them chat, watched Ray, really. He'd seen him dressed up for dinner, seen him in jeans and sweats, but never in a lightweight, slim black henley. It was a good look on him, showing off his muscle. There was a thread of silver running through the weave, making him shine. All the buttons were undone, capturing Michael's gaze at the base of his throat.

Libby kicked him, then, hard to the shin.

"Ow." He glared at her, then noticed the server. "Oh, right." He ordered an Old Fashioned and then, after some consultation, added a cheese plate to their order.

"So what are we celebrating?" Ray asked, and Michael had a paralyzing moment when he realized he hadn't told Ray anything about Libby's troubles. He'd just mentioned that hc met her on a case.

He looked over at Libby, who seemed unconcerned. "You want to tell him?"

She shrugged one shoulder casually. "From the top?"

"From the top."

Hearing Libby tell it all at once, from her parentage to the events of the day, was revealing. He'd heard it all, of course, but piecemeal and from people who weren't necessarily her. She had a way of making it all like an amusing adventure instead of the year-long horror show it likely was.

"So, wait, you're telling me you work at a sex dungeon?" Ray near-whispered it, but still managed to sound like he'd shouted.

The look of disgust that painted Libby's face was priceless. "Ew, no, there's no sex. At all. Ever."

"That you know of."

"No," she drew the word out. "Never. I won't say the clients don't get aroused, because I've seen it, but it's not about sex, not at the club. They take it all home to their partners." She eyeballed him, as if waiting for his reaction.

"That's just weird and wrong."

He had to step in before Ray dug himself any deeper. At this rate he wouldn't be able to introduce him to Claudine. "Think of it like physical psychiatry. Costs the same, and a lot of people would tell you it works better."

"I still don't know how you can work in a place like that and feel safe."

The pain on Libby's face was nearly heartbreaking. "It's the safest place I've ever been," she said, turning her glass in tiny circles on the table. "Aside from Michael's."

He couldn't help but return her shy smile.

Ray, on the other hand, was obviously uncomfortable. Michael had no idea how to help him, so he went for full disclosure. "Ray, my closest friend is a dominatrix at that same club. She's the most centered, self-assured, healthy person I've ever met. She has had my back in every way possible for nearly fifteen years." If he sounded a little harsh, well, he'd known

Claudine longer than Ray. If he had to make a choice, he knew what it would be.

Ray finished his drink, putting the glass down with a distinct thud, and for a moment Michael thought he was going to just get up and leave, but he didn't. He sat, clearly thinking it through. "Okay. I can reserve judgement." He watched Michael as he continued, "Just don't expect me to participate."

"That's not really my thing." Libby hadn't mentioned the bondage class in her story, and he didn't want to out her like that, but he also didn't want to scare Ray off. And it was the truth, mostly – he liked helping Libby, and he was proud of the work he did on making pretty patterns with the ropes, but it wasn't a dealbreaker. Not like it was for Claudine.

The conversation turned to other things, thank god, but when Ray eventually went to the restroom Michael apologized to Libby. "I had no idea. It's never come up before."

She plucked at a loose thread on her sleeve, tugging at it gently. "It's not unexpected, I guess? I just always figured it would be straight guys who freaked out about it."

"I guess everyone's got to have someone to feel superior about."

"Sounds about right." She rested her chin in her hand. "And it's not like I don't do it myself. Some of the clients are into stuff that...." She made a face. "Yech. But I like to think I wouldn't say it to their faces, or as if my preference was a fact, you know?"

"Maybe once you might have, though. Give him a chance to learn. Please?"

He'd dropped his hand between them when he turned to her, and now she picked it up and started playing with his fingers. "I'm not sure what kind of power you think I have, but sure. It's not my right to judge who you date."

"You've carved enough of a place in my life to at least get a say."

"How violently put."

"I was thinking more sculptor than serial killer."

She rattled the ice in her glass at him. "This conversation is going nowhere good. I need another drink. You want anything?"

Ray came back while she was gone, and Michael caught the flash of panic on his face until he saw her hat and gloves still on the seat. He turned it into a casual questioning look, but not quite fast enough for someone trained to read micro expressions. "She's gone to get drinks," Michael supplied. "And also I might be a serial killer."

Ray didn't hesitate to slide into his seat again. "Thanks for letting me know, but I won't fake an alibi for you."

"That's okay, I'm covered."

The rest of the evening went far more smoothly, at least until Libby started fading and went home and they were left alone.

Ray stared at him. "You're pissed at me, aren't you."

Michael examined what he was feeling. "A little bit," he said finally. "Maybe it's more like resentment."

"I forget you're not out at work."

"My boss knows. But no, no on else does."

"And I come in here all judgemental about something secret...."

"Yeah."

Ray took his hand, just holding it. "What can I do to make this right?"

"I don't know yet."

Twenty-One

Libby was home alone the next evening when Ray stopped by. "He's not here," she told him at the door. "He's babysitting, I think." He'd sent her a garbled text earlier about Claudine and an emergency and a seven-year-old, and that was the only way she could make it make sense.

"Actually I'm here to see you," Ray said, so she let him in. She'd been practicing and was still in that headspace, so she could be forgiven for not noticing the flowers until he handed them directly to her.

"Huh." It was pretty, a riot of multi-coloured cosmos and daisies. Not extravagant, but not a cheap street bouquet either. "Thanks."

"I did some thinking last night," he said, tucking his hands in his pockets. "And I'm sorry for what I said. I jumped to conclusions and," he chuckled ruefully, "I of all people shouldn't make assumptions." He scratched the back of his head. "Gay firefighter, you know?"

"Right." This she had not been expecting. "Forgiven, I guess?" She sent him an apologetic look. "I have no frame of reference for this conversation. So, sure. Thanks for the apology. Don't do it again." She waved an admonishing finger at him, hoping to make him laugh and stop looking so nervous.

She succeeded. He stopped fidgeting and looked at her, and wow, he had pretty eyes, a startling light brown, almost amber, with long blond lashes. "I'll try not to be an ass."

"Can I confess something?"

"Sure."

"Even after I started working at the club, hell, even after I worked as a sub in a bondage class, I wasn't the most open-minded about it. There are kinks I'm pretty sure I'll never accept casually. So I'd be a hypocrite if I didn't forgive you. And also the flowers were a nice touch."

"I'll keep that in mind."

It was her turn to be polite, so she invited him in. "I've got a pot of mint tea ready, if you're interested."

In reply he kicked off his boots and handed her his jacket.

She gathered up the score she had laid out on the breakfast bar and set it aside, replacing it with cups, teapot, and a jar of honey. "Pull up a stool and tell me your troubles, partner," she said, and watched him laugh again.

"Well, I've got this boyfriend...."

"You don't say." She poured the tea and offered him the honey, then took some for herself. It was wonderfully soothing after singing, probably more on an emotional level than physically. It reminded her of back home, days when she was sick. "Go on."

"He has this roommate." He glanced up at her, taking in her expectant raised eyebrows. "I mean, I knew he did, but I was startled when I actually met her and saw how young and attractive she is—and my boyfriend, he's way more bi than I am—anyway, I made an ass of myself. So now I've made up with her, but my boyfriend's still kind of pissed."

"Have you told him you apologized to her?"

"Not yet. You think that'll do the trick?"

"Well, I can't say I know your boyfriend, but my roommate would definitely take that as a positive sign. And he's totally besotted with his boyfriend, so it's not like he wants to be angry."

Ray nodded and drank more tea. "I'll tell him first thing." Then he registered what Libby said and his face bloomed into a wide smile.

"Oh my god, you're just as stupidly smitten as he is."

"So, how's your love life?"

"My sex life is great. The love part never works out too well."

He stared at her for a long second. "You're very open about these things, aren't you? I mean, just last night you were telling me about how you traded sex for a place to sleep, and now this."

"First off, I traded sex for sex as well as a place to sleep. Don't think I just picked up anybody off the street – although there's no shame in that either, Mister One Night Stand. Second, well, I was raised by quasi-pagan hippies. I don't have a lot of the hang-ups most people do." She wasn't going to tell him, not yet at least, that her first dildo—a beautiful carved wooden piece—had been a gift from the community on her fifteenth birthday. She'd learned quickly that most people thought it was icky for an adult to give a teenager sex toys, even if that adult was a parent. She wondered idly if the police who searched her room had any idea that the sculpture on her dresser had a use beyond being pretty.

"Sounds nice. How do they feel about being gay?"

"We are all as nature made us." She made a face. "Unless you're naturally a little plumper than community standards dictate." That still rankled. She had her grandmother's body, her grandmother the farmer who worked hard and had lived to be nearly a hundred.

He looked her over, as she knew he would. "You look pretty good to me."

"I remember. And you didn't get to see them but my thigh dimples are adorable."

"I'm sure they are," he said, as if he hadn't reacted at all. "Can I ask you something?"

She shrugged. "Sure, go ahead."

"Why did you stay here? After losing your home and everything."

She'd asked herself the same question more than once, early on. "Where would I go? Back to Picton? I don't have a degree. There's not much in the way of a theatre or music industry there." She paused to let him say something but when he didn't she went on. "Here I already had my job. I had busking. I was making money doing what I loved and I was close to the places I really wanted to work. Yeah, there are a lot of places I might have had a crappy little apartment, but I'd have been just as miserable in a completely different way." She noticed the bouquet still sitting to her left. "I should put those flowers in some water."

As she was hunting for something to use as a vase, Michael came home. He took in the flowers, Libby on a chair poking through a cupboard, Ray with a mug in his hands, and the corners of his eyes crinkled up. "Hey. I didn't expect you here." He kissed Ray sweetly and stole the last of his tea.

"Thought I'd come to make amends."

"He did a good job of it, too," Libby said. She caught a pitcher before it toppled off the shelf and decided it would do to hold a bouquet. She listened to them talk as she snipped the stems and cleaned up a few broken leaves. It was comfortable. Comforting.

"Congratulations. You have a place in the chorus if you're still available."

Libby had been bracing herself for yet another no, so she had to take a second to refocus. "Yes. Absolutely. I am still available." Opera Toronto. She didn't even remember auditioning, not really. She had a few blurry weeks of not sleeping and had let Benny, Dinah, and Mel drag her around to auditions without caring.

"Rehearsals for *La Traviata* start the second week of April. Is it okay if I email you the information?"

Libby agreed, then managed to get out of the conversation without embarrassing herself too much. The first thing she did after was text Dinah. The next thing she did was read up on the opera. It seemed pretty straightforward. As a chorus member she'd have to do a lot of standing around, but those were the dues you paid sometimes if you wanted to do more.

Her phone pinged, and they squealed at each other for a bit before Dinah had to get back to work.

Which raised another complication for Libby: work. She was okay with giving up busking; she'd miss some of her regulars but she didn't love it and she didn't want to risk damaging her voice again. However, she wouldn't be able to sing at the club anymore, not with daily rehearsals and then weekend performances, and that was a little bit heartbreaking. She texted Hazel, the club owner, asking for a meeting before her show on Friday and got an immediate reply: Everything okay?

Everything's great.

Now that she'd be making better money she'd be able to move out and stop taking advantage of Michael. She probably couldn't afford a place of her own yet, but Benny and Dinah were looking for a roommate and if they could stand to spend that much time together it might work out.

Something in her ached at the thought of leaving. She examined the feeling, connecting it to other moments, and realized she liked Michael more than she should. But even if he wasn't with Ray, he still wouldn't look at her that way. She was a charity case, a child he needed to protect. If she were five, ten years older it might be different. It was time for her to go, before she got too wrapped up in him. Basking in her melancholy, she started learning a new song.

The conversation that evening was more difficult than she'd thought it would be. She made dinner—she'd become a pretty good cook over the last few months—and cracked open a bottle of wine. To celebrate, she told herself, but as the hour drew nearer she needed the relaxing effects. She maybe had a bit too much before he got home, because she couldn't stop herself from hugging him at the door.

She'd always been a flirtatious drunk.

"You look like you have news," he said, and pressed his lips to her temple. "Good news?"

"Very." She let him go and went back to check the food in the oven. She'd just checked it, but she had to get away before she did something embarrassing. "Hey, we should have that dinner party before I move out."

All the little sounds he made as he shed his winter gear stopped. A few seconds later she jumped as he said, "Move out?" practically right in her ear.

She closed the oven and slid out from between it and him before replying. "I got a place in the chorus of a real opera company." She poured herself another glass of wine, then filled one for him, hoping she'd successfully diverted his attention.

From the sound of it, she had. "That's great," he exclaimed. He eyed the bottle of wine. "I see you've been celebrating."

"Hey, some of it went into the food."

"You still haven't explained the 'move out' part of what you said."

"Well," she said, hoping she sounded casual. She started getting out the dinner dishes as she spoke. "I'm going to be making more money now. I don't need to be a leech anymore."

He took a slow sip of his wine and watched her as she set the table. "I'm not even sure where to start. Do you want your own place?"

She couldn't say yes, not only because it wasn't true but because it wasn't possible. "I can't afford to live alone yet, if that's what you're asking."

"Do you want to get away from me? And it's fine if you do, just say so."

That wasn't true either. "No." She turned, leaning back against the counter. "I like being here. But I feel like I'm in the way of you and Ray. And that I'm taking advantage of the way you feel about me."

He sipped his wine again. "And how do I feel about you?"

She busied herself with the silverware, didn't want to see agreement on his face. "Like you're responsible for me. Like I'm a victim you need to keep saving." Like a little sister, she thought about saying, but would that be so bad?

"Libby." There was something like grief in his voice. She heard him set down his glass and then he was in front of her, hands gentle on her upper arms "Look at me, please."

She glanced up to his eyes for a second, then settled on his tie. Usually he took it off as soon as he got home, but she'd sidetracked him.

"Please."

So she forced herself to stop acting like a child and meet his gaze.

"I'm not sure you have ever been so wrong in your life." He gave her a small smile, warm and quiet.

"What?"

He dropped his hands to his sides. "Maybe at first I felt that way about you. Did I ever tell you about Jeanine?"

Where was he going with this? "Only that she was sick and died."

"She waited until I was away for a few days and then she took her life. She made it look like an accident, like a fall while hiking. I found a letter she left, in my sock drawer." His lips quirked up just a bit. "She was always leaving gifts in my sock drawer. Anyway, I've never told anyone. Except Claudine, but she's not just anyone."

It must have hurt to say that so bluntly; the lines in his face were deeper somehow than only a minute before, his voice lower by a few tones. "Oh."

"She had a degenerative disease and nothing I said could convince her to see it out, to spend a few more years with me, no matter what. The doctors said they could manage her pain, that the early deterioration was almost unnoticeable. That there could be a cure in only a few years.

But she was too proud. And she was scared, so scared of not being herself that I couldn't comfort her at all sometimes."

Libby wanted to ask questions, but the smarter, more sensitive part of herself swallowed them down.

"I saw a bit of that in you. Too proud to acknowledge that you needed help. Too scared to become dependent on other people."

"You're not wrong," she said, barely above a whisper. "But it's not fear. I'm just not used to having help."

"So yes, I wanted to save you again. And once I had, I realized that I genuinely like you."

The part of her that wanted to burrow into him shivered.

"You're fun. And smart. And a good roommate. I like to think of you as a friend." The last part was said in a questioning tone, looking for confirmation.

"Me too," was all she could say.

"So don't feel like you have to move out. If you don't mind Ray being over here then we're good."

A flutter started up in her chest. "And what will Ray think?"

"That's something he and I will work out together." He cocked his head toward the stove. "Smells like dinner's ready."

She took the out and opened the oven to retrieve the macaroni and cheese. "So, we should totally have that dinner party before I start working four nights a week."

Twenty-Two

Michael ran his fingers over the records, trying to figure out what he was in the mood for early on a Sunday morning. He'd just pulled Ziggy Stardust from its case when Ray came up behind him, resting his chin on Michael's shoulder. "Hey."

"Hey."

Michael jumped when Ray's hand slid down his ass, then nearly melted when it continued down between his thighs, stroking lightly over the flannel of his sleep pants before cupping his balls. "Ah." He leaned his head back, letting Ray take most of his weight.

Ray tightened his grip, chuckling when Michael started to harden. Michael moaned then, low in his throat, and he felt Ray smile against his neck.

"Oh, Jesus," he heard from the other side of the room, and he opened his eyes in time to see Libby rushing out, the back of her neck bright red.

"You know," Michael called after her, "for someone raised atheist you sure do swear by Jesus a lot."

She shouted her reply without looking back. "Bad habit I picked up in school."

Ray dropped his hand and laughed. "Forgot she was here."

A timer dinged in the kitchen. "Coffee's ready anyway." Michael finished putting the music on and stepped away.

"Can I come out yet?" Libby yelled from the bathroom.

"Nope, gotta stay in there indefinitely," Ray answered.

She came out anyway and glared at him, arms crossed under her breasts. "You promised to keep it to the bedroom."

Ray shrugged. "Sorry." Then he pointed at Michael, the traitor. "But he didn't stop me, either."

"You had your hand...I don't even know where you had your hand but from the look on his face it wasn't family friendly." She took the cup of coffee Michael handed her with a sullen glare at him.

"It was over the clothes," Michael explained. He wasn't quite sure why she was making such a fuss; from what she'd told him about her childhood she should be comfortable with PDAs.

"You're just lucky I love you," she said before burying her head in her coffee.

Michael hadn't been planning to cook breakfast, but figured it was the least he could do right now. Also he wanted to celebrate Ray's first time staying over. He tossed him a smile and got a grin in response.

"Fuck you both." Libby flipped them off.

Michael started working on pancake batter. Ray sat on the stool beside Libby and put his arm around her shoulder. "Not getting laid?"

He had to turn to watch for a second. Libby looked up at Ray with big, sad eyes. "Why do my fuckbuddies always end up in relationships?"

His eyes on his work again, Michael listened to them.

"Is it possible you've made them such great lovers that word gets around?"

She sighed dramatically. "I suppose. I am amazing."

Michael chanced another look at them, to find Libby nestled into Ray's chest. His breath caught in his throat – they were beautiful, and beautiful together. What was he even doing with Ray, when Ray could have someone like her? He stopped, went over that thought, and mentally slapped himself for being stupid. Ray was with him because Ray wanted him.

He tuned back into the conversation in time to hear something about Libby's magic vagina. He whirled around. "Okay I did not need to hear that." He put the pan on the stove and started it heating up.

Libby laughed at him, and at least that was a step up from earlier. He decided to give it another kick. "And stop canoodling with my boyfriend."

"He started it."

Michael cooked the pancakes while they bantered, feeling a wash of warmth and happiness like he hadn't had since before Jeanine got sick. This was perfection. If he could have this forever, he'd be good. But there was something he'd been putting off. "Guys?"

Two heads, dark and light, were bent over Ray's tablet. "Yeah?" Libby looked up. "Ooh, breakfast."

So Michael brought over the plate of pancakes and talked while they served themselves. "There's something I've been meaning to do, and I think I'm going to do it tomorrow."

"What's that?" Libby asked around a mouthful of food.

Ray caught on, though. "You're going to come out at work?"

Libby looked from one to the other. "Really? Wow. Are you sure it'll be okay?"

Michael had to shrug at that one. "I don't know. I know David won't have a problem with it because he knew before he hired me."

"And the others?" Ray asked.

"I can deal with a few assholes for your sake."

In response Ray ducked his head, a small smile gracing his lips.

"What about you, Ray?" Libby asked, breaking the moment.

Ray laughed. "Oh, man, when I came out, that was a disaster. But they eventually settled down."

"How did you do it?" Libby asked.

"I wanted to make a scene." Ray shook his head in dismay at his younger self. "So I brought a guy to the holiday party. A party full of drunk, nosy straight men."

"Ow. How did your date react?"

"Never saw him again." Ray got up to pour himself another cup of coffee. "And he was right. It was a nasty thing to do to him."

Libby turned to Michael. "So how are you going to do it? I'm assuming you're not going to get up on your desk and shout 'I'm gay!'" She even gave the statement jazz hands.

Good God, no. "I was thinking about having Ray take me to lunch. Remember that time you brought breakfast?"

Ray smiled at him, soft and sweet. "I was so sure you were gonna kiss me right there."

"I should have. And I will, tomorrow, if you're good with that."

"I am. I am so good with that, you have no idea."

"We just have to make sure a couple of people see, and then I won't have to say a thing."

Ray leaned over the counter to kiss him. Libby said nothing, just watched them with a small smile.

The plan went off exactly as they hoped. Ray flashed his badge and met Michael at his desk, kissed him hello and took him away to lunch. By the time Michael got back everyone who was in the office knew, and David gave him a thumbs up on the way past. And by the end of the day he knew that if anyone objected they were keeping it to themselves.

Claudine joined Michael for Libby's last show. Somehow news had gotten around to the members that she was leaving, so the bar was packed, but the two of them had managed to get a table in the middle. Libby didn't know they were there; it had been a last minute decision on Michael's part, when Claudine had invited him.

He was glad to be there. Of course he'd heard all her songs at home—she was rarely not singing while doing other tasks, now—but watching her perform them, full-voiced, wearing a smoky and seductive persona, was totally different from seeing her in yoga pants while cleaning the bathroom.

"You know I've never heard her sing?" As if reading his mind, Claudine continued. "Aside from to herself in the lounge. I've never bothered to come in and listen. I feel like I've missed out on something."

"She's got a job with a major opera company. With any luck they'll offer her a role out of the chorus. You still have time."

"So, when do I get to meet Ray?"

He knew this question was coming, and didn't have an answer. He shook his head at her. "Libby wants to have a bunch of people over soon. Probably then."

"You're being evasive."

"I know." He really didn't want to get into what Ray had said, no matter how contrite he'd been afterwards, and explaining why he was hesitating went right into that. "Can we just listen?"

She gave him her best exasperated face, but didn't object.

A glass of scotch, a good friend, and great music. Michael regretted that he couldn't have come here more often, and that he couldn't have brought Ray. But there was something intimate, almost nostalgic, about it being just the three of them. Two of them, after Claudine slipped out to meet a client. In the semi-dark room he could block out everyone else and focus on Libby. She was more beautiful now than he'd ever seen her, putting her heart into the song, this song in particular, one she must have been practising when he wasn't around, because he didn't recognize it at first. He listened more closely to the words; she looked sad, in a real way, a way she'd never looked in the other blues songs. He knew the song, it was Billie Holiday, *I Don't Stand a Ghost of a Chance with You*, but he had no idea Libby knew it.

It seemed so personal to her, like she was singing about herself. And for just a moment, when she sang meant for you she looked up, straight at him, then away. The look caught in his chest, the idea that she could mean him. She didn't, of course, it was just a silly fantasy, but it lodged in his head and he couldn't shake it for the rest of the song. She probably hadn't even seen him there.

Claudine came back in during the last song, kneeling beside Michael's chair instead of sitting at the table. She held a large, flat box, wrapped in green paper with a pink bow. "Michael, one of my guys just walked in and I'm going to give him a session." She handed him the box. "Will you give this to Libby for me?"

He nodded and took the gift, turning back to the stage as she slipped out. He'd debated leaving before Libby finished, but since he had the gift he decided to stay. At least he could give it to her and then go home while she finished up her goodbyes here.

The lights came up and there was a smattering of applause from those left. Applause was unusual, she'd told him, most people coming and going without really acknowledging her except through tips.

"I guess it's gotten around that I'm leaving, huh," she said into the mic. A few people laughed. "Well, thanks, and best of luck to you all. I'll miss this place."

Michael met her at the bar, where the bartender, James, had a gin and tonic ready for her. "Why am I not surprised that you're here?" She took a sip of her drink while James sorted out her tips for her. "And you brought a gift."

"It's from Adria. She was here for a while, but ended up having a client." He handed it over, watching as she carefully opened one end and slid two books out.

"Oh." In the dim light he couldn't tell if she was blushing, but her pursed lips and wide eyes indicated she might be.

"What is it?"

She turned the book around so he could see the title: *Shibari You Can Use.* The book slipped a fraction, revealing that she held the other behind it. "What's the other one?"

This time he could see her blush as she shoved both of them back into the paper. "Nothing important. Hey, do you want to come back to the lounge while I say goodbye? I've been told there's cupcakes."

"The others won't mind?"

"I don't think so. You've got me and Adria to vouch for you."

She didn't take long, saying goodbye. At midnight on a Saturday the place was pretty busy, but most of the dommes were able to stop in. Michael stood in the corner near the door, eating a vanilla and strawberry cupcake and trying to stay invisible. People would draw their own conclusions, of course, but he didn't want to fan the flames by sticking close to Libby. Usually he didn't care what people thought of them, but tonight the subject was...sensitive. Like a sore tooth he couldn't stop probing with his tongue.

Finally she was done. She grabbed her coat and collected Michael up and they went home. Once there, she seemed to come to a decision.

"Here," she said, and handed him the second book. Joyous Submission, it said. "It just wasn't a conversation I wanted to have in the bar."

She continued to talk while he flipped through the pages. "Did you know that most of the people in the bar are just members of the scene who go there to drink and talk to others like them? Maybe to pick up partners, but mostly to hang out in a safe space. A few of them would gleefully dominate me if given the chance."

He glanced up at her, and she nodded. "They've propositioned me. But for some strange reason I have trust issues – can't figure that one out. Anyway, if anyone had seen that book I'd never be able to go back."

"Is this," he raised the book slightly, "what you want?"

"I don't know?" Her hair fell over her face before she swept it back with one hand. "I mean, I think the whole master/slave thing is kind of over the top, but the rest of it? I think I might. I guess that's why she gave me the book." She pulled out the shibari book and held it up. "But this, this I really want. Let's do this."

"All of it?"

"Maybe. Okay, not the overtly sexual stuff, 'cause that's not how we are right now, but—"

She kept talking, but Michael was hung up on 'right now'. As if it was possible for them, at another time. Slip of the tongue, probably, but dangerous. Here be dragons.

He loved Ray, or at least he thought he did. These feelings for Libby didn't fit into that. That wasn't who he was. He had no problems with the idea, not for other people, but he'd never thought he was capable of loving two people romantically at once.

He put the idea aside, said good-night, and went to bed, closing the door behind him.

Twenty-Three

Faith called her first thing Monday afternoon. "I called you as a courtesy," she said, barely letting Libby say hello. "We're making more arrests in your case today. I'm on my way there now."

"To Picton?"

"To The Farm. The guys we picked up talked about everything but they didn't know motive. We've taken our time, made sure everything's in order before getting warrants. But we're almost there and the OPP are about to move in."

"Can you tell me who?"

"April and Jim Hollings."

Shit. April and Jim had always loved her and protected her. Why would they do such a thing? But Faith wouldn't be arresting them if she didn't have proof. Would she? Michael's job made her wonder, sometimes.

"Okay," she said, surprising herself with the steadiness of her voice. "Hey, Faith?"

"Yes?"

"Thanks for everything."

"You're welcome."

Libby didn't want to be alone. Michael was at work already, and so were most of the people she usually called on. "Ray's totally my friend now," she told Jeeves. "He gave me his number." She texted him, inviting him to her favourite cafe for coffee and cookies.

To her great surprise he was free. "I'm working nights this week. What's up?"

Libby stirred the foam on her cappuccino with a biscotti, watching the chocolate coating make dark swirls in white as it melted. "They're about to arrest my surrogate parents for kidnapping me." Her voice sounded too loud, even above the bustle of the café.

He dropped his cookie, fumbling it but managing to catch it before it splashed into his chai. "Okay, wow."

"Yeah. I need company."

"I bet. So who are these people?"

She ended up telling him more about her childhood than she'd told most people. "Think of The Farm like a commune. One commune in a system of communes. The Farm grows most of the food for Ontario. We had the greenhouses that supplied the others in the winter. Another raises sheep and makes textiles as well as cheese. Another has greenhouses to grow bamboo, which they make other products out of, and exotic produce. So it becomes a barter economy of sorts. When a kid gets old enough to work they go wherever they're needed. If they have a preference, they go there. No one wants a kid with pollen allergies working with plants, you know? Or someone who hates sewing making blankets. You have to enjoy what you do to live a life in harmony with the earth."

Ray nodded along. "I can buy that."

"Yeah, so can a lot of people, which is why the Church is so insidious. My parents lived primarily at The House, which is the administrative centre and also the hospital. That's where I was born – not because it's the hospital; generally you give birth in your home. But my parents moved around a lot. They both had jobs outside the Church, important ones. So I was sent to the Farm pretty early, because who wants to raise a kid in a hospital? They gave me into the care of the April and Jim, the...," she had to hunt for a word that would work, "the first among equals. Not quite leaders, but the most respected elders."

"So it's a meritocracy."

Not quite, but that wasn't a tangent she wanted to go on. "Sort of. It's more complicated, but on the surface that works. They were my guardians, although all the kids were free range, raised by whichever adult was around. It takes a village and all that. They'd both joined early and were elders already. It seemed like a perfect solution."

"Why would they have you kidnapped?"

She shrugged and finished her biscotti before answering. "I don't know. When my parents formally excommunicated me April and Jim were the first to vote in agreement. Then they cried the day I actually left. But so did my parents."

"They loved you," he joked, "they just couldn't live with you."

"I was doing exactly what they taught me. I was speaking truth to power, I was calling for change."

"What kind of change?"

"The kind where I got to go to college and become an opera singer."

"So what's with that, anyway? You always hear about celebrities who are members; they're all over the news talking about climate change and extinctions. So what's the difference?"

"It's just a huge double standard. See, if you're raised in the Church you're a worker and a true believer. You keep it running. You set an example for the rest of the world: look at us, if we can live this way you can too.

"The people who join from outside aren't expected to give so much of their lives. They're the figureheads, we're the guys chained to the oars. They give the money and work PR, we do the actual labour. I got selfish, stopped thinking about the greater whole and started thinking about myself."

"But they gave you exactly what you wanted."

This was the part that hurt the most. She'd only ever told Rain and Michael this part. "And in doing so they ripped away everything else I valued. I was never allowed to speak to my friends again. To them, to my parents, I was dead. Worse than dead, I had never existed. I was totally alone for the first time in my life. No support. Not a friendly voice or a hug for comfort. No one to cry to when I needed help, no one to share my success with. No money. Very little idea how to even use money, for that matter. I spent a lot of time those first few months just learning how to live in the world. I was a child given a list of things to do in a language I couldn't read."

"How did you even survive at first?"

"I already had my admission and scholarship worked out. All I had to do was show up." She could see his confusion. "What no one knew at the time was that there was a hole in the fence and on the other side of the hole was another farm. I slipped through one day to see the horses and met a girl my age. Corina. We became friends and I saw her as often as I could. She and her parents helped me out. Let me use their mailing address, helped me get a proper diploma, recorded my audition tapes. Her father was a symphony conductor, so his recommendation was vital."

Something flitted across Ray's face, an emotion Libby couldn't name. "Is that where you heard opera in the first place?"

"No, actually. We had records and an old turntable, a way to spend the evenings without poisoning our minds with new media. We had all the classic novels written before World War One, too. A lot of Dickens."

"So you never saw Corina or her parents after?"

"They moved away before I told my parents everything. I have no idea where they are now." She really should look them up, but with such a common last name—hell, it was the same as Ray's—she wasn't sure she'd find them anyway.

"Wow."

Libby pushed up out of her seat. "I need a glass of water. You want anything?"

She wanted a break from talking, as well as all the emotion she had to carefully control. The worst thing, right now, would be breaking down in public, because she had no idea what would happen if she did and she didn't want to put that on Ray.

When she got back with her water she changed the subject.

It didn't take long for Faith to get the truth from the Hollings. They'd told her the whole story: how much they'd regretted voting against Libby, how heartbroken her parents had been. How they'd come up with a plan to bring Libby back.

April Hollings: They never recovered from her leaving. They didn't show it all the time, but I knew. No one could feel good about their child running away like that. We had to do something to help them.

Detective Faith Strickland: So what did you decide to do?

April Hollings: First we thought we could just talk to Elizabeth.

Detective Strickland: We?

April Hollings: Me and Jim.

Detective Strickland: Go on.

April Hollings: I wrote her a letter telling her how much we all missed her and that if she just came back we could work something out. She could maybe record her singing and sell it at the farm stand like we sell the vegetables.

Detective Strickland: What did Elizabeth reply?

April Hollings: We never heard back from her.

Detective Strickland: What did you do then?

April Hollings: Jim got the idea that we should go get her and bring her back. But I said that wouldn't work, she'd just leave again or stay and pollute the kids, make them want to go out too. So we thought, well, we could re-educate her. Take her someplace and make her see what she really needed.

Detective Strickland: How did you go about that?

April Hollings: My nephew [Kyle Trent] works at a Toronto church. I gave him a picture of Elizabeth and told him where she went to school. He and his friends did the rest.

Detective Strickland: How did you decide where to take her?

April Hollings: Kyle's friend [Abel Lewis] grew up on a farm near Rice Lake. A neighbouring property had an old farmhouse on it that no one used; the old lady who lived there had dementia and had been gone for years. They decided to keep her there.

Detective Strickland: How did you plan to re-educate Elizabeth?

April Hollings: I told the boys not to hurt her, just to leave her alone a lot and feed her bad food. I thought she'd remember how it used to be, with all the family to love her, and fresh food properly cooked. That's all it would take for me, I know it.

Detective Strickland: Did they report back to you?

April Hollings: No.

Detective Strickland: How would you know if it worked?

April Hollings: Elizabeth would come back to us.

Detective Strickland: And if she didn't?

April Hollings: I never thought she wouldn't.

Detective Strickland: What did you do when Harrison Wyatt died?

April Hollings: I cried.

Detective Strickland: What decision did you make about Elizabeth?

April Hollings: It was even more important to bring her back. Paula went into seclusion. She stopped all her administrative work. She stopped visiting the communes. She even stopped eating for a while. Elizabeth was all we had left of them. We thought she could make Paula happy again.

Detective Strickland: Did you contact Kyle?

April Hollings: I had no way to. He was with Elizabeth.

Detective Strickland: What happened next?

April Hollings: Next thing I knew it was all over the papers that Elizabeth—they called her Libby, if you can believe it—was rescued.

Detective Strickland: And then you started planning for next New Year's.

April Hollings: What? No, we don't plan the New Year celebration until November.

Libby skimmed the rest of the transcript, but it didn't hold anything important to her. Trent and Lewis had already admitted that they planned the second kidnapping themselves in order to curry favour with the Church leaders and undo the damage of her magazine interview.

She pushed the pages across the conference table at Michael and took the transcript of Jim's interview. Reading it through she found nothing new or different from April's. She waited until Michael was done. He was more thorough than she was, but finally he leaned back.

"Dumbest kidnapping ever?"

He cracked a smile. "Close, but not quite. They might have gotten away with it if you hadn't come back to the city."

She looked at him, and then at Faith, who'd been waiting for them to finish. "I never got any letter. I would have replied if I had."

"It wouldn't have changed anything," Faith said. She collected the papers and put them back in the case file. "You would have refused to go back and they'd have taken the same action."

She didn't say what Libby was thinking, that it was obvious they cared more about her parents than they did about her happiness. Do the work you love and be in concert with the Earth didn't seem to mean anything real to them.

"Are they going to trial?" Michael asked, and it hadn't occurred to Libby that there was any other option.

Faith shook her head. "There's no point. They'll plead guilty and go straight to sentencing."

Same as Trent and Lewis, then. So easy. Hopefully their sentences wouldn't be.

Libby checked the time on her phone. "I've got to go," she told them. "I've got a lesson." And she really just needed to get out of there.

"Libby, if you're not going to focus you might as well quit and become a dog groomer." Andrea sounded more disappointed than angry, which Libby would have preferred for the sake of her composure.

"I'm sorry," she said, flipping the pages of her score back to the beginning. "I got some bad news. Well, news anyway."

"It doesn't matter. Take those feelings and swallow them down. Better yet, channel them into your performance, but don't let them get in your way. Who's your worst enemy?"

Libby licked her lips, tasting her watermelon lip balm. "Me."

"Who's the only person who can keep you down?"

"Me." She said it with more assurance this time.

"So get your head out of your ass and breathe."

She did better after that, not great, but better. Andrea stopped complaining and started teaching again and she actually made a little progress. She did channel some of her anger and despair into the aria, which was a love song, of all things. But what was love without a little fear and anger anyway?

Ms. Klein had told her masterclass that love was an amalgamation of all the emotions: fear of the unknown, joy of being with someone compatible, sadness that it will one day end, disgust at yourself for not deserving the other, pride in yourself for earning it, anger at the universe for keeping it away from you for so long. If you were lucky, joy outweighed everything else.

At the time Libby hadn't been sure she believed it but now, after reading April's confession, she thought maybe she understood. All those conflicting emotions sometimes led to bad decisions.

But all she cared about was the music, so she took that weird energy, that dichotomy of feeling, and put it all into her face. Because singing was about muscles – all of them. And even though she'd won a spot in the chorus didn't mean her competition had ended; every day would be a competition, if only with herself. One day she'd graduate and start auditioning for the big roles and everything she did now would make that day a little easier.

She went to her yoga class knowing she was on her way to the top.

Twenty-Four

Libby woke up three times before her alarm went off. At least she'd been sleeping, even if it had been on the couch. Rehearsal started at ten, her first rehearsal, and she'd set her alarm for seven so she'd have plenty of time. It was six-thirty when she finally gave up trying to get back to sleep.

Michael was up already, he'd been out for a run and was in the shower, so she made breakfast, a proper one, with oatmeal and fruit and tea because she didn't want to have coffee breath even a little bit and she always imagined she did even after brushing her teeth. She'd spilled water and milk all over the counter, split the lid on the plastic container of dried blueberries, and stepped on Jeeves's tail by the time Michael came out.

"Nervous?" he asked, handing her a tea towel to clean up the water.

She ripped the towel from him and dropped it over the puddle. "Of course not, why would you think that, I mean, it isn't like this day could make or break my entire career in any way at all, so why would I be nervous? I was never nervous for any of my auditions, especially not this one which I don't even remember. It's possible I was drunk or asleep and maybe they meant to hire someone else with my name." The thought was horrifying.

"Stop."

She stopped. Took a sharp, short breath and waited.

"I know we haven't talked about this, so you'll tell me if this is a problem, got it?" The power in his voice made her knees weak.

She nodded.

"Say it."

She lifted her chin and looked him in the eye. "Got it."

"Go, take one of the cushions off the couch and kneel in the living room. Clear your mind. I'll finish breakfast."

She obeyed. At first she couldn't control her racing heart or thoughts, but as she sat and concentrated on her body, her breathing, she calmed. Michael was taking care of everything. She didn't have to think yet. She didn't have to worry about anything because she'd made a list and Michael had seen it. He wouldn't let her forget anything.

"Do you have your corset ready?"

"Yes." She'd made sure it was clean and sitting out. Just the thought of it embracing her settled her more.

"Your copy of the score?"

"In my bag." She'd put it there last night. She stared at the bag, hoping for x-ray vision to kick in so she could check. "Can I double check?"

"I'll do it. Bend forward to put your forehead on the floor and stay there until I let you up."

It was an easy position, he'd seen her do it before. She couldn't see anything but the wood now, and Jeeves's little white paws. She concentrated on sound, instead: Michael rustling in her bag, the burbling of the oatmeal on the stove, Jeeves washing. She smelled the faint orange of floor cleaner, dust, Earl Grey. Food. Her stomach grumbled and Michael let her up.

"Sit at the peninsula and eat your breakfast. Drink your tea. You have plenty of time."

He ate with her, working on a crossword puzzle as he did. From time to time he'd ask her opinion on a clue, and that was the only time she spoke. When she was done eating he poured them both a second cup of tea. "Go get dressed. Get completely ready. When you come back out I'll dress you up."

It was what they'd started calling shibari, because he liked to make her pretty. The thought excited her and calmed her all the same. Usually they did it in the evening so she could sleep; the idea of doing it in the morning to calm her was tantalizing. Unexpected and subversive, and she liked the idea that no one at rehearsal would have a clue what she'd done after breakfast.

She came back out in loose pants and a tight t-shirt, completely ready except for her corset and the shirt she'd wear over it. A pile of ropes, all white, waited on the coffee table along with the safety knife. He'd moved the cushion away from the coffee table to give him more room to work.

"Go back to your position."

She knelt on the cushion again. He knelt beside her and stroked one hand down her braid, then continued down her back to stop at her waist. She stretched up into the caress, hardly thinking anything. As he wrapped the ropes around her and wove the knots he told her what he was doing, not only so she could move when he needed her to, but because he wanted her to approve. When he was done she was back in her kneeling position, forehead on the floor. Her ankles were bound together, and her wrists behind her back, secured to each other. Then he'd encased her from neck to knee in a herringbone pattern. She couldn't see anything but her own chest and the floor, couldn't smell anything but the bergamot in the cup of Earl Grey he'd placed near her chin. He'd reheated it to make it smell more and she breathed in the calming scent.

Distantly she heard someone come to the door, heard voices, but she didn't bother herself with it. She wasn't visible from the door so she didn't care. She was warm and quiet, neither happy nor sad, not agitated or angry or any other emotion. She just was.

Another sound broke into her awareness, closer, louder. The sound of liquid. She opened her eyes and saw Jeeves lapping at the tea. "Shit," she said, barely able to articulate. "Go 'way. Stop. Jeeves, stop."

He didn't stop drinking, the idiot. She came farther out of herself. "Michael?"

She heard him say something, so low she couldn't hear properly.

"Michael! Jeeves is drinking my tea!"

Michael laughed at the indignation in Libby's voice, then realized that he had no idea what caffeine or bergamot would do to a cat. He ducked around the wall and pushed Jeeves away from the cup. "Bad cat." He picked up the cup and turned around to see Ray, still and expressionless.

"What the fuck is this?"

"Is that Ray? Hi, Ray."

Ray's right hand clenched tight, then he spread his fingers wide. "What the fuck is this?"

Michael stepped between them, shielding Libby so he couldn't see her so vulnerable. "Can we talk about this later?"

Ray's mouth worked as he tried to form words. "No," he finally got out. "We can talk about this now or not at all." He took a step forward, into Michael's space. Michael couldn't step back, didn't know well enough where Libby was.

He could only hear a constant litany, the word shit over and over again. "Libby, please, breathe," he said as calmly as he could.

"You told me you weren't into this shit," Ray said, pointing one long finger at Libby.

Michael held up both hands. "I'm not, I promise. But Libby is and today she needed some rope therapy. That's all."

She gasped. "Michael untie me."

"Don't move," Ray spat, getting even more into Michael's face, and all his instincts screamed at him.

He kept calm, not wanting Ray to escalate. "I have to untie her. I have duty of care to her in this state." He glanced back to see her rocking back and forth. "Yellow?"

She nodded, repeating the word. He moved to untie her as quickly as he could, keeping an eye on Ray, but Ray only stared at him a moment longer before saying, "I'm done. Don't call me," and stomping out.

"I'm sorry," Libby said a while later, after the ropes were gone and he was rubbing the red in her wrists where she'd tugged at them. He sat before her on the floor, she was still on the pillow.

"It's not your fault." He shouldn't have answered the door. He should have known this would happen. "Maybe it's better this way. If I'm going to be your top," her eyes snapped up to his and her mouth dropped open, "then we needed to know how much of a problem he'd have before we got any more serious."

"Stupid cat."

He chuckled. "Yeah, stupid cat. What kind of cat drinks tea?"

"Maybe catnip tea."

He massaged her ankles, next, and she lay back on the floor. "How are you feeling?"

"Mmm. Still pretty fuzzy, despite all that. It's good."

"You should go put your corset on, try to maintain that feeling." He stood, holding out a hand to help her up.

She nearly catapulted herself into him, slinging her arms around his neck. "I'm sorry. Maybe once he has time to think he'll realize what he gave up."

Michael pulled her close, relishing the feel of her soft curves, the light, barely-there scent of her shampoo. "Maybe. I hope so." He kissed the side of her head. "You still have an hour before you have to leave. I'll stick around, make sure you don't go off the rails again."

"Thank you, you know? You don't have to do this for me."

"I know. But if I don't who will?"

Her laugh vibrated through him. "Claudine."

"She totally would." He gave her one last squeeze. "Go, get ready. I'll get you another cup of tea."

"I feel like I should be getting you something a lot stronger."

"I'm good for now." And he was. For now.

Ray felt like a fucking idiot. He should have known better, should have called it off right then in the bar the night Michael introduced him to Libby. He'd fucking noticed how close they were and a part of him had flailed but then he'd cursed himself out for biphobia—deeply stupid since he was a little bi too—and promised he'd do better.

He'd trusted Michael. He'd trusted Libby, and now they'd both betrayed him.

Ray slumped against the wall of the dry cleaner, fighting the nausea that threatened to dump his breakfast all over the sidewalk. He couldn't stop the images in his head, of all the other fucked up shit they probably did. Even if they weren't having sex. He'd heard stories, everyone had. Just because he didn't see any bruises on Libby didn't mean they weren't there. Or worse.

It was disgusting. He didn't know who led who down that road but they'd lied to him and God knows what perverted shit they were covering up.

But he'd liked them so much. Michael was everything he wanted in a partner and Libby had quickly become a friend, their new relationship wiping out the clusterfuck of their one night stand. He'd know better for the next time, that was for sure.

As he straightened up and began walking again his traitorous brain couldn't help but show him a picture of how beautiful Michael and Libby would be together.

Michael ghosted through the day, to the point where David called him into his office mid-afternoon and asked him what happened. He knew what David was expecting, that he was being harassed in some way, so he didn't spend any time avoiding the topic, he just told him outright, the whole story. If anyone could understand both his point of view and Ray's it would be David.

"Eesh," was what David said eventually. "You're coming over for drinks tonight, no arguments. We need to hash this out the old fashioned way."

Michael snorted at his pun. "Just tell me when."

Back at his desk he checked his phone and found a text from Libby: Ridiculous number of singers here who can't sit still. And then, How are you?

He replied with the neutral face emoji. I'm OK.

Nccd me to tie you up?

That pulled a laugh out of him. Thanks, no. I think I'll take off early today, though. See you at home.

Her reply was a string of little pink hearts. He loved how casually affectionate she was because it meant he could be too. He'd spent a long part of his adulthood restraining himself from all the little touches and friendly kisses he'd grown up with as normal. Libby had been raised the same way and so never misunderstood. Never recoiled or complained. She just accepted it as a part of him.

A distraction seemed in order, so he wandered around the streets for a few hours. He'd been putting off buying new shirts for a while, so that took up some time. Then he ventured into a hobby shop, only to realize that he didn't have any hobbies. His time was taken up with work, Ray, and shibari. He guessed that made shibari his hobby. The book Claudine gave Libby was good and it would take them a while to work through it, so he didn't need anything. That didn't stop him from spending some time in a high-end sex shop looking at toys.

He went home to an empty apartment, which wasn't as unusual as it seemed. Libby not only had been busking during evening commute several days a week, but she also had auditions and friends who kept her out later. He was used to coming home to only Jeeves, so why did it feel so strange right now? He put it down to his mood and busied himself making a sandwich for dinner.

After he ate his food he sat and read the news until it was time for him to leave. He was due at Claudine and David's at eight and it would take a half hour to get there. He'd hoped to see Libby before going, but she'd probably gone out with some of her new co-workers.

Claudine's house was as dichotomous as she was: conservative and classic on the outside, shockingly modern on the inside. He walked through the door of a Second Empire rowhouse and into an art gallery – sparse furniture, enormous paintings, dark wood floors, strategic lighting. The only thing galleries didn't tend to have were toys and books all over the place. Nor did they usually have a matched pair of Great Danes named Nick and Nora. Claudine had a love for Hammett which really, Michael couldn't fault her for.

The dogs greeted him at the door a step ahead of Claudine.

"Aw, Mikey, come on in," she said. She closed the door and immediately pulled him into a hug. She was a couple of inches taller than he was and enveloped him in big sister. He enjoyed the moment, taking in the scent of food and her lingering perfume. She backed off and kissed him before taking his coat.

"David putting the kids to bed?"

"Yeah, Lucy wanted a story only he could read, apparently." She shooed him away. "Go, sit. I'll bring drinks."

He patted the dogs and walked down the length of the house to the living room, only to stop short when he saw Libby taking up a big leather armchair. "Hello."

"Hey." She kicked a foot out and straightened up. "This house is insane."

"I know. Took me a while to get used to it."

"Is it really four floors?"

"Including the basement, yes."

He sat on the couch nearest her, within reach of the slapdash platter of snacks. He took a handful of pretzels and made himself comfortable. "What are you doing here?"

"David called Claudine, who called me to find out how you really were, and then invited me tonight." She carefully set down her drink. "Do you not want me here? 'Cause I can go home. Or wait outside."

"No." He reached for her hand. "It's good. How was your first day?"

He listened while she talked, watched the animation in her face, how she moved her hands. She'd changed so much since he met her, for the better, he thought. She was telling about one of the leads, who she'd seen and admired in several operas when Claudine walked in with a tray of drinks, David following.

"Claudine," Libby asked, interrupting herself, "why am I here?"

Claudine raised an eyebrow at her and set the drinks down before answering. "Because this isn't just about Michael's breakup. This is about Ray's reaction and your relationship," she gestured between the two of them, "in particular." She passed out the glasses. "We'll all need it for this conversation."

She took a big swallow and turned on Michael, who was starting to feel about five years old. "You. Why the hell didn't you tell him?"

He looked at Libby, who shrugged. "Because he was an ass about it earlier," he admitted. "When Libby told him where she worked he got all stereotyping and judgemental."

"He apologized for it, though," Libby added. "He promised to try to keep an open mind."

"And that made you think keeping it from him was a good choice?"

Michael took advantage of his own drink to buy time. "I didn't think it was any of his business. I wasn't doing anything wrong. I wasn't cheating on him or doing anything to endanger him."

David, who had seated himself in the chair beside Libby's, replied. "Look at it from his point of view. You're more than a little into women and you're doing something commonly associated with sex,"

"Violent sex," Claudine added.

"With a young, beautiful woman who lives in your apartment. How could he not take that the wrong way?"

Libby held up a hand to stop him. "Wait, no. I talked to Ray about the whole roommates thing. He was good with it. He didn't think we were fucking behind his back, not at all."

"Okay," David conceded. "He didn't. But you didn't give him a chance to understand before you dumped him in the middle of it."

"It was an accident." Why did Michael feel like he needed to defend himself? Oh yeah, because it was his former CO and his boss. "He was just about to leave when Libby called out."

He caught the miserable look that crossed Libby's face. "Damn it, Libby, it's not your fault. You were concerned about the cat."

"I could have, I don't know, headbutted him away or something." She sank down, her elbows on her knees, the glass in her right hand pressed against her forehead. "I could have waited."

Claudine turned the force of her glare on Michael. "And you. I should box your ears for leaving your sub alone tied up. What did I tell you that first class?"

"She wasn't gagged and she was within earshot. She was fine."

"I really was," Libby said.

"Neither of you is leaving without a hell of a lot more reading to do."

"Yes Ma'am." Then he winced, but sometimes those old reflexes kicked in and you couldn't help it.

"But the point," Libby said, having recovered her spine, "is that Ray was more worried Michael would want to dominate him, I think." She frowned at Michael. "Right? Isn't that what he was talking about at the bar that night? 'Just don't expect me to do it?'"

"That's pretty much what he said." Michael grimaced. "But I did say that wasn't really my thing anyway."

"And that's probably why he thinks you lied to him," David said.

"I didn't. It's not my deal, it's Libby's. I do it for her."

Libby's face went blank and this time Claudine really did cuff him. "You asshole."

"What?"

"If you didn't want to you wouldn't. That's it. You wouldn't even have come to that second class."

She was right. He did get a certain satisfaction from the act, in a way he hadn't bothered to examine. Whether it was because he was helping Libby or because he was creating something beautiful he didn't know, but he was pretty sure it wasn't the usual way people got satisfaction out of domination.

She'd read everything on his face—and since when was he that transparent?—he knew because her expression softened. "Idiot."

"I know. I just don't understand what I'm supposed to be feeling." He turned to face her more. "You've always said you do it because it's satisfying. How? What are you feeling when you're flogging someone?"

"Powerful. Protective. Like I'm giving them a gift. Sexy, but that goes along with powerful. Clever. Diabolical, sometimes." She paused, then added. "Rich. I do it for money, you know." She shared a long look with David, a look that had depths Michael couldn't read, the depths of a long and happy marriage.

"I doubt you'll get Ray back," David said after a moment of thought. "He's probably so deeply into his own head that he's painted all BDSM as evil."

Michael hoped not. Ray was more thoughtful than that. He might not come back to Michael as a lover, but he might, given time, realize he wasn't entirely correct in his read on the situation. "Maybe I'll send him some flowers," he joked weakly. He was exhausted all of a sudden, the whirlwind of emotions having caught up with him.

Claudine's hand landed on his knee, rubbing gently. "There's nothing I can say right now that'll make it better."

Michael didn't usually let his sarcasm get the better of him. "So you convened an intervention to yell at me about the way I treat my sub?"

The snort Libby let out wasn't exactly operatic.

David stared at her. "How drunk are you?"

"I'm not, I swear."

"She just laughs like that when I get snarky."

"The dominant/submissive relationship is all about respect, I hear," David said.

Libby waved a lazy hand at him. "Yeah, yeah, whatever."

Conversation sufficiently derailed, the evening ended up enjoyable, and Michael left feeling like he might make it through the grief.

Twenty-Five

Michael hadn't realized just how often he'd communicated with Ray throughout any given day until he couldn't anymore. It was ridiculous; they'd only been together a couple of months. Getting over him shouldn't be this hard.

"Maybe it's because he dumped you instead of the other way around," Libby said when he mentioned it. "That's always harder."

He winced at the word dumped. He wasn't trash. Except maybe in Ray's mind, probably in a lot of people's minds, he was. But what would that make Claudine, or Libby? He'd never allow them to be spoken of that way. "Maybe."

"Or maybe you just liked him a lot."

"I did, I really did."

Libby ate a handful of peanut M&Ms from the bowl on the couch between them. They were watching *Ghostbusters* and the dance scene was on. "Hey can I ask you something?"

"Sure."

"Could you have stayed closeted forever?"

He didn't have to think about it, he'd known the answer for a long time. "Yes. But that's probably because at any point I could have chosen to only date women and no one would ever guess."

"But if you were straight up gay?"

He chuckled at her wording. "I don't know. I don't know what it's like to not have other options."

"What about your family? Do they know about you?"

"I told them when I started seeing Oliver." He'd been in a state where, after losing Jeanine in such a horrible way, he thought he had nothing left to lose. "They took it well, on the surface at least."

"And not on the surface?"

"They're keeping it to themselves if they have any other thoughts about it." He picked a couple of red M&Ms out of the bowl. "They were thrilled when I told them about you moving in."

She chuckled, low and knowing. "You didn't mention my age, did you?"

"Nope."

"So they're assuming...."

"Probably."

"Okay."

He looked at her instead of the screen. She looked completely unperturbed. "It doesn't bother you?"

She blinked at him, puzzled. "Why would it? You're attractive, successful in an admirable way, caring, fun...what's wrong with that?"

"I'm nearly twice your age."

"First of all, no you're not. And even if you were, still not seeing the wrong." She held up a hand to forestall argument. "I know what other people see as wrong, but I don't personally understand it. Whatever consenting adults do is their business. I'm old enough vote, drink, and die for my country if I wanted to. Why do people think I'm too young and dumb to understand what it means to be in a relationship with an older man? My parents used to lecture us on paternalism in society. They were referring to the medical industry, but it applies here, too."

Suddenly Michael had a whole new problem to think about. They finished the movie in a comfortable, familiar silence, but afterwards Michael had little memory of the last ten minutes, consumed with wondering if he was falling for Libby.

He'd never been the type to fall for two people at once, but he'd never been in this situation before, dating one person and living with another he was attracted to. Yes, Ray had left, but Michael missed him, obviously had feelings for him, so how could he justify even thinking about Libby that way?

On the other hand, how could he not, now that he knew she might be open to it? But it wasn't fair to her when he was still hung up on Ray. He sat, eating the candy without really tasting it. Libby got up and turned off the TV, cleaned up their dirty glasses, gave Jeeves his evening kibble until eventually Michael heard her in the kitchen, talking to someone. To the cat.

Brrt?

"I know, but what can we do?"

Merow.

"That would be rude. I'm disappointed in you for even suggesting that."

Borrr-meh! Owowow.

"Michael, your cat has a filthy mind!"

"I taught him everything he knows," he called back.

Her laugh was full of music, and he wondered if she practiced that, too.

Libby remembered, mostly, where Ray lived. She had to go past, come at it from the east the way they went that night, but once she found the right street she knew which house it was. What she didn't know was his work schedule, so she might have made the stop for nothing, but it was worth a try, right? She double checked her memory and then gently pressed the doorbell.

It swung open almost immediately. "What?" he said, clearly already pissed off. Then he registered her presence. "Oh. I thought you were my neighbour."

She'd been working up a speech on her way, but he'd already derailed it. "You are a terrible human being," she said, unable to keep affection out of her voice. "Can I come in?"

Ray backed away, swinging the door wide. "Well, if you're going to sweet talk me." He might even have been happy to see her. Or it was residual pissiness. He always looked mildly annoyed, it was just the way his face was built.

"I'm sorry," she backtracked immediately. "You're not terrible. I don't know why I said that." She dumped her jacket on the floor in the hall, for lack of a place to put it.

"You're upset. That's okay." He led her into the living room. "Can I get you something?"

"I'm good. Sit, please?"

He sat across from her, leaning forward, elbows propped on his knees. "Does he know you're here?"

"No."

"Okay."

"I'm not sure I understand," she began slowly, trying not to misspeak, "which part of what happened upset you. I would like to.

Understand, that is." She chanced a look up at him, hoping desperately she'd said it right.

He sighed and ran a hand over his face. "I'm not even sure I know. It was the bondage, it was you, it was—"

She cut him off. "Wait, me?"

"You. You're young and attractive and fun and female and he was doing something sexy with you."

"Not really?"

"Which part?"

"The sexual part."

"Maybe not sexual but definitely sexy."

Libby's face heated up; she really needed to forget that she'd slept with the guy, right on the couch she sat on now. He was off-limits.

He picked up a coaster and fiddled with it, passing it from hand to hand. "Look, he'd be happy with you. You're tidy, you work stable hours, the cat loves you. He'll never get fired or shunted sideways for loving you. You're easy."

She raised a pointed eyebrow.

"You know what I mean. And you love him, I can tell. He loves you, too."

"Look, I've always had a thing for older men. When I'd sneak away to my friend's house to watch TV it was to ogle Jonny Lee Miller."

"That's not helping."

"But Michael saved my life. Maybe more than once. And he'd never take advantage of that."

"You're not denying anything."

"No, I'm not. Because it doesn't matter how I feel – he'd never do anything. And I'm kind of insulted that you think I'd seduce him away from you."

"Sorry. It's just, knowing he likes women, too...."

"He likes you. He misses you. That's what matters right now."

"I don't want you to be sad."

"It's not like I'm pining for him. I'm not holding out any hope and I'm not some child convinced she'll never be happy without The One. And I've been a lot worse than sad." She'd somehow managed to bring the conversation back to bondage. "The other thing, the bondage, that helps with the worse than sad."

He sat back, then, crossing his arms over his chest. "Tell me."

She told him everything, about the hopelessness of her captivity, about not being able to sleep alone anymore, about needing cash and doing Claudine's class. About how she'd been at peace for the first time in something that wasn't music. She told him about her panic attacks and her corset. And when she'd finished slicing herself open for him to examine and judge she waited.

Ray fidgeted when he was thinking. Libby had a lot of time to watch him and notice his little quirks, like how it was always his left hand he ran through his short hair, but he used his right hand for picking things up. It was his right knee that joggled up and down minutely and the creases between his eyebrows were different lengths. "I need to tell you something," he said eventually. "This isn't related at all, but I might not get another chance to tell you."

Libby put on an expectant look but said nothing.

"I grew up here, in this apartment. Two parents, a little sister, a dog, all of it." He glanced up at her as if to check her reaction. "A great childhood all around. Then my dad got a new job. I didn't want to leave the city. I was in college, I had a job at a clinic right down the street and I was going to be an EMT as soon as I was strong enough to make the fitness requirements. I needed to be here, near my job and my gym and my workout buddies. I also just didn't want to leave Toronto."

Having no idea where he was going with this story, Libby nodded.

"Anyway, the folks and my sister, they moved. Got some property out in the country, and I stayed here. The mortgage on this place was long paid off, so I wouldn't have to leave. Then my sister went off to university and my parents realized they hated living in the country. So my dad," he looked up again, this time holding Libby's gaze, "who was a conductor, got his old job back and they sold the farm."

Libby stopped breathing. The last name. She hadn't even considered it because the family were all his opposite: tall and lithe, dark-haired and eyed. And Lee was such a common name. "But you don't...."

"Look anything like them?" he offered. "I'm adopted. It's a long story."

He scratched the back of his head and scrunched up his nose. "Anyway, I remember, a little while after they moved, my mom telling me about this waif they'd semi-adopted, a girl from the next-door commune, who they were helping transition into the real world."

"That was me." No sound came out, just the shape of the words, but he understood.

"Yeah. As soon as you said your friend's name was Corina and she had a horse I knew it was them. I just needed to confirm with my family. And then that whole thing with the arrests came up and you were practicing so hard for your new job it just never seemed time. I was going to surprise you the next time Cory visits."

"I guess that not going to happen now."

He didn't answer, which she took as confirmation.

"That's okay. Thanks for telling me anyway. And thank your parents for their help. I'm not sure I ever did."

"No, yeah, they knew you were grateful." He stood up, Libby copying his movement. She knew the talk was over. "I'll think about what you said, but I'm not sure I can get past the lying." He shook his head. "And no matter how good that lifestyle is to you, I can't be a part of it."

She could even tell him that Michael hadn't been lying; they'd established that at Claudine's that evening. However inadvertent, it had been a lie.

Ray saw her to the door, and it was over.

Twenty-Six

Libby hadn't sung with other people as a group, trying to blend, since she was a little kid. They'd sung in school every day, songs about nature, about the importance of conservation, about the evils of industry. They'd focus on harmonizing, on working together to make something beautiful.

Then Libby had discovered that she had a talent that went beyond the other kids, and she'd forgotten how it was to sing as one of many. She'd discovered opera and standing out and being important and she'd never considered any other path.

Maybe her parents had been right about the dangers of exceptionalism, because she had a hard time adapting to being part of a group again. She had to relearn how to match consonants with the singers on either side of her, how to stagger breathing with them. But every so often she'd get it, that moment where it all came together, and she'd feel the gestalt as they all hit a chord just right. The room would buzz with a stunning energy, an almost perceptible emotional lift, a sense of community Libby had been for years desperately trying to regain. Those were moments she learned to live for and they happened more and more often as the weeks went on.

Most of the people around her had been in the chorus for years, had sung this opera many times before. She was one of only five new hires—last minute, late season replacements—and they had to catch up quickly.

She couldn't stick close to Dinah because she was an alto and Libby had been placed between two sopranos she could take cues from. It was helpful, sure, but lonely, too. Luckily Libby had never had trouble talking to strangers and making them into friends. Not that she'd be telling any of these people much about her life outside singing; she'd learned a lot about separating work and life at the club. In fact, she'd even glossed over singing jazz entirely. They knew about the busking but anything else was private, just for her.

The chorus's schedule was brutal. Two rehearsals a day for one show and when it went into performances they'd start rehearsals for a new one. So in the future she'd be singing upwards of eight hours a day, two different operas. She'd start at ten AM and finish whenever the evening's performance finished, with several long breaks in between.

"Is that even legal?" Michael had asked when she'd run down her hours for him. In response she'd showed him her employment contract, salary highlighted at the top. Rehearsals, shows, everything included, she'd be making nearly as much as he was if she was working the whole season.

His eyebrows shot up comically. "Makes me wish I could sing."

"You couldn't hack the hours, old man."

"Oh, yes, thank you."

Libby watched Dinah through morning rehearsal one day about a month in. They'd learned their music and were working on their blocking, so she could divide her attention.

Dinah's attention was somewhere to Libby's left. Libby tried to sneak looks once in a while, to find out just what or who Dinah was looking at, but every time she did she risked calling attention to herself. She hadn't been able to tell anyway. The only things to Libby's left were a few sopranos and basses and pieces of the set. To her right were tenors and altos, including the tenor she'd figured from the first that Dinah would be interested in, but nope. She'd never taken a second glance at him. But someone had her attention and the basses were all married.

Maybe it was someone off-stage? In any case, Libby needed to talk to Dinah because this was way too interesting to let go. As soon as they were let go she grabbed her arm and dragged her aside. "Lunch? Next door?"

"The hell? Quit it with the," she made a swirling motion, "the eyes."

Libby realized she must look a little frantic, gripping her arm like that. "Sorry." She dropped her hand. "I just need to get out of here."

Dinah immediately grabbed her bag and headed for the door. "Let's go."

The great thing about having friends who knew your story is that you never had to explain why you needed to leave. Libby mostly used her power for good. Unlike this time, when all she wanted was to get Dinah alone. They ordered and took their food to the park nearby, taking advantage of the warm spring sun.

The park wasn't so much a park as a concrete island with a landing strip of grass, three weak trees, and big planters full of spring greenery, but it was outside, a situation Libby craved more and more often now that she wasn't spending fifteen hours a day there. The practice space the chorus used didn't have any windows, it was a big, featureless room, and if it was any smaller it might give Libby hives. As it was she hated being in there alone. She'd prefer to wait in the hall looking out the window over the roof until someone else showed up.

The relief that swept through Libby when they got outside was so profound that she wondered if maybe she had been on the verge of an attack. Although the cleaning crew did their best, the place could get dusty and was always relatively dark during rehearsals.

So now she was out here with Dinah and she couldn't figure out a way to ask her what the hell she'd been staring at all morning. They chatted while eating until Libby finally gave up and said, "So, what the hell were you staring at all morning?"

Dinah took a last, huge bite of her sandwich. "Nothing," she said around it, her face all innocence.

"Bullshit."

She rolled her eyes, which Libby took as asking her to wait. Sure enough, when Dinah was finished chewing she answered. "I have kind of a crush."

"Please don't tell me it's on Emmett. Please."

"No, ew. Dude needs to bathe once in a while." Dinah fished around in her sandwich wrapper and pulled out a sunflower seed which she tossed to a passing robin. "Promise you won't laugh?"

"Swear."

Sometimes things that everyone knew, things they learned as kids, were what tripped Libby up. She'd just barely, with the help of Rain and YouTube, managed to catch up on the most quoted moves and TV shows, but the kid stuff was a minefield. So when Dinah stuck out her crooked pinky finger with an expectant look

Libby didn't know how to respond, and she hated having to explain why she didn't know things. All she could do was copy her and hope. Dinah linked their fingers, let go, and Libby breathed a mental sigh of relief.

"It's Sam," she said, then waited.

It took Libby a second to place the name. "Oh," she said, drawing it out. "I can totally see that."

"Really?" Dinah smiled at her, all her previous tension gone. "Most girls our age would just say 'ew'."

"Nope, not me." Libby would be a hypocrite if she criticized someone else for being attracted to a much older man. Sam was in his sixties, but the principle was the same. "That voice."

She sighed. "And the way he looks directly at you when he's talking. Pierces your soul."

"I couldn't take the deadly seriousness all the time."

"Everyone in my family thinks they're comedians. He's refreshing."

Libby crumpled up her wrapper and tossed it in the trash next to their bench. "Not my style."

Dinah glanced at her sideways. "Is Benny your style?"

Ugh. Libby knew this conversation would come but that didn't make it any easier. "No. And he feels the same, okay? We're good."

"Touchy." She checked the time on her phone and stood up.

Libby chucked her drink bottle and followed her out of the park. "I'm just tired of the assumption that every relationship has to be romantic. When I'm travelling all over the world I might not have time for romance. I know a lot of people manage it, but it can't be easy."

"Travelling?" They stopped for traffic and Libby got a good look at the confusion and disappointment on her friend's face. "You have a job in the chorus of a major opera house. There's no need to travel anymore."

They crossed the street, rushing to avoid the next wave of cars. Libby got to the door first and held it for Dinah. "I'm just here for the rest of the season to make a little money for when I go back to Pickford."

"Why would you bother going back to school? You're all set here. No one cares if you have a degree."

"Do you know what the chances are of us being picked out of the chorus for a solo role? Close enough to zero." She headed up the stairs to the rehearsal hall. "If I want a manager, if I want to win competitions and auditions I need to finish school. Maybe even go to grad school."

"Oh. You want to star."

"I thought you knew that." The hall was filling up but the chorus master wasn't in yet, so they rested just inside the door.

"I'm happy in the chorus," she said. "I just want to get paid to sing opera; I don't need the lead roles. It's too much pressure, too much stress. This is my place."

Libby could understand that. The chorus wasn't easy; the music was challenging enough and you had to constantly keep learning new pieces and styles. But you had a sense of your place in the world, you had a family, you had security. And although a part of Libby yearned for all that, a bigger part wanted the spotlight all to herself. Maybe someday she'd be happy in the chorus, just like maybe someday she'd be happy singing jazz in a club. But for now she had to try, just to prove that everything she'd been through, everything she'd lost, was worth the trouble.

"Hey, that guy didn't work out, so we still have a room if you want it."

Libby had said no before, but now she wondered if she should say yes. She'd been relying too much on Michael, and maybe now was the time to strike out on her own again.

Something was wrong. Something was different. Michael couldn't pinpoint it but the apartment felt off, fundamentally changed while he was at work. Jeeves greeted him at the door as usual then went back to his post at the window. Everything was in its place; even the blanket which Libby always left piled on the couch cushion was folded and draped neatly over the back.

He scanned the room. TV, stereo, laptop, all there. It was his turn to cook so the kitchen was clean. Nothing was visibly wrong. He poked his head into Libby's room. No shoes on the floor, no clothes or books on the chair.

No picture of her parents on the nightstand.

The closet was empty, as were the dresser drawers. The only proof she'd ever been there was a folded piece of paper on the bed, bearing his name. For a brief, terrifying moment he remembered Janine's note and his heart stuttered, but no, Libby wouldn't do that to him. He prayed she wouldn't do that to him as he opened the page.

Dear Michael,

I figure there's only one way to solve this problem, and that's for me to leave. You've taken care of me so now it's my turn to take care of you.

You can try to get Ray back, explain everything. Tell him anything about me that you need to.

He's a good guy, he'll come around. But only if I'm not living with you. Only if we're not doing that thing anymore.

I've got a place. Don't worry about that.

I'm not changing my number or anything, so feel free to keep in touch if you want.

Just don't try to convince me to come live with you again. It's better for all of us this way.

Libby

Well. Michael sat on the bed and read it a second time, hoping he'd missed something important. He should have known this was coming. He wondered when she made the decision, how long she'd been planning this. Why she'd decided that his love life was more important than her own mental health.

But ever since getting the job in the chorus she'd been better, learning how to stave off the panic as it started, using clothing as an alternative to bondage. She could sleep on her own now under most conditions. So perhaps she was right and she could take care of herself.

He tugged his phone out of his back pocket and pulled up the messaging app. *If all else fails, call me*, he sent to her.

A moment later she replied, *OK, but you're my last resort. And you'll ask Ray first.*

He wouldn't agree to that. If he couldn't convince Ray to trust him with Libby then they had no proper basis for a relationship anyway. He put his phone away without replying.

If Libby was perfectly honest with herself she'd admit that living with Dinah and Benny was a welcome change. They were loud, for one, fighting as siblings did, and although the apartment was tiny Libby didn't mind because they were never cruel about it and always shut up when she asked them to. The snack food was junkier, which she had mixed opinions about, and the alcohol was cheaper, but she never felt like a guest. She paid rent so she had the right to leave her towels on the floor and they had the right to yell at her about it.

It was good.

But leaning against Benny during movies wasn't like leaning against Michael. He didn't put his arm around her and he wasn't as solid and warm. The one time she'd tried to put an arm around him he'd just looked at her like she was an alien and she'd had to pretend she was brushing a spider off the couch cushion.

And having people around who would, who could, sing entire scenes with you? Was amazing. It made her want to start up her own commune full of singers, with maybe a few pianists thrown in for variety. They could buy a building, all live there as one enormous family, going to work and doing chores as they were best suited. No one would ever be lonely, except when they had to travel. But that would never happen. Dinah, when Libby suggested it as a joke, thought the idea was weird. Benny said he had no opinion, but he tended to side with his sister anyway. But even that rejection wasn't worse than her first month in Toronto, so she'd manage.

She got through the first week without any emotional explosions and was ridiculously proud of herself. She could do this.

She couldn't do this. In the two weeks since moving in with Dinah and Benny she'd actually grown lonelier. Benny was still in school and was spending all his time with his classmates preparing for their last year. Dinah's ridiculous crush on a married man was taking up all her energy at rehearsal, which meant Libby had to spend more effort making new friends in the chorus. It was exhausting in a lot of ways.

The worst, though, was the insomnia. Unlike her 'fall asleep, wake up screaming' PTSD this was pure guilt keeping her up at night. Michael and Ray still hadn't made up and she was responsible. They'd be happy together if it wasn't for her neediness, her helplessness.

"How can it possibly be your fault," Claudine asked her one day, after Libby broke down and called her, "if you weren't a part of their relationship? It's Michael's fault for not realizing the truth and it's Ray's fault for not stopping to listen."

"But they wouldn't be in this position at all if it wasn't for me. Michael would have had nothing to realize." Libby realized something herself. "Hell, they wouldn't have met if it wasn't for me. And now, instead of being happy alone or with other people, they're just miserable alone." Just the thought made her stomach ache.

Claudine sighed. "There's nothing I can say to make you feel better, is there?"

"Probably not."

"Then I'll just have to wait until you get your head out of your ass to have an adult conversation with you again."

Ouch. "Have we ever had a conversation where I sounded like an adult?"

"I think you do okay at times."

"Just not now."

"You kind of are making their choices all about you."

She was right. Libby never thought she'd be that self-centered, but you learn something new, et cetera. "I see your point."

"I think you made the right decision for you. Better to leave a fraught environment than get dragged down by it, right?"

Libby hadn't figured she was being dragged down, but that was not a discussion she needed to have over the phone, without the benefit of facial expressions. "Right. This way we can all have room to get balanced again."

She just hoped she could find her own balance soon.

Twenty-Seven

Opening night for *La Traviata* was in a week and the chorus was emotionally mixed about it. It was a remount, not a new production, so most of the chorus had done it at least once already and they were blasé about it. The second tier of emotion were the members like Dinah, who'd been performing all season but had never done this particular opera before. They were excited and apprehensive, but confident in their director and their group.

Then there was Libby and the few others who'd come on with her. This was their first performance of this opera, with this company, and they were nervous as fuck. It didn't help that they'd started rehearsing a different opera in the afternoons already and Libby was terrified of getting them mixed up. No matter that they were wildly different styles in different languages – that would just make it worse when she burst out singing into dead silence where the whole chorus should be.

"I have performed major roles to large audiences before," she told Dinah during the first technical rehearsal, "I have sung folk tunes at Union Station during lunch rush. I have sung jazz in an intimate bar when I was the only person on stage. So why the hell do I have stage fright now?"

Dinah patted her on the back, unconcerned with Libby's trauma. "Because you're a diva."

"Thanks. You're such a help."

"I aim to please." She put down her score and turned on the bench to face Libby. "You know exactly why you're nervous. But you'll get over it. You know how this works: you get out there, the music starts, memory takes over and you get it done. That's why we rehearse."

Libby groaned and put her face in her hands. "I know."

"Then stop obsessing about it. My first performance here I had my entire family in the audience, taking up a whole row. I did fine. I didn't even trip."

Oh fuck, she hadn't even thought about that. The first act had furniture everywhere. She wasn't used to wearing enormous skirts; what if she got caught on something when they exited the stage and she ended up dragging a chair or a tablecloth or another cast member with her?

"Stop it," Dinah said. "I can see the anxiety building up in your head. Take a deep breath and chill the fuck out."

Libby did, and it helped. "This is stupid." And then, "I don't hear you disagreeing."

"Nope. Understandable, but stupid. Stupid to give in to it, not to feel it." She dropped her score off to one side of the backstage area they waited in. "As stupid as me studying this score for the millionth time even though I know it. I think I know every part by now." She pointed to a cluster of singers by the stage door. "See Nick? How he's standing on one foot? That's what he does. Julia chain-eats mints. Paige doesn't have any nervous habits until show time, when she grabs a program and shreds it. Then she's fine. I study my score at every chance during rehearsal, but can't before performances. Find your thing. Then you'll be fine."

Easier said than done. "Sounds like something you just fall into."

"Probably. But everyone seems to, so you likely will too."

"You realize you've jinxed me by telling me."

"Then my work here is done."

The call came and the orchestra started the overture. "Newbies, over here," the chorus master told them. When they'd gathered he instructed them. "Today's not about you, so save your voices for dress. Concentrate on your entrances and exits, blocking, props, all that. And don't forget to act. This isn't bel canto; Nobody comes to see a block of wood, no matter how perfect its pitch."

The rehearsal went well, even if it was long and incredibly boring. Pickford productions hadn't been anywhere near as complicated as professional productions, and the length and tediousness of the rehearsal increased with the number of moving parts – which included people. At least the chorus got to sit back and play cards during a chunk of act two and all of act three.

"I get what you meant, now," Libby told Dinah while the stage hands were removing tables from an overcrowded set design.

"That instinct and memory take over?"

"No. Well, yeah, that too, but what you said ages ago about getting to sing and wear gowns and not have all the pressure." This was their first rehearsal with the soprano who was singing Violetta, only she hadn't shown up yet because her flight from London had been delayed. Her understudy was carrying rehearsal—and doing a great job, as far as Libby could tell—but it didn't take much to see the strain on her, and to imagine what Ms. Chao was going through wherever she was.

"It's a good life."

"If it didn't sometimes include ten hours of singing a day." She'd sometimes done as much as seven hours a day, four busking and two or three at the club, but there'd been times lately she wanted to do anything except sing. A week's vacation—a week's vacation without any other people so she wouldn't even have to talk—would be heaven right now.

Of course, most of the chorus would get the summer off. Some would find other places and ways to perform, sure, but Libby would be going back to school. They'd be starting a new season in September and she'd...still be in school. All of a sudden the prospect seemed disappointing. What was she thinking? She shook herself back to the present. She didn't have any decisions to make for months yet, but she had a job to do now and no way was she going to fuck it up.

She needed someone to give her a hug and then tell her she was making trouble for herself. She needed Michael. She missed Michael. She'd never noticed how much she watched him before, and even when she was at rehearsal she automatically looked for him when she had something to say.

It was embarrassing; she'd never thought of herself as that person who became so ridiculously focused on a crush. She just wanted to be with him all the time and he rarely turned down an invitation. Not that she passed up going out with friends without Michael. She'd never see them otherwise, because Rain was still a little uncomfortable around him and Dinah was disappointed on her brother's behalf. She just had to hope they'd get over it.

But the whole watching Michael thing was how she noticed the particular sequence of events: Ray would text Michael, Michael would smile sappily while reading it, Michael would look sad a few beats later. It was nice to see them communicating now, except for the results.

Libby couldn't say she didn't experience the same thing when she texted Ray. Getting to know him this way was different than when he was Michael's boyfriend. Less intimate, in a way, almost like they'd taken a step back in their friendship.

She'd send him a pic of the costume room, he'd reply with a story about one of the other firefighters and then she'd find herself smiling at the memory at odd times during the day, all the while hoping he'd text her again. Once Michael asked what she was grinning about and they ended up talking about Ray for twenty minutes.

Ray: *My grandma just texted me a photo of a Nice Romanian Girl she thinks I should marry.*

Libby: *Is she cute?*

Ray: *Pretty cute, yeah. Grandma likes that she writes a political newsletter. Says we'll have lots of smart babies.*

Libby: *What kind of politics?*

Ray: *Feminist/LGBT/green*

Libby: *Fuck being straight, I'll marry her. Tell Grandma you're dating me and M. That'll get her off your case.*

Nothing. No reply. She didn't realize until much later that she'd basically implied that she wanted to have Ray's babies. Which wouldn't be bad, but not for another decade at least. Shit. She was crushing on both of them now? Doubly ridiculous. They belonged together and she needed to get over herself. Her chosen career meant spending weeks, maybe months, away from Toronto, flying all over the world. The thought of getting to sing in Europe's opera houses with the greatest soloists of her time made her heart flutter. Then she ached almost to the point of tears at being without a family beyond the companies she'd work with. Stage families were great, but when you were the star they were short-lived and never as close as you'd like. Or so she'd gathered from reading their autobiographies.

She wanted both. She wanted a noisy, busy family like the one she'd grown up with and she wanted the life she was slowly making for herself. She just had no idea how to get there.

Twenty-Eight

Between his own work, which was taking up all his evenings right now, and Libby's schedule Michael felt like he hadn't seen her in weeks. Texting during work and the occasional phone call were their only chances to talk. How pathetic was it that those were the highlights of his day?

His team won their case, exonerated the client, and his first thought was that he wanted to tell Libby. His second thought was that he wanted to tell Ray. He thought about calling him after, but he'd never been the one to initiate their conversations, and Michael had never been the guy who put himself where he wasn't invited. Not in his personal life, anyway. He'd had to do that too often in his former job, force himself into people's homes, their lives. He was so often the bad guy, who broke up families, who arrested dad for killing mom or mom for selling drugs, who searched houses and revealed secrets.

Ray would learn about it on the news, just like everyone else.

Saturday, the day Libby's show opened, came around. He was home and she'd come over to, as she put it, "get out of the hell that is Dinah on opening night", and neither of them had anything to do. She'd warmed up her voice earlier and they'd both gone down to the gym, and now she was lying on the couch upside down, feet up on the back and head nearly touching the floor, pretending to read a book. He could tell she wasn't really reading it because she kept flipping back several pages to start over again.

"When do you have to be in?" The show started at eight, he knew that from his ticket.

"Six. An hour and a half to do hair, makeup, and costume, then warm-up."

"If we have an early dinner I can tie you up for a bit after, if you want."

She tumbled off the couch and landed on her knees, hair a mess of dark curls covering half her face. "Yes please, oh my god." She brushed her hair out of her eye. "Are you laughing at me?"

He couldn't deny there was something like a smirk tugging at his mouth. "You can ask, you know. You don't have to wait for me to offer." He gave her a hand up.

"I didn't know if you'd want to after what happened."

He rubbed his thumb lightly over the back of her wrist. "You can always ask. I can always say no. That's one of the rules, isn't it?"

"Yeah, I guess it is."

"Go get the book and the ropes and I'll start dinner. We can decide what to do while we're eating."

The neat pile of rope on the coffee table taunted him while he ate. For a bit he wasn't sure he could go through with it, so he examined the idea. What was bothering him? He thought about Ray, but that wasn't it. His mind kept circling back to before she moved out, during the movie. A little compartment in his head, the one that kept Libby the attractive woman out of his consciousness, had opened. He weighed Libby the attractive woman against Ray the attractive man and then gave up because it was not only pointless but almost embarrassingly equal.

Libby cleaned up their dishes while, on autopilot, he laid out his gear. She joined him wearing a tight tank top and the feminine version of boxer briefs, both in a deep, rich red that made her winter skin seem even paler. He worked quickly and quietly, watching her relax, listening to the ropes rasp against each other. The repetitive action was meditative for him, too, allowing him to stop thinking about anything but his subject and what his hands were doing.

He wasn't usually so aware of Libby's body, the strength in her legs, the muscle tone in her arms, the weight of her breasts, the curve of waist to hip and down to thigh. He accidentally over-tightened a knot on her sternum and in his haste to loosen it he brushed her breast with the back of his hand, something he'd done before, but never before had she gasped like that. "Sorry," he said, trying to ignore the rising urge to slide his hand down, around, to cup her breast and run his thumb over the prominent nipple.

"It's okay," she said, breathless, and he wasn't sure if either of them meant the brief pain or the resulting touch. "I kind of, kind of like the idea of going on stage with a mark you left on me."

He stopped breathing. "You...you want me to mark you?"

Her nod was more of a wobble, but her expression was clear. She drew one leg up, brushing his side as she did.

He sat back on his heels, away from her. All he could think to say was, "The rope marks won't last that long." His voice sounded too small and weak.

"My ankle," she said, drawing her foot into his lap. "Give me a cuff. No one will see it, but I'll be able to feel it."

Three strands of his highest gauge rope, woven, knotted around her ankle just above the bone, tight enough not to shift but not tight enough to cut off circulation to her foot. "Done." He gave her foot a squeeze, then cocked his head, watching her. "Something else?"

"If you want," she said, holding his gaze, "you could mark me here." She drew her finger up the inside of her left thigh, high up. "With your mouth."

"Jesus," he gasped.

"You said I should ask."

"I did."

"And that you could say no."

He made his decision, then. "I'm not going to."

He thought he heard her say 'thank god' as she relaxed back into her cushions. He still held her foot so he started there, drawing his nails lightly up the sole, feeling the shiver run through her. He kept going, the pads of his fingers tracing lines on her calf, catching on the slight stubble. He wondered briefly if she'd let the hair grow in if he asked. He used his nails again, feather-light, on the back of her knee, and she kicked out reflexively with a laugh. He kissed the spot in apology. The hair on her thigh was soft, unshaven, the skin supple and taut when he rubbed his cheek against it, loving the gasp she gave him as he darted his tongue out for a taste. "Where was that spot?" he asked, his mouth brushing her skin.

"Here," she replied with a catch in her voice, indicating a spot much higher than before.

He smiled into her skin then bit her gently. "Was it?"

"I swear." Her hand brushed his hair, then rested on his neck.

He nipped again at the spot, then sucked hard, and this time she gave him her full voice, deeper than before, in a wordless gasp. He worked at the skin with lips and tongue and teeth until the soft chime of her alarm made him stop. "Time to get ready," he said.

She sat up, dropping the leg he'd been holding to his side and straddling him where he knelt. "In a minute." She threaded her hand into his hair and pulled his mouth to hers.

He couldn't focus, her lips warm and wet, the weight of her resting on his thighs, his hands falling around her waist, to her hips and ass, feeling his ropes still decorating her. Then she was sliding away from him, standing. "Later," she said. "Because I feel fucking amazing and powerful and sexy right now and I really want to keep that."

"And also you don't want to be late." He stood up and helped her with the knots, all except the cuff.

"I'll meet you, after, in the lobby."

"I'll wait, however long it takes."

Michael barely enjoyed the performance.

It was excellent, from what he could tell—engaging stars, interesting set, no major mistakes that he could identify—but he kept thinking instead of paying attention. He'd be watching, listening, but then he'd see Libby in the background singing and flirting and pretending to have a great time at a party and his thoughts would get away from him. He'd think about what was under her skirt, the brand he'd left on her leg. He'd think about her lips on his, the slightest brush of her tongue when she pulled away.

He'd think about Ray. And that was the problem, there, because how could he do that to Libby? It was better if he didn't start anything with her, at least until he'd had some distance. His throat tightened at the thought that he might need distance from her in order to get some perspective. He could come up with some excuse, make up a reason to go see his mother, his sister. He could ask David if he was needed somewhere else, maybe out west. Not for long, not for more than a few weeks.

And then he'd see her on stage again and wonder what the hell he was torturing himself for. He wanted her, he could have her. As long as he was honest with her, why shouldn't he take that leap? If it didn't work out, well, they were adults. There might be fireworks, but it wouldn't be the end of either of them. And, to be honest with himself, he was just a tiny bit besotted with her. He had been since the first meal they'd shared, back in Cobourg, when she'd cracked a joke about him having to carry her out of the farmhouse, blushing the whole time.

First intermission came and Michael decided to reward all his hard work convincing himself with a glass of wine if he could find one. The first bar he came to was packed five people deep, but he'd wandered around earlier and found a little one upstairs that wasn't nearly as busy. He bought a glass of Gewürztraminer and nearly dropped it as he turned around to see Ray.

Ray was too far away for Michael to hear what he said, but it was clear he hadn't intended to meet up. Michael had to get away from the bar to let others in so he went left, towards the windows, away from the stairs Ray had just climbed. If he pretended not to see him, neither would be uncomfortable. Or so he told himself, anyway.

A reflection in the glass warned him he was wrong. "Hi," he told the glass.

"I should have expected to see you here," Ray's reflection said.

Michael half-turned, leaning his shoulder against the cold metal window frame. "I honestly didn't expect you."

Ray shrugged. "She was so excited about it. I thought I should come out and support her."

It was horrible, the feeling that Michael had then. The certainty that some day Ray would find out and if Michael wanted to salvage any kind of friendship with him he should come clean. He took a fortifying sip of wine. "You should know that we—she and I—. She kissed me. Tonight, before she came here."

"Oh." A woman in a short velvet dress bumped Ray from behind, forcing him to take a step forward.

Michael reached out to steady him, then dropped his hand. "There's something else I have to tell you, though. Nothing's changed about the way I feel about you."

Ray looked down, away, uncomfortable. "Does she know that?"

"She does."

"It's weird, but I knew how you two felt about each other, even when you and I were together."

"I don't know how I'd feel if you two started dating." Michael laughed, trying to push out the pain that threatened to rise up. "Probably like some pathetic slob in a soap opera."

"You said she kissed you."

"Yes."

"And you...what?"

Michael downed the rest of his wine and thought, what the hell. "Left a hickey on her thigh the size of an egg." A smile forced its way on to his mouth and he didn't bother to suppress it.

Ray laughed. He didn't look any less hurt, but he laughed. Maybe they could salvage this after all.

The five minute bell rang. "It's good to see you again," Michael said.

"Yeah. Tell Libby she looks great up there."

"I'm sure she knows. Anyway, you should tell her yourself."

"Yeah, I should." Ray gave him a brisk nod and walked away.

Michael waited another minute before following.

Ray didn't show up during second intermission and Michael didn't seek him out. At the end he waited in his seat, both to avoid the crush and because he had time. Libby wouldn't be out for a few minutes, even though the chorus hadn't been in act three at all. And he'd clearly made Ray uncomfortable, so he didn't want to push it by encountering him again.

As he waited he weighed his feelings, realizing that he'd made a mistake assuming the kiss meant more than that Libby was keyed up about the performance and in an intimate position. He needed to check in, make sure. The voice in his head that sounded like Claudine insisted on it.

When he did finally make his way out Libby was waiting for him, dressed to go out in a drapey red top and short black skirt, coat slung over her arm. She was even wearing make-up, a look he'd only seen at the club.

"Hey," she greeted him. Her eyes sparkled with energy. "A few of the other chorus members want to go for drinks."

"And you want to go with them."

"Yeah." She touched his elbow lightly. "Will you come with me? I want you to meet my friends."

He'd been so sure she wanted to send him home that it took a moment to process what she said. "I'd like that."

"Great. Let's go." She looped her arm through his and kissed him on the cheek before leading him away.

Libby finished her rhubarb fizz and thought about ordering another, but then she looked over at Michael, idly spinning his near-empty glass on the table, laughing at something Mariana said, and she realized they could go home instead. And then all she could think about was his mouth on her thigh, all hot wet suction, and she was suddenly, powerfully aroused.

She leaned against his arm, heat soaking through his thin cotton shirt against her bare skin. He looked over and smiled, then moved his arm and drew her close to his side. She let her right hand rest on his rib cage, her head on his shoulder, feeling the vibration as he laughed again. Mariana was telling her Rigoletto story, embellished for the non-singers among them. As she listened, Libby let her hand slide down to his stomach, then over his hip to his thigh where she left it, her fingertips resting against the inner seam of his wool dress pants.

She knew he got the hint; his hand on her shoulder twitched, his fingers biting into her skin. She scratched her nails against him and listened to his sharp inhalation. But he continued to listen to Mari, smiling and laughing at the right parts, not even looking at Libby.

Libby declared war. Her only problem was keeping the others from noticing, which pretty much meant keeping it under the table. She waited until he was distracted, asking a question, and then she gently slid her hand higher, letting her forefinger drift, and then his hand was on hers, dragging it down to his knee. She knew, she knew she was getting to him, but he'd never show it. He'd told her once that cops had the world's best poker faces and now she understood. So she settled in closer to him, wrapping her right arm around him and nestling her face into his neck. And if her breath happened to ghost over the skin showing at his open collar, well then.

"You seem like you want to go home," he said quietly, and she realized her eyes were closed. She'd been listening to his breath, his heartbeat. It was soothing.

"Yeah." She looked up, but all she saw was his jaw, smooth and square. "I'm actually pretty tired."

"Your place?"

"Yours," she replied.

"Then let's go."

They made their excuses and said their goodbyes and once Libby was out in the chill spring air she woke up again. Michael called a cab. As they waited he toyed with a lock of her hair. "There were times, just now, I couldn't believe how natural it feels to have you in my arms. It should feel different. I even thought it might feel wrong. But it doesn't."

She gazed at him, at the tender expression, the softness of his eyes. "That's because nothing's changed. We're adding, not subtracting." She stood up on her toes and kissed him, slow and warm, gentle. "We're good."

"Absolutely." But his mood had changed, now. "You know I still have feelings for Ray."

"I know. I can work around that if you can."

"I think I could manage," he said, a sly smile lifting the corner of his mouth. "Who next, do you think?"

The cab's arrival saved her from having to come up with a silly answer. They spent the trip home hand in hand, each watching the lights out the window, silent. Michael paid the cab driver, then took her hand again as they entered the building.

"You still love your job now that you've had a taste of the big time?" he asked. His voice echoed in the stairwell, bringing an unintended importance to the question.

"More than I thought. Being in the chorus is surprisingly satisfying."

"But you still want to be a star." He held the door open for her, not letting go of her hand.

She'd wondered about that herself recently, but now, being asked directly, she had her answer. "I really do."

Jeeves met them at the door, his fur shining in the low light from the kitchen. They'd done this, coming home at night, a dozen times before, but now the domesticity of it all had a different kind of importance. It had been their home together for months, but now it was stifling.

Michael was watching her with a frown. "You look like you're freaking out."

"A bit." She shoved the urge to leave into the back of her brain and finished hanging up her coat.

"Come sit down for a minute." He turned on the LED candles she'd bought after Jeeves singed his fur on a real one and sat in her favourite armchair.

He looked a little scared and so, desperate to reassure him, she placed herself in his lap, leaning back against one arm of the chair, her legs slung over the opposite. She could see his face from that position, could talk to him properly.

He stroked her hair and she tilted her head into his hand. He took the hint and scratched lightly at her scalp. She closed her eyes and enjoyed the sensation.

"What's up?"

How did she say this? She'd never had a reason to put it into words before. "I've never had a real, adult relationship before, you know?" He didn't respond, so she went on. "I've had week-long flings, I've had boyfriends for the sake of having a boyfriend, I've had friends with benefits. But I've never done the commitment thing." She wiggled down into a position where she could rest her head on the chair. "But we've already lived together and it's terrifying."

Jeeves jumped up on her stomach and settled in, purring. Michael stroked the fur on his ear, but still said nothing.

"It's not that I don't want this, us," Libby said, still working it out for herself. "I do. I love you and I want to be with you. But I'm twenty-six years old and I'm not sure I'm ready to be with one person for the rest of my life. I'm not sure I ever will be. Maybe it's just not in my nature."

She reached up, caressed his face, feeling the curve of his mouth. "You've done this before."

"Yes." His lips moved beneath her hand.

"And you want it again, that kind of stability."

"Yes."

"So what do we do?"

His right hand cupped the top of her head, comforting and warm. "I'm not asking you to marry me. I'm not asking you to sign a devil's contract pledging your eternal, singular devotion to me. I'm asking you what I'd ask anyone else I'd just started falling for: Give it a shot. We were friends first. If it doesn't work out, for whatever reason, if one or both of us finds someone else, we'll get through it. We've each handled much worse." He laughed, breathy and voiceless. "Besides, pretty soon you'll be off for months at a time, running all over the world to sing at the best opera houses. You'll never be bored."

True enough. She put on her saddest puppy eyes. "You mean you won't be coming with me?"

That got a genuine laugh out of him. "I'm sure I can perform my job perfectly well from the balcony at the Bolshoi."

Libby grabbed his tie and used it to pull him down, dislodging the cat as well. "You're hilarious."

"I know." He reached down the last few inches and brushed his lips over hers, teasing.

Libby knew he was getting her back for earlier, so she resisted. She darted her tongue out to taste his lower lip, daring him to take it further.

When she sat down her short skirt had slid up, baring her thighs, and he took advantage of it now, sliding his warm hand up her skin, dipping under the hem. She parted her legs for him, but he left his hand there, his thumb rubbing small, infuriating circles where it landed.

"Asshole," she murmured, sealing her mouth to his finally, desperately.

There was only so much of him she could touch from her position – his face and neck, the short hair on the back of his head. His shoulders were square, his arms firmly muscled, and she took advantage of the moment to touch them the way she'd wanted to for so long, running her hands all over as much of him as she could reach. He inhaled sharply when she rolled over his nipple.

"Have I told you how amazing you look tonight?" he said, pulling back, letting his eyes wander down. The draped neckline of her top had slipped at some point, and he traced a finger down her skin from her collarbone, skipping her cleavage to pull the loose fabric away for a better look. A waft of her perfume rose up, thick and musky, inviting.

"Nice view?" She knew the answer. It was a fucking amazing top, her favourite, which is why she'd taken it with her that night.

"Mmm," he replied. "Wasn't expecting the hot pink lace." He ducked his head and set his tongue against her sternum, leaving it there for a second before placing a sweet kiss on the top of her breast.

She dropped her head back and sighed, closing her eyes to enjoy the moment.

"I really like this top," he said into her skin.

"Hmmm."

"Libby?"

"Mh?" She'd fallen asleep. "Oh. Sorry."

Michael cupped the back of her neck and massaged his thumb into the muscle. "Let's go to sleep."

"Yeah. How did you get to be so perfect?"

"Just lucky, I guess."

Libby slid her legs off him, then wobbled as she stood. "Can I share your bed?"

Michael caught her hand, steadying her. "I was planning on it."

And in the morning, when she woke up before he did, she had time to plan what she would say – that she needed to be on her own for a little while longer. That he needed more time after losing Ray.

And he agreed with her.

Twenty-Nine

The day after the opera Ray had a few new things to think about. He'd managed to talk to Libby after the performance, asked her if she'd been nervous before going on.

"Not really," she'd said, then explained how she'd been nervous at dress rehearsal, then about her corset and the new braid around her ankle. How they calmed her and grounded her. He remembered what she'd told him, at his place, about the panic attacks.

Now he stared at a list of library search results, trying to figure out which of the dozens of books would be best. Even researching which books to take out gave Ray new insight into the whole subculture.

He wrote a few down, sure that once he read these he'd have a handle on it. Then he could decide how he felt.

Libby had chickened out with Michael, she knew that, but she also saw the relief in his posture when she told him she didn't want to start a relationship with him after all. They'd parted amiably, Libby confident that she'd made the right choice.

But she couldn't stop thinking about him, remembering his lips on her skin, his fingers stroking up her back, silky and hesitant, subtly different from the way he usually touched her. She heard his voice, smelled his aftershave, everywhere she went. She wandered through her days in a kind of stupor, and now it was affecting her work.

She sat in the chorus master's office and waited for him to get off the phone, trying to look like she didn't know why he'd called her in.

"You're getting sloppy," he said, before his phone even hit the desk again. "You're distracted, you're not learning your blocking as quickly as before. You have no life left in you."

She couldn't argue with the truth.

"At least you're still singing well."

Also the truth.

"If you were a permanent member this would be a formal warning." He stopped, then waited.

"But?"

"But I know you're leaving, so if you don't get it together I'll be rid of you quickly enough."

Libby swallowed, trying to wet her dry mouth. "You will." Best to just let him talk rather than hasten her punishment.

"I was going to put you in Fisherman, but I think you need a week off. When this run of performances is done go away, do something fun. Come back ready to start *Orfeo*."

She could only nod and leave as quickly as she could. They'd been doing a series of five one-act operas as an end of season special and she'd expected to be in two more. Scheduling meant that if she was in *Orfeo* she'd only get one role, which meant a lot less money.

But she couldn't deny that she'd been terrible these past few rehearsals and had barely managed to put out lackluster performances. A week off might be what she needed to work through everything. If she could get over Michael this summer she'd be able to start completely new at Pickford in the fall.

Her next problem was what to do with her time. She couldn't spend it all in the apartment, she'd go nuts. Maybe the best way to forget about Michael was to make sure he and Ray got together again.

She chose to spend her first day off catching up on the news. She'd gotten a little behind these past few days, busy with rehearsals, performances, and catching up with Rain after her show closed.

The apartment had a tiny little balcony, barely big enough for a single chair and an end table, but shady enough to use her laptop and protected enough to be comfortable. She started by poking through the opera blogs she'd neglected to read, then moved on to web comics, and by her third cup of tea was ready for actual news. Or so she thought until she was confronted by a picture of April and Jim under the headline KIDNAPPERS' INDICTMENT DELAYED. She waited for the reaction, the tight throat and quickened pulse, but it never came. Calmly, she read through the article, stopping at one point to reread: The Hollings's lawyer, Scott McClanahan, will present new evidence that may affect the charges.

Something niggled at her. Something about the transcripts she'd read, but was it in April's? Jim's? The two who'd actually done it? She'd noticed oddities but had disregarded them in her need to deny the truth. The more she thought about it the more she was convinced someone higher up had directed them. But who else could be behind it? No one else had the power. No one else knew where Libby was. Probably most assumed she was dead.

Except one. One other person could have done it. Libby knew what she had to do, so on the second day of her week off Libby caught a train to Belleville.

Ray knocked on the apartment door then shifted the bag of books to his other hand while he waited. He'd come here on impulse, wanting to talk to Libby about the reading he'd done. He knew she was off this week, but that didn't mean she was home. If she wasn't, though, he might not have the guts to come try again.

The door opened, revealing a young, Black woman—Dinah, he guessed. "Can I help you?"

He shifted the bag again. "Uh, yeah, is Libby around?"

Her jaw tightened. "What's your name?"

Okay, he could understand that. "Ray."

The door opened a little wider. "Michael's Ray?"

"In a way, yeah."

She relaxed against the door frame. "She's gone."

"Where to?" He didn't know she had anywhere to go.

"She said she was going back to the farm. Picton, I think."

Ray thought he said thank you and goodbye, but couldn't be sure because he was already halfway down the hall pulling out his phone to call Michael.

"Ray?" he answered in his usual mild voice.

"Yeah, look." Ray slammed the stair door open and ran down. "Libby's gone. I was just at her place to talk to her and she's left. Gone back to that cult her mother runs."

The pause on the other end weighed a ton. "Okay. She wouldn't do that on her own. Someone must be pressuring her."

"That's what I thought. Can you get time off to go up there?"

"I think so. You coming?"

"I'm already on my way to rent a car." There was a place a couple of blocks over, he saw it on his way in. "You know where we're going?"

"Not exactly, but that's what web searches are for."

"I'm pretty sure I do know." Silence. "I'll explain on the way. Get on a train and get over here." He gave him the address of the car rental and hung up.

Ray was just finishing the paperwork when Michael showed up. "Good, you're here. Is this stupid?" he asked as they walked to the car. "I think this might be stupid."

"It might be." Michael tossed a duffle bag into the backseat and climbed into the front. "But if she really is in trouble we can't just wait."

Ray started the car and pulled out. "I tried calling her, but all I got was voicemail. You?"

"Same. I'll keep trying."

The expressway wasn't far. Ray didn't know what to say, so pretended he had to concentrate on the midday city traffic. The GPS did all the talking for them until they got on the 401 and Michael leaned over to turn it off.

"Yeah, we don't need it now," Ray said, desperate to break the sudden silence. "Straight shot up to Belleville and then south on 62."

"Right. Ray," Michael began, then didn't go on.

Ray kept his focus on the road. "Can we just concentrate on this right now?"

Michael sighed. "Sure."

"What have you got in the bag?"

"Extra clothes in case we have to stay the night. How do you know where we're going?"

So Ray told him about the talk he and Libby had, and then the story of his sister and the girl next door.

"Huh," Michael said. Ray snuck a glance at him as he ran his thumb over his lower lip. "Small world."

Ray made a non-committal noise. "I just hope that's where she actually is. She said there's more than one commune. What if she went to a different one?"

"We have to start with the most obvious. If she's not there we can try them all if we have to."

Michael never asked what Ray was doing at Libby's apartment, which was great because he didn't want to open that can of worms. He needed to actually talk to her first.

When the car she hitched a ride with pulled into Picton it hit Libby that this was the first time she'd been back since she'd left the same way. She ate lunch at a cafe in downtown, then walked the twenty minutes to Prospect Avenue. She stood at the driveway to the farm, looking up as far as the curve would let her. The property was beautiful from the road, all trees and wildflowers, but if you looked closely enough you could see the solid brick wall rising fifteen feet up behind them. Up around the curve would be a heavy wooden gate with two people manning the little guard house. Smaller private properties flanked the drive, themselves another wall keeping the public out.

How many people in the area actually knew what was behind that wall? Most knew it as the old Lynch estate, certainly, swallowed up by forest over a century ago. The immediate neighbours certainly knew; you couldn't ignore the strangely-dressed people who came down the driveway and managed the roadside stand.

For a long time the community had thought they were Mennonite, which was actually fine until George Olin made the mistake of talking religion to someone from the church down the road. Then it came out that they were pagans, which was the best people could do at interpreting the commune's beliefs.

But greater Prince Edward County? Probably had no clue they were even there. None of the news articles had mentioned location more specifically than by province. The drive, the house, gate, it all seemed so normal, so innocuous. So why were Libby's hands shaking?

She straightened her spine and raised her chin and marched up the driveway. She wore her old clothes, which she'd kept out of some strange nostalgia—long grey wool skirt, unbleached linen blouse and jacket, straw hat. Her shoes were leather, but hopefully no one would be able to identify it on sight. If they did she'd lie and say it was waxed cloth. She'd stashed her bag in a locker at the station and her phone was in one of her deep skirt pockets, set on airplane mode so it wouldn't give her away. If she was lucky the guards would let her pass without looking at her closely.

She wasn't that lucky.

She barely got within sight of the guard house when one of the men—she didn't recognize him—walked out to meet her.

"I don't know you," he said, taking a long look at her clothes.

She panicked for a second that she'd got something wrong, but that would be like forgetting how to use a fork. Her acting training kicked in and she remembered her plan. "I'm from The Hospital. I'm here to see Mother Paula."

He still didn't trust her. "She's not here. No one knows where she is."

"Father William does." Let him interpret that how he wanted.

He glanced back at the roof of the house. "Does she know you're coming?"

Victory. Libby didn't bother to hide her smile. "No, Brother. It's an emergency."

He relented, waving her up to the gate and the second guard. "What's your name?"

"Beth." A common enough name in her generation, as newer members tried to curry favour with Libby's parents.

"Rowan. Brother Henry," The other boy looked up from the grasshopper he was studying, "I'll take Sister Beth inside and be back as quickly as I can."

He took her through the door in the back of the one-room shack they called the gatehouse and out into the main courtyard. The wild lawn was exactly as Libby remembered, dotted with flowers and striped with hand-mown paths, a cluster of solar panels in the middle. The herb garden nearest the gate had been enlarged and now included a greenhouse. The ring of bunkhouses, wash-houses, and equipment sheds remained the same, as did the old manor up the hill. The house, a big red brick building with a wide front porch and patchy slate roof, was their dining hall and community centre, library and school. She didn't realize how much she missed it until seeing it again. Life here had been good, for the most part.

Someone crossed in front of her, drawing her attention to the people who used to be her family. They walked quickly through the lawn with their hands full, hung out laundry, bent over the herbs. She recognized a few faces here and there, more as she got closer to the house. So far no one recognized her, or if they did they didn't show it. She didn't think she looked that different—her hair had been short when she left and she'd forgotten to take off her bra when she changed at the bus station, but her face was the same.

She didn't want to be recognized, didn't want her mother to have any warning, because she had absolutely no idea what Paula would do. Her throat closed up and she considered making up an excuse and turning back, even hesitated a step and pretended to be looking at a butterfly sunning itself in the border. But no, she'd come all this way and it might be her last chance.

She took a step forward, then another and another until a man stepped into her path. Facing her. Blocking her.

"That is not supposed to be here."

Shit.

Thirty

Michael had been working over his apology for weeks now but the time, the place, the mood of their conversations so far hadn't been appropriate. But now, in a car on a long drive, they could hash it out. Clear the air. "Ray," he said again, sure that he'd be ignored again.

Ray tightened his grip on the steering wheel, knuckles turning white. "Fine. Let's do this."

"I fucked up. I fucked up and you have every right to hate me," Michael said in a rush, ignoring his planned speech. "And I'm thrilled you're happy to talk to me as friends. But I can't stop thinking about you."

Silence, then a soft. "Go on."

"I miss you with an intensity I never expected." He folded his hands together in his lap, like a child or a penitent. Spoke to the dash in front of him. "After my wife died I thought that was it, I'd never really love again. Her suicide... it broke me. But I think what was worse was the realization that she didn't trust me to help her through her illness. And she couldn't even be honest with me about that."

Ray made a noise, indecipherable.

"And I suppose I did the same to you, didn't I?"

"You can't compare now to then," Ray said. "This is not the same at all."

"No, it's not. But when you reduce them to trust and honesty?" Michael tried to think through the muddle of his feelings. "I didn't trust you to even try to understand. And I wasn't honest with you." He chuckled. "It's been pointed out to me that lies of omission are still lies, which you'd think is something I'd know. So I'm a hypocrite, too."

"Aren't we all?"

"We can try not to be."

Ray glanced over, his expression unreadable. "Yeah. We can."

Libby's brain went blank, except for the man's name, Turner. She'd barely had anything to do with him in the year between his arrival and her exit, but he apparently remembered her.

"She's here to see Mother Paula," Rowan said, unwittingly coming to her rescue.

Turner didn't look at her, but Libby pretended she deserved to be there anyway. "It," he emphasized the pronoun, "was excommunicated," he told Rowan.

Rowan stared at her, examining her. "So what do I with her? It," he amended.

"Take it back to the street. See it off the property completely," Turner said. "Don't speak to it. Don't let it speak to anyone else." He then stared at Rowan until Rowan took her by the elbow and hauled her around back the way the came.

Libby didn't remember Turner telling him to shove her out the gate and into the street, but she was too busy picking herself up and brushing bits of asphalt out of her skin to complain.

Ray had only been to his folks' farm a few times in the years they'd lived there, but a little help from a map app got him and Michael there okay. His mother had pointed out the long driveway to the commune with its little roadside vegetable stand, telling him about what probably went on behind the walls. He drove past it, looking for a place to park, when Michael shouted, "There!" He pointed out his window at a stand of trees.

Ray was just about to argue with him that they'd passed the driveway already, but then he saw her, Libby, sitting on the verge. He pulled over, stopped, and let Michael rush out to get her.

She greeted him with a confused head tilt, putting up with him grabbing her shoulders and bending down to eye-level.

"What are you doing?" Ray imagined her saying.

"I thought we'd lost you forever."

She laughed. Ray continued their imaginary conversation in his head. "You have. I'm brainwashed again. I'll live out my life here in obscurity and hunger."

Michael glanced back at the car and Libby followed suit. "No. You can't. You must come back with us."

"Ray's here? Well, okay then. I owe this cult my soul but I owe Ray ten bucks and that's more important."

An SUV was coming up fast and the car was blocking the lane, so Ray honked the horn to get their attention before pulling up so he could park on the shoulder.

No point in staying the car while they talked without him, and their conversation had only gotten less friendly. Libby wasn't quite shouting, but her left arm was waving around at shoulder-level in an increasingly exasperated way.

"...hanging over my head for the rest of my life," she was saying when he got close enough to hear.

Michael was... Ray had never seen that expression before. Despair, maybe. Desperation. Maybe one part each and one of giving up.

"Ray," he said, his voice echoing his face, "please help me convince her not to go in."

But now that Ray was seeing her here, healthy and whole, dressed like one of them, he couldn't. "Are you going back for good?" he asked instead, and ignored the betrayal Michael showed.

He barely breathed when she levelled a sad look at him.

"Of course not," she said, and his shoulders relaxed. "Do you really think I went through all that just to give in to them now?"

He had to admit he might have. "You've always said how much you miss having family."

She reached out, first to Michael, then to Ray, and grasped their hands. "I have a family. You guys and my roommates and Rain, you're all family, too."

Michael stepped forward a pace. "Then don't do it," he pleaded. "Don't go in there and risk damaging part of our family."

"He means you," Ray provided. "You can't guarantee you won't get hurt or locked up."

She squeezed their hands again and let go. "I can ninety percent guarantee it. I'll have to sneak in the back since they already threw me out, but—"

"What?" Ray interrupted.

"You already went in?" Michael finished the question.

Libby made a face. "Yes? It's not like I knew you were coming to wait around for you." She stopped them from interrupting again. "I went in the gate, one of the members recognized me, they tossed me out the gate again. I was just planning another attack when you drove up."

Attack. Like it was a war she fought, maybe with herself. "Can you do this safely?" Ray asked.

"Yes. I managed to go in and out for a couple of years without anyone noticing. I never told anybody where the gap in the fence was."

Michael sighed and stared at his shoes. Finally he raised his head again. "And what if the gap isn't there anymore?"

"Then I'll come right back and I won't try again." Her right hand made a fist in her skirt, bunching up the heavy fabric.

Ray had one more question. "What do you expect to get out of this confrontation?"

Her answer was simple. "I need to ask her why." Realizing he didn't know what she was talking about, she added, "why my own mother had me kidnapped." With a deep breath she continued, "I'm going to do this, whether you approve or not. Now, will you still be here when I come back out or am I hitching a ride home?"

Of course they'd still be here, what was Libby thinking asking that? Ray clenched his teeth on his indignation and simply nodded along as Michael answered.

As Libby marched away from them, Michael, sounding more tired than Ray had ever heard him, said, "I'm going to move the car up to the main gates, out of the way," then he motioned at the cemetery down the road.

Ray nodded again. "I'll meet you there." He needed to move, slipping through an open gate into the cemetery for a walk through the trees. It wasn't terrible—at least there were standing headstones rather than the kind sunk into the ground, which always seemed to Ray like people pretending death didn't exist. And the path was easy to navigate. Too easy, maybe, because he didn't have any excuse to keep away from Michael for a bit longer.

And then of course Michael had to make it harder, by getting out of the car, spotting Ray, and meeting him halfway.

"Tell me," Michael said, stopping in front of Ray. "Why are you here?"

For a second Ray didn't know what he was asking. "I was worried."

"You said you went to her place to ask her some questions. Were you maybe thinking of...?" He let the question trail away.

Wrong place, wrong time, wrong person for that conversation. Ray deflected, going for the joke instead. "I was thinking of asking her out properly. See if we could work."

Hurt flashed over Michael's face, then a slight smile. "You do have lovely chemistry together."

"I know." Ray wanted Michael to hurt, just a little more, but he couldn't make himself do it. "But I still feel like I don't really know her. Not like I know you."

The smile widened, spread to the corners of Michael's eyes. "There's nothing stopping you from getting to know her."

"I want to try."

"And when you do?"

Ray hadn't thought about it.

Michael kicked at a loose stone, which rattled on the cracked concrete path. "Would you consider coming back to me?"

Yes, he wanted to say. "Aren't you and she a thing now?"

Michael shook his head, now studying a patch of fresh grass. "That was one time. I'll confess that I enjoyed it, and I could build a romantic relationship with her. But," here he looked up at Ray, "I can't stop wanting you, too."

Way to put him on the spot when they still had three hours in the car together. Ray felt like chickenshit, but all he could do was bail. "Hey, there used to be a Jamaican place near here. Why don't I go get us all some lunch?"

Michael blinked at him a second, then rebooted. "Sure. Surprise me." Then he turned away stare in the direction of The Farm.

Thirty-One

Libby's next trick was to get to the back fence without the neighbours (Were they home? She couldn't tell) catching her. She'd have to spend a few minutes on their land, in full view of their windows, before she could slip between their cedars and The Farm's fence.

Her clothes were bland enough that they wouldn't stand out, especially if she kept to the shadows near the trees. She moved as quickly and smoothly as possible, like a fleeing deer, concentrating so hard on remaining unseen that she nearly missed the patch of stray strawberries that marked the gap.

She'd always wondered about those strawberry plants and their perfect positioning.

The hole in the fence was really a pair of loose boards that stayed up with the help of a couple of cedar branches on this side and one nail each on the other. She carefully, slowly, pulled one board aside and peered through.

Nothing had changed. The shed that hid her escapes and entries still sat, weathered and peeling once-white paint, although now it smelled like it held compost instead of tools. She poked her head out a little farther to make sure no one was around, then pulled out the next board and squeezed through. She made sure to replace the boards so that no matter what happened to her, the next child looking to escape would have an option.

She paused at the corner of the shed and listened for activity, hearing nothing close enough to worry about, then peeked out to double-check. This might actually be easier than before, because the rows of strawberries that used to fill the field nearest her had been replaced with raspberry canes tall enough to hide behind. On each side of the canes were now solar panels, new and more compact. Were they planning to expand, or had they just upgraded?

It shouldn't matter to her either way, she reminded herself. As near as she could tell, no one was looking her direction, so she slipped out from behind the shed and walked along the raspberries, hat tilted to shield her face. She hadn't brought a basket to look like she was working here. She should have checked the shed.

Don't hurry. Don't look around too much. Eyes on the goal. The goal was the big house, the original manor at the opposite end of the property, the place the residents called home. It was barely visible, just a snip of the shiny black panels on the roof peeking out from the ancient conifers that surrounded it.

She passed steadily by the solar farm and across an area left wild for the grasses and beneficial insects. The leaves brushed against her legs under her skirt, familiar in a way that made her long to stay. But she couldn't stay, couldn't even stop to have a seat and enjoy the spring day, because there, right where it should be, was the solitary bee habitat and the start of her path through the woods.

She shivered as she crossed the line from sun to heavy shade. Ray had asked an important question — what did Libby expect to get out of this confrontation? If she was honest with herself she expected nothing. She expected to be refused, to be expelled from the property for a third time. What did she hope for? Acceptance? Perhaps. An admission of wrong-doing might calm some of her anger. As her feet thudded on well-packed soil and dodged tree roots she settled on her most basic wish: for her mother to say she still loved her. For an apology.

Knowing she wouldn't get it almost made her turn around and give up, but she would never get another chance to do this so she kept on walking the path she'd cut as a child.

It opened out into a clearing, a perfect circle of shade plants broken by ovals of disturbed soil. The burial ground. She searched for what must be her father's grave; it wouldn't be bare of growth, but it wouldn't have subsided completely yet either. That one, then, near the sassafras. That had always been his favourite tree. She stared at it for a little longer, then went on her way.

Behind the house was a stone wall, dividing what was once a formal garden from the forest beyond. Libby paused as she always had as a child, and tried to picture her grandfather, her great-grandmother, and generations back, growing up here, when the house and its occupants were envied rather than laughed at. She'd asked her mother once if she could try to restore the formal French garden, but she'd only been allowed to work on the herb garden. It was still there, she saw now, still tended, although it had outgrown her tidy borders.

No one was around, although if anyone watched from a window she couldn't tell. It was time to move. Up and over the wall as if she'd never left, follow it for a few metres to be out of direct view of the kitchen window, then straight for what used to be the servants' door.

The back stairs were empty of footsteps and voices, and Libby considered herself lucky. Most likely everyone was pruning and planting. The house still smelled the same, like shellac and wool and cooking. She dearly wanted to veer off and tuck herself into the window seat near the bookcase where she'd spent so much of her time. She'd stolen a book when she left — *Anne of Green Gables*. Was the gap on the shelf still there? Had anyone replaced the copy?

Instead she went upstairs, to the front room that looked out over the courtyard. Her mother's room when she was in town, and the only place she would be now if Jim's testimony could be believed. Libby couldn't imagine her bold, active mother so reduced. But it was true that she'd been out of society for at least a year, not even scheduled at any of the other facilities.

Best get this done. Three quick, quiet knocks on the door had Libby shaking again. She took a deep breath and opened it. Behind it the room was dark, only a thin sliver of light reaching between the curtain and the window frame, highlighting nothing. Her heart thumped, almost painfully loud to her, and she concentrated on the feel of the woven rope around her ankle to quell the rising panic. Better to just get it over with.

She pushed into the room and closed the door. "It was you, wasn't it?"

"Pardon?" Her mother, haggard, pale, worn down, sat in a corner the light didn't touch.

"My kidnapping. You planned it. You put April and Jim up to it. You're letting them go to jail for you."

Now that her eyes had adjusted to the dark Libby could make out more of the room—the rocking chair her mother sat in, the side table with a cup of tea on it, the dresser. No bed.

"They agreed." Her voice was as weak as her face was slack. "They did all the planning. They're as guilty as anyone else."

Libby reminded herself that her mother had once been an actor too, that she'd had time to plan this conversation. "How could you?"

Paula got up, leaving the chair to rock on its own, and came to Libby. "I needed to see you again. With your father sick—"

"It wouldn't have been necessary if you hadn't excommunicated me."

Her expression became resolute. Libby had seen it on her own face in the mirror enough times to know what would come next. "We're trying to build a utopia here. A pattern for saving the earth. Letting you go, condoning your destructive actions, would have set a bad example. A double standard."

"Do you have any idea what I went through, locked in that room for a month?" Libby gestured at the room around her. "It looked a lot like this, by the way. I was alone. Do you get that? The men you trusted to keep me safe? At the end they left me to starve to death."

"I'm sorry." Libby had to believe her. "I needed you here but I needed you to come back on your own. Permanently."

Libby took a moment to absorb all that. "It's time to give up on that dream. I'm a professional opera singer now. I succeeded despite you."

"I'm sorry about that too. I never wanted that life for you." Paula took Libby's hand, and Libby couldn't look away from the sorrow in her eyes. "Do you know why I set this place up? All I wanted was to get away. To forget that people like the ones I knew in Hollywood existed. And then I met your dad, who built a company to clean the oceans and take poison out of the land. His passion, his enormous vision of a clean and perfect earth, was like a miracle to me. We can prove to the world that our way is best. Elizabeth, I love you, but the church, the sanctity of our earth, always comes first. Humanity depends on us. Not you."

Libby swallowed down her raw anger, trying to keep an even voice even though she wanted to shout, to cry. "Humanity thinks you're a joke, Mom. You tell people they can cure cancer by rubbing herbs on themselves. You know what happens to the people who take that advice? They die of cancer. If Dad had gone to a real hospital, been treated by real doctors, he might still be alive. And guess what? It's all your fault. Dad believed in medicine before he met you."

A muscle twitched in her mother's cheek, but she said nothing.

As much as Libby wanted to continue she knew she wouldn't break through Paula's delusion. "I'm sorry I didn't get to say goodbye to him. I'll say goodbye to you now so I don't have that regret later." She rushed out of the room, the house, before anyone could stop her.

When Ray got back, hands full of fragrant paper bags, Michael was at the car, Libby in his arms, and Ray didn't know who to envy more. He nested all the bags in one hand, then rooted around in one to find his patty, which he shoved in his mouth so he wouldn't say anything stupid.

Libby didn't look happy, but she also didn't look hurt when she asked, "Are you ready to go? I want to change into my normal clothes."

"Yeah, let's go."

"We can eat in the car," Michael added.

After a stop so Libby could grab her bag and change they got on the road back home. Ray turned on the radio, some random music station, to kill the silence in the car and hopefully some of the guilt in his brain. He shouldn't have said all that to Michael, before. The topic was way too sensitive to joke about. But their situation struck him as funny, is all, except it was destined to end with one or all of them getting hurt.

As they ate she explained what she'd done, her realization, confronting her mother, everything including—and this made his chest seize up—how at home she'd felt while she was there.

"But I'm never going back," she said at the end. "I mean, maybe sometime in the distant future if they want me to help them become a lot less fascist, but not soon. And never to stay. I like myself too much for that."

"Good," Ray said. Then he remembered something. "You might want to call Dinah. I, ah, I think I scared her earlier."

"Did you accomplish what you wanted?" Michael asked Libby, leaning forward into the space between the front seats.

Ray risked a glance at Libby, who was chewing a fried plantain. "I'm not really sure?" she said. Ray turned down the music so he could hear her better. "I guess I wanted her to feel some guilt for what she did. Not only to me, but to the four people who are going to jail because she was too proud to contact me directly."

"Are you going to tell the police?" Ray asked.

She checked with Michael. "Do you think I should?"

"Ultimately it's up to you. It might get the Hollings's lighter sentences."

"And then she'd go to jail."

"Perhaps."

Libby was silent for a long while.

Ray spoke up. "I think you should. They were brainwashed and she took advantage of that. She manipulated them."

"It's not like that," Libby said, her voice rising. "She'd have asked, not ordered."

"And do you think they felt safe saying no? Would she have kicked them out, like she did to you?"

She went quiet again for a moment. "I don't know."

Michael leaned forward again. "Here's another question to think about: What's the fair thing to do?"

Libby made a frustrated noise. "I guess I'll call Detective Strickland when I get home." After a few seconds she said, "I wonder if it would have worked?"

"What?" Both of them, this time.

"Her plan. If she had showed up before you did, would I have gone along just to get out of there?" She shrugged. "I don't know. Maybe I would have."

"Really?" Ray couldn't help himself; it seemed so out of character for her.

"Maybe," she repeated, leaning her head against his arm. "I didn't want to die. I don't think I'm the kind of person who would die for her beliefs. Not like you two."

"You might not think so," Ray offered, "but I'm not, and I bet Michael isn't either. We'll make the sacrifice if we have to, but with any other option we'd choose to survive."

"Exactly." Michael undid his seatbelt so he could lean forward and see her better. "Survival is not a moral failing."

"Thanks." Soft lips brushed Ray's jaw, catching a bit on his stubble, and then out of the corner of his eye he saw her move to Michael. He risked a glance back to see her leaning her forehead against his cheek, her eyes closed.

"You two are goddamn adorable," Ray announced with absolute sincerity. They both laughed, which was his entire goal.

Thirty-Two

Ray just kept driving. One hour, two, slowed to almost nothing for construction. He tried not to let his frustration show, more than once forcing himself to relax his grip on the wheel. Libby poked through her phone and Michael was poking through.... Shit. "Don't open that," Ray said, but it was too late.

Michael had the grocery sack open and was pulling out the books Ray had taken to Libby's. "What's this?"

"Books."

Libby leaned between the seats, bumping Ray's elbow, to get a look. "Kinky books."

Ray resigned himself to the conversation. "I was going to ask you some questions. That's why I went to your apartment."

Michael passed one of the books up to Libby, who settled back in her seat. "Does this mean you're taking an interest?" He sounded so hopeful that Ray really wanted to be able to say yes.

"No. But I thought I'd try to learn about it before I go around insulting even more people I love." Well. That was out there. No taking that back now.

Neither of them commented on his word choice.

"So what did you want to ask me?"

Ray glanced back at Michael. "I wanted you to answer without him here."

He wasn't expecting Libby to swear at him. "Hey. What was that for?"

"I'm my own person. He doesn't get to control what I say unless I ask him for that specifically. Didn't you actually read those books?"

Right. He did remember something like that. "They also said that every relationship was different. I don't know what kind you have."

"Fine." She reached out to rub his arm gently. "Sorry."

He asked his questions and she answered, with Michael occasionally adding his own comments. They were just coming back up to speed after the construction when Libby asked, "Why don't you come watch sometime?" She looked back at Michael. "If that's okay with you."

"It's fine."

The thought kind of broke Ray's brain. On the other hand, it didn't repulse him the way it had when he'd walked in on them. "I think I can do that."

They'd crossed into Scarborough and were almost back in Toronto proper. Michael started reading excerpts from one of the more extreme books—Ray hadn't known it was so negative when he ordered it from the library—aloud in a dramatic voice, which got them back to the rental place.

Car returned, Ray hesitated, not entirely sure how to say goodbye after the day they'd had. Libby seemed to be having the same problem.

"I'm twitchy," she said, proving it by bouncing slightly on her toes.

Examining her more closely, Ray could see she was shivering too, although the air was decently warm.

Michael touched her elbow with his fingertips, forehead wrinkling in concern. "Do you need anything?"

And suddenly Ray was an outsider, unaccustomed to their personal language of trauma recovery. He stepped back, trying to give them some privacy, but Libby stopped him by grabbing his shirt cuff.

"I don't want to go home," she said, directing it to Michael. Then to Ray, "I don't want to have to explain today yet." She was still hanging on to his cuff, so Ray supposed he must be included in whatever they came up with.

Michael replied, "My place? Dinner, a couple of movies?" He looked over at Ray, eyebrows raised expectantly.

Ray shrugged. "Sounds great to me."

Libby didn't even have to answer, she just slid her grip to Ray's hand and guided Michael by the elbow in the direction of the nearest subway station.

At Michael's, Ray hung back. "If you need to..." he waved his hand aimlessly around the apartment, "you know. Go ahead."

Libby shot him a confused look while taking off her shoes. "Oh. No, that's not necessary. Just come sit with me while Michael cooks." She grabbed up the cat and led the way to the living room.

"While I cook?" Michael protested. "You promised you'd cook next time."

Libby's expression was entirely innocent as she said, "But I haven't planned anything! And I don't live here anymore, so I have no idea what you have on hand."

She winked at Ray and he chuckled as he sat down beside her. The cat wiggled out of her grip and shot off to visit Michael in the kitchen.

"I don't even know what I have right now." But Ray could hear cupboards opening and closing, followed by the fridge, so he must have found something.

Meanwhile Libby had curled up beside him, close enough that her knees perched against his thighs and he could feel her still shivering. Before he could, she reached for the blanket draped over the arm and wrapped it around herself as much as she could. She aimed the remote at the TV and settled back against his side.

"Let me know if this bothers you," she said as she brought up Netflix, and he was sure what she meant until she added, "I don't want you to think I'm a tease." She didn't look at him as she paged through her account listings.

"I'm thirty-two years old, you'd have to do a lot more than lean against me to tease me," he said. To drive the point home he wrapped his arm around her, nestling her in closer. The blanket was too warm against him, but this was obviously what she needed given the smile on her face after.

The smile grew wider and significantly more evil as she hit play on a long-running cop show with a distinctive theme song, then cranked the volume.

"Turn that shit off!" Michael appeared in the hall like the ghost of a wet cat. "You know I don't allow that kind of crap in my home." He disappeared again as Libby buried her giggles into Ray's shoulder.

"I only keep those shows in my list for him," she murmured, "and I don't use my evil power very often."

"I think he secretly likes it," Ray confessed on Michael's behalf. "Or else he'd delete your account."

"Probably. But I'm sure he knows I'd only fuck with his list if he did."

"I do know that, thank you," Michael said, setting down a plate of apple slices and a small bowl of peanut butter, as well as a bowl of pretzels.

Libby immediately grabbed the apples and peanut butter, saying only, "Comfort food," to Ray before dipping one in the other.

"I think I'm going to have to move in with one of you just to get ahead on something." It was a little dazzling how well they knew each other. He couldn't help but feel lost.

Libby held up a wedge of apple-PB to his mouth and he took it just before she announced, "Well, I've never had Michael's dick in my mouth, so you're ahead there."

While Ray laughed and tried not to spit out his half-chewed food Michael just shook his head and grabbed the remote from her. "You get used to it," he said to Ray. "At least I hope you will."

Having finally swallowed, Ray leaned over to murmur in Libby's ear, "I think you should change that. It's a pretty nice dick."

Her only response was a pair of waggling eyebrows and a sly smile.

Thirty-Three

After Libby and Ray went home the night before, Michael was kept awake by one penetrating thought: That evening, with all three of them, was the best date he'd ever been on.

The small, shamed part of him that was raised in a very traditional community screamed at him that it was wrong, that everyone would be hurt when it ended, which it would because no relationship like that could sustain itself.

So he did what he always did and invited Claudine out for dinner to get her advice.

"Have you ever looked at those ropes you use?" she asked while they ate. "They're not one strand, or two, but three. It takes three strands to make a rope. It's stronger that way."

He put down his fork, thinking. "I just can't help wonder what people will think."

"Who? Which people? Me? David? You know what we think. You met our last girlfriend. The others at work will follow David's lead if they ever find out. But you know what? Even if people see you together they won't believe it. We have an amazing capacity to rationalize anything to fit into a pre-existing worldview." She gestured at the tables around them, the white cloths and soft candlelight. "I bet you anything everyone here, except maybe our waiter, thinks we're on a date. They would never guess the truth of either of our lives."

He looked around at the other diners, the pairs and quartets, the occasional singleton. How many of them were in unconventional relationships? "How do you make it work, though? The logistics are kind of blowing my mind, here."

Claudine pointed her steak knife at him. "Talking. Negotiation. Making sure everyone's needs are met. Every poly relationship is different, you have to work out your own rules." She stopped aiming a deadly weapon at him and went back to cutting her meat. "And yeah, it'll feel weird and forced at first. But so do a lot of couple's relationships before they work out boundaries."

She wasn't wrong about that. "It just seems so selfish," he said, feeling pathetic even as he did.

"Michael. You were in Afghanistan at the same time I was. You served on peacekeeping missions in East Timor and Darfur. After all that you've seen and learned, tell me, how can anything that increases the amount of love in the world be wrong?"

He couldn't disagree.

The next morning, Sunday, they'd planned to meet again to ease Ray into the world of shibari and submission. Libby arrived first, early, and immediately made herself a cup of tea.

"I can't believe I'm nervous," she said, taking across from him at the peninsula.

Michael swiped the last of his toast through a blob of jam and ate it. "I'm pretending not to be."

"It'll be fine, right? He's coming into this with more knowledge and of his own free will."

"Sure."

Libby sipped her tea, wincing when it burned her tongue. "Have you decided what to show him?"

"I thought I'd try to recreate what I was doing that time he showed up. And then maybe show him that pretty foot dress we found online."

"Good plan," she said with a grin. "Try something new to show him how it's not all suave movie confidence."

"How do you know I haven't been practising on myself?"

She leaned to one side to peer at his feet, currently bare, then popped back up. "I'd actually like to see that."

"It might be easier if you did the tying."

"Would you be up for that?"

It was a new dynamic, but it wasn't like Michael had any ego tied up in being the dominant partner. "I don't see why not."

Ray arrived then, looking possibly more nervous than Michael was if his bouncing foot was any indication. "Let's do this," he said, and watched as Libby went into the spare room to change.

He wouldn't meet Michael's eyes, which was odd, but he had a big smile for Libby when she came back and arranged the couch cushions on the floor.

"Sit here," she told him, patting one of the cushions at her side. "You'll get a good view and," she emphasized, "you'll get to hear Michael swear at himself when he gets something wrong."

Ray sat where Libby pointed, cross-legged, back straight in a way that seemed almost formal, in contrast to the red toes and little dalmatians on his otherwise black socks. He caught Michael looking and shrugged. "Gift from my sister." Then he sighed dramatically. "You think they're adorable don't you."

Michael wanted to kiss that condescending look off his face, but settled for the truth. "I think you're adorable."

Libby flopped backwards on to her cushion. "Oh my god, just get back together already."

Michael wound his biggest rope around his hand, saying, "Do I have to start by gagging you?"

She flipped him off and settled into her usual neutral position. "He doesn't ever gag me, by the way," she told Ray, "that's strictly off limits."

That led to Ray asking specifics about limits, which Michael took as a sign they should get going with their demonstration.

He tried to concentrate on his hands, on what he and Libby were telling Ray, on the ropes themselves, but his gaze kept wandering to the anklet he'd made for her, then up to the spot on her thigh that used to carry a bruise. They hadn't done this since that night, since she'd kissed with such promise and voracity and no fucking way could he let Ray know what he was thinking and ruin all the trust they were building again. But she was even wearing the same light perfume and he wanted to bury his face at its source between her breasts.

He'd feel like an asshole if he didn't see the way her fingers stroked her own skin periodically, or the way Ray leaned in closer than he needed to. It would be so easy to turn this explicitly sexual, to have both of them right here on his floor. He wanted it so desperately he didn't even try to hide his increasing arousal, hoping one of them would take the bait.

But neither of them did and that's not what the morning was about anyway, and the next thing he knew it was nearly noon and Ray's phone was buzzing.

"Hey, I gotta get going," he said regretfully. "I promised I'd be available to help a friend and he's calling me on it."

Michael eased his way to his feet, mindful of the fact that he'd been kneeling for too long. He wobbled slightly and Ray and Libby grabbed him from both sides. "Trouble?" he asked.

"Nah. He just failed to plan properly and now needs another set of hands to help him pack up his apartment before the movers come."

"Besides," he continued as he laced up his boots, "any more of this tension between you two and I'd have to leave anyway." He shrugged into his jacket and half opened the door before turning back with a sly wink. "Maybe you should do something about that."

He left before Michael could get his brain back in gear. "Well."

"Huh." Libby was warm at his side but he couldn't stop watching Ray until he disappeared around the corner. "You know, this is the second time he's done that."

Michael closed and locked the door, then leaned against it. "Pushed us at each other?"

"Yeah."

"He's not wrong about the tension."

Libby snorted. "Believe me, I know." She patted his chest and then quickly removed her hand, raising a finger to him to wait. "I'm going to put some real clothes on before we talk this through."

Fully dressed, Libby came back out and settled on the coffee table opposite Michael, their knees touching in the open space. She slid her feet to the outside of his, trapping him there, then for good measure leaned both hands on his knees. "I have an idea," she said, holding his gaze, serious and steady.

Needing to do something, Michael slid his fingers under her right hand then left them there, holding on with his thumb. "Okay."

"You, Ray, me. All three of us. Together." She waited.

Michael almost laughed. He couldn't possibly be that easy to read, which meant she'd come to the same conclusion without him even hinting.

She gave him a weak smile. "You don't think so?"

"It's not that I don't want it. It just seems like such a big step."

"I don't see why it has to be any bigger step than two people hooking up. We like each other a lot and want to see where it goes." She twisted her hand and grasped his fully, then laced their fingers together. "I know you miss him. I miss him too. And we have a lot of fun together. If he wasn't your ex I'd be over at his place asking him out again."

"And how does he feel about it?" His fingers twitched, almost pulling away, but she held tight.

"I haven't said a thing. I was waiting to see how today went."

"He might bolt and never talk to us again." It wasn't without precedent.

"Then that's his choice." She edged closer to him. "But maybe he won't this time. Maybe he'll stop and think about it. Maybe he's already thought about it too."

Michael pressed a kiss to Libby's palm, then dropped her hand. "I'm not saying no. But I need a few more days."

She nodded and stood up. "Okay. But I'm back to work day after tomorrow, so we'll have scheduling problems again." She aimed a light kick at his shin. "Which is another good reason to have all of us in the same place."

"Wait, you've already got us living together?"

"Why not?" She was out the door before could even start thinking about reasons.

Thirty-Four

Ray: *Did you take my advice?*

Libby: *Which advice?*

Ray: *Either one. They were both good.*

Libby tried several times to reply, starting with "They really weren't," then deleting that and switching to "Don't you know how screwed up you have us?" After deciding that was both too accusatory and exclusionary she replaced it with, *Not without you there.*

Then she waited. Not the best subject to bring up over text message, but she had a history of it so maybe he wouldn't be too shocked.

She was at work, taking a break between scenes, so maybe he was at work too, and just got called out. Or maybe he'd read her text and deleted her number.

Eventually her phone buzzed in her pocket and she took it out as covertly as she could.

Michael: *What did you say to Ray?*

Libby: *He didn't tell you?*

Michael: *He called me and gibbered at me for a minute then said he had to think.*

Libby: *I may have, over text message, implied I wouldn't fuck you without him there.*

Michael: *You may have.*

Libby: *Yup. Got to go.*

Her phone was back in her pocket before the chorus master saw her, she hoped. It wasn't the worst offence, because she wasn't even in the scene that was starting, but she didn't want to tempt fate after his threats before her vacation. So she sat through her phone buzzing several more times before falling silent. They were grown men, they could work it out themselves.

Apparently they did, because they were both waiting for her when she got out of rehearsal at 5:30, just standing there on the steps, looking like models and twitching like children. At least, Ray was. Michael was watching Ray with fond amusement; Libby knew that expression well. They both looked up when she approached.

"Hi?" she said, confused. "Are you ganging up on me?"

Michael shrugged. "We thought it was about time."

"He did," Ray said, gesturing at Michael with his thumb. "I'm terrified of your revenge."

"Okay...." But when Michael held out his hand to her she took it and let him lead the way down the stairs to the sidewalk. "Where are we going?"

"Neutral territory," Ray answered.

That narrowed it down to only most of the city, so Libby went along, curious but hopeful.

Just having the three of them together again, especially after awkward conversations, meant the world to her. Ray walked slightly ahead, turning periodically to chat with Michael, so Libby got a good chance watch him. He'd calmed somewhat since she joined them, and she admired him in his dove grey t-shirt and tight black jeans. Between him and Michael in the remains of his work clothes, she probably looked like a slob and she couldn't believe she got to have either of them, let alone possibly both.

It turned out they were going to St James Park, pretty much the definition of neutral territory, and a good choice for having a private conversation in public. Conditions weren't the best—it had rained the day before and the ground was still too wet to sit on the grass—but with any luck they'd move on quickly to Michael's or Ray's place. They ended up in a shaded area, the kind of place Libby would have chosen to nap in back when, and stopped when they'd put a decent distance between them and other people.

Libby waited – this wasn't her party and she didn't want to risk anything by taking over. To her great surprise it was Ray who chose to speak up first.

"Okay, so," he began, watching Libby for her reaction. "After I hung up on Michael and paced for a while I figured I didn't know what you meant when you said that. So here we are." He scratched the back of his neck and grimaced. "I feel like an idiot, but I miss being with Michael." He clasped his hands together and looked away, up at the tree behind her. "But I don't want to destroy things between you and him."

Ray's confusion stabbed at her, so she answered as clearly as she could. "Look, I like you, you like me, we both love Michael. Let's give it a shot."

"Your solution is a threeway? Or sharing Michael?" His confusion turned lighter, more amused, but didn't lessen.

"More than that. You know what ménage a trois means? A household of three." She took a deep breath and dove in, despite his frown. "Maybe we can be a family. I know you want a relationship with him, but can you have one with me, too?"

His frown turned puzzled, then he chuckled. "I should be the one asking you that."

Desperate to lighten the mood, Libby joked. "You're going to keep dangling that over my head, aren't you? I have money now, you know. I don't need either of you." And neither of the guys realized how good it felt, to be independent again, to be able to choose her life based on what she wanted, not what would keep her alive another day.

"I think I get it," Ray replied, "why you left that night. Especially since you told me about your family and everything." He took a few steps towards her and quirked his mouth up in an embarrassed smile. "And it's possible you weren't wrong about me."

She couldn't resist hugging him then, wrapping her arms around his waist and resting her head against his chest. "Possible. Not great, but I'll take it."

"And what do you think?" he asked Michael, who pushed himself off the tree he'd leaned against to join them.

Michael idly stroked her back as he spoke. "I think it's worth trying. We don't have to make any promises except that we talk to each other about what works and what doesn't. Like any other relationship."

Joy welled up in Libby's chest as Ray nodded. He leaned down to kiss her, quickly, gently, then repeated the gesture with Michael. "Well," he said, "I cannot believe I'm doing this, but I guess I'm dating two people at once."

Libby resisted squealing like a child. "I have so many fantasies, you guys, oh my god." She actually felt a little faint as she grabbed their hands. "Let's go home."

Ray stayed over that night. Libby had suggested that it would help them bond as a threesome if they all got used to being in each others' space, and it seemed like a good enough idea. And Ray hadn't spent much time with either of them recently, so he'd been feeling a bit touch starved anyway. The guys at work were great, but he was wary of getting as handsy with them as they did with each other.

Michael's bed was barely big enough for the three of them, but they managed to get to sleep with a minimum of jostling and poking at each other. When he and Libby woke, though, Michael was gone—they found him sleeping in Libby's bed.

"You two put off way too much heat," he said when they woke him. "And Libby kept kicking me."

Ray looked up at him from his position on the floor, arms crossed on the bed near Michael's head. From here he could see his delicate eyelashes, the specks of gold in his brown eyes. "So what I'm hearing is that we need practice at this whole sleeping together thing."

Michael reached out and grazed Ray's cheek with warm fingers. "We'll get there."

"But at least this time Libby didn't run out on me."

A knuckle jabbed into his rib cage where Libby was cuddled up into his side. "Watch it, buddy. I'm still new at this whole commitment deal."

"Yeah, don't scare her off." Michael rolled off the other side of the bed and their day went on as usual.

Days, plural, it turned out. One after another they would get together when they found time but they'd stagnated already, only a week into their relationship. Ray paid attention: Libby touched Ray, Libby touched Michael, Ray touched Michael, Michael touched Ray, but Michael never touched Libby first. He'd respond enthusiastically, sure, but he'd never instigate. After a bit Libby noticed the habit, too, but she never said anything, so Ray never said anything, and they both backed off a bit, assuming Michael was still uncomfortable with the arrangement. They'd spend quiet evenings on the couch barely acting like friends let alone lovers.

Until the night Ray broke. They were again on the couch watching a movie, this time a little friendlier than usual. Ray and Michael sat side by side, with Libby leaning against the arm, ass in Michael's lap and feet in Ray's. Jeeves was cuddled up to Ray's other side purring so loud Ray could barely hear the dialogue. It was nice.

But that was it. Nice. Until Libby started idly, unconsciously, scratching her toes against the inside of Ray's thigh. Flick up, dig down. Flick up, dig down. It was aggravating and enticing and he slowly reached out, grasped the offending foot, and slid it up to cover his dick, which was starting to chub up against his thigh.

A glance over showed her flushing a pretty pink and she pressed gently where he was holding her, shifting a little to manage it. Under her, Michael was oblivious to their actions, although when Libby shifted he did too, in a way that Ray knew intimately.

Surprising even himself, Ray stood, dumped Libby's legs off his lap and clapped his hands together, the sound almost painful in the near silence. "Okay, this has to end. I'm tired of this pussyfooting around."

He thought he heard Libby murmur "oh, thank god" but he couldn't be sure because the confused look on Michael's face was both hilarious and pathetic.

"I'm sorry?" Michael said, glancing between Ray and Libby in his search for meaning.

"This," Ray replied, gesturing among them. He pointed at Michael's thumb, gently stroking Libby's hand. "This high school flirting."

Libby nodded vigorously.

"We're all too afraid or too polite to make the first move, so here I am, making it. Let's all just go into the bedroom, take our clothes off, and see what happens."

"Seconded." Libby stood and tugged lightly on Michael's hand. "You coming?"

The slight bulge in his pants said yes, but he hesitated. "Somehow I thought this would be more romantic."

"I am the least romantic person in the world," said Libby, as Ray replied,

"We can do romantic another time, once we've worked out the mechanics. I've never had a threesome before. Plus I kind of have a history of weird first times with you two. This could be complicated."

"So I'll save my strap-on for another time?" She was looking at Ray so she didn't notice Michael's eyes go dark.

"You have a strap on?" Micheal asked, his voice breathy.

She swung around to take in his expression. "Nope. But I've always wanted one, so I guess that's incentive." She tugged on Michael's hand one more time. "Come on," she said. "The only thing keeping me from rubbing myself all over you is respect for Ray."

Ray mocked offence. "You don't want to rub yourself all over me?"

"Pfft. I already have." She waved a thumb at Michael. "He's new territory."

Michael clearly worked out his issues and joined them. "Fine. But don't blame me if I end up spanking both of you."

Ray dragged Libby who dragged Michael towards the master bedroom. "Not my kink, but have fun, you two."

"Just to be clear, that's not for me, either," Libby said.

Once in the bedroom they stalled again, until Ray went with his comfort zone and peeled Michael's shirt off him, trusting Libby to keep up. He got a little distracted when Michael kissed him, lips as soft and warm as ever. This, he knew. The solidity of a male chest against his, strong hands grasping his waist, drifting low to slip inside his jeans, confident and teasing. And then another hand snuck in between them, smaller and more delicate, fiddling with something that must be the button on Michael's jeans, then more considering the gasp stifled in Ray's mouth.

Michael pulled back a touch. "Sorry," he murmured. "Back in a minute." He turned around then, ass pressing against Ray's cock as he grabbed Libby and pulled her up into a kiss fit for the golden age of film.

As he watched, Ray's teeth found their way into Michael's shoulder, just scraping for a moment until someone twitched and he bit down too hard. Michael yelped and dodged away from them both.

"Sorry," Ray said nervously. "Sorry." But Libby had her hand over her mouth, eyes merry, and he couldn't stop the laughter that bubbled up to join hers.

"Oh god," she said. "Our first injury."

"When you put it that way I feel like I should make a scrapbook," Ray replied.

"You two will be the death of me." Michael stalked away from them both to strip off the rest of his clothes. "There. Didn't we say that the last one naked had to watch?"

"What?"

"No!"

Somehow Libby managed to scramble out of her clothes faster than Ray, even though she was wearing more layers. He dropped his boxers and asked, "If I kiss you will you run away again?"

She made a face like she was thinking. "Nope. Promise." But she was the one to move, to step up and wrap her arms around his shoulders and brush her lips to his. God she was soft, melding against him like bath water. The first time they'd done this she was overpowering and frantic, now she was still in control but more patient, languidly stroking his lips and tongue with hers, making him feel precious. If this was how she'd kissed Michael then no wonder he wasn't able to choose between them.

A noise behind them drew their attention to Michael, spread out on the bed having just fetched a bottle of lube out of the bedside drawer. Ray watched him flick the cap open and drizzle a little into his hand before grasping his cock and going to town.

"Carry on," Michael said, grinning wickedly. "Don't mind me."

Libby straddled Ray's leg and ground down against his thigh when he angled it for her, even though she was still watching Michael's show. Ray tensed a muscle and she gasped, leaving a streak of wetness behind. He ached to lift her up and sink into her, let her envelop him completely, and he was probably strong enough to make it work for a few strokes, but he had better ideas. He leaned down to whisper in her ear.

She launched herself up on her toes to plant a firm kiss on his cheek before sliding off him and heading for the bed.

It had taken a moment for Libby to understand what Ray wanted, but when the penny dropped she'd nearly gone woozy at the idea. She didn't want to just, as Ray had put it, "sit on Michael's face" without warning, so she took some liberties and hoped he'd get the point. Just the memory of his lips and tongue, the hot suction on her thigh the night of the premiere, nearly had her groaning in anticipation and she slung a leg over him and settled on his belly.

"Hi," he said, smiling fondly up at her. His hands echoed the sentiment, grasping her waist and sliding down to cup her ass, fingertips trailing heat as he tipped her forward.

She caught herself with hands on either side of his head, as eager for his lips on hers as anything else. The hair on his belly dragged pleasantly over her clit as she slid back and she gasped into his mouth.

"C'mere," he mumbled against her lips, tugging her thighs up.

Following his lead, she raised up, gripping the headboard, and allowed him to position her vulva over his mouth. "Oh god," she gasped, even before he touched her with his tongue.

Ray kissed her on the ear as the bed dipped behind her, then murmured, "We had a nice discussion about kinks one night."

As if knowing what she needed, he slid his arm around her waist, holding her up against him, bracing her trembling thighs against his. She barely noticed his erection against the small of her back; all her focus was on Michael's lips, his tongue, slick and strong, teasing, sucking, dipping in, his own moans and sighs echoing her own, eating her out like he wanted nothing more in the world, and soon she was lost to the rest of the room, nothing left of her but a bundle of nerves and gasping cries.

She slumped against Ray, catching her head on his shoulder. "Can you do that too?"

He chuckled into her hair. "Maybe not as well, but I'm a pretty quick learner."

"Good."

She reached back and grasped his erection, which was slick with lube. "You want to come like this?" she asked, tightening her grip as he thrust.

"Sure," he said, his careless tone warring with the breathiness of his voice.

Michael chuckled beneath them. He was smug, so pleased with himself that he was happy to be neglected for a while longer.

Libby nipped at Ray's jaw and said quietly, "When you're done here," she squeezed a little more for emphasis, "wipe that look off his face."

Ray laughed, then a moment later his movements went ragged and hot wetness flooded her skin. It was filthy and exciting and like nothing she'd done before. Careless of the mess, he pulled her back against his chest, posing, she realized, showing the both of them off for Michael, but she just couldn't hold that position anymore and slid sideways out of his grasp to tumble on the bed beside Michael, who was laughing along with her.

"I'm done," she said. "I can't feel my legs anymore. One of you will have to do all the work now."

"Got it," Ray said, already moving down to lie between Michael's spread legs. It didn't take long for Michael to start panting and shaking, and Libby decided she liked him like that, not so in control all the time. He was running his hands over Ray's shoulders in a random, thoughtless way, then tapped him twice, a signal, she guessed, for Ray to stop.

His eyes were bright when he turned his head towards her. "Can I be greedy?" he asked with a wicked smile.

"Please," she replied, ready to move over as he scrambled up and over her to grab a condom.

She took a second to grab some lube and finger herself with it, kickstarting what might become another orgasm, but even if it didn't it felt really good, especially when he tilted her hips up and sank in smoothly. He didn't drape himself on her, which she appreciated; she could never be sure what would send her into a panic attack these days and now would be a bad time. Soon she couldn't think anymore, eyes tightly shut, just enjoying the full sensation, squeezing against it, the slick motion against her clit that must be Ray's finger and this orgasm washed over her gently as Michael worked through his own.

After that it was easy, being together, like a chorus all hitting their notes perfectly so the sound hangs in the air, transcendent.

Thirty-Five

Libby woke to the sound of pigeons cooing at the open window and Michael breathing gently by her side. She sat up and sneaked a peek at him, sheet shoved down to his waist, hair mussed. A ray of sunlight touched the headboard and she watched the dust dance in its path from the window.

"You getting up?" He hadn't even opened his eyes yet and his voice was still froggy with sleep.

"First day of classes," she replied.

"You'll do great."

She planted a kiss on his forehead and slid out of bed, hearing his breathing deepen again as she pulled on her robe.

Jeeves waited out in the hall so she detoured to the kitchen to fill his bowls. The front door opened and she leaned out into the hall to check that it was Ray. "Hey."

"Morning." He kicked off his shoes and kissed her, firm and warm and a little wet. He smelled like chili spices, which meant he had an uneventful shift. "You excited?"

She nodded, but she wasn't totally sure the feeling was excitement. "Excited more about the fact I'll have a degree by Christmas than going to classes themselves." It was anyone's guess how the other students would react.

"You'll be fine." They'd had this conversation so many times before that Libby didn't blame him for skipping to the end.

"I know. And if I'm not I can just come home to you."

Ray glanced at the closed bedroom door. "Michael not up?"

"He was out late, too." Libby kissed him again. "Anyway, I'm going to get dressed and head to my dorm room. I've got to pick up my books and stuff."

When she came out of the bathroom dressed and ready Ray was nowhere to be seen but a glass of juice and a little bakery box sat on the island. The box contained a cinnamon roll and a message written in red ink, smeared with icing, on the inside lid:

*If these five minutes are the only ones we get
it will still have been a perfect day*